Wild As You

SHELBY STORME

Content Warning

This book contains content that may be troubling to some readers, including, but not limited to:

Death

PTSD

child abuse

Gaslighting

Alcohol

Pregnancy

Talk of Abortion

To those lost in the darkness, hoping for a light,
and the sunshine souls who are afraid to burn too bright. You are seen, you
are loved, you are beautiful.

CHAPTER 1
All The Time

MAVERICK

Twenty years ago

A half-full beer bottle sailed across my field of vision and shattered against the wall with a thundering crash, the broken shards of glass glistening like raindrops as they pattered all over the shag carpet in a spray of warm beer. I ran to the kitchen, ripping open the cabinet under the sink. My hands shook as I grabbed a spray bottle filled with carpet cleaner.

If this gets out blood, it'll get out beer. My hands shook about as much as the small voice in my head did.

I snatched a dish towel off the counter and raced back to the living room, finding Ellie Mae staring down at the mess, a look of fear and confusion glistening in her teary eyes. Worry ate at me. Dad hated seeing us cry. Hated it more when he heard us crying. He did bad things when that happened.

"Ellie, go back to the room. You're gonna get in trouble," I warned, my voice trembling only a bit. "Be careful not to step on the glass."

"O-okay, Maverick," Ellie Mae choked out, even as silent tears slipped down her cheeks.

She was only four. She hadn't had to watch many beer bottles go flying through the house yet. Wasn't used to it like me.

I strode to her side and squeezed her in a quick hug before gently propelling her towards our room. "Get your shoes on and get ready to go. Just in case."

There was no telling what Dad would do when he was this angry. Sometimes he left, storming out of the house and slamming the door so hard it would fall off the hinges. Sometimes he'd break things. Throw things. Hit things. I rubbed at my cheek absentmindedly with the back of my arm. The bruise had finally yellowed, a step up from the black and blue it was a few days ago.

As Ellie fled the living room, I knelt to the task of cleaning up the spilled beer and broken glass, careful to set aside the larger pieces of the bottle, and cautious about picking up smaller splinters stuck in the carpet.

Mama was still in bed. She'd said she didn't feel good this morning. Probably from the fight with her and Dad last night. Something about money and food and other things that were 'none of my damn business,' according to Dad.

"What in the fuck do you think you're doin', sissy boy?" Dad's harsh voice cracked like a whip as it cut through the air. He stumbled over from the beat-up recliner, a mean firestorm dancing in his jade eyes. *My eyes.* "Women's work? Figures. Get up off your fuckin' knees."

"Don't you talk to him like that, Eli!" Mama slipped from the darkness of the hallway like a wraith. Her brown hair was frizzy, her blue eyes dull and haunted. She looked nothing like the cracked picture that hung off-center in the hallway.

But that was four years ago. Dad wasn't as mean then. Didn't drink as much. Hadn't lost his job yet.

Dad struck a hand out toward Mama before I could even open my mouth and beg him to stop—fast as a cottonmouth. She crumpled to the floor, one of her hands going to her face. When she pulled it away, her cheek was a bright angry red and tears shone in her eyes.

My heart thumped like a war drum in my chest, anger and fear pumping through my veins. I made to rise from my crouched position, pushing past the fear and resolving myself to stand up against Dad, knowing fully well what the consequence would be. Mama's wild gaze landed on me; she shook her head once.

And as much as I hated it...as much as I wanted to do something, I listened. It wouldn't do any good anyway. He'd just hit me too.

Dad whirled to me, noticing Mama's attention, and pegged me with an angry glare. "God damn it, I said get up off your knees!"

He grabbed me by the shirt and hauled me to my feet, his fingernails digging into the soft flesh of my shoulder. Pain shot through me, my arm still sore from when he'd thrown me into the wall a couple days ago, but I bit back the tears pricking in my eyes.

Tears only ever made him angrier.

"Your ma will clean that shit up later," he slurred. "We gotta get to this fuckin' jackpot so I can make us the money for the fuckin' rent, cuz your fuckin' mom can't do a goddamn thing, and neither can anyone else." It took a moment to make sense of the words—they'd started slurring together. "Get your fuckin' sister. Get your asses outside. And get the trailer hooked up. I swear to God, boy, if you forget to hook the damn lights up again, I'm gonna beat you so bad you won't be able to sit down for a fuckin' week!" Spittle flew out of his mouth and sprinkled against my cheeks. That drunken, stupid anger smoldered on his red face as he glared down at me.

I nodded, hoping, praying, he didn't see the fear in my eyes. I must have been getting good at hiding it. Or maybe he was just that drunk that he couldn't tell anymore.

"Eli, he's eleven. You gonna have him drive you there next? You can't leave. You're drunk," Mama protested.

I turned for the door though, not waiting to hear his answer. If Dad said we were going, we were going. There was no stopping him. Not when he was like this.

I caught Ellie Mae's blonde hair in my peripheral and turned her way as she slipped out of the hallway with her pink boots on the wrong feet, quietly sobbing. My heart squeezed. Rushing to her, I grabbed her hand and led her outside, away from Dad's yelling and the smell of beer soaking into the carpet.

3

"Maverick, Mama and Daddy are fightin'." Ellie sniffled, hugging her stuffed unicorn to her chest.

"No shit," I snapped. They were always fighting. The only time they weren't was when Dad was passed out. Ellie flinched, her blue eyes wide as she gazed at me. I sighed, hanging my head. "I'm sorry...It's gonna be okay. Come on. I need you to help me hook up the trailer."

"But Mama and Daddy are fightin'," she repeated.

I placed my hands on her shoulders. "Ellie, please... if we don't get the trailer hooked up Dad's gonna be *really* mad."

She stared at me for a long moment, like she didn't know what to do. I knew she didn't understand what was going on. Why everything was the way it was. I *still* didn't know why Dad was angry all the time. Didn't know why he stayed when he threatened to leave at every turn. Most times, late at night, when I couldn't sleep because my body hurt so bad, I hoped, wished, prayed he'd just leave. But then I'd wake up and he'd be sleeping in the recliner or passed out on the couch. And we'd just repeat the same cycle over and over. Day after day.

Ellie Mae finally wiped at her tears. "Okay, Maverick," she squeaked before looking down at her faded pink unicorn. I needed to wash it again for her and sew up the hole she'd made from pulling on one of the strings. "Come on Wild Star, let's go hook up the trailer!"

———

PRESENT DAY- LATE JUNE

My eyes shot open, my heart and mind a war of emotions. Twenty years and my brain still knew when to let those ugly memories surface and haunt me. But of all the days... I could have used a break today.

I glanced over to the clock on the nightstand. 3:46 AM. My alarm would go off in fourteen minutes. I blew out a slow breath. How much could I get done before it went off?

As I dressed, I tried shaking off the images from the dream. They lingered like cobwebs in the back of my mind. I wished I could forget. But some things you just couldn't. They stuck with you forever. Like a tattoo.

Or an armful of burns.

I glanced down at my arms, my gaze scanning over the canyons and rivers of mottled, scarred flesh. They didn't hurt anymore really, but every now and then phantom pain slithered up and down, reminiscent of the flames in the accident.

I shivered, shaking off the memory as I pulled a clean pair of jeans out of the bottom drawer and drew them on, tensing my toes against the starch that fought so valiantly to keep the legs pressed shut. I snatched a pair of black socks from the top drawer and a crisp, white tank from the middle. From the closet in my room, I selected a black, long-sleeved button-up shirt and shrugged it on, trying not to wrinkle it before sliding on my leather belt with the buckle I'd won in Nashville. My gaze settled on the plastic hat box tucked away on the corner shelf of the closet. I pulled it down and grabbed out my black felt cowboy hat. A little hum fell from my lips as I inspected it, brushing away some dust before setting it on my head.

I glanced at myself in the mirror leaning in the corner of my room by the armchair. Another hum of approval as I tugged on my sleeves before going to the chair and pulling on my work boots. Good, old-fashioned Ariat cowboy boots made for riding and working. Like me—they weren't fancy, but they did the job.

I slapped the *OFF* button as the alarm finally caught up to me and strode out into the kitchen of my new home. The lights were still out at the barn. So, Cash hadn't fed yet. Unsurprising.

He wouldn't be up until I all but broke down the door and forced him out of bed. I'd deal with him later, right now I needed a minute for myself. A minute of peace without his loud, obnoxious ass chiming in on some bullshit.

Pressing the *ON* button on the coffee maker, I moved to the front door and stepped out into the warm Texas darkness.

CHAPTER 2
Before He Cheats

CHEYENNE

You've gotta be kiddin' me.

Voices echoed in my trailer as I made my way towards the front door. Correction...*moans*. Yep, those were moans coming from my trailer, and they sure as hell weren't mine.

Fury scorched through me, bubbling up from my stomach.

Really?

Nate had the audacity to sleep with someone in *my* trailer. I wish I could say I was surprised, but I'd known his reputation and been stupid enough to sleep with him anyways. We weren't really official, but still... you'd think he'd at least have the decency to try and be discreet with his other lovers, instead of, you know, screwing them in my home.

I rolled my eyes as I paused under the awning. My *Howdy Y'all* wreath looked a little sad, the hot Texas sun washing out the color of the bright, fake flowers I'd arranged around the wreath. The trailer still creaked and swayed, the god-awful melody of moans and grunts making me want to throw up.

I'd been gone for an hour. One damn hour and he'd been stupid enough to bring someone here. He deserved every bit of scorn I dredged

7

up inside me, ready to unleash on him in just a moment. But catching him in the act, yelling at him, maybe even throwing out his things just didn't seem like enough for this bullshit. No, this deserved something a bit more dramatic. And Daddy always said I got my attitude from my mama...who was a petty bitch.

Turning on my heel, I strode for my truck, Brandy, my red Australian Cattle Dog, right on my heels. At least I could depend on *someone*. She sat dutifully at my side as I rifled through my backseat. After a moment, I found what I was looking for. A sadistic smirk tugged on my mouth as I grabbed the cattle prod off the floor. With fire in my eyes and ice in my heart, I stomped back toward my trailer, those moans rising, rising, rising. I all but ripped the door open, cutting their little love making short.

Nate had some brunette bent over my kitchen table—*eww*, I'd have to deep clean literally every inch of this place now—as he plowed into her from behind. His horrified gaze met mine, all the desire dying in his eyes like embers fizzling out beneath a spray of water.

Good. Glad to know I'd ruined this moment for him. Just like he'd ruined my Saturday morning. The brunette's brown eyes met mine, terror and guilt and confusion shining in the dark depths.

I crossed my arms over my chest, putting the cattle prod on full display as I leaned casually against the doorway. "Oh, don't let me interrupt...please, continue," I said with a calm I definitely didn't feel. Not as pure, unbridled rage thrummed through my veins.

How I managed to not go absolutely bat-shit crazy was beyond me. I never had been the type to have a lot of restraint. But I managed, somehow.

Nate's mouth bobbed open and closed like a fish gasping for air. "I... Chey...I—"

The girl's horrified expression said everything I needed to know. She had no idea this wasn't his trailer. "You weren't expectin' me, were ya?" I asked, meeting her gaze.

She moved in a flurry of motion, shoving Nate off her and trying and failing to cover herself with her shirt that she still wore. Tears shone in her eyes. I almost felt sorry for her. Almost.

"Get out of my trailer." My voice held a steely resolve to it. "Now."

Funny... On the inside I trembled with rage—pure, fucking rage. But on the outside, I was cold. Numb. My muscles felt frozen, or like someone had poured cement on me and it had started to dry.

"Chey..." Nate fumbled with his jeans, trying to pull them up around his hips. "It's not what it looks like."

Something snapped in me. One minute I was cool, the next, I was seeing red. Violent, blood red. I pressed the button on the cattle prod, letting it crackle and spark. The brunette let out a shriek, followed by a string of curses, something about me being a crazy bitch.

Right then, I *felt* crazy. But it also felt good—good to let it out.

A low, wicked chuckle rumbled in my chest. "Oh, I know exactly what it looks like. You have thirty seconds to get out of my fuckin' trailer before I shove this cattle prod so far up your ass it'll come out your mouth."

His eyes widened, his Adam's apple bobbing as he stopped fussing over his pants and stumbled for the doorway. He nearly knocked over the brunette, who looked just as terrified. They scurried past me and down the steps of my trailer as I moved out of the way. Brandy snapped at Nate's heels for good measure—she never had really liked him.

I smirked, taking three slow steps down the stairs and onto the concrete slab outside my trailer space.

"Cheyenne. Come on, let's...let's talk about this."

"Fuck off, Nate," I said, crossing my arms over my chest once more. "I ain't playin'."

"At least give me all my shit back!" he whined, buttoning up his pants. He was still shirtless. He must've left it somewhere in the trailer.

As if he deserved any of it. But after what he'd just done, I didn't want a single thing of his in my space. Didn't want any reminders of him. I doubted he'd like the way he got his things back though.

With a shrug, I stomped up the stairs, grabbing up anything that was his before tossing it all out onto the ground. A crowd of nosy neighbors had gathered, Mr. and Mrs. Perkins from the spot next door right there with a front-row view. They'd been nosy from the minute I'd pulled in beside them, but I didn't mind much. They were sweet, and Mrs. Perkins made the most delicious fried chicken I'd ever tasted.

"Hi, Mr. and Mrs. Perkins." I grinned, waving from my doorway.

"Everythin' goin' alright, sweetie?" Mrs. Perkins asked, her brows raised so high they disappeared beneath her grey bangs.

"Oh, you know, just takin' out the trash," I said sweetly, cattle prod still in hand.

Nate picked his clothes up off the floor while spewing out curses under his breath. The brunette had already gotten into her car, leaving his sorry ass behind as she all but peeled out of the trailer park.

"Cheyenne," Nate huffed, a look of regret on his face.

Nope, it was too little too late for that. Way too damn late.

Tears pricked in my eyes. Not of devastation or sadness. No... can't say I was surprised this had happened. A part of me was impressed that he'd gone this long without me catching him in the act. No, these were tears of rage. Of embarrassment. My anger coiled tight like a snake in my chest, making it hard to breathe.

Dear God, why did I have to be an angry crier? I hated that about myself. People never took you seriously when you cried.

I took a couple steps his way, pressing the button on the cattle prod once more. "Last chance, dickhead. Get your shit and leave." I even went so far as to aim the prod his way. Not close enough to let it touch him, but enough to make shock and terror shine in his shit-brown eyes.

He let out the most pathetic yelp that stopped my tears in their unshed tracks, a laugh escaping me. "Maybe next time you'll think before you sleep around in someone's home."

By the time he'd scrounged up the last of his things most of the trailer park watched from the street. Mrs. Perkins had settled at my side, fussing over me like a mother hen. I let her do it, smiling and thanking her for her kindness the whole time, but the truth was, I just wanted to be alone. With each minute that passed, the adrenaline pumping through my veins trickled out. I didn't want anyone around when there was none left.

"You sure you're okay, sweetie?" she asked, rubbing my shoulders reassuringly when Nate finally drove away.

I nodded. Truth is, I was fine. Okay, not *fine*—the betrayal stung even if we weren't official—but I wasn't going to go sob myself into a pile of mush either. To be honest, I was mad more than anything. Mad at him, but mostly mad at myself for being stupid enough to expect anything more from him.

Brandy fidgeted and whined at my side, sensing my mood. I'd owned quite a few dogs in my lifetime but this pretty girl... She just got me. Dutiful, loyal, obedient. Everyone deserved a dog like her.

I stretched out my hand and she brushed her head against it, leaning fully against my leg. I smiled at Mrs. Perkins. "I'm okay, Mrs. Perkins. Nothing I can't handle."

Her husband came up to us, his glassy blue eyes full of sympathy. "Let us know if you need anythin'."

I nodded, thanking them again for their kindness, and reassuring them at least three more times that I'd be okay. By the time I closed the door to my trailer, shutting myself securely inside, I was completely drained. My social battery and patience for people was at a whopping zero. I slid to the linoleum floor, cupping my head in my hands. My temples pulsed with a dull ache that already started to radiate across my forehead. *Great.* Another damn headache. They were becoming more and more common these days. I'd had what...like five in the last week.

A familiar weight settled on my legs, followed by wet, slobbery kisses.

"Stop," I grumbled half-heartedly, even as I pet Brandy, letting her calming energy soothe some of the chaos in me. "He was always a dumbass, wasn't he, girl?"

She didn't answer, because of course she didn't, but her head tilted to the side in that way of hers that made me swear she knew what I was talking about.

I blew out a breath and stood. Maybe cleaning would clear my mind. It was one of those mindless activities that made me feel productive, but also didn't take a lot of mind work. Finding a station on the radio, I blared something heavy and angry from the speakers and set to work.

Only my anger didn't dissipate. It lingered like a damn cold that didn't want to go away.

I'd scrubbed the counters, swept and mopped the floors, changed the bedding and tossed the old ones—who knew where all they'd been while doing the deed. But still, I couldn't get rid of the knot of frustration cloying for purchase in my chest, my heart.

Maybe I needed a distraction.

With a sigh, I pulled out my phone and scrolled through my Instagram, my gaze landing on a photo of Charlie and Ryder posted from this morning.

Ooh, Ryder must be home.

Charlie had mentioned he was coming back soon the last time we'd talked. June had been busy for him now that he'd gotten sponsored, but they seemed to make it work so far.

She answered on the second ring, her soft, cheery voice warm and buttery. "Hello?"

"Hey girl, what are y'all doin' tonight?"

CHAPTER 3
Cowgirls

MAVERICK

This heat can fuck off any time now.

I wiped sweat from my brow with my free arm as I lugged Betty's saddle into the tack room. It wasn't even July quite yet and the Texas heat made me want to move somewhere north. Like Wyoming or Montana. Yeah, Montana sounded pretty damn nice right about now.

I huffed. Who the hell was I kidding? I'd never leave Texas. Better yet, I'd never leave Cash. He'd get in too much damn trouble without me. At least, that's what I told myself.

My cousin might be the most obnoxious, cocky dickhead I'd ever met, but the bond we shared ran thicker than our blood. He'd saved me in a time I didn't think I could be saved.

Speak of the devil...

Cash's crow of laughter echoed through our barn as his and Ryder's silhouettes strode down the center breezeway. I made my way to Black Betty, who I'd tied up in the center of the aisle, and began brushing her down. Flicking a glance over my shoulder, a little niggle of dread coiled in my chest.

Cash's lips were pulled up into a wide grin. I knew that grin. Knew it well, and knew that I wasn't going to like the reasoning behind it.

I sighed, though it did little to ease the knot forming in the pit of my stomach. "No," I said with finality, turning back to Betty and focusing all of my attention on brushing out her sleek, black coat.

Cash scoffed. "You don't even know what we were goin' to ask."

I didn't look at either of them as I spoke. "I already know I ain't gonna like it."

Ryder's low laughter pulled my attention. "That's fair," he said with a nod.

"Aw, come on, Mav!" Cash groaned, taking a step toward me.

Betty snorted and pinned her ears in warning. The mare was possessive, and there was nothing she hated more than Cash. He was too loud, too...over the top for her. She'd always needed calm, quiet. It's why we worked so well together. I ran a hand over her neck, shushing her under my breath. Some of her tension eased, even as she eyed Cash like a hawk.

"We were thinkin' 'bout goin' up to San Antone for the night. Drinks and dancin'."

I bit back a groan. None of that sounded fun—being in the city, around people. Hell, especially dancing. "Y'all just need a ride, don't ya?"

I looked at Ryder for confirmation, but it was Cash who spoke. "What're you talkin' bout? Of course we want you to come. You and your shinin' personality."

I huffed, my lips pulling up into the ghost of a grin. "Who all's goin?"

"Just us, Charlie, and Cheyenne. She invited us up there."

Cheyenne.

Girl was a firecracker. About as pretty as she was wild. Like a mustang. That girl could probably give Cash a run for his money. Tonight, would be trouble, I could guarantee it.

It'd be good for you, a hopeful little part of my heart begged.

It wasn't that I didn't want to spend time with them all. Sure, going out wasn't my thing, but I liked being around my friends. It's just...

"I can't," I said, refusing to meet Cash's gaze.

His brows furrowed, a frown replacing his grin. "Why?"

"I got plans." I shrugged, hoping he'd leave it be.

"Plans with who?" Cash's voice turned cold, a true feat as hardly anything ever pissed him off enough to change his voice from carefree and cocky.

I swallowed hard and blew out a breath. I couldn't bring myself to look at him. Couldn't bring myself to face his disappointment.

He answered before I could bring myself to respond. "You're fuckin' kiddin', Mav."

My brush stilled against Betty's side, and I pursed my lips.

Even Ryder joined in, though nowhere near as pissed. "I thought y'all were done?"

I braved a look at him. Disappointment and pity shone in his black eyes, but it didn't get to me like it did with Cash. Maybe because there was hardly anything on this planet that truly disappointed my cousin. Knowing that I could with just the mention of Ashleigh damn near wrecked me.

"We've been talkin'. She wants to work things out."

Cash shook his head, a string of muffled curses falling from his lips as he turned away and smacked a hand against one of the bars of the nearest stall. Betty snorted and pranced in place. Murmuring to her quietly, I ran a hand over her coat until she calmed.

Ashleigh and I had been on again off again for almost as long as I'd lived with the Mooneys. Since the summer of the crash twenty years ago.

Fuck...it'd been twenty years since the accident and yet still it haunted me.

Every day. Every night. The smell of the fire. The sound of metal crashing against metal. My sister's screams. *Damn—the screams.* I don't think they'd ever go away.

Cash's wild glare snapped me from my thoughts, but when he spoke, his voice was cold, defeated...which was almost worse. "Come on, Mav. She's usin' you. Girl's a goddamn spider and you're stuck in her web."

"Watch it, Cash," I growled, the sound a low rumble in my throat. He didn't have to like her. Didn't have to approve. But I'd not have him speak ill about her. Not around me.

Cash didn't seem fazed in the least. Which was unsurprising. Not much fazed him.

Ryder placed a hand on Cash's shoulder. "Hey, it is what it is. He's got plans. We don't gotta like 'em."

Cash shook off Ryder's grasp, muttering under his breath as he stalked out of the barn without a backward glance.

Guilt gripped me...and shame. So much damn shame. I hated disappointing him.

Ryder sighed and waved him off, offering me a sympathetic smile that didn't quite reach his eyes. "He'll be alright."

I blew out a breath and nodded. "I know."

"You sure you want to hop back on that train, Mav?" He pulled his ball-cap off and speared a hand through his hair before replacing it atop his head. "She messed you up pretty good this past Christmas."

I didn't have the heart to look at him as I spoke. "I love her," I breathed as I ran a hand down Betty's neck once before reaching for the clasps holding her in place.

"I know, but—" Ryder's voice held no anger, no annoyance, just a hint of desperation.

I hated that my choices made him and Cash feel this way. Hated that I disappointed them... But of the two, Ryder would understand. He damn near gave up his career for Charlie.

Maybe one day I'd get tired of chasing after Ashleigh. But until then...

"If she's willin' to make it work, I'm willin' to try. I gotta."

Ryder dipped his head and nodded, a weak, resigned smile on his lips. He clasped me on the shoulder and gave it a reassuring squeeze. "Alright. I can't say I understand what you see in her, but it ain't my life. You do what you gotta do. We're gonna miss you tonight."

I offered him a guilty smile in return. "Sorry I couldn't be your designated driver."

Ryder chuckled, his lips pulling into a genuine grin. "See you tomorrow."

"Take care of your bonehead best friend, okay? I don't wanna hear how much trouble Cash got into since I wasn't there," I called as he started down the breezeway.

He turned to me, walking backwards a few paces, his laughter echoing off the stalls. "I'll do my best."

With a sigh, I turned to Betty. She nuzzled my stomach, pushing me backwards with her aggressive demand to be loved on. "Hey, knock that shit off, pretty girl," I muttered, but as she calmed, resting her head against me, I ran a hand over her forehead.

Was I making a mistake? Probably. Ryder was right...what she'd done at Christmas...It still felt like a dagger was lodged in my heart. Just the thought twisted it, causing more lingering pain.

I didn't drink. Didn't do drugs. But even I had a vice... and Ashleigh was mine.

Leading Betty into her stall and closing the door, I pulled out my phone. No calls or texts from her. We hadn't settled on a time really. She'd said she'd be here sometime this afternoon.

Ain't nothin' wrong with just callin' and checkin' in.

It was a four-and-a-half-hour drive from Houston, maybe she'd want a distraction.

Finding her name in the call log, I pressed it and listened for the dial tone.

My pulse danced in anticipation, each ring sending my nerves skyrocketing. What if she didn't answer? What if she forgot?

No. She wouldn't.

Five rings. Each seemingly longer and louder than the last. Five rings that all but shattered my resolve, then...

"Hello?" Ashleigh's light, airy voice sent a rush of relief through me.

"Hey. How's it goin'?" I asked, pacing up and down the breezeway.

"Look...Mav—"

My heart sank right then and there. I already knew where this was going. Knew and couldn't do anything to stop it. "You forgot?" I offered.

"No, I—I got called in last minute for a shift, and I—"

I bit back the disappointment. "Ashleigh, it's okay," I soothed, "you don't gotta make excuses."

The line crackled as she exhaled a breath. "I'm sorry, Mav. Really. I just...forgot. Time slipped away from me and it's just too late to come now."

I didn't mention the fact I'd lost count of how many times I'd dropped what I was doin' right then and there to drive to her whenever she called. It wouldn't do any good anyway.

"No, it's okay, I get it..." I hung my head, kicking at a clump of shavings that'd fallen in the breezeway. Little pieces scattered around, fluttering on the breeze, looking about as pathetic and helpless as I felt.

"Maybe let's try for next week?" she asked, her voice still holding that airy note to it, but she sounded rushed... As if she were trying to get me off the phone.

I found myself replying yes. I didn't say that the reason I'd specifically asked for tonight was because I didn't want to be alone. Didn't want to have to relive the memories of this day from all those years ago.

She knew what today was. At least, she should.

The anniversary of when my family died. The day *I* almost died. Phantom flames licked up my arms at the thought. I bit back a curse, rubbing my free hand over my left arm, feeling the scars hidden beneath my long sleeves.

She didn't say anything now, though. Maybe she didn't remember. Twenty years was a long time ago, after all. But it still felt raw, fresh in my mind.

"I gotta go, Mav, but I'll call you later, okay?" No doubt about it now, she *was* trying to get me off the phone.

I mumbled a goodbye, lowering the phone from my ear just as a male's voice picked up on the other end of the line. "Who was that, babe?"

The sound of the next word on Ashleigh's lips sent a spear of ice straight through my heart. "Nobody."

My thumb fumbled for the *end* button, the blood in my veins turning to ice. *Nobody.* That was almost worse than catching her two timing me...again.

Crushing defeat settled on my chest, spearing and twisting in my heart like a blade. My pulse thrummed in my ears as I dipped my head in shame.

I should have known. Should have known this would happen. It always did. It was the same ol' story with her and I. The same cycle. The same game of cat and mouse. And yet, I couldn't let her go. Aside from the Mooneys, Ashleigh had been the first person I'd made a connection with after losing my family.

She'd been my first everything, really. First friend. First kiss. First love.

My emotions warred within me like a hurricane—wild and raging. I hated this feeling. Hated feeling so out of control.

Fisting my hands at my sides, I made my way towards the stairs leading up to the hayloft we'd converted into a workout room. I didn't bother taking off my shirt or hat as I stomped over to the punching bag. Didn't bother wrapping up my hands. Settling into a defensive stance, I centered my breathing and began punching.

—————

I DON'T KNOW HOW MUCH TIME PASSED. IT COULD HAVE been five minutes or five hours, but when I finally pressed my head against the punching bag, sweat coated my brow and blood stained my knuckles.

Ryder and Cash were right. She'd only ever need me until the next best thing came around. I'd been a fool to let her in. A fool to think things had changed.

That's the last time.

As much as it hurt, I needed to put her in the past.

Cash would be happy to hear that, at least. I thought of him and how he'd stormed out of the barn. There wasn't much that disappointed him. So, when something did...especially something *I did*... fuck, it stung.

Good thing about Cash was he had a short attention span. He didn't stay angry for long.

Blowing out a breath, I glanced down at my phone. 5:05 PM. They probably wouldn't leave for another hour or so. I might be able to still join them.

Thumbing through my phone for Cash's name, I called him, not even bothering with a greeting as he said hello. "Y'all need a driver still?"

—————

I BLEW OUT A BREATH AS RYDER PULLED UP TO COWBOY'S, the neon sign glowing like a beacon. Trucks lined the parking lot, while people milled in and out of the dance hall and bar. Plumes of smoke dissipated into the night air from those puffing on cigarettes and vape pens.

My stomach did a flip flop even as Cash clapped his hands together in the back seat, that million-dollar grin curling his lips. "It's gonna be a good night!"

I wasn't quite as optimistic as him, but I was here, so figured I might as well try to make the most of it. Charlie and Ryder were lost in their own world, hardly paying Cash or I any attention. A pang shot through my heart. I wanted what they had. The way Ryder looked at her...and the way she looked right back. They were like two magnets, drawn to one another. You could *feel* the pull they shared.

I wished mine and Ashleigh's connection had been that strong, that pure. Ours was just toxic.

Stop thinkin' about her.

Right. I rolled my neck, trying to release the tension, and opened the truck door. Cash all but bounced beside me as the four of us made our way toward the entrance.

The place was dim inside, save for the dancefloor lit up by blue-hued lights. People hung out at the multiple bars strewn throughout the place, while others stood around in the back left corner, cheering on those drunk or dumb enough to brave riding the mechanical bull. A large number two-stepped across the dancefloor. Some country song drifted through the dancehall. I didn't know the name of it, but I'm sure Cash did. He listened to all that new shit.

We ambled through the throng of people, my nerves coiling tighter and tighter. Crowded spaces always made me feel uncomfortable.

A familiar smokey and feminine voice drew my gaze, sending a trickle of relief through me. "Hey y'all!"

Cheyenne's bright smile rivaled Cash's in its intensity. Her pale blonde hair bounced all the way down to her hips in wild ringlets. And those eyes... Like twin chunks of turquoise, they bore into me as she met my stare.

She reminded me of wildflowers and whiskey. Gorgeous and wild and potentially trouble. The harsh blue lighting did little to wash out her sun-kissed tan, which paired well with the bright pink denim flares she wore along with a white cropped tank top that hugged her chest.

I'd never met anyone as confident to wear the things she did, save Cash. The two possessed a confidence I'd never know. And like twin rays of sunlight, it felt like the entire bar was drawn to them. Eyes scanned us from all around, taking us all in with their veiled scrutiny. Probably wondering what the hell I was doing in the mix. Ryder and Charlie held a light, a pull, a magnetism all their own, the most intriguing blend of western and edgy with Ryder's cowboy getup and Charlie's tattoos.

Which left me, a shadow, a stain of darkness among the group. I didn't belong. That much was clear.

I didn't drink, but, fuck, the thought of something right now to drown out my nerves almost sounded tempting. Almost.

But the group would all be dancing soon enough, leaving me to disappear among the shadows, just the way I preferred. My lips curled, my prediction correct as Charlie and Ryder strode for the dancefloor after a quick hello to Cheyenne, while Cash did a slow turn, taking in the dancehall, his gaze landing on a group of girls there for a bachelorette party—by the looks of their matching outfits.

Oh, dear Lord, he'd have fun with them. With a knowing grin aimed my way, he strode for their table.

"How's it goin', Maverick?" Cheyenne's bright eyes pegged me in place.

I fidgeted under her stare. Cheyenne Harris intrigued me about as much as she terrified me. She held a predatory grace and charm that left the fearful, quiet side of me trembling in my boots. I'd gone up against men twice my size, come out on top, but I'd bet this five-foot something spitfire could bring a man to his knees with little more than a smile.

I thought of what happened earlier with Ashleigh. Of what today meant to me. A million different horrible thoughts flashed through my mind even as I lifted my shoulders in a simple shrug as I answered her question. "I'm alive. And you, Miss Cheyenne?"

She scrunched her nose up at the formality. "Just Cheyenne, please. I'm definitely no miss."

My lips quirked in the corner. "Alright. How's it goin', Cheyenne?"

Her shoulders mirrored mine in a matching shrug, but the smile on her face, the glow in her eyes was pure mischief. "Oh, you know, just caught this guy I was seein' cheatin' on me this mornin'."

"Well, damn. I'm sorry." Why anyone would cheat on her was beyond me. Girl was gorgeous. Beyond, really. A girl like her wasn't meant to be hurt, she should be treasured.

She lifted a single shoulder. "Eh, it's okay. I chased his sorry ass off with a cattle prod. You should have seen the asshole's face."

I coughed, blinking back my surprise. "You what?"

She repeated herself, her voice light, her demeanor open and casual —as if chasing people with cattle prods was an everyday thing. It might be for her. Barrel racers were their own brand of crazy, and I'd heard stories of Cheyenne.

I couldn't help the low chuckle that escaped me as I shook my head.

Her brows furrowed, the light in her eyes dimming as she crossed her arms over her chest, her lips dipping down into a frown. "What's so funny?"

I held up my hands in a placating gesture. "I just like the confidence, is all."

"Oh." Her features softened, just like the anger replaced with intrigue. "Charlie said you weren't comin' earlier, what made you change your mind?"

A part of me was tempted to say something about Ashleigh, to vent to someone other than Ryder or Cash about my situation. Someone who didn't know our history, our toxic story. But I'd never been good with words or expressing myself or talking in general, so I just shrugged again. "My plans fell through."

She whistled low, a hint of a smirk lining her plump lips as she pressed a plastic whiskey tumbler to her mouth. "Boy, you always talk this much?"

Dear Lord, she reminded me of Cash with the unabashed level of confidence. I didn't know what to say, so I just nodded once more.

A low chuckle left her. "It's okay, you don't need to talk to dance. Come on, cowboy."

My heart hammered in my chest, my legs seizing up and freezing as if I were stuck in a chunk of ice. I hated crowds, but more than that, I hated dancing. I'd never been good at it. I was too tall. Too lanky. It always felt odd. Robotic. I didn't have a rhythmic bone in my body.

Neither does Cash.

But Cash had something I'd never have enough of. Confidence. It poured off him in buckets. That and alcohol.

"I uh...I don't dance," I muttered, fidgeting under her gaze.

Something flickered in her stare, that pout returning. "What're you talkin' about?"

Another shrug of my shoulders. "I don't dance."

She rolled her eyes, one of her hands drifting to her hips as she jutted it out to the side. Challenge danced in her gaze, in every inch of her petite frame, actually. She was fiery, that one. I fought the ghost of a smile pulling on my mouth.

"You can't dance or you won't?"

"Does it matter?"

She huffed. "Of course, it does! One suggests you *can* learn, the other just shows me you're stubborn and unwillin' to."

I chewed my lip a moment before lifting my shoulders into yet another shrug. "You ever seen a frog fly?"

She frowned, rocking back on her heels in confusion. "No."

My brow quirked up. "Then you got your answer."

She sucked in a slow, deep breath, that turquoise gaze searing every inch of me. "Well, that's a damn shame."

Another shrug. Dear Lord, could I do anything other than that? But it was true. I didn't think myself a particularly good dancer, and it was too much attention for my liking. Best to just leave the dancing to Ryder and Cash. The two of them loved it.

She blew out the breath she'd been holding and asked, "What about gettin' a drink then?"

"I don't drink."

She groaned, her head tilting back, those long ash blonde ringlets falling down her back and brushing against the curve of her ass. "You're killin' me, Maverick. Do you know how to have fun at all?"

I huffed, a low chuckle rumbling out of my chest. "You sound like Cash."

She rolled her eyes, even though warmth lingered in her features. "And *you* didn't answer the question."

"I'm afraid if you're lookin' for fun, I ain't the one you should be talkin' to."

Something shifted on her face. The light remained, but her gaze hardened a bit, the corners of her eyes tightening ever so slightly. She blew out a deep breath through her nose and sighed. "Fine. Be boring then." And with that, she strode away.

She didn't even make it ten feet toward the dancefloor before some guy stopped her, asking to dance. Unsurprising. She was like a beacon of light in this den of shadows. A sun among a midnight sky.

I leaned against the table we'd claimed, letting out a sigh as I glanced around the dancefloor. Ryder and Charlie twirled around, both of them smiling and laughing as they tried and failed to work on a new spin. I wasn't surprised to find Cash by the bar still, two girls on either side of him, eating up every word he said like he'd hung the damn moon.

I swear, if he weren't family, I'd probably hate him. The ease and confidence with which he held himself. Not that I agreed with nor wanted to flirt with multiple women at one time, but...well, flirting or small talk just never had really been my thing.

Maybe that's why I'd always hung onto Ashleigh. She was as familiar as my favorite pair of boots. I hadn't won her over all those years ago with my charm, but from honesty. Before she'd been a lover, she'd been my friend.

The idea of doing what Cash was doing now, of putting myself out there like that...I just couldn't. It wasn't me. I didn't have the charisma, the charm. I wasn't the type of person for light conversation. Peopling was hard. Words were harder.

My mind drifted back to that first year after the accident. Of the countless doctors' visits with Bad and Aunt Violet. Of them saying nothing was physically wrong with me, but that sometimes when a person went through a traumatic experience they'd just stop talking altogether.

I pushed the brim of my hat up, rubbing at my forehead before righting it once more.

Why was I even here? I wasn't good company even on the best of days. But today...?

A bright blur of pink drew my gaze.

Cheyenne's lips were pulled up into the most radiant smile I'd ever seen—one of pure sunshine—as the same cowboy who'd asked her to dance spun her across the floor. I wasn't the only person watching her. At least half the dancehall did too, as she dipped and twirled and two-stepped to the beat. She held a magic all her own, drawing everyone's attention.

A part of me envied that. That light that she so easily possessed. Why couldn't I have fallen for a girl like her? Sure, the cattle prod chasing, barrel racer part of her scared me a bit, but it had to be better than Ashleigh and her two timing ways.

There was no way a girl like her—who was pure light—could fall for someone with as dark and tainted a soul as me.

With a huff, I pushed off the table and made my way toward the exit.

I needed a smoke.

CHAPTER 4
Cowboy Killer

CHEYENNE

I t was harder than I'd anticipated to get my dance partner to leave me the hell alone. Sure, he was decent looking and a great lead, but he wasn't the cowboy I wanted.

What was it with Maverick?

I'd been aware of him watching me on the dancefloor, mostly because I was painfully—I mean painfully—aware of him the entire time. Hoping, praying that maybe seeing me dance with another man would force him to act.

But no such luck on that front.

Either way it sucked and turned my mood sour. And I didn't want to be in a bad mood tonight. Nate had ruined my day. I wouldn't let my night be ruined as well. But as the song ended and the cowboy asked me for another dance, my gaze flicked to our table...only to find Maverick gone. My heart sank a bit at that, a burning need to find him taking over.

Why was I so desperate to cause myself pain tonight? Was I a masochist? I had to be, because there was no explanation I could think of that sent me searching for him. Why dance with a perfectly capable,

29

perfectly handsome man when you could pine over a broody, emotionally unavailable cowboy, right?

But there was more to Maverick Holstrom than that. I just knew it, and I wanted to be the one who was able to pull back his layers and find the real Mav underneath. I'd wanted to know more about him from the moment I'd met him a couple years ago at one of our rodeos. He'd just always been so closed off and unapproachable.

He wasn't at any of the bars—unsurprising—or the mechanical bull area, so I made my way outside. I scanned through the throng of people standing around smoking before my gaze landed on him. He leaned against the wall, away from the fray—again, unsurprising. It's like he was allergic to people. Why even go out at all?

I ignored the random looks from strangers, a few catcalls, a couple whistles as I made my way towards him. My leather soles clacked against the cement.

"There you are," I said, coming to stand before him.

He lowered his hand from his mouth and blew out a puff of white smoke, the sweet scent of tobacco hitting me. It gave me pause as I thought of Daddy. I hated the smell of cigarettes, but Black and Milds were like getting hit by a wave of nostalgia. My eyelids fluttered closed for a moment as I inhaled.

"Cheyenne? You okay?" His voice was a low, deep rumble in his throat. It should be a sin to have a voice like that. Honestly, everything about Maverick should be a sin. It was like he'd been designed to bring women to their knees.

"I was just comin' out here to check on you, is all," I said.

"I was just havin' a smoke."

My lips drew up into a knowing smirk. "I can see."

Something shifted in his gaze, almost like guilt. "I only do it sometimes."

I let out a low chuckle. "You don't gotta justify it. Lots of people smoke. There ain't nothin' wrong with it. Besides, my Daddy smoked Black and Milds, you'll never find me complainin'."

He nodded, pressing the cigar to lips once more, and inhaled.

"*So*, havin' fun?" I asked, trying to find a way to get him to say more than a couple words. Did he even understand that I was trying to flirt with him—*trying* being the keyword—or that I'd come out here searching for him because I liked him? His eyes, his stoic face was so closed off that I couldn't even tell. Which was infuriating.

He shrugged, blowing out another puff of smoke.

A flicker of annoyance escaped me, the edge in my voice peeking from beneath the surface. "Is that all you can do? Just...just shrug?" What do you know? Another. Damn. Shrug. I let out a disbelieving laugh. "You're something else, cowboy."

Those jade eyes settled on me, holding me in place. "Why're you out here, Cheyenne?"

God, the way he said my name. I know there was nothing sexual about it, but, damn.

I braved a step closer to him, our bodies close but not touching. In order to hold his gaze, I had to tilt my face up towards his, putting our faces close. "I came out to see you," I said, my voice low, sultry.

His brow furrowed, the usual scowl on his face deepening. "Why?"

"Dear God, Maverick...do I really gotta spell it out for you?" I asked, meeting his stare once more.

His head cocked to the side, a look of pure confusion on his face. "Spell what out?"

Ugh. Case and point. With a loud sigh, I rolled my eyes and pressed a hand to his chest. Maybe he'd get *that*. "I've been trying to flirt with you all night, from the moment you walked in. Why do you think I asked you to dance? To drink? Why do you think I'm out here talkin' to you?"

"Why me?" That frown dipped lower, those light eyes full of disbelief. On one hand, it was absolutely adorable that he was that humble, that earnest, and oblivious, but on the other... It would be nice if the guy could take a hint.

I shook my head, my hand still pressed to his chest. His hard muscles feathered beneath my touch. Dear God, the guy was cut. What I'd give to run my hands over his chest without his crisp, black, long-sleeve on. Despite the deer-in-the-headlights look in his eyes, something else lingered there too. It was deep, but there was no doubt in my mind, desire lurked there. "Do you even know what a catch you are, Maverick? Tall, dark-haired, broody...hell, all your missin' are some tattoos and

31

shadow magic and it's like you'd have stepped out of a fantasy romance."

"I don't...I don't understand." He shook his head, managing to back out from under my touch, placing at least a foot of distance between us.

Annoyance, and, let's face it, a bit of embarrassment, welled within me, choking some of the confidence I'd worked up coming out here.

"You know what?" I snapped, some of my anger getting the best of me as I threw my hands up in the air. "Just forget I said anything." I turned on my heel, muttering a string of curses under my breath as I stomped back for the main doors, passing by a whole group of cowboys staring my way.

Too bad they weren't the cowboy I wanted.

I'd barely made it inside when I bumped into a familiar face.

"Whoa there, darlin. Why you look so pissed?" Cash's words were light and slightly slurred as he bumped into me. Those hazel eyes of his held a glassy sheen to them. He wasn't drunk yet, but definitely buzzing.

I sighed, glancing back over my shoulder, like I could still see Maverick through the doors, and rolled my eyes. "Your cousin is either an absolute idiot, or just too damn nice to tell me he ain't interested."

"What happened?" he asked, a winning smile lighting up his face.

I shrugged, throwing up my hands. Damn, I needed a drink. Or five. Five sounded like a fun time. "I guess I came off a little too strong and scared him."

Cash barked an obnoxious laugh and put his hand on my shoulder. "What do they call them people that can't read?"

"Cash Mooney?" I guessed, quirking an eyebrow at him.

Another laugh. *God, he sounds like a donkey.* "No... itinerant....illigerent?"

"Illiterate?" I frowned at him, not sure what he was trying to say.

"That's it!" He lit up. "Maverick is like...illiterate of women. Like he can't read you at all. Doesn't mean he doesn't like y'all, he just doesn't understand."

"Okay?" I started to walk away but he moved in front of me.

"It's like—I heard...Or, well, someone told me there was these books where—" He paused to chuckle. "Where like elves fuck and stuff. Like just a bunch of beautiful elven women with big tits fucking all the time, ya know? And like, I wouldn't probably be able to read one, not cuz I'm illiterate or nothin', just cuz I don't read so good. Can't keep my attention. But it doesn't mean I wouldn't want to hear the story. You know?"

"No." I shook my head. "I have no idea what the hell you're talking about."

"He likes you." Cash swayed on his feet. "I can tell. He just...He can't. Ya know? *He* don't realize it cuz he's all hung up on that fuckin' Ashleigh bitch. Ya know?"

I wondered who Ashleigh was. Maybe that's why he'd been so weird. Was he dating someone else? No... Maverick didn't seem the type to cheat or two time. Maybe she was an ex he was hung up on. Either way, it didn't change anything. Not really.

"Thanks... I think."

"You okay?" His smile faltered.

I shrugged again—*ugh, how very Mav-like*. "It's fine. I'm just hot is all. Gonna go get myself a drink."

His lips pulled up into an apologetic smile. There was none of the Cash Mooney flare, no obnoxiousness as he said softly, "Don't give up on him just yet. He's been through some shit."

The way he talked about Maverick...you could tell that he meant a lot to him. I knew they were cousins, and very, very close, but it was deeper than that. The bond they shared...it was different.

I let out a deep, slow sigh. "Haven't we all, Mooney?" I clapped him on the shoulder. "You go find yourself a fun time."

And just like that, Cash was back with the usual energy. A confident smirk curved his lips as he winked my way. "Happy drinkin'," was all he said before striding for the door.

I huffed a half-hearted response before aiming for the bar.

CHAPTER 5
Blazin'

MAVERICK

"**H**ey dumbass!"

I groaned, tilting my head skyward as I blew out a puff of smoke.

What the hell did Cash want? That was such a loaded question. There was no limit to what dumb shit that dickhead could want. Each scenario that played out in my head worse and worse than the last.

"What'dya want?" I muttered, my gaze flicking to him as I pressed the cigar to my lips once more.

"You done fucked up," he said, sauntering over and smacking me square in the chest halfheartedly.

I batted his hand away. "The hell are you talkin' about?"

Cash shook his head, a hint of a smirk lighting up his features. "You remember our first rodeo?" he asked, voice casual as he leaned against the wall beside me, stealing my cigar from my hand and taking a drag.

I frowned but nodded. "Yeah."

Smoke billowed around him as he spoke. "Remember how we were all set up. Everythin' was good to go. That shoot opened, the steer shot out the gate. We went tearing down the arena after it, and you just kept

35

swingin' and swingin' and swingin' your rope. You were right there. One fuckin' throw away from catchin' it, but you just...kept on swingin'."

What the hell was he gettin' on about? He was spending too much time around his dad. Only Bad ever told stories like that.

I shrugged. "Yeah, I remember."

Cash pushed off the wall and turned to face me, placing a hand on my shoulder. "You just did the same shit right now with that girl."

I scoffed, my brow furrowing tightly. "You talkin' about Cheyenne?"

Another smack to my chest. "No fuckin' shit I'm talkin' about Cheyenne, dumbass." He shook his head, his usually playful gaze holding a seriousness it almost never possessed. "Girls like her don't come around too often. You gonna sit there fuckin' with your rope and let her get away, or get ya some fuckin' money?"

I sighed. I still didn't quite know what to feel about the interaction her and I had just had. I know I'd come off like a dick...I hadn't meant to. I was just *shocked* is all. I still didn't understand... Why me? What about me seemed worth getting to know? Worth wasting her time over? I wasn't funny and cocky like Cash. I wasn't inquisitive and confident like Ryder. I was broken and boring. It was hard to think why she'd approach me. Not when she could spend the night with any number of guys. I didn't miss the way people watched her. Hell, *I* couldn't even stop watching her.

When she'd gotten up close, pressing a hand to my chest, and I'd inhaled her citrusy scent, something had sparked in me. She had an electric touch. One that brought the broken, shattered pieces of my soul back to life for a moment.

That is until I'd pissed her off and she'd walked away, leaving me feeling cold as ice.

I thought of Ashleigh. Had I ever felt that electric touch with her? That...spark? It'd been so long since I'd felt anything but hopelessness with her, I couldn't even remember.

Stop thinkin' bout her. We were done. Had been for a while, if I were bein' honest. I pulled another cigar and my lighter out of my back pocket and lit it.

"Goddamn, Mav. Why you still thinkin' about that bi—"

A low growl rumbled out of my throat, the protective part of me refusing to let anyone bad mouth Ashleigh, no matter what misdeeds she'd done to me. I wasn't one to talk shit, and I'd not let others do it about the people I cared about.

Cash raised his hands in a placating gesture. "Sorry... Look I know you don't wanna hear it, but I'm tired of watchin' that girl hurt you. Time and time again she fucks you over. And you just take it. Again and again. Not even realizing you got somethin' way better right in front of you. Cheyenne ain't the type to chase after someone...and yet she chased after you."

I shrugged, blowing out a deep exhale of smoke. "I don't know why."

Cash huffed, shaking his head as he all but rolled his eyes. "Fuck, Mav. You always gotta be so fuckin' self loathin'? No wonder she's so pissed."

"You talked to her?" I asked.

I wondered what she'd said. Probably a whole string of curses. Girl had a mouth on her, especially when she was pissed.

"She came stormin' in a few minutes ago. Look...ain't nobody sayin' you gotta marry the girl, but at least give her a chance. You've been so hung up on Ashleigh for so long, it's like you don't even know how to interact with a woman."

I hated when Cash made sense. When he sounded reasonable. I hated it more when he was right. Cuz when he was, I was usually the one in the wrong.

I pursed my lips, grumbling around my cigar, "I get your point."

Cash took a final drag and put his cigar out against the wall. "I sure hope ya do."

I snorted a laugh, rolling my eyes. "Get off the damn soap box, Cash. Reasonable ain't your best look."

That confident, cocky smirk lit up his face once more. "Nope, but drunk sure is."

"You're a fuckin' idiot."

"Nah, not tonight, bud. You earned that role fair and square."

"Get fucked," I huffed, flipping him the bird, even as my lips curved into a grin.

He winked, that smirk pulling into a full-fledged smile. "Oh, I plan to." He started backpedaling as he called out, "Go, talk to her."

I waved him off, taking another drag as I thought of Cheyenne. I still didn't know what she saw in me, but Cash was right. She didn't seem like the chasin' after type. At the very least, I wanted to know more about what she found so intriguing about me.

Making my way towards the double doors, I put out my cigar and threw it away. Looked like I had some apologizing to do.

———

It didn't take long to find her. She sat on a stool at one of the bars across the way. I leaned against the table we'd reserved for the night, trying and failing to work up the nerve to go talk to her.

Go. Just go. But it's like my feet were stuck in concrete slabs. No amount of self-encouragement could move me even an inch. What if I'd blown it? What if she told me to fuck off? I wouldn't be surprised if she did. She seemed the fiery type. The kind of girl to have a short fuse.

Go.

Drawing up every ounce of willpower, I took a step forward...and then another...just as a guy slid into the seat beside her, angling his body toward her as he dipped his face toward her to start a conversation.

I sighed, the breath leaving me in a slow whoosh. *Looks like you lost your chance, dumbass.* The damn voice in my head reminded me of Cash —maybe not quite as obnoxious, but still annoying, though.

I shrank back against the table, whatever sliver of confidence I'd mustered up withering away to ash. *Probably better this way anyway.* She'd realize pretty quick I wasn't kidding when I said I was no fun at all.

I was just about to go back outside when two familiar voices came from my left.

"How's it goin, man?" Ryder's voice drew my gaze.

He and Charlie came to a stop before me, Ryder's arm wrapped around her waist, her hand in his back pocket. The two of them were slick with sweat, but a lightness danced on both of their faces, in their eyes.

I shrugged. "It's goin'. Y'all look like you're havin' fun."

Charlie smiled, leaning into Ryder, who seemed to pull her closer to him. She was barely pregnant, way too early to be showing, but I couldn't accurately describe Charlie as anything less than glowing. She'd always been a knockout, but the happiness and light in her eyes made her truly something to behold. They weren't lying when they talked about a baby glow, I guess. That, and since she and Ryder had gotten back together, both of them had been on cloud nine.

She looked up at Ryder. "Mind grabbing me a water?" she asked, leaning up and pressing a kiss to his lips.

He kissed her back before nodding. "Of course, darlin'." Ryder glanced at me. "Want anythin'?"

I shook my head, muttering a thanks.

"So...what's got you down?" Charlie asked, sliding into a seat beside me, nudging me with her shoulder.

I grunted, but the softest smile curved my lips upward. She and I had gotten close since Ryder joined the PBR team. Turns out, Charlie sucked at cooking, so I'd been giving her lessons... Well, that's what she liked to call them. She'd just sit on the counter chatting away about any and everything that came to mind, while I cooked.

It worked though. I liked to cook, and she liked to talk. She didn't hover or pester me like Cash, and I didn't interrupt her stories. It was a win-win.

I shrugged, then thought of Cheyenne and how she'd called me out on that. Did I really shrug that much? I guess I did. I fought the urge to shrug again. "Nothin'," I muttered.

Her head tilted to the side, her soft smile dipping into a scowl as she placed a hand on her hip. "You're as bad at lying as Cash it at staying sober."

"So basically, shit at it?" I offered lightly, a crooked smirk forming on my mouth.

"Yep." She laughed, before sobering a moment later. "Seriously though, what's going on?"

My gaze flicked to Cheyenne across the bar, talking animatedly to that same cowboy. Letting out a breath, I glanced back at Charlie. "I fucked up."

Her brow furrowed. "How? With who?"

"With Cheyenne." I drummed my fingers against the polished wood tabletop, trying and failing to keep from looking back at her. But I was little more than a moth drawn to a damn flame.

"Ah...you finally realized she was into you?" Charlie's lips pulled up into a knowing smirk.

Had everyone known she was into me but me? Was I really that oblivious? I launched into an abbreviated retelling of what had happened between us outside, even going so far as to mention how she'd even said something to Cash about our conversation.

"I don't even know what to do at this point," I huffed, my shoulders curling up into a shrug.

Charlie pursed her lips before settling on a soft smile as she pressed a hand to my forearm. "Oh, Mav.... She wants you to chase after her. To talk to her. To play the game."

"I ain't good at games," I admitted.

Clearly, Ashleigh had been playing games with me since we were kids and I still always lost in the end. Besides, I didn't *want* to play games. I wanted...hell, I didn't even know what I wanted.

Charlie squeezed my arm. "Then just go talk to her."

"About what?"

She chuckled. "About anything. Her. You. Your interests. It doesn't matter. Just...talk to her."

Ryder returned just then, a bottle of water for Charlie in one hand and a beer in the other. "What'd I miss?"

"Mav was just saying how he was gonna go talk to Cheyenne."

I speared her with a harsh glare, my mouth popping open. "No, I—"

Her lips curved into a challenging grin, even as Ryder clapped me on the shoulder. "Good on ya, man. It's about damn time you noticed her."

Seriously, had everyone known but me? Maybe Cheyenne was right. I *was* oblivious. That, or I'd just been so wrapped up in Ashleigh I hadn't really been paying attention. My gaze settled on Cheyenne once more. Well, I was paying attention now.

A flicker of jealousy writhed within me as I watched her across the way. She laughed at something the guy said, but from the tightness in her smile, the way she sat turned away from him, how she'd stopped drinking her cocktail... I knew she wasn't into him.

Was it bad of me that I wanted to go over there? That I wanted to be the one who made her laugh? Earlier today all I could think of was Ashleigh, and now here I was, jealous over a girl I didn't even know?

Charlie nudged me once more, pulling my stare. "Go save her, Mav."

"She don't look like she needs savin'," I muttered, some of my nerves getting the best of me.

What if she was still pissed at me? What if she was actually enjoying herself and didn't want me to interrupt her?

What if...what if...what if, the little voice in my head mocked.

Ryder came up beside me, gripping my shoulders and giving a reassuring squeeze. "She may not need savin', but that don't mean she don't want it. Go get her, before you lose her."

I inhaled slowly, drawing in every scared, negative, worrisome emotion inside me, and blowing it out. Resolve welled up as I nodded. "Alright. I got this."

With newfound confidence—however misplaced—I pushed off from my spot at the table and made my way toward her. My slow, sure footsteps were in direct opposition of my wildly thumping heart. It all but galloped out of my damn chest.

And then she stood up, flashed the cowboy a smile, and waltzed toward the exit without a backward glance.

Fuck. Chasing her sure wasn't going to be easy.

CHAPTER 6
Pretty Little Poison

CHEYENNE

I leaned back against the stucco-sided building and sucked in a lungful of fresh air...and all but choked on the humidity. Summer in Texas already in full swing and June wasn't even completely over yet. It felt like I was wading through hot sauce. But at least I'd escaped wannabe Morgan Wallen's unrelenting advances. If I had to listen to him try any more of his shitty pickup lines on me, I might've keeled over and died of disappointment.

Maybe I should just go home... Except the whole reason for coming out tonight was so that I didn't have to be stuck in my trailer feeling sorry for myself. Yet, here I was, feeling sorry for myself. Maybe I should just forget about Maverick. Maybe there was a reason it hadn't worked out with him yet. Maybe it never would.

Some things just weren't meant to be.

"There you are."

My body seized up, a spark of excitement igniting in my chest at the sound of that familiar voice—deep, smooth as velvet. It made my stomach do little somersaults.

I turned to take him in—from his black cowboy hat down to his black boots. Dear Lord, he was hot. He wore the same usual scowl, the same hooded, closed-off gaze. He always seemed so mysterious. So grumpy.

"Maverick," I said with a nod, looking forward once more and settling back against the wall. I let my eyes flutter closed as I feigned disinterest, even as my heart fluttered like it was full of a swarm of butterflies waiting to be released. The air moved beside me as he settled on my left—close, but not quite touching. A ripple of desire coursed through me. I didn't open my eyes though. Not yet. I was still being petty.

The scent of him—tobacco and leather—filled my nose, reminding me of home. My heart panged at that.

"So, I uh...I got a few babies I'm workin'... There's this one...Blue Zeus, he's uh, he's this little blue roan. Cason named him. But uh..."

Why was he talking about horses? I'd hoped that if he ever worked up the nerve to talk to me it would be to flirt...not talk about the babies he was breaking.

I sucked in a deep, sharp breath through my nose, preparing a flippant response, but the moment I glanced over at him, I paused, mouth half open, the words dying on my lips. His usually guarded gaze was open, earnest, his face holding none of the usual dourness he almost always possessed. Vulnerability lingered throughout every inch of him.

I blew out the breath I'd been holding, all of the anger leaving me as my heart all but melted. A smile toyed on my lips as I turned to face him, angling myself closer so that my body brushed against his.

He fumbled over his words, his gaze widening—in fear or nervousness, I wasn't quite sure—for a moment as he noticed my movements, but still he continued on. Something shifted in him the longer he spoke. I wouldn't necessarily call it confidence, but maybe...certainty. He spoke about the babies he was breaking with a surety and knowledge I could only dream of possessing...and I'd grown up with horses. But the way he spoke about them...I'd never seen him talk so much. So animatedly or passionately.

It was cute and innocent and sweet, and it melted me even more. I hadn't expected that. Maverick didn't seem the type to melt your heart. He was broody and grumpy and closed off, more the kind of guy to break a heart than melt it, but beneath that, I realized, was the sweetest soul. He reminded me of Ferdinand the bull, who only wanted to sit and smell the flowers.

Only all this cowboy wanted was to talk about horses.

A full-fledged smile spread across my mouth, and I don't know how or what possessed me, but one minute I stood there, the next, I was leaning up on tiptoe, pressing a quick kiss to his lips.

He all but jumped back, a look of pure bewilderment on his face, those jade eyes flashing with disbelief. "Wh–what'd you do that for?"

I shrugged and smirked, raising a tentative hand and placing it against his chest. His heart thumped beneath my touch—a fast, erratic beat. "You're cute when you talk so much."

Something ignited in his gaze, which was sharp and intense as it pegged me in place, but still he made no move toward me.

I bit my lip, my voice dipping low as I asked, "Can I kiss you again, cowboy?"

I almost thought he wouldn't react. That he'd just stand there and let me flounder again.

Oh no. A rush of disappointment washed over me. Had I gone too far? Scared him off completely?

His hands, calloused and rough, cupped the back of my head and scraped along the small of my back before hooking around my waist, pulling me to him. His mouth met mine once more, holding a possessive, demanding note to it that had my toes curling in my boots. When he finally pulled away, both our chests rose and fell in heavy breaths. He didn't let go of me, which was more than a bit surprising. I half expected him to run away already. In fact, I *still* half expected it to happen any moment.

"You taste like tobacco and trouble," I murmured, tilting my chin up to meet his hooded gaze. His hat cast his face in shadow.

He chuckled, tucking a piece of hair behind my ear. "No, you're the one who's trouble."

I grinned, pulling his face down toward mine once more. "I'll take that as a compliment," I said against his lips.

He surprised me again, brushing his lips against the corner of my jaw, the words low, husky as he whispered, "Figured you would."

He claimed my mouth with his, his grip on the back of my head tightening with the slightest pressure as his fingers knotted in my hair. A moan escaped me.

This. This was exactly what I needed. What I'd wanted from the minute I'd met him.

And he sure as hell didn't disappoint.

I don't know why I'd expected timidness—okay, scratch that, I knew *exactly* why I expected that—but I was more than pleasantly surprised when he matched me with a passion I'd only dreamed of.

No, he wasn't just matching me, he took the damn reins completely as he pressed me back against the wall, his touch, his kisses possessive, hungry, wild.

I liked this side of Maverick.

And I wanted more.

The hand that'd been wrapped around me slid up my waist before brushing along the swell of my breast, finally settling lightly around the side of my neck. A touch that proved Maverick wasn't as sweet and innocent as he appeared.

As he pulled away, I bit his bottom lip, pegging him in place with a scalding stare.

The look on his face nearly knocked the breath from me. This wasn't the same man who'd all but trembled in his boots when I'd told him I wanted him. This was a man who knew what he wanted and had no problems doing whatever necessary to get it.

I'd never been more attracted to him.

"Well," I huffed, my hands resting against the planes of his chest. "Gotta admit, I'm more than a bit surprised at that."

"Is that a good or bad thing?" Even though that sexy look in his eyes still remained, his voice gave him away. There was a hint of worry laced in his words.

Grabbing a fistful of his shirt, I leaned up once more and kissed him softly. "Don't worry, Maverick," I whispered against his lips. "It's a very good thing."

He chuckled, low and deep, his light green eyes taking me in. I don't know what it was about that look, but it filled me with confidence.

One of my hands snaked up his chest to cup the back of his neck, even as his hand clutching my throat drifted down to hook along the curve of my hips. "So, what'dya wanna do?"

The corner of his lips pulled up into a lopsided grin, his light eyes swimming with desire now. Anticipation thrummed through me. Was this really going to happen? Was I finally going to get Maverick all to myself?

"How 'bout a dance?" he asked, surprising the hell out of me.

It was my turn to frown. Okay, was I in some weird episode of the Twilight Zone? The guy who'd *just* said he didn't want to dance earlier now wanted to dance.I studied his face, searching for anything to help me understand the shift in his decision.

"You're serious?"

He shrugged—his trademark gesture. "You wanna dance, and if I say no, some other guy's gonna come over and steal you away."

I highly doubted they'd be able to steal me away, but I didn't say that. No, I just started counting on my finger.

He frowned. "What are you doin'?"

"I think that's the longest sentence you've strung along all night... that was, what, eighteen words?"

A true, genuine smile pulled on his lips, damn near stopping my heart. Sullen Maverick was hot as fuck, but happy Maverick...he might just be my favorite. "Well, now I ain't dancin'," he said with another shrug.

"No!" I pulled him closer to me, a pout drawing on my mouth. "I'm sorry."

His smile vanished, a seriousness washing over him like a rogue wave. The shift in his demeanor was so quick it left me breathless. He tightened his grip on my waist, his other hand moving to tilt my chin up, forcing me to meet his gaze. "No, I'm the one who's sorry."

"For what?" I asked, my heart thumping so hard in my chest I could barely talk, let alone breathe.

"For bein' an idiot." He claimed my mouth in another soul-stopping kiss. One that stole the air from my lungs and made my nerves tingle. Dear Lord, if he kissed this good, I could only imagine what else he could do.

"All's forgiven, cowboy," I murmured against his lips. "Now let's go dance."

He groaned, even as a ghost of a grin warred with the shadows lingering on his face.

CHAPTER 7
Spin You Around

MAVERICK

The bar all but swam with people, the dance floor a sea of bodies two stepping and twirling to a fast, thumping beat that rivaled that of my heart. Cheyenne all but bounced beside me, flashing me questioning glances every couple minutes.

She finally turned on me with a sigh, her hands coming to rest on her hips. "Ugh, come on, Maverick. It's been like five songs." Her lips drew down into a pout, those turquoise eyes filled with challenge. "*You're* the one who asked *me* to dance, remember?"

My lips tugged up slightly in the corners. She was a demanding little thing. Fiery. Feisty. Completely opposite of me.

But she was right. I *had* asked her to dance. It's just...well, there were just too many people. I'd had a moment of temporary insanity, and, like a damn fool, asked her to do the one thing I hated most. *Why?*

Hell, I was still trying to figure that out.

"They're all too fast. I said a slow one," I grumbled.

She rolled her eyes, even as her lips pulled up into a smirk. "You're so difficult."

I shrugged, making her shake her head as she grabbed a shot of

51

Crown off the tabletop and brought it to her lips before tossing it back and slamming it down. A grimace marred her features a moment.

I'd never understand why anyone would willingly drink something that obviously tasted so horrible.

The song ended, Morgan Wallen's "Spin You Around" replacing it. Cheyenne's gaze lit up like a firework on the Fourth of July, a smile brighter than the sun curving her lips.

"Ooh! Well, would you look at that, cowboy? Ask and you shall receive. It's time to dance."

She slipped her hand in mine, all but dragging me toward the dance floor. I didn't have a choice but to follow. She was a beacon of light, a ray of sunshine, and I found myself drawn to her.

My feet felt like they'd been coated in cement or lead, each step heavy, unnatural. But not her. She all but floated around me, leading me through the motions in a way that made me feel like I wasn't a complete idiot... But then I looked around.

People watched us. Correction—her. They watched her, because who could resist? I'd only ever met a few people in my life who held such a grand presence—her and Cash being among them. A part of me envied them, for the ease and confidence with which they held themselves. But that would be too much attention for me. Even now, with all these eyes on us, my pulse raced. A weight settled on me, making my chest constrict. My stomach clenched in knots, my nerves coiling tighter and tighter.

PTSD was a real bitch. I never knew when it was going to rear its ugly head. When it would pop up out of nowhere and ruin my time. There wasn't much that could stop it though once it came around. Every inch of me, from the top of my head to the tips of my toes, tingled as a wave of heat made its way through me. Sound warped and wobbled, the music all but disappearing as my pulse thrummed in my ears. My breathing shallowed, making it hard to get in a deep breath.

Fuck.

Every inch of me screamed to run, to get the hell out of there and away from everyone's gaze. My movements slowed, damn near stopping completely.

"Hey." Cheyenne's smokey voice sounded far away as it tried to cut through the chaos in my mind. "Maverick. Hey, look at me."

Warm hands snaked up my chest and wrapped around my neck. It was enough to dispel the cloud of panic cloying for dominance in my mind. I inhaled sharply, the sweet, citrusy scent of her grounding me a bit. My hands trembled as I held her.

Those gemstone eyes of her swam with understanding. She placed a soft, tentative kiss to my lips. "Don't worry about everyone else right now. It's just you and me, okay?" She began swaying to the music once more, and it was then I realized sound had returned to normal.

"Sorry," I muttered, my gaze falling to my boots in shame.

She tilted my chin up, forcing me to meet her gaze. Resolve and determination blazed in the depths. "You got nothin' to be sorry for. If this is too much we can stop."

I shook my head, my grip on her tightening a bit. "You want to dance, though."

She shrugged, her tone light as she replied, "But you don't want to."

It was my turn to shrug. "I don't wanna do a lot of things."

She laughed, the sound a lilting melody that rose over the song. "Well, what *do* you like to do then?" she asked, still dancing slowly to the beat.

I moved with her, settling my hands back in their proper position. "I like whittlin'—you know, woodcarvin'. And um...well, I like workin' with the horses and keepin' my hands busy. I like to build things. Work on cars. Fish. Cook. Every now and then, I'll pick on a guitar."

She grinned. "And you said you're no fun."

I huffed a low laugh, more of the tension leaving me as I focused on her and her melodic voice. Her calming touch. "I ain't."

She rolled her eyes, trying and failing to hide a smile. "You're an idiot."

"What about you? What do you like to do?"

Her face turned contemplative a moment, her brow furrowing together. "Hm...well, I love craftin'...even if I gotta do it for work. But makin' candles, wreaths, essential oil blends, t-shirts, knittin' blankets...I love it all. And then there's always rodeoin' and ridin'. I mean, it's been a minute since I've ridden for pleasure, but who doesn't love a good trail ride?" She bit her lip a moment before a soft, almost shy smile tugged on her mouth. I'd never expect to see that look on her face. "Sometimes, when I have a minute, I like to read."

I scoffed. "You read?"

That smile dipped into a scowl, her gaze hardening. "Um...*rude*. Are you callin' me illiterate?"

I chuckled, pulling her a little tighter to me. "Nah, I ain't sayin' that at all. Just surprised. You don't seem like the type to want to sit and read."

Her scrutinizing gaze held me in place as she said, "Well, I *love* to read."

"What kinda books?"

The song ended. Something a bit faster picked up, and I surprised the hell out of myself by speeding up my pace, all while still keeping her firmly in my grip. It was like if I let go of her, she might disappear altogether. What if we stopped dancing and she lost interest? As much as I hated dancing, I didn't want this moment to end.

Her cheeks flushed slightly, but her gaze, her words, blazed with confidence. "Mostly fantasy romance."

My brow scrunched up. "Is that like...Lord of the Rings with porn in it?"

Laughter bubbled out of her; she curled in on herself nearly stumbling in my arms. "Oh my God, no! Think fairy tales but with spice."

"What the hell is spice?" It was like she spoke a different language.

I don't think I remembered the last time I'd picked up a book for pleasure. Maybe never? Sitting down, doing nothing but turning pages seemed counterproductive to me. I needed to be doing something, using my hands.

She rolled her eyes, a giggle escaping her. "Ugh, you know nothin', Jon Snow. And as for spice, it's like...how much smut's in a book."

My brows furrowed together. "Smut?"

Another flush of her cheeks as a coy smile tugged her lips upward. "Basically, how much romance a book has. You know...like sexy scenes."

"So, it *is* porn."

"It is *not* porn." She smacked my chest playfully, a huff of laughter escaping her.

"Sounds like it." I couldn't help but smirk.

"Well, it ain't," she replied, her mouth drawing up into a playful snarl.

I spun her, my body instantly missing her warmth, even if only a moment later I was pulling her back into my arms. "I think you're gonna have to prove it."

Her face scrunched up, a confused laugh coming from her even as she didn't miss a beat, falling into step as we danced. "You want me to read a smutty book to you?"

It was odd...in the course of a few moments, a few dozen words, the panic was gone, all but a whisper. It still lingered in the corners of my mind. I didn't think I'd ever be lucky enough for it to go away completely, but some of the worry, the darkness, had receded.

I shrugged, moving with her and the music. "Well, I gotta know for myself what smut means."

Her head fell back, laughter bubbling out of her like a babbling brook. That happiness, that light was infectious. Pure, dazzling light that chased away the shadows. How could someone be filled with so much? I wanted to bottle her up and save her for a cloudy day. She sobered after a moment, but her eyes still swam with warmth. "I could do that, cowboy. Got any plans after this?"

I swallowed. The thought of going home with her sent a rush of excitement through me. And also, surprise. My mind for the briefest moment drifted to Ashleigh. Hadn't I just been trying to see her tonight? Yeah, she'd been screwing me over, as usual, but I loved her... didn't I?

I didn't even know anymore. Maybe I just loved the idea of her. Of what we were so long ago.

I focused on Cheyenne once more, and while I expected guilt, I only felt resolve. Maybe that's why I found myself saying, "Only plans I got are this right here."

Cheyenne's grin sent shivers of anticipation down my spine, a look of pure mischief glimmering like stardust in her eyes. "Well, how 'bout we get on out of here, then?"

"I thought you wanted to dance?" I asked, twirling her away from me.

This wasn't actually too bad. Not as she spun back into my arms, her body settling close to mine once more. Her sweet scent enveloped me, her gaze holding mine. It's like everyone else had melted away and her and I were the only ones on the dance floor.

"I'd rather see where this goes more," she replied, that bright gaze full of desire pegging me in place.

Well, damn.

CHAPTER 8
Barn Burner

CHEYENNE

Excitement thrummed through my veins like an electrical current, setting my leg bouncing as I sat in the passenger seat of my truck. Maverick drove, his gaze settled on the road before us. Not gonna lie, he looked hot as all hell sitting there. Not many people drove my truck. Call it an ego or control thing, I didn't really care. I was just a bit territorial with my things, is all. But I couldn't drive home... I mean, I definitely *could*, but I didn't want a DUI.

Even if I'd been okay to, though, Maverick wouldn't have settled on being a passenger princess. He'd been adamant on driving me home, and I was too stunned that he'd actually agreed, that I hadn't put up a fight.

I *had* talked the majority of the ride back to the trailer park though, only pausing every so often for him to mutter out a sentence or two in reply to one of my questions. For the most part, he didn't seem to mind me talking. In fact, since he'd agreed to coming home with me, there was a definite shift in his demeanor. He seemed more open, more alive. He still was one hundred percent himself when it came to being closed off and tight-lipped, but he didn't seem so wound up anymore. He watched me with a warmth in his eyes I'd rarely seen before tonight, amusement dancing in the light irises.

Whatever the reason for this shift, I'd take it.

My trailer park came into view, and the desire simmering inside me turned up to full blaze. The anticipation of what was to come made me fidget even more. Between that and the amount of whiskey I'd consumed, it was no surprise I reached over and trailed a hand over his thigh, making sure to brush my fingertips over his cock beneath his starched denim jeans.

His knuckles whitened around the steering wheel, his entire body tensing up as a low, deep rumble, reminding me of rolling thunder, quaked from his chest. A shaky breath escaped him as he slowly slid his gaze to me.

The strangest mixture of emotions glimmered in his gaze—surprise, lust, worry, excitement, challenge, confusion—as he opened his mouth to speak. "Which spot's yours?"

"Six...." My fingers brushed over his cock once more.

He chuckled softly, pegging me with a gaze that mirrored my desire. "Careful, trouble. Or I may just pull off right here and drag you in the backseat."

"Don't tempt me with a good time," I clapped back, offering him a wink as I stroked him once more.

A shudder passed through him, his entire body tensing beneath my touch, those light green eyes of his telling me everything I needed to know. Maverick wanted this. Wanted me. And I sure as hell wanted him.

The desire vanished on his face in a heartbeat, worry and concern replacing any lighter emotions. "What the hell?"

'Red lights flashed, casting his face in a crimson glow. *Wait...why are there—*

I followed his gaze, my chest constricting as I took in everything.

Fear—cold, paralyzing fear—turned the blood in my veins to ice. It traveled through me, from the top of my head to the tips of my toes, settling like a frozen chunk around my heart.

Flames licked toward the midnight sky as a crew of firefighters worked on putting them out.

My trailer... What the fuck? Why? How?

"Oh my God...Brandy!" My voice sounded far off, like I was stuck underwater. Maverick hadn't even stopped the truck as I slipped off my seatbelt, opened the passenger door, and launched myself out and towards the commotion.

"Brandy!" I rushed forward, fear eating a hole through my chest. I had to find her.

"Ma'am!" A firefighter stopped me, "Ma'am! What're you—"

"That's my trailer! Where's my dog? My dog! Brandy!"

All that mattered. All I could think of was her. Where was she? Was she okay? Heat licked at me even from a distance, the smell of smoke irritating my lungs.

"We haven't seen or heard a dog, Ma'am. We checked inside."

My stomach writhed and twisted, like a snake coiling tighter and tighter and tighter. I couldn't breathe. Couldn't think or feel anything other than icy terror. I shivered despite the heat. "She doesn't do well with strangers, she's probably hiding! Please, please, sir. I have to go get her! Brandy!"

I pushed past him, but he caught me around the waist.

"Ma'am—Ma'am, calm down. We checked. There ain't no dog."

I lost it. Completely and totally lost it.

I started swinging. Flailing. Screaming as tears poured down my cheeks and smoke tore at my raw lungs. No. Brandy wouldn't leave. She was loyal to a fault, which meant she *had* to be in there. She had to.

"Cheyenne, what the hell's goin' on?"

That familiar, deep voice cut through the chaos, and my wild gaze found him. He stalked toward me, a look of murder on his face, his dark silhouette reminding me of some fallen angel come to earth.

My chest screamed at me—from the panic and the smoke inhalation —as a raw, broken cry left my lips. "Maverick, it's Brandy! She's in there!"

A second firefighter had joined his buddy to keep me at bay as I struggled beneath their grip. If I could. Just. Get. Free.

I knew she was in there. I knew it. I felt it in my bones.

Maverick's shadowed face met mine, but some unnamed emotion blazed in his eyes as he met my gaze.

And then he raced toward my trailer...

CHAPTER 9
Burn It Down

MAVERICK

Every nerve ending in my body zinged with fear as I saw the flames.

God must've had a sick sense of humor. Twenty years to the day, and then this.

Cheyenne jumped out of the truck before I could even slam on the brakes. Panic surged within me, swelling and rising with each breath I sucked down. My lungs stopped working. My body seized up. I didn't even know how I managed to stop the truck and park it.

Just like that, it was like I was eleven years old again. Fear pinned me in place as I just sat there for a moment staring at the flames. Cheyenne's screams cut through the night, louder than the roar of the fire.

No one talks about how loud it is. The sound. It ain't peaceful like when you sit before a fireplace or a bonfire. It's like the fire...it's alive. It's angry. And it wants to consume any and everything.

Cheyenne's wails—raw and visceral—dragged me from my thoughts, spurring me into action. Just like Ellie Mae's had all those years ago.

Fuck.

I swallowed past the growing lump in my throat and slammed the driver-side door open before racing toward Cheyenne. A crew of firefighters fought the fire, aside from the two she struggled against.

"Maverick, it's Brandy! She's in there!" The pure, undiluted terror in her voice, written plainly on her face, made the lump in my throat grow larger.

I needed to do something. Had to. Had to stop the terror in her tone like I should have done all those years ago for Ellie but couldn't. Fear and determination warred within me, sending a jolt of adrenaline straight through my veins.

I hadn't been able to save Ellie Mae, but I'd be damned if I didn't save Cheyenne's dog.

I don't know if anyone chased after me as I ran headfirst toward the flames, sweat already coating my brow as the heat assaulted me. Covering an arm over my mouth and nose, I tried to breathe in through the fabric of my shirt—whatever I could to save my lungs.

The door was open already, fire snaking out like gnarled fingers as it consumed and destroyed every bit of flammable surface in sight. My eyes stung and watered, my vision blurring as I raced up the steps and into the main aisleway.

"Brandy!" I coughed as I tried to call for her, inhaling a lungful of smoke.

My body seized up, fear gripping my heart so tight I thought I might keel over and die. The heat, the smoke, the smell, it brought back every painful, terrifying memory. A swell of panic chased away whatever adrenaline had spurred me onward a moment ago.

Just like that, I was back in the car. Just like that I didn't know what to do.

One minute I stood there, the next I was on the floor. My eyes blurred with tears—of terror or from the smoke, I couldn't tell you.

"Mavie!"

Ellie Mae's screams cut through all the chaos. Mom and Dad lay hunched lifeless in their seats. Flames licked at them. Licked all around us, destroying everything in their path as they made their way for Ellie Mae and I.

One of my arms hung useless at my side, pain—blinding pain—

pulsing from my elbow down to my fingertips. My head swam, my vision doubling, tripling during some moments. I just wanted to sleep. Sleep sounded so nice. It beat this hell.

But Ellie Mae's screams turned shriller, pained. I turned and clawed at the seatbelt straps of her car seat. Instead of buying her a proper one, like Dad said he would, he'd resorted to tying the straps from when he'd gotten angry and cut her out of them once when he was drunk. I struggled with the knots, flames searing my fingers, my hands, my arms.

But the pain would never compare to the screams.

A whine broke through my thoughts, followed by a distant, weak yip.

I blinked through the tears as I pushed up from the prone position I'd landed on the ground.

"Brandy?" I croaked out before falling into a fit of coughs.

Another whine.

I scanned through the smoke and flames, my gaze landing on her directly under the bed at the other end of the hallway. She whined again, even as her tail wagged in a single thump. On my hands and knees, I scrambled over to her, a trickle of hope pulling at my heartstrings.

"Come on, girl," I choked out as I made my way toward the foot of the bed.

She whined and thumped her tail again but made no effort to move. She could have been hurt, could have just been scared stiff, and as much as I wanted to ease her out from under the bed, I just didn't have time.

A loud creak groaned from the trailer and then a loud boom as the window above the bed exploded. Glass and ash rained down on me, pain prickling along my face.

Fuck. Fuck. Fuck.

I needed out of here. I couldn't die like this. No, I wasn't ready.

"Come on, girl, I got you. I got you," I repeated again, reaching out a hand and grabbing for her collar.

Please don't bite me.

She didn't, thank the Lord, but she also didn't help much either. Despite being a small thing, she sure weighed a ton as I scooped her up in my arms and made my way for the front door.

My lungs screamed, my eyes burned and I was so hot I wasn't even sure at this point if I was on fire or not.

"Come on, pretty girl," I murmured as I crawled toward the door. Poor thing trembled in my arms as I went.

The smoke hung like a shroud, choking in its intensity, and while the fire raged around me, all I could think, all I could hear, all I could see was Ellie Mae. Her screams. The tears in her eyes. The feel of her fingernails clawing at my arms as I tried to pull her out.

Tried and failed.

Failed.

Panic settled around my heart, suffocating me more than the smoke in my lungs. Ice slithered down my spine, my mind going foggy. My vision blurred, darkness closing in around the corners.

Not again. I couldn't pass out again.

I still don't know how I survived the accident. The firefighters and paramedics were just as surprised. An act of God maybe, or probably just dumb luck. But I didn't think I'd be as lucky this time around.

Something warm and wet bumped my cheek, a soft whine following it. How had I ended up laying down again? Brandy's brown eyes, full of terror, pegged me in place.

Fuck.

I tried to suck in a calming breath, but no cold air slithered down my throat or swelled in my lungs. Only a scalding trail of smoke and ash, searing every inch of me. I coughed, my vision blurring once more, the screams in my head getting so loud I couldn't think straight. Would they ever go away again?

Brandy nudged me once more, a whine escaping her. I shouldn't have been able to hear it over the blaze, but I did. It broke the paralysis in my limbs, giving me strength I didn't think I had left in me. One second, I was on the ground, the next scooping her up again as I stumbled forward. A curtain crashed down beside us over the kitchen table, raining down more ash and embers. Just as we got to the door, a hulking figure in a turnout held out a hand, shouting something through his oxygen mask at me as he pulled us out. I couldn't make out the words, my brain a haze of smoke. My lungs barked in agony as I struggled to get air down. But as he dragged me away from the flames, the scorching heat of the fire was replaced by the damp, summer night air. Not quite the relief I was looking for, but better than before.

My vision blurred, sound wobbling in and out of focus before going quiet all together as memories bombarded me.

Ellie's screams. Her face full of tears. That last look we shared before I was ripped out of the truck by some stranger. My outstretched hand reaching for her as I roared and cried and flailed to get back to her.

She had been all that was good and light in the world. Neither of us had been dealt a particularly good hand at life, but Ellie never cared. Never understood how bad we had it. She'd only been four. She didn't deserve to die. Didn't deserve this fate.

She deserved a good, long life. A mother and father who loved her. Cherished her. Not this.

Darkness threatened to overwhelm me completely, the yawning black abyss of oblivion a welcome sight. Maybe now, I'd finally get to be with her again. My body didn't hurt anymore. My lungs didn't burn.

I'm comin' Ellie.

A hum cut through the silence. I couldn't make it out entirely, but it was soft, feminine. *Ellie.*

Warmth came next. The touch soothing, gentle but insistent.

And finally, light. Like a ray of sunlight in a dark, gloomy, shitty world. I moved toward the light. Hoping, praying, that wherever I went to next was wherever Ellie Mae was.

But the blinding light softened, the touch became more insistent, and the voice—not Ellie's after all—held a worried edge to it.

"Maverick! Maverick, it's okay!"

I woke up with a jolt, sucking air down my throat, only to dissolve into a fit of coughing. Soft hands gripped my shoulders, the brightest set of gemstone eyes fixing me in place.

"Cheyenne," I choked out.

CHAPTER 10
Deeper Than The Holler

CHEYENNE

I don't know how long Maverick was in the trailer for. It could have been two minutes, but it felt like twenty. Longer even. Each second that ticked by felt like a lifetime, fear gripping my heart tighter, tighter, tighter.

I'd stopped fighting the firefighters the minute Maverick raced for the trailer, my body suddenly paralyzed in place. He'd run into a burning building for my dog. He didn't even know Brandy. Not really. He was either crazy or a goddamn super hero.

Some of the terror eased in my chest as the firefighter dragged him out and away from the flames. As soon as he was on the ground, Brandy bolted out of his arms, her wild gaze searching for me.

"Come here, girl," I urged, squeezing her to my chest as she barreled into me. Running my hands over her fur, I scanned her for injuries. Nothing that I could see, though she smelled god-awful. But the relief was short lived as they dragged Maverick's motionless body toward the ambulance.

My hands trembled, my breathing hitching in my throat. *Oh my*

God. Please let him be okay. On legs that felt like jello, I raced forward, Brandy hot on my heels.

A medic was already strapping an oxygen mask to his face, tearing his burnt shirt off as they checked for injuries. I gasped as I took him in. Burns coated him. Canyons and crevices of all shapes and sizes, spanning from his wrists to his chest. The left was worse than the right, but not by much.

"A-are those from now?" I gasped, my hands muffling the sound.

The medic didn't even deign to look at me as he shook his head and responded. "No, ma'am. These don't look fresh." And then he was back to working, pulling things out of his pack, cleaning and wrapping Maverick's wounds. All the while, Maverick lay unconscious, the only sign of life being the rise and fall of his chest.

I ran a hand over his close-cropped hair, eyeing the deep cut slicing through his eyebrow.

"Is he gonna be okay?" I asked, casting a worried glance at the medic.

He met my stare this time at least. "He inhaled a lotta smoke, but aside from that it's mostly cuts and bruises..." he glanced at the cut above Maverick's eye. "Well, except that one. May need a couple stitches."

I blew out a sigh of relief. Not completely in the clear, but I'd take that verdict for the moment.

"I don't know whether your boyfriend's just plain stupid or incredibly brave," the medic went on, gaze flicking back to his task. "Likely a bit of both."

I didn't bother to mention Maverick and I weren't dating. It seemed such a trivial thing in the moment. Not when he still hadn't woken up. My heart hammered in my chest. I know the guy said he was okay, but... what if he wasn't? What if he ran in there and saved Brandy and ended up seriously sick or hurt or dying?

Panic gripped my stomach, twisting it in knots and making me tremble. Fuck, I hated this feeling. So...so out of control. He had to be okay. I couldn't take that guilt. Not like I'd had any control in stopping him, but I'd all but begged him to do something. Anything.

Please let him be okay. Please let him—

He fell into a coughing fit, his chest crumbling in on itself as he fought and flailed to pull the oxygen mask off. I pressed my hands to his shoulders. "Maverick! Maverick, it's okay!"

Panic—pure, undiluted panic—shone in his light gaze as it settled on me. "Cheyenne." his voice was raw, his breath ragged. His chest rose and fell as the paramedic spouted off something, but I wasn't paying attention.

"Hey," I breathed out, my voice a broken squeak. "It's okay. You're okay."

His wild gaze flitted around, searching for something. "Brandy?" he choked out from behind the oxygen mask.

I glanced down at her before settling on him once more, my hands still holding him steady. "She's okay. You..." my throat closed in on itself. A lump forming. "You saved her."

I don't think I could ever thank him enough. Could ever repay the kindness and bravery he'd shown me. Brandy was my everything. My good girl. My road dog. My best friend. Without her...God, I didn't even want to think about that possibility.

I didn't even realize I was crying until he raised a shaky hand to my cheek. "I couldn't—" another coughing fit "—let her die."

My heart squeezed. And thank God the paramedic interrupted me, or else I might have done something incredibly stupid like rip the mask off and kiss him. Or even worse, tell him I loved him. Because I just might be in love with him after that selfless act.

———

THE NEXT FEW HOURS WENT IN A BLUR AFTER THAT. THEY got the fire under control, and finally out. All of my stuff was ruined though. Everything I owned, aside from my tack, in that trailer. Thank God, I'd left it in the back of my truck.

At some point, a couple Sheriffs showed up, asking a whole bunch of questions I had zero answers to. No, I hadn't left any candles on. No, I hadn't left the stove or oven on. No, I hadn't left my curling iron on— I didn't even own one. Had they seen my hair?

Each question felt more like an interrogation, making me frustrated and defensive. I hated that I felt like the suspect. I hadn't done anything wrong, and I wasn't some dumb idiot who just left something on and forgot to turn it off.

"Do you have any problems with anyone? Someone who'd wish you ill will?" one of the deputies asked.

I frowned. That gave me pause. Would Nate be that much of a dick? He was certainly fucking capable of it... But, arson?

You did chase him with a cattle prod, the traitorous little voice in my mind offered.

But chasing off someone with a cattle prod and arson were on two completely different levels. And if he had done it, why the hell would I tell the sheriffs? He'd likely just retaliate more in the end. Even if he did do it, I honestly just wanted nothing to do with him.

With a shake of my head, I said, "No, sir."

They interviewed Mr. and Mrs. Perkins, who hadn't seen anything. But they had heard Brandy bark once—though that wasn't completely out of the ordinary for her. With nothing else to really do, they talked about getting security footage from the trailer park, but that'd likely take a day or two, so until then it was just sit and wait.

I'd have to call and file an insurance claim on the trailer tomorrow, but that would do me little to no good in the here and now. Basically, I was homeless and broke. Cool.

I bit back tears as the deputies and fire department finally pulled away. The paramedic had already finished patching up Maverick a while ago. Despite their best attempts, he'd refused to go to the hospital to have the cut on his eyebrow patched up as well as a breathing treatment.

The scent of fire still remained, though little more than soot and broken shrapnel littered the ground where my home had once been. My chest constricted, a lump lodging in my throat as my entire body trembled. What the hell was I going to do? How was I going to come back from this?

I glanced over at Maverick sitting on the tailgate of my truck, the lump in my throat thickening. He'd been so quiet. Painfully quiet since waking up. And with the constant barrage of questions from the firefighters and sheriffs and neighbors, I hadn't had a chance to say more than a few words to him.

"Come on, Brandy," I murmured, making my way toward him.

Brandy trotted past me, completely unfazed by the events of the evening. I wished I could bounce back like her. She hopped up onto my tailgate, plopping herself onto Maverick's lap. He didn't even react, save for stroking a hand along the back of her neck, his gaze fixed on something on the ground. It's like he wasn't there, but reliving some memory from a different time.

My voice trembled as I came to a stop before him and said, "Hey."

The look in his eyes, on his face was haunted. My heart splintered in my chest. This was my fault. God, how had today gone to such shit?

He didn't respond, but he did give me a stiff nod.

I reached out to place a reassuring hand on his knee but stopped myself. Something in his gaze told me not to. He looked like a spooked deer. Ready to bolt at any moment.

"I'm so sorry for tonight. It's late, too late to drive you back right now. I'll find us a place to stay and we can call Charlie and the guys tomorrow morning."

"I already got us a hotel," he muttered, "I'll pull up directions." He sounded so hollow. So broken.

"Thank you. I'm good to drive."

He shook his head. "I will." The finality in his voice, blazing in his gaze, left me nodding.

I opened my mouth to say something—I don't know what—but I closed it. I'm sorry just didn't seem like enough.

I know that everyone dealt with trauma differently, but I hadn't expected this from him. This...lifelessness. I thought of the scars marring his arms. His chest. He'd dealt with fire before. Had I brought him back to that?

Bile rose in my stomach. *Oh, dear God, please don't throw up.*

I sucked a shaky lungful of air down my throat, praying like hell it soothed my nausea.

He didn't speak as he slipped off the tailgate of my truck. Didn't so much as look at me as we settled into the front seats. But as Maverick placed his hands on the steering wheel, I noticed the whites of his knuckles, the trembling in his hands. His jaw was clenched so tightly, a part of me wondered how he hadn't cracked it.

"No," I breathed, turning to face him fully, causing Brandy to shuffle beneath my feet.

Maverick turned to meet my harsh stare, his brow furrowed in confusion.

"No," I repeated, gesturing for him to get out. "You ain't drivin'. We ain't gettin' a hotel. I'm takin' you home."

"I'm fine," he said through a clenched jaw. But his haunted gaze gave him away. He was still stuck in whatever memories he'd been reliving. I couldn't let him drive. No matter if it was just down the street.

"Maverick..." I pressed a soft hand to his forearm. He flinched beneath my touch, a newfound horror burning in his eyes as he noticed my hand against his marred skin. "Please, let me help you."

A string of emotions warred within his gaze, but finally with a broken sigh, he all but pried his fingers from the steering wheel. With a dip of his head, he turned and opened the driver-side door.

———

I'D CALLED CHARLIE AS SOON AS WE'D GOTTEN OUT OF SAN Antonio and were headed towards the ranch. They'd all just been getting home, and the moment I'd mentioned a fire, Cash had taken over the call, all drunkenness having left his tone as he asked, "How long 'til you're here?"

With each passing moment, with every mile that we came closer to the ranch, the quieter and more withdrawn Maverick became. He was like a ghost. A wraith. A shell of a human. His body was here, but there was no light inside. That same glassy look had returned to his eyes, and even though he was sitting next to me, petting Brandy methodically with one hand while clutching mine in the other, I knew he was somewhere faraway.

I didn't know what to do. Didn't know what to say. Not that I thought saying anything would help at that point anyway. So, I did the only thing I could think of that eased the tension. I sang.

———

IT WAS NEARLY TWO IN THE MORNING WHEN THE Mercenary Ranch sign came into view. Relief trickled through me, but it wasn't enough to quell the trepidation clawing in my chest. The lights were on in Charlie and Ryder's house, and before I'd even fully made it up the drive, three dark figures dashed down the front steps and toward the circular, gravel driveway. As I pulled to a stop, Cash all but ripped open the passenger-side door. A seriousness I'd never seen had settled around him like a shroud, shining him in a completely new light.

This wasn't the man-whore who was as obnoxious as he was attractive. This Cash was new. Fierce. Valiant.

"Maverick." Cash's voice was both soothing and stern all at once as he loomed in the passenger seat doorway. "Oh, shit—"

Brandy growled at Maverick's feet. It hadn't taken long for her to deem herself his personal protector. Cash took a step back, worry and determination to help his cousin fighting for dominance in his features.

I stroked a hand down Brandy's back. "Shh, it's okay, girl. Let him help."

Brandy's brown eyes flicked to mine, a silent question lingering there. I gave her another pet and nodded. All of the tension left her in a moment as she turned back to Maverick and Cash. She still eyed the brown-haired cowboy warily, but she wasn't growling, so there was that.

Something about Cash's voice broke whatever catatonic state Maverick was in enough for him to glance at up. And I don't know what happened, or what silent conversation the two of them shared, but after a moment Cash nodded, the look in his face as haunted as Maverick's.

"Fuck." He blew out a breath. "Okay, Ryder, help me get him into the house."

Worry gnawed at my stomach, my heart. What had happened to Maverick? Why was Cash so scared? I hopped out of the truck and came around to the other side, where Charlie wrapped me in a tight hug.

"I'm so sorry," she whispered. "What happened? Here...let's get you cleaned up and you can tell me, okay?"

I nodded, snapping my fingers for Brandy to come. She hopped out of the truck and settled at my heels. We hadn't even made it a few steps toward the house before I noticed Maverick's unmoving frame. "What's goin' on?" I asked, coming up to Ryder and Cash.

Cash cast a confused, worried glance my way. "I think he wants you with him."

"Me?" I frowned. "Why?"

Surely, Cash and Ryder could take care of him better than me. Especially Cash. He'd dealt with something like this before, obviously. He moved and handled Maverick with a purpose, a surety, yet softness that I'd never seen before. He didn't need my help. Probably not even Ryder's, to be honest.

But as my worried gaze settled on Maverick, I noticed panic in his eyes despite his stoic stance. It was odd. Seeing so much silent emotion swirling in the jade depths, but not an ounce of it transferred to his body, to his face. He didn't cry. He'd stopped trembling. But emotion brewed from within.

Guilt ate at me. This was my fault. I hadn't forced him into that fire, but if he hadn't come home with me, he wouldn't be like this. Had he not come with me, though, Brandy would likely be dead. He'd saved her. Charged into a blazing trailer with no second thought.

So, when Maverick reached out a silent hand, the look in his eyes pleading, I took it.

———

GETTING MAVERICK INTO THE HOUSE WAS EASY ENOUGH. Charlie broke off toward the kitchen, mentioning something about getting some coffee going. I couldn't think of drinking or eating anything right now, though. Not with my stomach tied in knots and the lingering scent of smoke stuck to the back of my throat. I kept my hand in Maverick's calloused one, my thumb tracing reassuring circles along the back of his palm in a silent show of comfort. Cash moved on certain steps through the main living room and off to the right—toward the long hall of bedrooms, if I was correct. I hadn't been here much, but I remembered Charlie and Ryder giving me the tour during their engagement party a couple weeks ago.

Hanging left through the first door, Cash brought us to a guest bedroom with a bathroom attached. He turned to me, concern still shimmering in his hazel stare before he focused his attention on Maverick.

"Let's get you cleaned up, okay, bud?"

Maverick didn't move as Cash disappeared into the bathroom. A moment later, I heard the spray of water as he turned on the shower. I glanced up at Maverick. "I'm gonna let you get showered, okay? I'll be right here waiting."

He didn't answer, but his grip tightened around mine, his body tensing ever so slightly as his eyes flashed with panic.

My brows knit together. "You want me to stay?"

Another squeeze of my hand.

Well, that was settled. I nodded, and blew out a soft breath before saying, "Okay, come on then."

Cash came back out as I took a step in his direction. "Alright, shower's ready, bud."

"I'll get him cleaned up," I told Cash, noting the confusion on his face.

His head cocked to the side before glancing at Maverick. The two of them shared another one of those silent conversations for a moment before he looked back at me and stepped out of the way. "I'll go grab some clothes. Holler if you need anything."

I led Maverick into the bathroom, the only sound that of our boots against the hardwood floors and the shower going. Oh, and Brandy's toenails click-clacking against the floor as she followed dutifully behind. She wasn't about to let me or Maverick out of her sights anytime soon. "Stay, girl," I told her, nodding at the little rug in the corner of the room beneath a comfy looking armchair.

She gave me a reluctant look, but plopped down with a huff.

I turned back to Maverick, the harsh light of the bathroom revealing just how haunted he looked. He was covered in ash; smudges of dark soot smeared his face. The cut on his eyebrow looked angry and puffy beneath the butterfly bandage that he'd begrudgingly let the medic put on him. His white tank wasn't even white anymore, but some disgusting shade of grey with splotches of dried blood soaked into it. And in the

77

light, his burns were more gruesome than I'd first thought. Okay, not gruesome, just more extensive.

I trailed my fingers down one of the mottled scars, admiration and awe gripping my heart like a vice. I couldn't even comprehend what hell he'd gone through to get these. And he'd risked everything again for me. A stranger, basically.

He flinched away from my touch, a look of horror written plainly across his face.

"I'm sorry," I said, whisper-soft, pulling my hand away. "Come on, let's get you in the shower."

In the end, I had to get in with him. It's almost like he was terrified if he let go, I'd suddenly disappear. So, after stripping both of us down, I settled under the spray of water before him. It should have been odd, being in a shower naked with a guy I had no intention of hooking up with—at least not tonight. But getting in with him, helping him in this moment was more important than my worry or any self-consciousness.

"Is this too hot? Too cold?" I asked, searching his face for any sort of emotion other than the icy hollowness shining back at me.

He shook his head, his gaze lowering to the tiled floor of the shower. God, I wished he'd talk. This...silence. It was deafening. He'd never been a talker before, but, fuck...what I'd give to hear him say something, *anything*, right now.

I chewed my lip a moment, feeling awkward and worried and concerned but not having a single clue how to fix any of it. Wiping water from my face, I reached for the loofah and a bottle of body wash. With trembling hands, I began scrubbing the soot off of Maverick, singing softly under my breath.

With each pass of the loofah over his skin, with each new verse I sang, the tension melted off Maverick. Not completely. Not even by a long shot, but he wasn't stuck in his head anymore. His pale green eyes weren't so glassy and glazed over. He regarded me in silence, letting me scrub and sing without interruption.

"I used to think when I grew up that I wanted to be a singer," I said, finishing up the chorus of my favorite Randy Travis song.

His brows knit together questioningly, though he didn't speak.

I shrugged, understanding what he was asking. "Because I'm not *that* good. And...I don't know. I did choir in high school, but it just wasn't my thing. I've gotten asked to sing the National Anthem at a couple rodeos, though. That was pretty cool."

His face softened more as he regarded me, his eyes warming just a bit.

Hope and...some other emotion I couldn't quite name swelled in my chest. It was good to see him not so dead inside. I focused on his arms, my fingertips brushing the patchwork of his scars once more.

"You always wear long sleeves to cover these up, don't you?"

His gaze darkened, his jaw tightening. *Well, that was stupid of you, Chey.*

Damn. I'd never been that great at learning to quit while I was ahead. But I'd gone and done it anyway, so might as well run with it.

"You know you don't need to, right? They aren't ugly. Not at all."

His answering scowl told me everything I needed to know.

"It's true," I said softly, though I pegged him with a hard stare. "Scars are beautiful in their own way. They show strength. Endurance. Resolve. They show that whatever tried to kill you failed. That's pretty impressive if you think of it that way."

From the look on his face, I'd say he didn't agree, but at least he wasn't scowling still.

"Maverick...What can I do? I—" my voice broke, my throat tightening with emotion. I wanted so badly to help him. To make him talk. To make him smile. To make him...anything at this point.

Cash didn't seem all that fazed at Maverick's silence. Had this happened before? And for how long? I'd have to talk to Cash, that was for sure.

Blowing out a breath, I met Maverick's gaze. "Alright, you're all cleaned up," I murmured after urging him under the spray of water to wash off any lingering suds.

He held out a hand, nodding at the loofah. I frowned and raised it up in question. He simply nodded once more, and grabbed it out of my grip. He worked some body wash into it, then took over doing the same thing I'd done to him.

Whatever shred of resolve I'd kept in place to keep the dam of my emotions from crumbling shattered completely. A single tear fell down my cheeks. I'd only allow myself one.

Yes, I'd lost my home. Yes, I'd lost all of my things and my livelihood. But I still had Brandy. And whatever I'd gone through tonight couldn't be worse than what Maverick had and was currently going through.

So, one tear. I'd allow myself this one tear to fall in front of him.

Later I could come apart. *Later.*

Another five minutes, and we'd both dried off and gotten changed. Charlie had been kind enough to let me borrow a pair of sleep shorts and an oversized t-shirt while she washed my clothes. Maverick changed quickly into a long sleeve shirt and pajama pants, thanks to Cash.

"Want me to go get Cash?" I asked him as he sat down on the foot of the bed.

He shook his head.

"Do you want to go to bed?" I asked. God knows I did. It was late. Like, almost three o'clock in the morning late. Or early, I guess, depending on how you wanted to look at it.

A nod this time.

"Okay, I'll leave you then." I said pressed a gentle hand to his shoulder and gave him a reassuring squeeze. "I'll be in the living room if you need me."

His strong grip on my wrist held me in place. Worry settled around him, tensing up his shoulders and making his gaze sharp once more as he offered me a pleading look.

"I—I can stay if you want," I offered, moving to pull down the blankets before settling myself among the pillows, urging him to lay down with a soft pat of the bed. He obeyed silently, curling up beside me. There was something so earnest, so pure and innocent about the movement, I almost smiled.

He rested his head on the pillow beside me, our bodies touching. Under normal circumstances, I'd be all about this level of closeness, but there wasn't anything romantic about this right now. Hooking up was the last thing on my mind. Not when his jaw was still clenched, and I could all but feel every single tensed muscle in his body.

I turned on my side to regard him, taking him in for a long moment. "I'm sorry," I finally choked out in a whisper. "For everything."

He lifted his shoulder in a shrug, grabbing one of my hands and giving it a gentle squeeze.

I shook my head, a soft smile toying on my lips. Ever the gentlemen, even when he was falling apart at the seams. I ran my fingertips across his forehead, careful to avoid the cut on his eyebrow. "Girls will love this one," I murmured.

Something darkened, hardened in his gaze as he shook his head.

I huffed. "I'm pretty sure I speak for most girls when I say eyebrow scars are hot."

He didn't answer, just shrugged his shoulders silently once more, his gaze fogging over a bit. He didn't withdraw to the depths he'd been in. And from the look on his face, he wasn't in such a desolate, lifeless state, but I still didn't like that it was so easy for him to fall back there.

"What can I do?" I asked, clutching his hands in mine.

I wished he'd answer. Dear Lord, I really did, but he didn't. A soft hum came from his lips, though. The closest thing I'd get to an answer. It took me a moment to realize what he was doing. I recognized the tune of "Deeper Than the Holler", which I'd been singing in the shower with him.

I smiled softly. "You want me to sing?"

A nod.

My heart warmed a bit, a welcome replacement to the worry and concern brewing in my chest. "I can do that," I said, sitting up slightly to make myself more comfortable.

And then I began to sing.

Between the close proximity and the lack of anything to distract me like in the shower, my heart thumped in my ears like a drum beat, causing my nerves to ratchet up higher and higher the longer he held my gaze. I was so painfully aware of his quiet presence. It'd been a long time since I'd sung for anyone. Probably Daddy when I went to visit him for Christmas last year. But I'd never sung for anyone like this.

Someone who listened to me as if their life depended on it.

While it made me self-conscious, it also felt...nice to be so needed. To know that what I did mattered to someone. Even if it was something as simple as singing a Randy Travis song.

With each verse, his eyes grew heavier, the tension in his limbs smoothing out as sleep descended over him. He fought it to the very end —tooth and nail—making him seem boyish almost. It was cute and innocent.

I slid from the bed carefully, so as not to wake him. He stirred for just a second, stopping me in my tracks, but only to turn over and snuggle into the blankets more. I tiptoed across the room toward the bedroom door.

"Brandy," I whispered, looking to her at the foot of the armchair. She hadn't left the spot since before the shower. I nodded toward the door—a silent command I had no doubt she understood.

She stood up slowly, making sure to stretch every limb in her entire body like the dramatic girl she was, earning an eye roll from me. I swear, if she woke him up. "Really?" I hissed under my breath, gesturing to the door once more. "Let's go."

Brandy began padding over to me, her toes click-clacking on the ground. I grimaced at the sound. *I hope Mav's a heavy sleeper.*

But instead of coming to my side, Brandy hopped up onto the bed, her brown gaze filled with challenge as she hovered over Maverick's sleeping body.

I gritted my teeth. "Get down," I hissed in my best quiet, take-no-shit voice.

Her only answer was to spin around once and plop down beside Maverick, even going so far as to lay her head atop his side.

I rolled my eyes. "Fine, you wake him up, you're dealin' with it."

With a final glance at the two of them, I slipped from the room and eased the door closed.

CHAPTER 11
Daylight

CHEYENNE

I tiptoed down the hall and into the living room. Charlie and Ryder sat on the couch, their voices little more than hushed whispers as they talked back and forth. She held a mug of something hot in her hands, her legs tucked up under her. Ryder held her in the crook of his arm. Despite the worried looks on their faces, they could pass for appearing alright. But Cash...

Cash was a mess.

He paced the living room, his boots damn near burning a path into the hardwood. He'd taken off his hat and kept scrubbing his hands up and down his shadow beard and back through his hair. Completely opposite of the confident, cool-hand-Luke I'd come to know him as.

"How is he?" Even his voice held a desperate note to it I'd never heard before.

"He's okay. He's sleepin'," I said, coming to stand in the center of the room. Sitting felt too casual, but I wasn't so amped up that I needed to pace like Cash did. I settled on trailing my left hand up and down my right arm, though.

Cash blew out a breath and nodded, but it was Charlie who spoke. "Here, come sit. Tell us what happened. Are you okay?"

I waved her off on the offer, though I did take a few steps her way. "I'm fine..." I said with a shrug, my voice sounding foreign and weak.

And then I told them. About the sirens. The flames. How the firefighters couldn't find Brandy. My pulse quickened as each memory filled my mind. "...I freaked out when they said she wasn't in there. That's when Maverick ran in."

Cash huffed a cold laugh, a ghost of a sad smile tugging on his lips. "Figures. He's like a goddamn fairytale princess when it comes to rescuing animals. He never can just leave 'em alone."

As horrible as I felt that I was part of the reason for Maverick's silence, I would be forever grateful that he'd been so brave and valiant, and charged in and saved her.

"Do they know how the fire started?" Ryder asked, his voice calm, though his black gaze swirled with concern.

"No. The Sheriffs are gonna try to get camera footage from the trailer park, but they said it'd take a couple days probably."

"Well, you gotta place to stay here while you get everything sorted out," he replied.

I exhaled slowly, offering what I hoped but doubted was a grateful smile. Cash began pacing again.

"Those burns on his arms... This happened before—or something like it, didn't it?" I asked.

Cash's forlorn gaze said it all. He nodded at me. "Twenty years ago to the day."

My heart squeezed, wrenching all the air from my lungs. "What?" I don't even know if the word came out, I couldn't breathe.

"He was just a kid. His dad was drivin' 'em all to a jackpot ropin'... drunk. He went head on with a semi. His parents died on impact. His uh..." Cash shook his head and ran his tongue over his teeth. "His sister burned alive. State Troopers pulled him out of the truck while he was tryin' to get her out. They couldn't save her."

A pathetic sound clawed its way up my throat as I cupped a hand over my mouth. Holy shit. He'd gone through that as a kid. And then, twenty years later to the fucking day this happened?

Tears streamed down my cheeks, blurring my vision as I struggled to control my breathing. I hadn't even realized I was crying until then.

This was all my fault.

I needed air...or to get out of here. Just *something*. The phantom taste of smoke slithered its way down my throat, choking me. A wave of nausea hit me like a ton of bricks, and I took deep breaths through my nose. *Please don't throw up.*

Brandy's whine pulled me from whatever the hell episode I'd lost myself in. I took off for Maverick's room, wondering what state I'd find him in. Cash was hot on my heels, Ryder and Charlie close behind.

CHAPTER 12
Pain Won't Last

MAVERICK

Twenty years ago

I lurked in the darkness of the dimly lit hallway, quietly eavesdropping on Aunt Violet and Uncle Bad. My eleven-year-old hands trembled as I pressed them to the wall. Poking my head just far enough into the doorway, I found Aunt Violet standing at the kitchen sink, washing the last of the dishes while Bad dried them off and put them away.

"How was the kid's appointment today?" My uncle's sandpaper voice cut through the quiet.

"The doctors are impressed with his progress from this round of skin grafts. There's not much they can do for the scarrin', though. It's..." Her shoulders slumped, her voice shaking as she spoke, "it's just so extensive." She sniffled and wiped at her eyes with the back of her arm. "His broken arm's almost ready for that cast to come off, though. Which'll be good for him."

Bad nodded. "What about the talkin'? What'd the doctors say?"

Aunt Violet turned to Bad, her face a mask of sadness. "There's no damage to his vocal cords. Nothin' physically wrong with him. It's a

89

mental thing. They said sometimes when someone goes through trauma like that, they can just stop talkin'."

Bad blew out a breath. "They say how long it'll go on like that for?"

"There's no tellin'. He may never talk again. It's completely up to him." She took a steadying breath in and blew out slowly, the look in her gaze turning wary. "They wanna put him in therapy and have a psychiatrist look at him."

"You mean they wanna pump him up with drugs and make him look at ink blots?"

I noted the layer of anger brewing in the depths of Uncle Bad's voice. He wasn't a huge fan of doctors in general, always said if it couldn't be cured by a saddle or a bottle of whiskey, it couldn't be cured.

"I don't know." Violet shook her head. "Maybe they figure it could do him good."

"Kid doesn't need a headshrinker, Violet. He needs time to heal, time to process."

"That's what they're trained to do, Clint. You and I are out of our depth here."

Bad placed the towel down on the counter—so different from my dad, who'd have reacted with an explosion and likely broke something. But Bad was scary enough just with the tone of his voice. He rarely raised it, but with the slightest change in his emotions, you could pick up just how angry he was.

"You said that boy may never talk again. And you wanna send him to some stranger to *talk* about his trauma. He barely spoke before the accident, now you think he's gonna open up to some doctor?"

"They might get through to him." Aunt Violet didn't sound convinced though. "With enough time."

"Time is one thing we *got* plenty of. But the money to pay someone else for theirs?" Bad shook his head.

Guilt gnawed a hole in my chest. I hated being a burden. And that's all I'd been since the accident eight weeks ago. Why couldn't I have just died? Things would be so much simpler. I wouldn't hurt every day with just a shift in the wind or my shirt scraping just the right way. I wouldn't have nightmares. I wouldn't hear Ellie Mae's screams. Uncle Bad and

Aunt Violet wouldn't have to put up with me. And Cash and his younger brother, True...well, they wouldn't have to deal with my silence.

Not that Cash seemed to mind. He could talk to a wall and have a conversation; he didn't need me to entertain him. But I think I scared True a bit. It was the scars, I think. Made sense though, kid was only four and a half and the burns were pretty gross.

Aunt Violet frowned, challenge brewing in her gaze. "So, what do you suggest?"

It was moments like that when I could see the resemblance between her and my dad. They both had a fire in them. But that was where the similarities ended. Aunt Violet was fierce, but fair. She wasn't mean and rotten, like Dad had been.

And while my mom would have backed down to my dad if he'd looked at her like that, Bad didn't falter an inch. He matched her with a quiet fury blazing in his hazel depths. "Give me three weeks. Three weeks with me and them horses and some fresh air. If he ain't doin' better by then, then you can hire a damn shrink."

Some of the worry eased in my chest. I didn't want to put them out of money. Not that I was entirely convinced that Uncle Bad would be able to help either. But being with him and the horses sounded better than being with a shrink. I'd do my best to be better. To talk.

But I had nothing to say. Nothing to tell that seemed to matter. It hadn't mattered what I'd said before the accident. My words were nothing more than wind...so why waste my time saying anything now?

I'd lost everything. I didn't really feel like I was here. My body was, but my mind, my heart...they'd died in the crash. I might be alive...but I sure didn't feel like I was living.

The two stared one another down for a long moment before Aunt Violet finally let out a weary sigh. "Okay," she muttered with a nod, going back to scrubbing dishes. "And if he doesn't get better? You gonna take him out behind the barn and shoot him?"

Bad chuckled. "Him? No. That nag of a mare of his dad's? Maybe."

"*Clint*!" Aunt Violet chastised, pegging him with a harsh glare. "She can't be that bad. It's just a horse."

He shrugged and grunted once more. "I think that *horse* is one of them ones from Revelations. *I saw a man that sat upon a black horse, and Death was his name and Hell followed with him*? Something like that. Black horse of death."

"It's a pale horse. And don't be dramatic." Violet chided him.

"Dramatic, hell! The bitch tries to run me down every time I go near her and she's only *got* three good legs to do it with. I don't know what she'll do if she ever gets sound again."

"You can't shoot the horse, Bad." Violet shook her head.

"I bet Cash would do it if I asked him to."

A lump lodged in my throat and tears burned in the back of my eyes. Black Betty and I were the only survivors of the accident. She'd come out of it almost as bad off as me, maybe even worse. Though she wasn't burned all over like me, she'd tore a tendon pretty bad in her right back leg and cut herself up pretty good. Not the worst injuries the vet had ever seen, but if she didn't let someone heal her up and help her, there'd be no point in keeping her alive. She'd always been skittish, from the moment that Dad pulled her out of the stock trailer from the auction. But a year under his hand...well, let's just say, Eli Holstrom left his mark on all of us.

After the accident, she wouldn't let no one touch her. Anytime someone came near her stall she went crazy, messing up any progress to her leg again.

Hot tears slipped down my cheeks and I fled from the doorway before my muffled cries could give me away. True was already asleep, Cash was up playing with his Legos in the room we were sharing, but I didn't want to go up there. He'd just start talking. I didn't mind it most days, but right now, I needed to be alone.

With a blurry field of vision and my heart feeling like it would thump out of my chest, I raced for the barn. It was quiet there. The ranch hands were likely all in the bunkhouse now, drinking, playing poker, or heading off to bed. No one would come bother me in the barn.

They'd put Betty in the final stall on the left, away from the other horses. Partly to keep her calm, partly because she tried to kill any she came into contact with.

She snorted, those sleek black ears of hers pinning back as she noticed me slowly placing my hand on the latch of her stall. She pawed and struck out, a whinny peeling from her lungs as I undid the latch.

"Shhhh," the sound was foreign, scratchy in my throat, but it was all I could do. It bothered my vocal cords, reminding me of all the smoke that seemed coated to the back of my throat for weeks. Every now and then I still felt it. Tasted it.

This is stupid. What are you trying to prove? Reason warred with the storm of emotion in my chest. But I had to do this. I couldn't give up on her. No one had given up on me yet. Not Aunt Violet, Not Cash and True, certainly not Uncle Bad.

And maybe I needed to prove she was worthy of saving because self-consciously, I wondered if I even was.

Taking a deep, steadying breath, I kept my head lowered, my gaze not directly on her, and one hand out as I took my time opening her stall.

Her wild, terrified gaze flittered about as she snorted and pawed. I didn't shush her. I didn't have it in me to say anything anymore. Even that had been too much. But I stood in her stall with my hand out. Waiting. Waiting. Waiting.

My heart, in tandem with the stomp of her hooves as she struck the barn floor, began to slow. I forced calm, measured breaths from my lungs and met the mare's gaze. Fear and anger and just about every other emotion blazed in those brown eyes, reflecting my own feelings. I saw so much of me in her. In a new place. With new people. With all this hurt and terror eating away at my sanity.

I was her and she was me.

And maybe she understood that. Maybe she recognized all of the brokenness in myself within her...maybe that's why when I reached out my hand, steady despite how I felt on the inside, she didn't bite it off, but pressed her nose to my palm.

Emotion swelled in my chest, silent tears spilling down my cheeks. She moved closer, nuzzling my stomach.

I'd never felt so seen. So accepted than I had in that moment. She knew what I felt. She felt it too. We didn't need words to talk. To understand.

I don't know how much time passed. Could have been minutes or hours. We just stood there, her head resting against my stomach as I absent-mindedly stroked her neck. The motion was soothing...for the both of us.

I finally pulled away, meeting her dark, steady stare for a moment before glancing at her back leg. She favored it, keeping it up unless she absolutely needed to. I'd need to start hand-walking her. Slowly. For little amounts of time and gradually build that tendon back up again.

Tomorrow we'd start.

I ran my hand down the bridge of her nose a final time before backing out of her stall. As I latched the door, she snorted, pinning her ears back.

My shoulders sagged. What had I done? But she wasn't looking at me, I realized.

"Well, I'll be damned..." Uncle Bad's gruff voice sent me jumping back a step. "You got magic in them hands of yours, boy?"

I shook my head.

Bad spit some dip out the side of his mouth, his lips pulling up into a satisfied smirk. "You got somethin'. That's for damn sure." He turned for the front of the barn, waving me on to follow.

I did so in silence, falling into step beside him as we walked outside, the moon shining down on us from a star-flecked sky.

"You heard us in the kitchen?" he asked, his boots scraping against the dirt.

For a split second, I almost shook my head. But I knew the consequences for lying. Dad beat that into me. Literally. Unable to meet Uncle Bad's gaze, I nodded.

Bad cleared his throat, pulling off his cowboy hat to run his hands through his light brown hair—the same color as Cash's. I could see so much of my cousin in him. They were like carbon copies of one another.

"I appreciate the honesty."

Another nod from me.

"Hey, look at me." His voice always held a sharp edge to it, even when he wasn't angry. It was hard to read. And I liked to think I was pretty good at reading people cuz of my dad. But I never knew with Uncle Bad.

I took a shaky breath, my gaze finally settling on him. My hands trembled, the nerves tingling painfully.

"I ain't mad, and I ain't gonna hit ya."

I flinched on instinct. I couldn't help it. I was so used to my dad doing it that just the word set me on edge.

His hard hazel gaze softened, and he nodded as if he understood. He reached out a hand, like he was going to grip my shoulder, but pulled back at the last instant. I appreciated that; the burns still hurt.

"Your dad...did he hurt ya?"

I shrugged.

Bad shook his head, a streak of anger flashing across his face like lightning. He spit out the side of his mouth once more. "Well, you don't gotta worry about that no more." He looked to the ground, kicking at the dirt with his boot a moment before meeting my gaze one more? "How much did you hear?" he asked. "All of it?"

I nodded.

"Yeah, that's what I thought. So, you know about the deal between your aunt and I."

I dipped my head, even though it wasn't so much a question as a statement.

"Think we can make some progress in three weeks?"

I nodded once more, even though a traitorous part of me whispered little bits of doubt in my mind, my heart. What if Bad couldn't help? What if he was wasting his time? I didn't want to disappoint them. Not after everything they'd done.

I have to try.

He rubbed his stubbled jaw a moment before spitting once more. "Alright. Your daddy let you ride much?"

I waved my hand in a so-so gesture, pulling my shoulders up in a shrug once more, hoping he'd understand I meant a little bit.

"We'll find out," he replied, glancing back at the barn behind me. "Starting tomorrow, your job is to rehab that mare. She's your responsibility. I want you soakin' that back foot twice a day in Epsom salts, and hand walkin' her three times. That's includin' weekends. If we can't get her walkin' again, we'll have to put her down. And no one else can go near her."

I nodded. I could do that. Better yet, I *wanted* to do it. Busying myself always gave me a sense of purpose. Made me feel valuable.

Uncle Bad's lips quirked up as he gestured toward the house. We fell in step with each other again as he spoke. "You ever worked with babies before?"

I shook my head.

He blew out a chuckle. "Well, ain't no better time to start. Day begins at 4 am tomorrow mornin'. Sound good?"

Another nod.

Bad's lips curled up into a grin. "Ain't too many kids eager to wake up that early. You just might have what it takes to be a true cowboy, Maverick."

———

PRESENT DAY

Smoke filled my nose; it burned a path down to my lungs. Panic surged to life in me, the memory of Bad and I rippling and morphing into something else entirely. *Flames. Screams. Pain.*

I thrashed and called out, but choked on the taste of ash in my mouth. It coated my tongue, my throat. A warm, heavy weight settled on my chest, but it did little to ease the panic brewing within me.

Wake up. Wake up. Wake up.

My eyes snapped open, my breathing labored and shallow. No fire or smoke greeted me. Only darkness. Darkness and a soft whine.

I squinted, reaching out a hand toward my chest and feeling fur. A dog. Whose dog? Memories came flooding back through my mind. Cheyenne. The fire. *Brandy.*

I sat up and pet her softly, letting her lean into the touch. She smelled like smoke. So, that explained the scent.

I focused my breathing, urging it to slow, to even out. I didn't want to start coughing again. My throat still felt tight, like any second my lungs would seize up and stop working all together.

You're okay. There's no more fire. It's okay.

But it's like my mind and heart weren't speaking the same language.

I *knew* I was okay, that the worst had passed, but my heart, my irrational heart, just couldn't comprehend.

A voice cut through the quiet, just as light spilled into the room, chasing away the darkness. Standing there in the doorway with her hair a wild mess of curls and bathed in warm, buttery light, Cheyenne might as well have been an angel.

"Maverick. You okay?"

CHAPTER 13

Iris

CHEYENNE

My heart clenched at the sight of Maverick. He had that deer-in-the-headlights look in his eyes, terror lining his face, making him look somehow both older and younger in the same instant. Brandy leaned against him, as if she'd been trying to console him, but despite her best attempts, it wasn't working.

Maverick's wild gaze settled on me, and he let out an audible sigh.

"Hey," I soothed, stepping into the room, repeating my last question. "You okay? Did you have a bad dream?"

I let out a soft gasp as he grabbed my hand and pulled me toward the edge of the bed where he sat. There was a desperate feel to his touch as he wrapped his arms around me and dipped his head to rest against my stomach. He didn't speak, though I didn't expect him to, but his shoulders shook, his entire body trembled.

Tears pricked in my eyes and I pursed my lips. I couldn't cry. I couldn't let him see how much this killed me. Knowing that this was because of me.

"Everythin' alright?" Cash's voice drew my attention. But not Maverick's. Maverick remained still, his face burrowed against me.

I shared a look with Cash. Worry knit his brow, causing a frown to curl his lips downward. I offered him a soft shrug, before saying, "I think he had a bad dream."

Cash blew out a breath, rubbing a hand over his stubbled jaw, and nodded. He regarded me for a long moment before saying, "Will you stay with him?"

I blinked my surprise. Cash obviously knew how to handle Maverick in this sort of situation, he was probably the better one suited for the job, to be honest, but the fact that he knew that and still asked me to take of Maverick said everything.

I nodded. I wouldn't let him down.

With a final, weary look, Cash stepped back out of the room, closing the door and cutting off the light. Darkness descended over us. Charlie and Ryder's muffled voices rose in the silence. Not enough for me to make out, though.

What if I somehow set Maverick off? I appreciated the confidence in Cash, but...what if he was wrong to place his trust in me?

Maverick still held me tightly against him, though his shoulders had stopped shaking quite as much. I ran my fingers through his short hair, reveling in the softness of it as a song fell quietly from my lips. It was all I could think to do. I couldn't stand the sound of the silence lingering around us, and it seemed to help earlier.

It's funny, you always hear about the power of music, and I'd definitely felt its effects on myself before, but witnessing the magic unfold right before my eyes was truly a sight. Maverick's trembling stopped first. Then his breathing evened out. The vice-like grip around my waist loosened as the tension left each of his muscles, until he just held me against him. His hands began tracing little paths up and down my sides, the gesture soothing.

His palm drifted up over the fabric covering my ribcage, his fingers brushing feather-soft against the bottom of my breast.

I gasped, stilling in his grasp, the song dying in my throat. I couldn't help it. The moment, the touch, it was so intimate and so unexpected.

Stop it. It was nothing. He didn't mean to.

"Maverick..." My voice trembled only slightly as I tugged his chin up with a finger. His green eyes clashed with mine and my breath hitched in my throat. The air in the room shifted. His eyes held an intensity that sent a shiver down my spine, and not at all the bad kind.

His right hand drifted up from my side to cup the back of my neck, and with a certainty I didn't expect from him—at least not right in this moment—he pulled my mouth down to his.

I melted into the touch, savoring the feel of his lips against mine. The kiss wasn't rushed or brutal or filled with wanton need. It was soft, slow, but no less intense.

A sigh left me as I wrapped my arms around his neck, deepening the kiss. All of the tension left me then. Dear God, this felt good. Like really damn good.

A groan of approval rumbled up from his chest, making my knees week as his free hand drifted over the curve of my ass. He leaned back against the bed, dragging me down with him so that I had to straddle him. My damp hair fell like a blanket around us, and I lost myself in the feel of his calloused hands scraping against my skin as he dipped a hand beneath my shirt.

I wanted him. Needed him. And from the way he held me, the way he kissed me, I think he needed me too.

Something cold and wet pressed against my side and I let out a yelp, nearly jumping out of my skin. I sat up, still straddling Maverick, my gaze landing on Brandy, who sat beside us, her head tilted to the side in that way of hers.

"Fuck, Brandy!" I hissed, my heart dancing in my ribcage for a completely different reason than a couple seconds ago. "Get off."

I let out a sigh as she begrudgingly hopped off the bed and aimed for the spot by the armchair once more. Rolling my eyes, I set my sights on Maverick. "I'm sorry."

A hunger still lingered in his gaze as he reached a hand up to pull me back down to him. I let him, pressing my mouth to his. There was something so incredibly attractive about the possessiveness in his touch. I liked this sure, assertive side of Maverick. His free hand toyed at the hem of my shirt, slipping beneath the fabric so that his fingers feathered up along the side of my ribcage.

I moaned at the touch before flicking my tongue against his as I tried to deepen the kiss... But my mind chose that particular moment to see reason.

Should we be doing this? I mean, I knew everyone dealt with trauma in different ways, but was this going too fast? Would he regret this tomorrow? Lord fucking knows I wouldn't, but...

"Mav," I murmured, drawing back to look down at him.

His dark brows knit together in question.

I pressed a soft hand to his chest, right over his heart. And as much as I didn't want to say it, I managed to ask, "Should we slow down?"

Confusion rippled across his face.

"I'm not sayin' I wanna," I reassured, "I absolutely want you. By all means, kiss me, take me, use me, if that'll help...but I want it to be because *you* want it. Not because you feel obligated." I traced my fingers lightly down the side of his face. "I don't want to take advantage of you."

He sat back up, my legs still wrapped around him, and cupped my face in his hands. One of his thumbs gently stroked back and forth along my jaw as he regarded me in silence. My eyes had adjusted to the darkness, but even in the dim light I could make out the myriad of emotions swirling plainly in his eyes.

The desire still burned, hot as coals, but something akin to appreciation loomed there as well. He wanted this just as much as I did—there was no doubt now—but I think Brandy's little cockblocking episode had stolen the moment away.

He pressed a kiss to my lips, whisper-soft, before resting his forehead against my own. We sat there like that for a long moment, our breathing aligning as we clung to one another. And then he wrapped me in his arms and drew me down to rest my head among the pillows. He held me to him, his arms cradling me after he'd pulled the blankets up around us. His warm breath tickled my neck with each inhale and exhale, but I didn't mind. Not as a sense of calm settled around me.

So much had happened today. So many emotions still writhed and clawed for dominance in my chest. I felt the worry and panic and anxiety lingering on the outskirts, looking for the perfect moment to strike. But it never came. Not as my eyes grew heavy and began to flutter closed.

And as sleep descended on me, one thought remained—which should have scared the absolute hell out of me—*I could get used to this.*

CHAPTER 14

East Side Of Sorrow

MAVERICK

I didn't sleep long. Not because of nightmares or anxiety, but because of my damn internal clock that just didn't know when to quit. I'd woken before dawn for twenty years now. You just couldn't cut habits like that so easily, no matter the reason.

My lungs burned still from the smoke, but it didn't send me into a panic like it had the night before—a small win.

Cheyenne slept next to me, tucked against my side like how we'd fallen asleep. She didn't even stir as I slipped quietly from the bed. I grabbed my boots and phone that had been left in the bathroom last night. I nodded as I checked the time. 3:58 AM.

Grabbing my boots, I tiptoed back into the room. Brandy watched me from the floor. I looked between her and Cheyenne, who still slept soundly and nodded toward the door. The red heeler didn't need words to know my request. Padding on silent steps to the door, I paused with my hand on the knob. Brandy rose and stretched before making her way to my side. My gaze flicked to Cheyenne for a moment.

Damn, she was beautiful. And kind. And she had the voice of an angel—even if she didn't seem to think so. A part of me, a large damn part, wanted to crawl back in bed with her and hold her until I fell back asleep.

The way she'd taken care of me last night... I wish I had the words to tell her how much it meant to me. I would. Eventually I'd tell her. But right now...I just couldn't. There was no explaining it, really. I just... didn't have it in me to talk. It felt like such an insurmountable task.

Speakin' of tasks...

Those chores wouldn't do themselves.

With a final wistful look, Brandy and I crept out of the room.

───────

I'd beaten Ryder and Cash to the barn. Unsurprising. Ryder was always out closer to 5. Cash...well, I was lucky if Cash even made it out before 8 AM. I'd already finished throwing hay to the horses in the barn and gotten through cleaning all but one of the stalls when the clink of spurs and the scuff of boots pulled my gaze.

Well, I'll be damned...

It wasn't Ryder striding down the breezeway at a quarter past five, but Cash, looking bleary eyed and drinking a Monster. His light gaze met mine, his lips drawing into a scowl.

"What the hell are you doin' up?" His voice held none of the light-heartedness he usually possessed. He sounded pissed.

Made sense.

He'd seen this before. Saw the toll it took on me and everyone in the Mooney family. Hell, he'd been the one who'd dealt with the brunt of it. Barely seven years old, bunking with a cousin who wouldn't talk. He'd never admit it, but I'd caused him hell. I'd caused all of them hell...

And here I was, doing it again.

I blew out a breath and paused in my raking long enough to offer him a shrug.

"Go back to bed." Not a request; a demand. "I got the rest of this."

I shook my head, shrugging with upturned hands.

"Maverick, why you gotta be so stubborn?" His voice sounded about as weary as he looked. It wasn't a look he wore well.

Guilt ate at me, but I still couldn't find the words to ease his worries.

When I was a kid, even before the fire, I could go days without talking. It was easier than saying something that could set Dad off. Not talking wasn't that hard to do. It was pretty easy actually—almost like auto-pilot. I could do the motions, interact if I needed to. But I found that it was the easiest way to deal with the torrent of anxiety that lived within me.

I shrugged at Cash once more before finishing up raking the stall. Latching the door, I slipped into the breezeway. He bit his lip, running his tongue over his teeth like he always did when he was annoyed. Ryder appeared then, saving me from whatever tirade Cash had been preparing.

"Sorry. Charlie was sick again," Ryder said, adjusting his ball-cap as he came to a stop at Cash's side.

"Ain't she sick every mornin?" Cash asked.

"Yeah, that's why they call it mornin' sickness, dumbass." Ryder's tone was light though, the smirk on his face a welcome sight. At least someone was acting normal. Cash's lips pulled up into an answering grin, but it didn't reach his eyes.

Ryder nodded at me, his smile falling. "I wasn't expectin' you up."

I shrugged.

He seemed to get it, or maybe he didn't, but he went on to ask, "You get the buckin' horses fed yet?"

I shook my head.

"Alright, I'll go throw 'em a bale." He nudged Cash. "You comin'?"

"Nah, I'll stay back. Finish the rest of the stalls."

I waved him off. I just had one more to do anyway.

Cash scowled at me. "Well, fine. You're always bitchin' about how I don't do shit, but then when I offer to do it, you gotta be all valiant, so I may as well go fuck off." He stormed out of the barn, murmuring curses to himself under his breath.

I pulled off my hat and blew out a sigh as I wiped the sweat off my brow. Pain blossomed and I winced. Fuck. I'd forgotten about the eyebrow cut. It pulsed, but the pain was nothing compared to the regret I felt.

Ryder offered me an apologetic smile. "Hey, he'll be alright. Last night just scared him. Scared us all."

I nodded.

I wanted to say something, but again words failed me. Thank you just didn't seem like an adequate response. It seemed hollow. Weak. Better to just say nothing at all. Ryder knew how much I appreciated him. He didn't need words to know that.

He clapped me on the shoulder, giving it a reassuring squeeze, before strolling out of the barn. I made my way toward Betty's stall, the last on the left—what can I say, I liked routine—when I heard the sound of rope hitting plastic.

Cash must be ropin' the dummy.

I ignored the almost rhythmic sound as I unlatched the mare's stall. She barely lifted her head up from her flake of hay as I walked in and began raking. So different than twenty years ago. She'd been all hellfire and brimstone then—Cash, Bad, and just about everyone else would argue she still was, but we'd come a hell of a long way. I paused a moment, leaning the rake against the stall door and ran a hand down her neck.

It was just like when I was eleven all over again. Coming into her stall, seeking her quiet comfort. I focused my breathing, matching it to the strokes I made down her coat. Working with Bad had taught me many things, but the healing power of horses would always be his greatest lesson.

CHAPTER 15
Sad Songs For Song People

CHEYENNE

I awoke alone. Completely and utterly alone. No sign of Maverick, or Brandy for that matter. Worry gripped me, twisting my stomach in knots. Where were they?

I couldn't tell how late or early it was since there weren't any windows in the room, but it *felt* early. I could have sworn I'd just curled up in Maverick's arms and then here I was. My lungs burned from all the smoke I'd inhaled last night, but I ignored it as I got up.

I needed to find them. It wasn't like Brandy to leave me, and with the night Maverick had, I wouldn't have suspected him being up so early.

I padded out of the room and down the hall, the familiar aroma of bacon, hash browns, and something sweet filling the air. As I turned the corner down the hall, the living room came into view, and directly beyond it, the open dining room and peninsula separating the kitchen. Ryder and Charlie sat at the peninsula, while Cash leaned against the wide door frame between the dining and living room. They all stared on in silence toward the large, open kitchen.

Well, if they weren't cooking that meant...

My heart slowed a bit as I spotted Maverick's tall frame before the stove, but the worry and tension coiled tight in my belly still remained.

"Hey," I said quietly, making my presence known. "Has anyone seen—"

The familiar click-clacking of Brandy's toenails sliced through the thick silence, and everyone's gaze shuffled to me. But I was only focused on a single green-eyed gaze. I regarded him for a long moment, searching for any signs of...what exactly I wasn't sure. Was he more back to himself today or still silent?

He wasn't in the clothes Cash had lent him last night. He wore his usual getup—starched black wranglers, a black long-sleeve, and a black felt cowboy hat.

I bypassed everyone, weaving my way into the kitchen and around the large center island to come to his side. I hovered next to him, longing to reach out and touch him, but was unsure if it was the right thing to do.

"Hey," I repeated, my voice gentle as I tried to gauge his expression. "How're you doin'?"

From this close, I noticed the tension in his shoulders, saw the sadness and lifelessness in his gaze. Another piece of my heart shattered. Looked like whatever progress we'd made last night had all but vanished. He lifted his shoulders in a weak shrug and nodded at me.

It was surprisingly easy to understand him even without words. "I'm okay. You scared me. I didn't think you'd be up so early. And when I noticed Brandy gone too... She doesn't usually leave my side."

His gaze turned apologetic and he tilted his chin toward the window in the kitchen looking out at the barn.

I frowned. "Are you sayin' you woke up to go do chores?"

A nod.

I huffed. Of course, he'd go through some harrowing experience and then wake up the next morning like nothing was wrong, back to choring away. Well, not that he was back to normal, but still.

Ryder's voice pulled my attention. "He was up first, as usual. Had almost the whole damn barn fed and cleaned before we got out there."

I can't believe I'd slept through him leaving and not even heard

Brandy's loud steps on the hardwood. I'd never been a light sleeper, but maybe after last night, my body just went into rest mode.

I looked between Ryder and Maverick. Maverick just shrugged and met my gaze once more. He nodded at the food then quirked an eyebrow.

"I'm a little hungry," I replied.

He nodded and held up a hand.

"Five minutes?" I asked after a moment.

Another nod.

"Can I help with anything?"

He shook his head, his gaze appreciative as he turned his attention back to the stove. I took that as an opportunity to make my way back to the rest of the group.

Charlie offered me a warm smile as she gestured toward the island. "Want something to drink?" she asked. "There's orange juice and sweet tea, or if you're a coffee drinker, Mav started a pot already. I've got some of Mrs. Mooney's hot cocoa too. Oh, there's also some Monsters in there."

"Hey, those are mine," Ryder groaned, even though warmth lit up his handsome face.

Charlie rolled her eyes and leaned into him. "Oh stop. She can have one."

Ryder sighed, but a smile spread wide on his lips as he spoke. "Fine."

I grinned and moved toward the island, grabbing an empty mug. "I'll have some coffee, thanks."

At least the two of them seemed normal enough. I felt their worry still, but it wasn't like last night. I appreciated the semblance of normalcy, though. Tension like this tended to trigger the fight or flight response in me, making me want to run away. It's what I was good at. What I'd always done.

But while Ryder and Charlie tried to be normal, Cash was sullen, broody. It was so unlike him, and it made me fidget with nervousness.

The room descended into silence once more, the tension so thick I could cut it with a knife. Having poured myself a cup of coffee and mixing in a bit—okay, a ton—of creamer, I made my way to Cash's side.

Dipping my voice down low, I asked, "Has he been like this all mornin'?"

Cash's hazel eyes settled on me, a what-do-you-think look on his face. "It's like he's here, but not," he murmured quietly.

I held the coffee mug up to my lips and blew out a breath before taking a tentative sip. The first sip of coffee was always my favorite. That shock of heat, of sweetness, of delicious goodness. "What can we do?"

Cash's face softened and he sighed. "Not much more than what we're already doin'. He'll open up when he's ready."

I frowned. "What if he doesn't?"

Cash's eyes hardened with determination as his gaze shifted to his cousin. If Maverick heard us, he didn't let on. He worked in silence at the stove. Flipping French toast, scrambling up the eggs, checking the hash browns. "He will. Give him time."

I took another sip of coffee worry swirling in my chest. *I sure as hell hope so.*

Cash nudged my shoulder a moment later, an appreciative look on his face. "Thank you, for last night. I can't imagine how hard that was for you too."

I shrugged. "I just feel bad. I wish I could do more."

Cash dipped his head like he knew exactly what I was talking about. He probably did. "You're doin' plenty. Thank you."

I nodded and leaned against the wall beside him. Brandy ambled about the kitchen, going back and forth between checking on me and Maverick. Oh God, I hadn't even asked if Charlie and Ryder allowed dogs in the house. I know Ryder had a dog, but I hadn't seen her.

"I'm so sorry," I said, drawing Charlie and Ryder's attention, "I didn't even ask if y'all were okay with Brandy being in here. I can put her in the room or the truck if you want."

Charlie's smile was soft as she waved a hand at me. "It's fine. Dutch is outside in the yard for now. We didn't want to introduce them without you here. We can let them out together later."

I sighed in relief. "Thank you."

Maverick moved away from the stove and started putting things onto platters and plates before bringing them to the kitchen island next to all the drinks.

"Looks like breakfast is ready," Charlie said, slipping out of her chair and grabbing plates and utensils for everyone.

Maverick hung back, gesturing for everyone to grab food before him.

"Want me to make you a plate?" I asked.

He shook his head, the look on his face grateful though. I almost did it anyway, as Charlie handed me a plate, but in the end, I wasn't sure what all he wanted. The scent of food filled my nose, making my mouth water. I hadn't eaten since early yesterday evening, and my stomach growled in answer.

Each of us sat around the dining room table in silence, the tension growing thicker and thicker by the moment. Maverick was the last to take a seat—at the opposite head of the table from Ryder on either side of Cash and I. I stole a quick glance at Cash, his gaze burning bright with frustration as he glared at his plate.

The only sound was that of forks and knives scraping against the glass plates. Cash's shoulders were tense. He wasn't even eating his food. He just shifted his gaze between Maverick and his plate, the tension rising. Rising. Rising. Until...

"I can't fuckin' take this shit anymore. I ain't eatin'." And then he was up and storming out of the back door in the kitchen toward the barn.

I watched him from the large bay window as he grabbed his practice rope and started roping the plastic dummy cow. Over and over and over.

I didn't exactly know why he was so angry, but I felt for him. Maybe he hated the tension as much as I did. Maybe he couldn't deal with the normalcy of everything after the events of last night. Or maybe he just hated the silence. God knows I did.

Focusing back on my plate, I took a forkful of eggs—they were the only thing I hadn't tried yet—and bit into them just as a wave of nausea hit me full force. "Oh, fuck..." I cupped a hand over my mouth and launched out of the chair. I barely made it to the bathroom before vomiting up all the contents in my stomach.

Okay, that was totally weird.

As disgusting as it was, the taste of ash stuck to the back of my mouth. Maybe I'd inhaled more smoke than I'd realized. I waited for the nausea to pass, a dull headache blossoming as I cleaned up and made my way back to the table.

Maverick eyed me worriedly.

"I'm okay," I offered. "I think I just ate too quickly and from all the smoke it just left me feelin' sick."

There wasn't really any other way to describe it, and now that I'd thrown my guts up, I felt fine. Completely fine. I didn't eat much more, though, but settled instead on the coffee I'd made myself.

Charlie met my gaze from across the table. "I wish that was my reasoning for the constant nausea episodes," she said lightly. "I knew about morning sickness, but I wasn't expecting it to be such a pain in the ass."

"Do you get it often?" I asked.

Ryder didn't look up from his food as he nodded, but Charlie was the one who answered. "Every fucking day. It's such a bitch. I can't eat eggs anymore. They smell so good being made, but the minute they touch my lips..." she made a face. "Nope. Just nope."

"That doesn't sound fun. How much longer are you in the first trimester for?"

"A bit. I'm just now eight weeks. I have my first official doctor's appointment tomorrow." She glanced at Ryder and smiled. "We'll get to hear the baby's heartbeat then."

The two of them shared a look that could melt even the iciest heart. They were so perfect it was almost sickening.

I smiled, taking a sip of my coffee. "That's awesome."

I wondered if I'd ever be in love like that? If I'd ever look at someone like that? It was hard to imagine being that into someone that I'd settle down and have a kid with them. I'd never been the type to stay somewhere for too long. It's why I didn't really do exclusive relationships. Long-term hook ups, sure. But a relationship? Marriage? Babies?

I snuck a glance at Maverick, and something softened in my chest. He was hot and kind and everything good in a man. We had something between the two of us that made me want to explore more...but it was too early to know what all would unfold. He clearly had baggage, and I had my own. Two broken people together wasn't always the best combo.

His eyes locked onto mine, and a shiver went down my spine. I wondered what he was thinking. I wanted to ask him, but it'd be useless, and I wasn't going to try and force words out of him.

He nodded to my plate, a questioning look on his face.

"It's amazing," I said softly, understanding what he meant. "I've never been a French toast fan before, but yours is delicious."

He eyed my half-eaten plate like he'd disagree.

"I'm only not eating because I'm afraid to throw up again. Not because of your cooking." I offered him a reassuring smile, hoping he believed me.

Charlie and Ryder guided most of the conversation throughout the rest of breakfast. They talked and laughed as if nothing had happened last night. I appreciated it, and I think Maverick did too. He'd settled back into his chair, drinking his coffee—blacker than a midnight sky.

I turned to face him more fully as I asked, "How the hell do you drink that shit?"

He eyed me, a questioning look in his eyes as his gaze traveled between me and his cup.

"How do you drink it black?" I clarified, making a face. Daddy used to drink it like that. Not a drop of sugar, milk, or creamer. It always reminded me of oil in a cup. Just the thought sent a wave of nausea to my stomach again, but I pushed it down, taking a sip of my sugary drink to wash away the thought.

His lips pulled up into the barest ghost of a smile and he shrugged, taking a large sip from his mug.

I stuck my tongue out and shook off the disgust.

Charlie laughed, tucking her feet up under her and holding her mug in her hands. "I've asked him the same thing."

"It's disgustin', isn't it?" I asked. "Like, it needs some sort of sugar or creamer or milk."

She laughed, pressing her mug to her lips. "I wouldn't know. I can't stand it even with those things in it. I'm a hot cocoa or energy drink kinda girl."

"Not an energy drink girl *anymore*," Ryder added, offering her a stern look. She rolled her eyes in mock annoyance, though a smile toyed on her lips.

We cleared the table not long later, but when I'd silently begun drying some of the dishes, Maverick shooed me out. I think he'd peopled enough for a bit and needed a moment to himself. I'd tried to fight him on it, but given up in the end. Ryder and Charlie went to go get ready to pick up Cason from Charlie's mom's house, which left me with nothing to do.

The sound of rope against plastic cut through the painful silence and I remembered Cash. He hadn't stopped roping since he'd gone outside half an hour ago. With a sigh, I found my boots and made my way outside.

———

CASH THREW WITH PERFECT ACCURACY. HE HANDLED HIS rope with the finesse and comfortability of someone who'd been doing it their whole life. I sat on the bed of an old, falling apart pickup truck that I questioned could even run, watching him in silence for a few moments.

His right hand was stained red, crimson droplets falling to the dirt. He didn't seem to notice, or maybe he just didn't care.

"You're bleedin'," I called out as he roped the horns once more.

He paused, looking down at his hand for a moment. A surprised frown tugged on his mouth, a grunt of disbelief escaping him. "Well, shit."

He rolled up his rope and readied for another throw. Completely unfazed.

God, it was almost harder dealing with his silence than Maverick's. Cash wasn't quiet. He wasn't sullen, or broody. He was loud and talkative and the center of attention.

Maybe I should leave. Coming out here had been a mistake. I didn't really know why I'd decided to check on him anyway. Maybe because he'd gone through this with Maverick before and possibly had some insight on how to navigate this... Though, from the way he was acting, that proved otherwise.

I should go get my things and... *and what?*

My trailer was gone. All my things were little more than ash. I had

Brandy and I had Country Road, but she was back in San Antonio, so it's not even like I could just hop in my truck and go ride her for a little bit then come back. That would be an all-day excursion.

But anything beat being here right now. Charlie and Ryder were leaving. Maverick wasn't going to be talking anytime soon, and Cash was even worse company than his cousin.

I was about to hop off the back of the tailgate when he turned to me, cradling his bloody hand. "I'm sorry, I know I'm bein' a dick..."

I shrugged, glancing toward the house and spotting Maverick working at the kitchen sink before looking back at Cash. "You're worried about him. I get it."

I was too.

Cash tossed the rope into the bed of the truck and took up a seat beside me. "I'm worried about how long he ain't gonna talk for again."

Well, that settled my question. "It happened before?"

He nodded. "After the accident. He just stopped talkin'."

"How long did it last?"

Cash blew out a breath, his gaze glazing over a bit as he stared unseeingly ahead. "Almost a year."

"Fuck," I breathed. A year? I couldn't imagine not talking for more than a day...let alone a year.

Cash nodded, rubbing absentmindedly at his hand.

"What pulled him out of it?" I asked.

"I ain't really sure," he said with a shrug. "I think a lotta different shit played into it, ya know..." A soft smile came to his lips, that glassy look in his gaze deepening. "I remember his first words, though."

I smiled, turning towards him. "Tell me about it?"

I got the feeling he needed to talk about it as much as I wanted to hear it. Brandy hopped up beside me and I began petting her absentmindedly.

"It was the weekend of my eighth birthday. We were at a youth rodeo in...well, I guess it don't matter where. Some kids in his age group were bullyin' him. Particularly this one asshat." Cash's lip curled up into a snarl. "Bodi fucking Johnson...shithead couldn't rope then, and he sure as shit can't rope now."

My lips quirked up. I knew the guy. He *was* an arrogant asshat.

119

He waved a hand through the air. "Anyway, that ain't the point. Him and his dumbshit friends were pickin' on Mav. Callin' him simple and shit cuz he didn't talk." Cash shook his head, rubbing at his stubbled jaw with his free hand. "Mav was like four years older than me and didn't need no help standin' up for himself, but I just remember hearin' the things they were sayin' and seein' red. I went after Bodi. Lost my shit completely."

"Really?"

A flicker of the Cash I knew blossomed in the shit-eating grin that spread across his face. His eyes lit up, making them glow almost a burnt gold. "Fuck yeah, I bit him and everythin'."

I scoffed, an incredulous laugh escaping me. "You bit him?"

"Sure as shit did." He nodded, that grin pulling wider.

"Oh my God." I giggled. "So, what happened next?"

"Well, Bodi and his fuckin' friends were a hell of a lot bigger, so it wasn't too long 'til I was gettin' the absolute piss kicked outta me...but then Mav stepped in."

Cash's smile pulled wider, and it was easy to see why girls fell for him as quickly and as hard as they did. Cash Mooney had a magnetism about him that reminded me of a celebrity. That poise and confidence and just...debonair attitude. "Maverick knocked Bodi out cold with one swing. Just...boom. Lights out. His friends went runnin' to tell on us, so we got outta there like bats outta hell. We hid in the back of Dad's horse trailer."

He rubbed at his bleeding callouses even as that smile still loomed on his lips. "I remember Mav was pacing back and forth—he does that when he's stressed out—hands on his head... I remember tellin' him what he'd done was awesome, and he'd just looked at me in that way of his. You know, with a whole bunch of judgment in his eyes... And then he said, 'you're a fuckin' idiot you know that?'"

Laughter bubbled up out of my throat, even as tears sprang in my eyes. I couldn't help it. I didn't even know why I was crying really, but I couldn't stop the tears from welling.

Cash huffed a laugh. "Shit...are you cryin'?"

"No!" I said, wiping the proof from my cheeks. "Maybe...okay, yes."

"Why?" he asked with a chuckle.

I sniffled. "I don't even know. I can just completely see Mav sayin' that to you. The look he gives you. The way he said it. And... I don't know the way you talk about him, it's...it's really sweet. You guys are more like brothers than cousins."

"We might have different parents, but he's my brother at the end of the day."

My heart squeezed, not in sadness, but from exploding with warmth. More tears hung in my eyes before falling down my cheeks.

Cash's laugh was genuine as he shook his head. "What the hell's wrong with you, girl? Why you cryin' now?"

I shoved him, even as I laughed. "Fuck off." Then after a moment another laugh bubbled up out of my chest. "I can't believe you bit Bodi Johnson."

"You know him?"

"I rodeo, remember?"

"Ah shit, yeah, I forgot." He nodded. "But yeah, I bit him."

I chuckled, shaking my head. I could just imagine a pint-sized Cash biting Bodi in a fight. "You fuckin' heathen."

He smiled even as he eyed me long enough to make me fidget under his gaze. My brows knit together in question.

"You're good for Mav, you know that?"

The warmth in my heart spread through me at the mention of his cousin, but also a trickle of fear. Maverick was different than any other guy I'd ever known. Even before this shared trauma of the fire... things were different. And that scared me.

I didn't do relationships. It just...it wasn't my thing. But without even thinking about it, I could see potential for one with him.

The warmth won out in the end. "You think? Better than quote unquote, that Ashleigh bitch?"

Cash rolled his eyes, a scowl marring his handsome face. "Fuck her."

"Harsh words."

He pegged me with a hard stare, his hazel eyes looking more green in that moment than gold. "You ain't met her."

"Is she, like, his ex or somethin'?"

"She's a snake if I ever saw one, that's what she is. A goddamn cottonmouth ready to sink her fangs into him whenever he starts to get out of her reach."

I frowned. Maverick didn't seem like the type to play games. Probably wasn't even capable of it. He hadn't even realized I was flirting with him at first last night.

"What'd she do to him?"

He blew out a breath before running his tongue over his teeth. "She's done so much I can't even keep track anymore... The biggest stunt she pulled was this past Christmas."

"What happened...if you don't mind me askin'?"

He shrugged, hopping off the tailgate to pace back and forth. "He proposed to her on Christmas Eve. She said yes, everythin' was goin' fine, but she got drunk at my parent's Christmas party and made a fool of herself, then blamed Mav for it. She stormed off, and he found her in the bunkhouse hookin' up with one of the ranch hands... in Mav's fuckin' bed."

I hated people like her. Cheaters deserved their own special place in hell, and people who fucked over nice people...I hated them just as much. And the fact someone could do that to Maverick... "What a fuckin' bitch."

He balked at my foul language, surprise brewing in his gaze for a moment before that familiar shit-eating grin lit up his face. "I knew I liked you."

I smirked, appreciating the support. "You think Maverick would really take her back after that?"

"He was goin' to!" Cash shook his head, grabbing for his rope once more. "She and him were talkin' this past week. He wasn't even supposed to go out with us last night. He was supposed to see her, but he caught her two timin' him again."

It felt like I got hit by a ton of bricks. "Oh..." Was that the only reason he'd kissed me last night? Because I was a rebound. "So, I was just a distraction?"

Realization dawned in Cash's gaze and he shook his head emphatically. "Nah, Chey...it ain't like that. I promise."

"You sure about that?" I scoffed, a flare of anger sparking in my chest. I wouldn't be someone's sloppy seconds. I wouldn't be the alternate. Never had. Never would.

Cash placed a hand on my shoulder, the one not bleeding, thankfully. "Maverick doesn't play games like that. He wouldn't have kissed you if he didn't like you. Believe me."

I chewed my lip, irrational fear warring with logic in my heart. I wanted to believe him. I *think* I believed him...but that doubt wouldn't be squashed until I spoke to Maverick. And being that he wasn't talking, I'd probably be waiting a while.

Why was I even upset about that, though? It's not like we were together...

But I think he'd proven he wasn't just trying to rebound with me. Besides, actions spoke louder than words. He'd run into a burning trailer to save my dog. And the way he'd kissed me last night. The way he'd held me until we fell asleep...

I sighed. "I shouldn't even be worried about that right now. I've got bigger fish to fry with this whole fire situation."

"You got any clue what you're gonna do?"

I shook my head. "None. I've gotta call the insurance company, but I doubt I'm gonna get shit for the trailer. And until I can restock all my products and replace my printer, I've got no income."

"Stay here 'til you figure shit out." He shrugged and moved away, rolling his wrist to flip his coils and open up his rope loop.

"I can't impose like that on Charlie and Ryder." I frowned, hopping down off the truck bed. "They just got engaged and have a baby on the way. Not to mention, Cason. They don't need an extra person takin' up room in their house."

Cash went back to roping, swinging the loop over his head in three quick turns before throwing it over the plastic cow's horns. A perfect throw. "So, stay with me or Mav," he said, turning to look at me. "Actually...maybe not me."

I cocked my head to the side. "Why not you?"

"It don't look good to have a girl already in the house when I bring another one home."

I shook my head and laughed. "Jesus, Mooney."

He shrugged, a smirk blossoming on his lips. He seemed a lot more like himself now. "Stay with Mav." He waggled his eyebrows. "Might do you both some good."

I rolled my eyes even as I bit back a smile. "You can't just offer me up a place in Maverick's house without even talkin' to him."

Cash rolled up his rope once more and readied it for another throw, bloody hand completely forgotten. "So go ask him. He ain't gonna say no."

"And what if he does?" I asked, crossing my arms over my chest.

Cash looked me up and down, that smirk still on his lips. "Then he's a fuckin' idiot and never deserved you in the first place."

CHAPTER 16
The Painter

MAVERICK

I'd just finished cleaning up the kitchen when Cheyenne and Brandy made their way toward the back door. She'd been laughing with Cash—a welcome sight for the both of them. But another emotion stirred within me—a touch of jealousy. I couldn't do that for her. I could barely even keep myself from falling into a panic attack at any given minute, let alone make her smile.

The both of them had gone outside sad, morose, and after a few minutes the two were smiling, talking, teasing —it looked like—from the shoulder bumps and the playful scowls.

Hell, they even looked good together, if I were being honest.

I shook off the thought as the knob to the backdoor turned and Cheyenne walked back inside.

"You're still cleanin'?" she asked, her brow rising and concern echoing in her tone. "I'd have helped."

I waved her off and placed the cleaning spray and rag underneath the counter before turning back to her. I lifted a brow and nodded in her direction, hoping she understood.

Her face scrunched up a moment, her gaze turning contemplative.

"I'm...okay, I guess," she said with a sigh. "I uh...I wanted to talk to you."

I frowned and nodded for her to go on.

"I can't stay with Charlie and Ryder. There's too much goin' on. I feel like I'm imposin'."

Worry swelled within me, constricting around my middle. I didn't want her to leave. Besides, she had nowhere to go, no belongings. Where would she go?

"Cash and I were talkin'..." her voice sounded weak, weary.

Here it comes.

He'd worked his magic on her, hadn't he? I wanted to be mad, but I couldn't even blame her. Either of them, really. Maybe our kiss last night had meant nothing. A response to the trauma we'd both shared. I hung my head, already knowing where this was going.

"Would you be okay if I stayed with you?"

My head snapped up and I fixed my gaze on her intently. She was closed off—her eyes, her face, her posture. I couldn't read her.

"It wouldn't be for long. Just until I get the money from the insurance company for the trailer and find myself a place and a job while I can get the etsy shop runnin' again." She blew out a breath and ran a hand through her wild blonde curls. "If you're not okay with it, that's fine. I can figure somethin' out." Her head dipped, her gaze falling to the floor. "In fact, this was stupid. I'm sorry. I know what I'm askin' is a lot."

What? Not at all.

She had no home. Nothing to call her own. And after last night... I *wanted* her to stay. Something fluttered in my chest at the idea of that. Of having her in my house. Of waking up, knowing I'd see her there when I came back in at the end of the day.

I moved around the peninsula, coming to stand before her. She was so much smaller than me—I liked that. I gripped her chin between my thumb and forefinger, tilting her face up to look at me. I shook my head.

"No, what?" she asked. Her eyes were like twin pools of worry. "No, you want me to go? Or no, you want me to stay?"

How could she not understand? I still couldn't find the words within me, so I did the next best thing. Cupping her face in my hands, I kissed her. Slow, unhurried.

A little gasp escaped her before she melted against me, her hands pressing against my chest.

The fluttering in my heart quickened as I pulled away enough to look down at her. Her breathing was shallow and labored, her turquoise gaze swirling with some emotion I couldn't quite place. A warm smile crooked on her pouty lips. "Was that a yes?" She bit her bottom lip. "I may need a little more convincin'."

I smirked and shook my head before flicking her nose gently.

"Hey!" She batted my hand away, a smile lighting up her face. My heart fluttered again. I liked seeing her smile. Liked even more when I was the reason for it. It was like a sun on the horizon, warming everything in its path.

I stole another kiss from her. Just a whisper of one.

She smirked a moment before sobering, a sigh escaping her. "Well, now that that's settled...I should probably go buy some clothes. I *should* go work Country Road...we have a rodeo this weekend, after all."

I nodded, pointing a thumb toward my chest.

"You too?" she asked, then went on to answer herself. "Of course you do." Worry stirred in her gaze as she bit her lip. She couldn't do things like that. It did something to me. "Do you think it would be too much to ask if you trailered her up there for me? We'd have to go get her Thursday or Friday morning to get out for the first night of events."

Why wouldn't she just bring the horse here? I frowned and cocked my head to the side. Pursing my lips, I tried to figure out a way to convey what I wanted. In the end, I settled on pointing at the barn.

Her brow furrowed as she looked between the barn and me. "What are you suggestin'?"

I sighed. Damn, I didn't remember this being' so difficult when I was eleven. Grabbing her hand in mine, I led her toward the back door and out to the barn. Cash eyed us, a hint of his usual smile on his lips. Not as wide and shit-eating as usual, but mischief glimmered in his eyes. I'd take that as a win.

I hated seeing him unhappy at my expense.

"Make sure to use some protection, y'all," he called with a chuckle, not pausing in roping.

He needed to fucking cool it if he wanted to be able to compete this weekend. I didn't want to hear him bitching when we didn't win because he'd gone and been a dumbass and fucked up his hand.

"Cash!" Cheyenne hissed, even though laughter fell from her lips.

The shade of the barn was a welcome reprieve from the hot summer sun. It wasn't even nine and the temperature was already climbing. Dear Lord, Texas summers were a bitch. I led her down the breezeway and to one of the empty stalls. Stopping before it, I nodded.

She frowned a moment. "Are you sayin' I can board her here?"

I nodded.

Her mouth gaped open, a little gasp escaping her. "But—but that's too much. I'm already crashin' at your place. I can't possibly ask to board her here too."

I rolled my eyes, giving her my most are-you-kidding look. I wouldn't have her driving an hour and a half one way up to San Antone just to ride her damn horse. There was more than enough space here. We could buy a couple barrels and she could practice as much as she needed.

She worried with her bottom lip again, sending a shot of desire through me. "Are you sure?"

Another nod. I gestured between the two of us, and pointed westward. Toward San Antone.

"You wanna go now?"

I shrugged. Why not? Might as well bring her here, give her time to adjust to the new setting, especially with the rodeo this weekend.

Cheyenne seemed to share the same thoughts, repeating them aloud. "It makes sense to bring her now." She sighed. "You sure you're okay with this? I can pay for her board. And rent. I ain't a freeloader."

Absolutely not. I didn't need her money. Didn't want it. Her being here with her dog and horse wouldn't affect me financially. I shook my head and waved away her offer.

She loosed a breath and met my gaze, unshed tears hanging in those gemstone eyes. "Maverick...this is too much. I can't." She dropped her head, her shoulders shaking.

No. I didn't want to see her crying. Not because of this. Not because of anything, really, but especially not this. I tilted her chin up once more, wiping away the twin tears rolling down her cheeks with my thumbs.

She sniffled. "I can help with chores. And the cookin' and cleanin'. I don't got a lotta experience, but I've worked babies before. I'll earn my keep."

I didn't need her to do those things, but the desperation in her voice, in her gaze had me nodding. She couldn't be worse with the babies than Cash, who had little to no patience, and hopefully she was a better cook than Charlie—bless her heart.

Cheyenne's lips drew up into a weak smile. "Okay. Let me see if I can get my clothes from last night and I'll be ready."

CHAPTER 17
Fearless

CHEYENNE

By the time we got me some more clothes and unloaded Country Road at the ranch, it was late afternoon. Maverick drove us in silence past the barn and down a paved road that split in a V. He took the right-hand road, which was lined with blooming jacaranda trees on either side. A gorgeous little house came into view a moment later. It was slightly smaller than Charlie and Ryder's, but I loved the look of it—very log cabin-y. A large garage sat directly to the right of it, and parked before it was a gorgeous classic truck.

I could just imagine him out there, working on it whenever he had a chance.

My nerves wound tight as I got out of the truck, Brandy at my side while Maverick grabbed the bags of clothes and household items we'd bought while we'd been out. I don't know why I was so nervous. It was just temporary. Just until I got on my feet again.

I followed behind Maverick as he unlocked and opened the door. Everything was immaculate. I don't think a single fleck of dust was out of place. It made me bite back a smile.

So very Mav-like.

Everything was grey or black. Again, unsurprising. Black leather couches sat before a grey-washed wooden coffee table, atop a black, and white geometric patterned rug. But despite the monochromatic color scheme, the house wasn't devoid of life. It still possessed a welcoming air. It was just...well, it was just so unapologetically him.

The house had a very open floor plan to it. The kitchen, dining, and living room all taking up technically one large space.

"This is really nice," I murmured, admiring the only decoration in the room—a gorgeous antler chandelier hanging above the dining room table.

He nodded in thanks and put my bags down near the door, motioning me to follow him toward the hall on the right.

A guided tour, then. I trailed behind him as he showed me the spare bathroom—simple, plain, and again monochromatic—and then the spare bedroom. It was a decent size, with a queen size bed taking up most of the wall opposite the window. Sunlight spilled in, bathing the dark polished concrete floor in light.

He nodded to the room. So, this was mine? All in all, it was almost as big as my trailer. Crazy. But despite the spacious size, it felt cold, lonely, not cozy and roomy.

Stop being picky. You're homeless, remember.

I smiled softly. "And is your room across the hall?"

He nodded and waved me on to follow once more. There was a small hallway off to the left of the dining area, which had a laundry room hidden behind little folding doors and then a door to the right. He opened it and led me in.

It still held that dark color scheme, but there was something elegant and masculine about this room. Maybe because it was actually decorated—if you could call it that. The massive bed was made of black polished wood, and had a black and white gingham-style comforter on it with matching pillows. A large cow skull hung centered above the bed on the wall. Two dark wooden sconces accompanied the piece on either side. An armchair sat near the large window looking out on a small pond about a hundred or so yards away. An impressively large cowhide rug took up the space before the bed. But the glint of silver and gold caught my eye. Buckles lined these really cool shelves that looked to be made of old barn wood on the wall opposite the bed above the flagstone fireplace. There had to be at least forty or so of them.

"You won all these?" I asked, moving further into the room to admire the wall. A little pang went through me. Most of my buckles were lost in the fire...but my collection had been tiny compared to his.

He rubbed the back of his neck and nodded, looking bashful.

I smiled, glancing around the room, finding two more doors. One hung slightly ajar to what I assumed was a bathroom. I voiced the thought aloud, looking back at him to confirm. He nodded toward it, silent permission to take a look.

My jaw just about dropped. A massive—I mean *massive*—claw foot tub sat before glass French doors that led onto a private back porch. Off to the right, was a walk-in shower with three—not one, but three— shower heads. Not to mention, this room alone could easily fit the living quarters of my trailer into it.

"Holy shit," I murmured, turning to look at where he lingered in the doorway. "This is really fuckin' nice."

He nodded, appreciation written plainly on his face. Moving to him, I grabbed one of his hands, tracing patterns over his callouses and the lines along his palm. I couldn't remember the last time I'd stayed in such a nice place. My trailer had been old when my dad had given it to me for my eighteenth birthday. It'd been seven years since then.

"Thank you for your hospitality," I said, whisper-soft. A lump lodged in my throat.

His warm hands cupped my cheeks as he tilted my face up to meet his stare. Warmth and desire and other emotions I couldn't quite put my finger on swirled in the light depths. He pressed a soft kiss to my forehead.

And as I melted into him, as I breathed in what was becoming the familiar scent of him—tobacco and leather—I thought that maybe having a roommate might not be so bad.

———

THE SPRAY OF HOT WATER DID LITTLE TO EASE THE GROWING knot in my chest. It was easy to ignore when I was with Maverick and the others, but since we'd gotten back to the house for the night, it grew and grew and grew.

A lump lodged in my throat.

I had no home. Only a few things to my name, even. For so long, I'd never needed to rely on anyone for anything. I'd taken care of myself. But now...now I was completely reliant on everyone else. Especially Maverick. Which I was super grateful to him for, but it wasn't exactly how I'd imagined a relationship with him starting.

Were we even in a relationship? Did he even want to be in a relationship? Did I?

A pulsing headache settled just over my left eye socket—*ugh, please not another migraine.* They'd been coming so often lately. I couldn't even blame it on the smoke inhalation either. It'd been this way for the past week, at least.

Maybe sleep would help. A solid eight hours could do me some good.

I finished up in the shower, then dried off and padded to the spare room. I'd bought a couple throw pillows while we'd been out to liven up the place a bit. But the *you are my sunshine* pillow just seemed sad in the room.

And I don't know what it was about it, or if it really had anything to do with it at all, but I lost it. Completely and totally lost it.

Big, fat tears rolled down my cheeks, a weight settling around my shoulders like a ton of cement blocks. The knot in my chest constricted so tight that I couldn't breathe. Wrapped in nothing but a towel, hair dripping wet still, I sunk to the floor, sobs wracking me so thoroughly I thought I might die of the pain. Brandy nudged me, raining kisses on my face, but I ignored them. I appreciated the love, but couldn't accept it. Not right now.

You see, when you're seen as all sunshine and wildflowers and everything light and happy, everyone just expects you to be strong and keep your cool in hard situations. And for the most part, I strived to uphold that belief. But sometimes that optimistic, golden girl just couldn't fight the darkness.

I'd been so worried about taking care of Maverick, of making sure he was okay, that I'd used it as a Band-Aid to not worry about myself.

But seeing that sunshine pillow against a mound of grey and black pillows was the saddest, most accurate depiction of my life right now.

Only problem...I didn't have many happy thoughts to keep me shining. Okay, that was a bit dramatic, but a girl could feel, right?

I'd woken up yesterday unknowing of just how much my world would be flipped upside down in a day. At least Brandy was okay, at least I still had my truck and Country Road, but now I'd ventured into unknown territory.

A home made of brick and mortar, no wheels to just up and leave. The need to get a job—yet another thing tying me down to this place... Not that Mercenary Ranch wasn't nice or that I was ungrateful for Maverick, Charlie, Ryder, and Cash's kindness and hospitality. But it was all so new and foreign and...

Brandy started barking. Barking. Barking.

"Brandy!" I sobbed, but she just kept barking at the door, and I was too much of a mess to stop her.

A knock came a few moments later.

"I'm fine!" I called, biting back a torrent of emotion and tears as I tried to get myself up off the floor. I'd barely stood when the door slowly opened inward, Maverick's tall frame taking up the entirety of the doorway.

Maverick's eyes, swirling with worry, landed on me, a silent question lingering there—*What happened*?

CHAPTER 18

Dig

MAVERICK

I was working in the garage when I heard the barking. Incessant, insistent barking. The kind meant to get your attention.

Brandy.

Dread coiled in my stomach as I dropped the wrench on the table, not bothering with putting it away.

Was Cheyenne okay? What was wrong? She'd seemed fine when I'd left her in the house a bit ago.

My feet ate up the distance to the house, through the living room, and down the hall. Each step sent my pulse rising, the fluttering in my heart beating faster than damn hummingbird wings. My knuckles rapped on the door to her room.

"I'm fine!" Her voice sounded weak, broken, the words a choked-out sob.

The dread turned tighter in my stomach. She wasn't fine.

I opened the door gingerly, too worried to wait for an invitation, and found her standing in the middle of the room, clutching a grey bath towel to her chest. Her hair was wet and she smelled like my soap. I know it was indecent of me, but she looked so beautiful and so broken in that moment.

My lips pursed as I lingered in the doorway. Brandy whined and spun around, looking between Cheyenne and I. Tears leaked down Cheyenne's cheeks as she clung to her towel, her eyes deep turquoise pools of emotion.

"I-I'm s-sorry," she sobbed. "I t-tried to c-calm her d-down."

I frowned, shaking my head, even as I pulled her into my arms. Did she think I was mad at Brandy? She was a dog. That's what they did. In fact, she deserved some extra attention for letting me know something was wrong. Cheyenne all but fell into my touch. It's like she had no more strength in her.

"I-I'm sorry," she murmured, over and over and over.

I held her to me, lightly rocking side to side—a little trick Aunt Violet taught me. I opened my mouth to console her, to reassure her, just...*something*, but no words came. None.

I didn't need to ask her, though, to know why she was crying. I could see it in her eyes.

She reminded me of this one mustang I broke once. She had that same wild, terrified look in her eyes that he did when I first brought him to the ranch and put him in a stall. Despite the shavings, the quality feed, that mustang hated the barn. It wasn't his home.

Hell...it's almost like how I'd felt when I'd lost my parents and sister, my home. I'd had the Mooneys at least to help me through. It didn't seem like Cheyenne had anyone.

She'd had everything taken from her in the blink of an eye. And I could only imagine how hard that must be for someone as wild and free as her.

Her entire body trembled as she clung to me as if her life depended on it. I just held her in my arms, pressing soft kisses to her forehead as I ran my hand down her damp hair. But it didn't seem to help. Nothing did.

I wanted to help her. I needed to help her. And standing there in a towel wasn't going to do her any good. Scooping her up in my arms, I carried her back out the hall and all the way into my room—the only sounds that of my boots and Brandy's toenails on the polished concrete, along with Cheyenne's muffled sobs against my chest.

I flipped on the dimmer switch, turning the lights down low, and sat her on the bed.

"Wh-what? Why did you bring me here?" No accusation lingered in her tone, just mere curiosity.

Standing before her small frame, I tilted her chin up, forcing her stare as I cupped her face with my palm. I hoped she understood the silent question that I couldn't bring myself to say aloud.

With a soft nod, my gaze flickered to her mouth then back up to her eyes just as I ran my thumb over her bottom lip. In an instant, the devastation in her gaze darkened to a glimmer of desire. She sucked in a sharp breath.

Slowly, painfully slow, I dipped my mouth to hers.

CHAPTER 19

Burn

CHEYENNE

Maverick's touch was magic.

It had to be.

Because with each passing moment, every fear and worry and thought withered away like ash under his scorching touch.

I clung to him as he kissed me, his mouth moving against mine in soft, unhurried motions. Lazy almost in nature, giving me the opportunity to decide what I wanted. Allowing me the chance to set the pace. I appreciated the thought, the respect, but I didn't want that. I didn't want to think, let alone make a decision. I just wanted to *feel*. Feel his touch, his kisses on my skin. Wanted to feel those calloused hands over my flesh.

I slid my arms around his neck, pulling him in and deepening the kiss. He answered after the briefest moment of hesitation, laying me back flat against the bed. He moved to partially cover his body over mine, my towel completely forgotten as it fell around me. One of his hands still rested against my cheek, even as his other drifted down my neck, and slowly, slowly, slowly, over my breast.

I hissed at the touch, arching into him.

This. This was exactly what I wanted. *Needed.* No talking, no coddling, just...action. Action always spoke louder than words anyway. Maverick was a living, breathing testament to that. I didn't want him to console me, to tell me it would be alright. I wanted him to kiss me, use me, wreck me. I wanted him to make me forget why I was crying. Who I was, even.

Maverick's hand cupped my breast, his thumb flicking over the peaked nipple. A shiver skittered through me and I let out a moan. "Fuck."

His lips stretched up into a satisfied smirk as he pulled away.

Goddamn, he was sexy. But he was still wearing too much. I wanted to touch him, feel him. Feel those scars—those beautiful fucking scars—beneath my fingertips. To see his strength and bravery right there carved into his flesh. Not yards of black fabric.

I hastily tugged at the pearl snap buttons on his shirt, exposing the white tank beneath. He stilled, a look of concern washing over his face.

"Let me see you, Maverick," I begged. In silence, I watched as a war played out on his face. "Please." The word was but a whisper on my lips as I raised a tentative hand to his chest and began slowly pulling at his shirt.

Apparently, asking nicely was all I needed to do.

He stilled beneath my touch, giving me a stiff nod. Moving slowly, purposefully yet gently, I helped him slide the shirt off, revealing his toned arms and burns. I ran a finger up and down his arm lovingly, a silent show to him that he didn't need to hide. I held his wild gaze, my hand moving up along the curve of his shoulder before cupping the back of his neck, holding him to me. "Beautiful," I murmured. "Absolutely fuckin' beautiful."

Something shifted in him then. No...broke. The restraints of his self-control shattered. His mouth descended on mine once more, his kiss holding a desperation to it I wasn't anticipating.

Fuck yes.

As he kissed me senseless, his hand drifted lower. Lower. Lower. His fingertips feathering over the planes of my stomach before brushing along my hip and toward the apex between my thighs.

The first stroke at my core sent a ripple of desire through me and a moan falling from my lips. My head fell back against the bed, my back arching into the touch as I gripped the bedsheets. Maverick's lips trailed along the curve of my jaw, his breath fanning against my skin even as his fingers teased and taunted me with a magic all their own.

My eyes fluttered closed as he stoked me higher and higher, like pouring gasoline onto a fire. God, he made me burn. Bright and hot. He moved with the same surety, the same precision and quiet confidence he did with everything else. I'd never thought it more fucking attractive than I did now.

His name was a breathy whisper on my lips.

A hum of approval rumbled through him, sending a shiver down my spine. It was the only sound he'd made so far, and knowing he'd made it because of me... Dear. God.

His free hand cupped one of my breasts and squeezed, wrenching a moan from me as I arched into him.

More. I needed more.

He seemed to understand that. His touches, his kisses, they turned more insistent, possessive. I didn't want soft and timid, I wanted wild, chaotic. And without needing words, he delivered.

Still cupping my breast, his mouth found my nipple and he sucked it into his mouth. All the while, his hand at my core never missed a beat. Never faltered. Another wave of blazing heat seared a path down my spine and all the way to the tips of my toes. One of my hands drifted up to cup the back of his neck again, a silent demand for more. More. More.

He paused, pulling back to look at me.

What? No. No, he couldn't stop.

But as his heated gaze met mine, I let out a gasp. Fire. Fire and lust and need burned in his eyes. A silent promise of what was to come. The sexiest smirk I'd ever fucking seen blossomed on his face before his lips trailed kisses down the planes of my stomach, along my hip, and down the inside of my thigh. His breath teased me, setting my nerve endings into overdrive. I was so. Damn. Close.

So close to that ledge of no return.

His mouth on my core sent a wave of pleasure rippling through me so intense I thought I might shatter apart right then and there.

But it's like he knew, knew how close I was and didn't want this to end.

He dipped a finger into my core, his tongue working a special kind of magic as he sent me higher. Brighter. Hotter. I felt like a livewire beneath his touch, my skin, my blood, my nerves all but sparking with need. I clutched the bedsheets, my back bowing off the mattress. It felt so good it was almost painful, teetering that line between pleasure and pain. Every time the flames of my orgasm rose too high and I thought I might shatter apart, he eased up, slowly starting the process all over again.

I was on fire. I had to be. The fact the bed hadn't erupted into flames was a goddamn miracle. I burned. Burned for him.

"Maverick," I growled through clenched teeth as another wave of heat rippled through me. He paused at my core and glanced up at me, those green eyes sharp.

"Please," I all but begged.

His mouth on my core was answer enough, his tongue finding the sensitive bundle of nerves there, teasing taunting, just as he inserted a second finger and pumped in and out. Again. And again. And again.

I came so hard I saw stars, a breathless scream tearing from my lips. My vision blurred and blackened around the edges, each wave of my release scorching through me like a wildfire.

I collapsed against the bed, the air sawing in and out of my lungs as I tried to calm my breathing. Maverick laid beside me, brushing a stray piece of my damp hair back off my face as he watched me in silence.

"That was..." I sucked in a shaky breath and let it out slowly. "That was amazing."

He offered me a soft smile while he continued to run his fingers through my hair. I turned to face him more fully, pressing a kiss to his lips.

What he'd done for me...

I hadn't even realized I was having a panic attack until it was too late. Hadn't even realized how overwhelmed I was. But he'd pulled me out of it. I couldn't thank him enough. Words just didn't seem to be enough. But I could show him without words.

I deepened the kiss, one of my hands drifting down his chest and toward the pant line of his jeans. Even as his breath hitched, he halted me with a hand over mine.

I met his heavy, hooded stare. Despite the desire in his eyes, he shook his head.

I frowned. "But don't you want this?"

He gripped my chin and pressed a feather-soft kiss to my lips before giving a nod.

I narrowed my gaze. So then why wouldn't he let me do anything? Did he not want to have sex? We didn't have to do it. I could do...other things. This didn't need to escalate that far. I voiced the concerns aloud.

His gaze was soft, his kisses softer, as his mouth met mine once more. I melted into the touch, still completely baffled as to why he didn't want more. But as he broke the kiss and his light eyes held me in place, they seemed to silently say, *soon*.

I blew out a loud sigh, to which he smiled. He nodded toward the pillows at the head of the bed and stood up long enough to pull off his jeans and socks, leaving him in a pair of boxer briefs, before sliding beneath the covers. He patted the bed silently, a soft look on his features.

I relented, completely ignoring the fact I was butt-ass-naked, and slid beneath the covers. Maverick pulled me to him, wrapping me snugly against his chest. The scent of leather and tobacco filled my nose. He must have been smoking outside. That familiar scent soothed me, and within a few heartbeats, my eyes began to drift closed.

CHAPTER 20
Right Now The Best

MAVERICK

Cheyenne was still asleep when I came back in from feeding and working the babies around 7 AM.

Good. She needed rest. She slept soundly, wrapped up in the bedsheets, looking like some blonde-haired goddess—it was the only thing that seemed fitting to call her.

Last night... She'd been perfection. Complete perfection as she'd shattered apart from my touch. *My* tongue. Just the thought—damn, I'd take her right now. The irrational side of me wanted to. It had wanted to last night, and now it all but bellowed to have her. But the rational side of me won out in the end. I hadn't done what I'd done in the hopes of compensation. I'd done it because it was what she'd needed, and I was more than happy to give. Besides, I wasn't going to wake her up for that. There'd be other opportunities. More chances.

Casting a final glance her way, I left her in the room, heading for the kitchen. I wondered if she was a breakfast person. What all had she'd eaten yesterday? She'd seemed to like everything but the eggs.

No eggs, then...how about pancakes?

I set to work mixing up the batter and getting some bacon fried up, losing track of time as I worked. It was what I liked so much about cooking. I was so focused on creating something, that my mind sort of... blanked on all the rest.

I'd just about finished up the last of the pancakes when a soft touch drifted down my shoulder and settled at the small of my back. My breath hitched in my throat.

"Mornin'." Cheyenne's smokey voice was thick with sleep.

I turned to face her, my heart pitter-pattering against my ribcage. *Must've gone through my drawers.*

She wore one of my t-shirts. I wasn't one who typically liked people messing with my things, but it was something I'd overlook because of how goddamn gorgeous she looked in my shirt. Her hair spilled down her back in wild ringlets, her turquoise eyes heavy still. Her sun-kissed skin all but glowed against the white fabric.

I pulled her to me, desire sparking to life in my veins. That indecent, irrational side of me began bellowing again. I didn't have the will to resist this time. Not as my lips dipped to hers. She didn't seem to mind, though. She welcomed it even. Met me stroke for stroke, even sliding her hands up along my shoulders before snaking them around my neck.

God, I wanted her. Right here. Right now. I was just about to grab her and hoist her onto the countertop when she froze in my grasp, a strangled groan escaping her. "Oh, God. I—" She tore from my grip, dashing through the living room before disappearing down the hall. The guest bathroom slammed shut a moment later followed by the muffled sounds of vomiting.

I frowned. That was the second time she'd been sick. I wondered why. Was it from smoke inhalation? Stress? She'd seemed okay yesterday, though she'd mentioned having a headache in the evening. I'd have to keep an eye on her.

I debated whether to go check on her or leave her be, when she finally came back out a few moments later.

"Sorry." She sighed. "I um... I don't know what's wrong with me."

I glanced between her and the food before offering her a questioning glance. *You hungry?*

She pushed a stray curl off her face and nodded as if she understood. "Yes, please. I'm starvin'."

Starving was an understatement. She all but wolfed down four pancakes and almost half a pound of bacon. Even as I ate my own breakfast, I half expected her to run off again and throw it all up. But she never did.

We remained in relative silence as we ate—obviously, since I didn't have anything to say. I could tell she did, though from the unspoken questions burning in her eyes. In the end, she just focused on her food. Guilt ate at me. I hated that I couldn't ease her worries, her fears. But talking wasn't my strong suit even on the best of days.

"So," she finally said, grabbing her mug of coffee and pressing it to her lips. "Can I help you with anythin'? Cleanin'? Workin' horses? What do y'all do here at the Mercenary Ranch?"

I gestured at her empty plate; my brow knit in question. I didn't want to rush her off if she wanted more.

"Oh, I'm done, thank you. It was amazing," she replied after a few seconds of trying to understand what I asked.

Nodding, I rose from my chair and grabbed her plate, placing it into the dishwasher along with the other dirty dishes.

"You didn't have to do that." She frowned at me when I waved her off. After I'd finished putting away the last bit of leftovers, I grabbed her hand and led her outside.

If she wanted to see what I did for a living, I'd gladly show her.

CHAPTER 21
Leather

CHEYENNE

I'd just finished putting Country Road away from working her when commotion over by the round pen drew my attention.

"She's gonna kill you, Goodie." Cash's dad, Clint Mooney, stood before the pipe-stall round pen, resting his arms and one of his feet against the rails in a casual stance. His large sunglasses shielded his eyes, but a grin tugged on his lips. Cash stood beside him, in a similar stance, though not all of the usual Cash flare and energy was present. He was still worried about Maverick. I could tell.

But standing like that, next to his father, it was like taking a glimpse into Cash's future. The two looked so incredibly similar.

I made my way over, the little girl in me nervous as all hell. Clint "Bad" Mooney was big here in Texas as a successful cattle rancher, but I'd grown up watching him bronc ride. He was a legend. A celebrity in my mind. And I was sort of, kind of sleeping with his nephew.

I bit back a giddy squeal. I didn't want to interrupt, but who the hell would miss out on the opportunity to watch one of their heroes work?

"Either shut up, or help me, dammit." the man in the round pen,

Goodie, Mister Mooney had called him, grumbled back, not daring to drag his eyes away from the red filly angrily circling him in the round pen.

The two looked similar, though the other was maybe a few years younger and more clean-cut. His alligator boots were too nice, his periwinkle paisley shirt looking more like something he'd wear beneath a nice sports coat than to ride in, and his belt buckle gleamed just a little too brightly. Like it didn't get enough wear and tear. He was a businessman if I'd ever seen one.

Brothers, then.

"I told you not to go in there." Mister Mooney chuckled as the filly rushed at his brother.

Goodie sidestepped the horse before shooting a curse out. Okay, so he wasn't *all* businessman. I'd seen plenty of city slickers try their hand at riding horses. This guy knew what he was doing. Which made sense if he was brothers with the famous Bad Mooney. "I gotta get this *fuckin'* pig workin', don't I?"

Mister Mooney shrugged, a smile lighting up his face, making him look extra Cash-like. "Can't get her workin' if she kills you, dickhead." Just then, Cash's dad turned to me, and he nodded my way. "Come on over here, girl. I see you lurkin'."

My heart hammered in my chest, excitement brewing like a storm. I'd not gotten to officially meet Mister Mooney. I mean...there was the one time Cash had given Charlie that horrible, but equally funny shirt —that she still proudly wore, might I add—but I'd never gotten to, like, actually talk to him.

"Sorry, sir," I managed to squeak out as I came to his side.

He pulled down his sunglasses for a long moment, eyeing me with an intensity that made me want to fidget before turning back to the round pen. He didn't speak for a long time. So long I thought he wasn't going to say anything at all. Should *I* say something? Should I tell him what a big fan I was of his? How I'd watched damn near every rodeo he'd competed in and had his whole final season recorded on tapes in a box somewhere that my daddy kept safe for me. No. That just made me sound like a crazy person.

Maybe just introduce myself, then? I looked to Cash, who still stood beside him, for something, anything, but he was more focused on the arena.

I opened my mouth to speak, but Mister Mooney stopped me with his gravelly voice. "So, your trailer burnt down?"

I opened my mouth, shut it, opened it again. It was so blunt and direct, and I wasn't quite sure what I'd expected, but it hadn't been that. "Yes, sir."

"I'm sorry to hear that."

"Thank you, sir."

"Cash says you been helpin' Maverick?" He glanced between Cash and me.

I thought of last night. I could argue that he'd been the one to take care of me, but I nodded once more, another, "yes, sir," falling from my lips.

He nodded just as Goodie's growls of frustration echoed on the wind. "Speak of the devil, Where the hell's Maverick?" Goodie railed. "He's the only one can get anythin' other than piss and vinegar out of this goddamn nag."

"Maverick's got his own babies to worry 'bout." Mister Mooney waved him off with a dismissive hand. "And this horse ain't Maverick's problem, she's yours."

"Yeah, well Maverick's baby doesn't have a burnin' keg full of black powder for a fuckin' brain." The little red filly raced by, flailing out her hind leg as she tried to kick him for emphasis.

I looked between him and Mister Mooney. "Can...can I ask why he's in there, sir?"

Mister Mooney's face sliced into a grin. "When the boys bought this group of babies, we decided to place a wager. Each of us would break one. The most broke and rideable one that sells for the highest dollar wins...This here's Goodie's charge. We was gonna call her Widowmaker, but...well, Goodie is gonna die alone, just like he's lived his entire life so, it doesn't fit."

"Shut up," Goodie groaned.

Mister Mooney nodded back to the red filly before focusing his attention on his brother once more. "You should spend less time bitchin' and more time workin' that horse before she turns your head

155

into a canoe. What good is it doin' ya to yell at me about how you hate her? She hates you just as bad. More maybe. Did you try hittin' her in the head with a shovel?"

The first smile on Goodie's face was like a sunrise on a new day, bright and refreshing. Holy shit, no wonder Cash was a cocky sonovabitch...look at his fuckin' dad and uncle. "She bent the shovel and snapped the goddamn handle in half."

The chink of spurs drew my attention and suddenly Maverick stood behind us. A shiver traversed the length of my spine as I took him in. He wore his usual all black, his aviator sunglasses hiding his eyes from me, but the look he snuck my way wasn't any less scalding.

Mister Mooney let out a string of curses. "God damn it, Maverick, don't sneak up on me like that. You're gonna give me a fuckin' heart attack and then Cash, here, is yours and Ryder's fuckin' problem. Do you want that?" He nodded at his son for extra emphasis.

Cash grinned, but it didn't reach his eyes. He wasn't wearing any of his godawful, obnoxious sunglasses like usual. It was like the light in him had dulled, dimmed.

Who'd have thought I preferred the brash, brazen brunette over this. Give me back the Cash who perpetually stuck his foot in his mouth and somehow miraculously got laid, not this sullen, sad, serious version.

Maverick's lips peeled back into a smirk as he shook his head before gesturing toward Goodie in the round pen with the red filly. He still didn't talk, but it's like Mister Mooney understood him anyway.

"I think he's tryin' to get himself killed." Mister Mooney chuckled. "Course, he's just as bad at that as he is at everything else."

Goodie clapped back, a glare on his face. "Fuck you, Bad."

Mister Mooney laughed once more, glancing back at Maverick. "Whatdya think, boy? What's the problem here?"

Maverick's lips pursed as he took a step up to the pipe-stall between his uncle and I. Still silent, he slipped his sunglasses down, his eyes sharply focused on the arena for a long moment before he gave a single shake of his head. Mister Mooney's voice drew my attention. "He's undoin' all the shit we spent yesterday fixin', right?"

Maverick nodded, gaze still focused on the filly.

Goodie turned and bolted for the fence as she raced past him, trying to climb out and charge him again. He hauled himself up the metal piping and fell over with a thump just beside Cash. "Well, if you're so good, *you* handle it." He stabbed a finger at Maverick.

Dear God...she was psychotic. Worry knit my brow, a scowl curling my lips downward, my heart thumping faster as Maverick looked at Mister Mooney, an unspoken question in his eyes.

"Get in there and see if you can calm her down." Mister Mooney nodded.

He was going to get in there with her? That hell beast?

Maverick climbed the fence and dropped down on the other side, his gaze never leaving the horse, who snorted and pawed the earth. I gripped the pipe-stall, watching. Waiting.

He didn't rush. In fact, he didn't do anything at all. He just stood there, watching her as she watched him. He waited, as if he didn't have a single other worry in the world. Nowhere to go. No place to be.

Mister Mooney moved to help Goodie up. "Only thing that fuckin' horse is good for is target practice," Goodie groaned as he brushed himself off. "Let me go get my Henry rifle and punch a couple air holes in that nag's head."

Mister Mooney settled back at my side once more and nodded at the arena. "Maverick'll get her sorted out."

"I don't think so, Bad." Goodie settled on the other side of me, his fancy cologne drifting on the wind and filling my nose. He even smelled of money. Wealth. He reminded me of that old Marty Robbins song, *The Cowboy In The Continental Suit,* except he hadn't ridden no brute. "Last time I seen a horse that was both that mean *and* that stupid was that old broodmare dad used to keep in the pasture to keep the coyotes away from the sheep."

"Maverick's got a way with the wild ones," Bad said, pulling a leather pouch out of his back pocket. "He'll calm her down."

Goodie glanced past me to see what Mister Mooney was doing as he pulled some rolling papers and a bag of tobacco out. "I thought you quit smokin'?" Goodie asked before looking at me. "I'm sorry, Miss. Where are my manners?" He offered out a hand to me. "Goodfellow Mooney."

I smiled, placing my hand in his and giving it a firm shake. "Cheyenne Harris, sir."

"You one of Cash's girls?" he asked. So, he hadn't heard Mister Mooney and I talking then.

"She wishes..." Cash sidled over to my side and bumped me in the shoulder, a glimmer of his usual self peaking through.

I rolled my eyes and laughed, nudging him back. "If I recall correctly, I'm the one who turned you down, remember, sweetheart?"

His grin pulled wider and he nodded. He'd shot his shot the first time Ryder introduced us all, but even then, I'd been interested in Maverick. Cash and I were too similar. Yeah, he was attractive, but a little too himbo-ish for me. I liked my men grumpy, or broody, or both.

Maverick couldn't fit the bill any more perfectly.

Cash wrapped an arm around my shoulder for a moment before letting it fall. "Nah, she's Maverick's."

A little trickle of...of something went through me at that. I wasn't sure what it was, and honestly, I wasn't quite ready to know what it meant, but it did something to me.

Goodie's eyes widened as he glanced between me and Maverick. "Really?" A soft smile played on his lips. "Well, it's nice to meet you, miss."

I gave him a soft smile before movement in the arena drew my gaze. Maverick made his way slowly into the center of the round pen as the horse sprinted off angrily around in circles, tossing her head and snorting up a storm.

"I told Violet I quit smokin'," Mister Mooney finally answered his brother, his gaze similarly glued to the arena as well. "She said I had to either quit smokin' or quit drinkin'. I figure I can smoke in secret a hell of a lot easier than I can drink in secret."

"And if Violet finds out?" Goodie asked, shifting his focus to Maverick as well. Cash's gaze never truly left his cousin. He'd been watching like I hawk since the moment he'd gone into the pen.

"Then I'll work that red filly next time and let the bitch run me over," Bad quipped, fidgeting with his hands. I glanced over as he sprinkled some tobacco into a piece of paper.

"How do you get the shit to roll your own cigarettes?" Goodie asked. "Aren't you afraid she'll see the charges on the card?"

Bad glanced over his shoulder at Cash beside me, a sly grin on his face. "Turns out my son ain't unreliable in *every* way." He winked. "Cash buys me the stuff and doesn't tell his mama. And I don't tell her I caught him in the hay barn with that Karkula girl again last week. Win, win."

In the round pen, Maverick finally made a move towards the horse. She'd been running herself ragged for a while now, sweat all but dripping off her. Maverick slowly worked his way out from the center towards the far fence. The filly saw him and turned to charge.

My heart squeezed even as my mind told me to calm down. Everyone always talked about Maverick being an excellent horseman. And from the way he moved, the way he watched the horse, I knew I didn't need to worry.

But my heart still fluttered as Goodie shouted out. "Maverick, look out!"

Maverick paid him no mind. He just stood his ground. A silent sentinel.

"You know why a horse will never run itself into a tree or off a cliff?" Mister Mooney asked no one in particular, lighting a cigarette.

Goodie was the only one to regard him. "What?"

"A horse won't run itself into a tree or off a cliff because instinctively the horse knows that tree or that cliff won't move. And if it keeps goin', it ain't gonna end well for the horse."

I glanced between Mister Mooney and Maverick, a soft smile coming to my lips as Bad pointed at the dark-haired cowboy. "Horse knows, instinctively, that Maverick ain't gonna move either."

The filly charged within a few feet of Maverick and stopped. Just stopped. Maverick didn't take a step back or to the side. He made no indication of any kind that his life was in danger. He just stood his ground, staring at the horse.

"Every time I look that bitch in the eye she tries to bite my face off." Goodie shook his head on my right.

"You challenge her," Mister Mooney answered. "You raise a question of who's in charge. Maverick don't do that."

"So, they just know he's in charge?" I found myself asking.

Mister Mooney regarded me for a long moment. "With Maverick it ain't about who's in charge. The horses trust him. Like nothin' or no one I ever seen before."

"Why?" Goodie wondered aloud, mirroring my own thoughts. I'd never understood people who had that deep of a connection with an animal. Hell. He'd only been around Brandy a couple times and I already had to worry she'd replace me with him.

Mister Mooney just shrugged. "I don't know. I've never understood. But I *do know* I ain't ever seen anyone calm a horse as quickly and efficiently as that boy."

I shifted my focus back to Maverick as he approached the horse on her right side and slowly reached out his hand to run it along her back. It wasn't fear or trepidation slowing Maverick's hand. It was that smooth, sure confidence. The horse flinched as his hand came into contact with her flesh. Maverick didn't speak as he methodically ran his hand up and down the horse's side, working his way leisurely up to her head. She pinned her ears back, threatening to bite, but he ignored her. He met her gaze, never faltering. It was like he was communicating with her through some unspoken language.

Made sense. Him and I managed to understand each other pretty well without words.

The filly relaxed a bit as he came to stand beside her face. A dangerous place for anyone else to be. Maverick stood like he belonged there.

I'd ridden my whole life; I'd watched men and women ride and train and compete. But I don't think I'd ever seen anything like this. It was like in those movies, the cheesy horse girl ones where the untamable stallion all but bent the knee for some angsty teen.

Except this wasn't a movie, and Maverick wasn't an angsty teen. Well, I guess you could argue he might be a bit angsty, but that was beside the point.

I glanced over my shoulder at Cash. "You're right. He *is* like a fairy-tale princess."

Cash's lips pulled up into a grin, his gaze never leaving Maverick. "It's crazy, isn't it? The connection he has with them."

I nodded. "It doesn't seem real."

"It's real alright," Mister Mooney added.

We all watched as Maverick took a step back and held out his left arm to gesture across the pen. The filly arched her neck, and for a heart pounding moment I thought she might rear, but with a snort, she started forward in a brisk trot. Maverick clicked his tongue at the horse, the only sound he'd made so far. As if understanding his request, the mare sped up into a gallop, though not quite into the balls-to-the-wall run she'd been at when he'd first gone in.

"So does he speak horse or does the filly speak English?" Goodie asked.

Mister Mooney blew out a puff of smoke. The sweet scent of tobacco enveloping me. I breathed it in deeply, savoring the familiarity of the smell. "Neither the one, nor the other. They don't speak the same language at all. They just understand one another." He nodded toward the arena again. "See, watch."

Maverick lowered his hands then, and stilled in the center of the pen. Even went so far as to drop his head down toward his chest. He didn't say a word, but it was like the air shifted. I sensed it. Bad and Cash and Goodie sensed it as well. Especially the horse, as she stopped in the arena and looked to him—ears forward, harsh lines of her face softening a bit. Maverick took a step to his left, moving out past her head. Taking a step back, she turned around, starting in the other direction at a slow jog.

Maverick clicked his tongue once more, urging her faster. The filly obliged.

Goodie sighed. "I'll be damned."

"Likely." Mister Mooney blew out another puff of smoke and chuckled. "Very likely."

I watched, in awe, as Maverick worked the filly for a few more minutes, stopping her and turning her around every so often. She was steaming and dripping sweat, but relaxed into the work instead of trying to find a way to get loose and go on a killing spree.

Maverick stilled once more. The horse stopped and walked towards him, meeting him in the middle of the pen. He petted her face for a long moment before turning and walking back towards us.

I'd always thought he was attractive, talented. But fuck...there was something so fucking sexy about what he'd just done. That calm, quiet confidence. It made me think of last night. Of the way everything he'd done had been with purpose and that same, slow surety. A shiver went through me.

"If I turned my back on that pig, she'd put hoofprints on it," Goodie marveled as he climbed back over the fence toward his charge.

Maverick shook his head, but Mister Mooney's voice drew our attention. "She ain't a pig, you're just a dumbass."

"Well," Goodie sighed. "You know what they say. If it looks like a pig and acts like a pig, it's probably a red mare."

"And what does that make you?" I asked, immediately cupping my hand over my mouth. Shit. I hadn't meant to say that out loud. Damn my big, fat mouth.

Cash and Mister Mooney burst out laughing. A smile even graced Goodie's face. Maverick just cast a meaningful glance back at the horse, now sniffing around the pen. After a moment he nodded toward Goodie.

We all frowned. I didn't know what he was asking. Looking to Cash, I wondered if he understood, but Cash glanced at me and shrugged.

Mister Mooney was the one to speak. "No, you ain't takin' on another baby, Maverick. You've got Blue Zeus, and Goodie has that red filly. You don't have time to work 'em all and I don't want Blue Zeus endin' up like this one."

"Are you suggesting I can't break a baby?" Goodie demanded from beside Maverick.

"Who got the filly to calm down?" Mister Mooney shot back.

Maverick shook his head once, before lowering his eyes to the ground.

"You think she's too much horse for your uncle?" Mister Mooney asked. I don't know how, but he seemed to speak fluent *Maverick*. I guess it made sense. Maverick lived with them, he probably had to get good at reading his body language to know what he was thinking, but it was still impressive as hell. Not even Cash could do that.

Maverick nodded before casting an apologetic look at his other uncle.

Goodie dipped his hat. "No, I agree."

Mister Mooney stomped out his cigarette, a scowl forming on his lips. "I don't. Goodie's gotta learn how to communicate with pigs just like Maverick did—" He glanced at his brother, before turning and leveling his nephew with a pointed stare "—and Maverick's gotta learn to let other people figure some shit out for themselves."

Maverick looked like he wanted to argue, his dark brows knitting together as his jaw clenched. And I don't know what came over me, or what the hell possessed me to open my mouth, but there was no stopping it once the words fell from my lips. "I'll take over."

Everyone stopped and stared at me. Cash with surprise, Goodie with straight up disbelief, Maverick with soft appreciation. But Mister Mooney's heavy gaze on me almost had me eating my words. The weight of his stare was crushing, and with his sunglasses blocking his face, I couldn't read his emotions.

"I'll take over for Goodie," I repeated when it was clear no one was going to say anything. "You said there's a wager, right? How much money we talkin'?"

"Two grand," Goodie said. "You sure you wanna kill yourself over that?"

If only he knew just how desperate I was right now. The insurance company still hadn't gotten back to me yet, but I doubted I'd be getting much. And while two grand didn't seem like much, it could set me up with a nice new heat press and sublimation printer to start up my shop up again.

I looked to Mister Mooney. "So...can I take over?"

He scratched at the stubble on his chin and regarded me for another long moment, finally offering me a nod. "Alright."

I grinned, my gaze flicking to Maverick. His lips curved up into a soft smile and he nodded. I wonder if he knew why I'd decided to do this. It seemed like he did. It felt like he did...if that made any sense.

Mister Mooney huffed out a loud sigh and nodded at Goodie and Maverick. "Well, should we get back to the ranch and doctor up those calves in pasture three?"

Cash frowned. "What're you talkin' bout?"

"I asked Maverick if he'd help me with some of the new calves back home," Mister Mooney said with a shrug.

"Mav's done enough today. I can help." There was an earnestness, a desperateness to his voice that was so wholly un-Cash-like that had I not known *why* he was acting this way, I'd be worried.

But I understood the sudden want—no, need—to make sure Maverick was okay. I felt the same too.

Cash's dad shook his head, a frown on his lips. "You got a fever or somethin', boy? You ain't ever volunteered to do shit for free in your life, unless it involves gettin' your pecker wet."

I bit back a laugh, even as a scowl formed on Cash's lips.

"Besides," his dad went on, "you're too rough with the babies, and I asked Maverick."

A muscle tightened in Cash's jaw, his hazel gaze narrowed on his dad, but after a long moment he blew out a breath. "Fine."

Mister Mooney nodded to his brother. "Get your ass outta that round pen before she kills you, Goodie. And give Maverick your keys. We ain't waitin' out in this fuckin' heat for your sorry ass."

I looked between Mister Mooney and Maverick. I didn't want him to leave. Firstly, what the hell was I going to do here by myself? And secondly, he still wasn't talking. Wasn't fully back to himself. There were glimmers now and then, but he was still so quiet and stoic. His smiles were few and far between.

"Can I come along?" I asked. "I've worked with calves before."

While Mister Mooney's gaze wasn't harsh and cold as it had been toward Cash, there was a firm finality to it. I knew the answer before he even opened his mouth. "You got that red filly to work with."

I sighed, disappointment writhing in my chest, but I lowered my gaze to the ground and nodded. "Yes, sir."

The jangle of keys and the rhythmic chink of spurs drew my attention. Maverick had climbed over the pipe-stall and made his way toward me—Goodie following behind, albeit a bit slower. Maverick didn't speak as he placed a soft hand on my shoulder, his sunglasses stare holding mine for a long moment, but he didn't need to. I knew what he meant well enough. *It was okay and he'd be back soon.*

I offered what I hoped was a reassuring smile. "Text me if you need anythin'."

He dipped his head, a soft smile coming to his lips

as he flicked my nose gently. I waved him off, a huff of laughter escaping me. He turned and clapped Cash on the back before nodding to Mister Mooney.

"Be right there," Cash's dad responded, waving a hand at Goodie and Maverick. "Y'all head to the truck."

Without a backward glance, the two headed off for Goodie's pearly white King Ranch edition Ford F-350.

As soon as the doors shut, Cash whirled on his dad. "Why're you makin' him do this? Ain't he been through enough shit? He don't need your bitchin', and we all know what a prick you can be when you're doctorin' them cattle."

Mister Mooney took off his sunglasses, the hazel depths swirling with some unknown emotion I couldn't place. A smug smirk coated his lips, though. "I ain't actin like nothin', boy. That's the thing...you two are the ones makin' it seem like somethin's wrong with him. I'm treatin' him like I normally would, which is what he wants. What he needs. He don't want no coddlin'. No fussin'. He just wants things to be as normal as possible."

He took a couple steps, his focus on his boots, before nodding and replacing his glasses. It was a contemplative stance, one that I noticed Maverick doing on occasion. When he looked up, he fixed Cash with a soft smile as if he was lost in old memories. "Wanna know why that boy started talkin' again? It was you, dipshit. You, who treated him and talked to him like not havin' a voice was no big deal at all. Like words weren't needed to communicate. In those ten months, you talked so much, you spoke for the both of ya's. You gave Maverick a voice and made him feel normal. That's what he needs now."

It made sense. Letting him come out of it on his own. A part of me worried that it would only make him withdraw further into himself if we just let him, but that was just my fears talking. Logically, it made sense. Give him time to process and come to terms with things, and he'd open back up.

165

"Do you think it'll last ten months?" I asked, worry trickling into my tone.

He shook his head. "Nah. Last time, Maverick wasn't just dealin' with the trauma of the accident. He was dealin' with a whole bunch of other shit. Shit he's come to terms with since then. I say a month tops." He gave us both a pointed look. "A lot sooner if y'all start treatin' him like normal and don't coddle the piss outta him."

I lowered my head. "Yes, sir."

It was hard not to treat him differently. What he'd done... I still couldn't believe he'd done that for me. I couldn't fully shake the guilt that it was my fault. Deep dow,n I knew it wasn't, but tell that to my stupid head. My heart.

A warm, heavy hand settled on my shoulder. I looked up to find Mister Mooney holding me in place with his stare. "Chin up, darlin'. You didn't know. How could you possibly? But do me a favor, don't be so busy tryin' to take care of him, you don't take care of yourself."

I frowned. "What do you mean?"

"You went through shit too. And pushin' it aside to take care of him ain't gonna get rid of it. At some point it's gonna pile up, and shit always rolls downhill."

I blew out a breath and offered him a soft smile. "Thank you, sir."

"We're havin' dinner at the house tonight," Mister Mooney said, glancing at Cash. "Tell everyone to come. Your mama's making fried chicken."

Cash grinned. "What'd you do to convince her to make that? A new gun?"

Mister Mooney grinned. "She don't even know yet, but if she won't do it for Maverick, I think your idea just might work." He looked between the both of us and pointed at me. "You go work that filly and take care of yourself. And you—" His finger landed on Cash. "I hate to say it, it'll give you a bigger head than you already have, but bring some of that Cash sparkle when you come over...or else you ain't gettin' nothin' but burnt pieces."

"Like fuck I am," Cash huffed, some of that said Cash sparkle returning to his gaze.

CHAPTER 22
Ranch Hand

MAVERICK

Most people hated work. Hated the monotony. The daily grind. And I knew it was corny as hell, but how did that old saying go...? If you did something you loved, you'd never work a day in your life—or something like that.

But it was true. At least for me.

From that first morning Uncle Bad woke me up at 4 AM, I'd loved it. Every bit of it. Moving cattle, doctoring calves, working horses, hell, mending fences or even shoveling shit...I loved it all. Every day—despite its certain routines—always had something different to offer. Every day I woke up, I never knew exactly what the day would bring.

I'd always be grateful to Bad for that work ethic. Lord knew his son didn't feel the same way.

Sweat dripped down my brow as the afternoon sun beat down on me. It was hot as hell, not even taking into account the humidity, but I'd long since stopped caring. We'd be done soon enough.

"That's the last one," Goodie shouted over the lowing of the cattle. I wiped at my face with the back of my sleeve and stepped away from the calf as it bolted upright and bounded off toward its mother.

Bad took off his hat and ran an arm across his face. "Alright, let's pack up this shit and head on back."

Goodie muttered something about needing a beer as he headed for the horses. He hauled himself atop his dapple-grey gelding with a huff. Bad and I followed. The wind felt good against my face as we walked across the pasture. It was still warm, but cooler than when we were at a standstill, so I'd take it.

"So, that girl..."

Here we go. I'd been waiting for this conversation. Bad liked to say he minded his own business, but he was a sucker for drama, you'd never convince me otherwise. And with Cheyenne coming into my life like a whirlwind and changing everything, well, hell, I'd be interested too.

Bad's gaze met mine for a moment. "She's a pretty thing."

Goodie snorted and cracked open a Coors from in his saddle bags. "Pretty's a bit mild for that girl, Bad. She's a cowboy killer if I ever saw one."

My lips tugged up at that. She *was* a cowboy killer. I bet she'd love hearing that too. I could even see her wearing it on a shirt proudly.

Bad looked at me. "Cash told me she's stayin' with you. Is this a romantic thing or just 'til she gets on her feet?"

I lifted a hand from my reins, waving it side to side. It was a bit of both, honestly. I definitely liked her. But I could tell the thought of settling down scared her. She didn't seem like that type really. She was wild, free, and I wasn't stupid enough to try and tame her. I think it would only make her run.

But as long as she was here, for however long she wanted to stay, I'd have her. Have her in any way she wanted.

"Both?" Bad guessed.

I nodded.

"And what about Ashleigh?"

I stilled at the name. I hadn't thought of her since Saturday evening, to be honest. But the memories came flooding back...as well as the hurt. I couldn't believe I'd let down my guard again. Let her into my heart, only for her to just crush it beneath her feet at the first opportunity.

I hardened my resolve. I was done with her. Done with the second, third, fourth chances only to be left disappointed.

I glanced at Bad, holding his gaze as I shook my head. The ghost of a smile drew on Bad's mouth. "Good. I want you to be prepared though for her to come back around. If she catches wind about you and Cheyenne, she'll be back here in a heartbeat tryin' to tear you two apart."

I nodded once more.

"You know I ain't the type to tell you boys what to do when it comes to relationships, but I feel compelled to tell you right now that you'd be an idiot if you let her ruin things with this one."

I nodded.

I understood. I understood his fear. I knew everyone hated Ashleigh, and I didn't use hate lightly.

"I like this girl," Goodie said, coming up on my left. "She's got charm and balls. Anyone willin' to take on that bitch of a horse has got my vote."

Bad chuckled, pulling a rolled cigarette out of his shirt pocket along with his lighter. "I gotta agree. I like her spirit. I think your aunt'll like her too."

Goodie scoffed. "Name a handful of people that woman likes, Bad. One handful."

"She likes Charlie and Cason." Bad lit his cigarette and blew out a cloud of smoke. I nodded at him, a silent request if I could have one.

Bad's only response was to fish another cigarette out of his pocket before handing it to me along with the lighter.

"I don't think I know a soul that doesn't melt being around those two," Goodie replied. "Sweet as pie, I tell you...the both of 'em."

Uncle Goodie and I didn't always agree, but we could on that. Charlie and Cason *were* sweet as pie.

The two of them shifted on to talk about something else for a few moments, leaving me in silence as I smoked. I appreciated it though. This was my happy place—atop a horse, nothing but land around me, and relative silence...I couldn't ask for anything better.

I preferred this to rodeoing, to be honest. Always had. I didn't eat, breathe, and love the sport like Ryder did. Didn't love the attention and notoriety like Cash. I enjoyed it, and I was good at it, but ranching was my passion. Not the rodeo. I'd only started because Cash asked me to be his header. And we all knew there was almost nothing I'd say no to him about.

"So—" Bad's voice cut through my thoughts. "This girl, she rides, obviously. She rodeo too?"

I nodded.

"What event—" Bad seemed to come to the conclusion on his own. He rolled his eyes, puffing out another plume of smoke. "Ah, hell, she's a fuckin' barrel racer, ain't she? Damn it. I take it back. I ain't lettin' no barrel racer ruin my damn horse... fuckin' hell, boy."

My shoulders shook with silent laughter, a grin coming to my lips. Goodie laughed beside me. "Well, you did say Mav's got a way with the wild ones."

"Let's fuckin' hope." Bad huffed, even though a smile drew on his lips.

———

I FIDGETED AT MY SPOT AT THE KITCHEN COUNTER AS I washed all the dishes. Aunt Violet bustled about, a flurry of motion as she got things ready for dinner. She'd been oddly quiet since I'd gotten back—a true feat for her, as she gave Cash a run for his money.

It meant she was thinking of what to say.

"Mav, honey..." Her voice held a tentative edge to it.

I glanced over my shoulder at her, soapy water running down my hands.

"So, your uncle says you have a new roommate?"

I nodded.

"You like her?"

Another nod.

"And she's nice to you?" I knew what she meant but wasn't saying. *Was she like Ashleigh?*

Did everyone hate her that much? Had I just been completely oblivious? I knew everyone had their issues with her. Cash hadn't liked her from the moment he'd met her. I'd always just thought it was because Cash could be territorial and he didn't like that when Ashleigh was around, my focus wasn't solely on him. Bad and Aunt

Violet were better about hiding their dislike, it wasn't until the second time she'd broken up with me that they started expressing their thoughts.

Cheyenne was nothing like Ashleigh, that was for sure.

But would she and I even last though? And what even were we? Saturday night I'd have thought just a hookup and been okay with that. I'd still be okay with that if that's all she'd wanted. But then the fire happened, and now she was livin' with me, and I wasn't talking, and didn't know what she wanted or what we were.

Maybe she didn't even want a relationship. Maybe she planned on leaving the minute she got enough money to buy herself a new trailer. I didn't know. I had so many questions that needed answers, and the only reason I didn't have them was my own damn fault.

Frustration welled inside me. I wanted to talk. I really fucking did. But it was like the connection between my brain and my mouth had been severed. A trauma response from my PTSD.

I don't even know exactly how I'd started talking back when this happened before. All I remembered was watching Cash get his ass kicked for sticking up for me, and us running like hell to hide from Bodi Johnson and his little minions. I'd been thinking about how Aunt Violet was going to kill us for starting trouble, and Cash had given me that famous grin, said something about what I'd done being so awesome, and I'd just called him a fuckin' idiot.

Some of the frustration had dulled, I realized. But I still didn't know *why?* Was it because I'd been so mystified that Cash would do something like that for me? Was it because for as dumb of a thing for him to do, I was eternally grateful for his undying support?

I didn't know, and it drove me mad. I wanted to talk. To ask Cheyenne what she wanted. If this was just a situation of convenience or if she wanted to explore something more. She seemed like it last night, and this morning before getting sick...but, well, I just didn't know.

I turned off the running water and dried off my hands before facing Aunt Violet fully. I gave her a firm nod, hoping she understood I didn't think Ashleigh and Cheyenne were anything alike. She offered me a smile and returned my nod, saying, "Good. I'm lookin' forward to meetin' her."

Bad strolled into the kitchen then, moseying around looking at everything Aunt Violet was working on.

"Nope. You just go find yourself somethin' to do. You ain't gettin anythin' until dinner, so don't even," Aunt Violet admonished, snapping her tongs at Bad for good measure as the chicken sizzled in the frying pan.

He chuckled as he made his way to the fridge, opening it to grab himself a Coke. "Want one?" he called over his shoulder to me.

I waved him off.

"You ready for this weeken—"

A sound reminiscent of a gunshot went off in the kitchen as the backdoor swung open and smacked against the wall with a crack. A familiar crow followed. "Big Daddy's in the house!"

Cheyenne stepped through the threshold next, looking like a ray of sunshine in her yellow crop top and cut off jean shorts. Charlie, Cason, and Ryder followed right behind. Cheyenne's familiar smokey voice filled the room. "Jesus Christ, Cash. Do you have to be so damn loud?"

"Lord's fuckin' name!" Bad said, cracking open his can as he leaned against the counter top.

Cheyenne stopped in her tracks, clapping a hand over her mouth, her cheeks turning pink. Cash, Ryder, and Charlie laughed though.

"Hey! That's what Uncle Mav says!" Cason chimed in, running up to Bad and Aunt Violet to give them each a hug.

"Where'd you think he got that from?" Bad asked, tousling Cason's hair. Charlie had agreed—begrudgingly—to let him grow it into a mullet for the summer.

Charlie, Ryder, and Cash all made their way around the kitchen, saying their hellos while Cheyenne stayed a step behind, hovering between me and the door. While she didn't look spooked, there was a flightiness to her gaze. I moved to her side and nodded toward Aunt Violet.

Cash noticed and chimed in, "Here Trouble, this here's my mama. Mama, this is Cheyenne... Mav's girl."

Mav's girl. Something sparked in me at that, but I pushed it down. It was too early. Too preemptive.

Cheyenne tucked a curl behind her ear, one of her sunshine smiles lighting her up from within. "It's nice to officially meet you, Mrs. Mooney. I do apologize for what I said a minute ago." Cheyenne rifled in her cowhide purse a moment before pulling out a glass jar. "Here. I uh... I made this candle for you. It's magnolia scented." She glanced down at the simple candle and shrugged. "I was just messin' around, so it's nothin' fancy."

Aunt Violet was always hard to read. Her eyes never gave anything away, and she was the type who could smile and wave and hold up an entire conversation while silently judging you and you'd never know. She eyed Cheyenne as she grabbed the candle and raised it to her nose. Her eyes fluttered closed for a moment, her face softening almost imperceptibly. Opening her eyes once more, a smile blossomed on her lips. A genuine one.

Something in my chest loosened. A breath I hadn't realized I'd been holding. I didn't even realize how much Aunt Violet's approval meant to me. Not that Cheyenne and I were anything yet really, but...still.

"My lord, child, you made this?" She took another deep inhale.

Cheyenne beamed and nodded. "Yes, ma'am."

"This smells absolutely lovely. Thank you. Please, make yourself at home. Would you like some sweet tea? Water? Soda? Cash I'm sure brought some beer."

"I'm good for now, Mrs. Mooney. Thank you, though."

Aunt Violet smelled the candle once more. "I can't wait to show the ladies this at Bible Study tomorrow night. Can you make more of these? I have a friend in town who owns a little shop on Main Street, and these would be a *hit*!"

Cheyenne's grin was more radiant than the sun peeking out from behind the clouds after a storm. "Absolutely, ma'am. That would be amazin'!"

"Hey!" Cash all but yelled. "Less talkin', more cookin', Mama. You're gonna burn it."

Aunt Violet whirled on Cash, snatching up her tongs and brandishing them at her son. "You don't tell me how to cook in my own kitchen, boy. I don't care if you're a grown ass man, I'll still beat your ass raw with the wooden spoon."

Cash at least had the decency to look afraid as he all but ran out of the house and into the backyard, earning laughs from the rest of us.

Aunt Violet shooed as all out shortly after. Bringing up the rear, I glanced back to find her sneaking another sniff of the candle before setting it down. There was no possible way Cheyenne could have known that magnolias were my aunt's favorite, but call it sheer luck, a good guess, whatever...she'd won points with Aunt Violet, which made me inexplicably happy.

Cash and Ryder were already setting up for a game of horseshoes as I shut the door. "Mav! You and Trouble over here are a team against Ryder and I!" Cash shouted, a beer already cracked open in his hand.

The old Cash was back, thank God. I couldn't deal with the sad, depressed version. Call it crazy, but I preferred his usual, wild, pain-in-the-ass antics over him being all morose and shit. That just wasn't who he was, and seeing the light leave him...especially because of me...I hated it. I don't know what happened after I'd left with Bad and Goodie, but I was grateful.

Had to be Bad.

Now that I thought about it, I was certain. He was one of the only ones ever able to get through Cash's thick, stubborn skull.

"Why the hell is my nickname Trouble?" Cheyenne chimed in, drawing my attention.

Cash grinned. "You're trouble if I ever seen it, darlin'."

She rolled her eyes, even as a smile lit up her face. "Whatever... Hey, we can't just leave out Charlie. That's not fair."

Charlie already sat in one of the deep-set lawn chairs a few away from the group. "It's honestly fine. This heat is God awful, I feel nauseous as hell, and the thought of having to move around more than I have to right now makes me want to die."

Cheyenne flashed her a sympathetic look. "I'm sorry. That doesn't sound fun. Oh! How was your doctor's appointment today?"

Cason bolted past with Brandy and Dutch hot on his heels as I made my way over to the group. I didn't know who enjoyed this new arrangement more—Cason or the dogs.

Ryder stepped up to Charlie's side, placing a hand gently on her shoulder. Charlie tilted her face up to look at him, a loving smile on her lips. He dipped his mouth to hers for a quick kiss. I was happy for him. For them both, actually. The love they shared...I wanted that someday. The type of love that could be seen, be felt, without the need for a single word.

All you had to do was take a moment and watch them together and know they were meant for each other It's like they were soulmates or something—if you believed in that sort of thing.

I came to a stop beside Cheyenne and opposite Cash. She didn't look up at me as I approached, but settled into the crook of my arm. Funny how comfortable it felt. I thought of Bad's question earlier. Was this the beginning of a relationship or just a situation of convenience? I truly didn't know, and with each passing moment, with every touch, every look, every seductive smile on her lips, I wanted to know the answer more and more.

"Everything looks good," Charlie replied, dragging me from my thoughts. "Heartbeat's strong, its measurements are tracking at the right age. We have another appointment in four weeks." Charlie looked up at Ryder once more. "And then a week or two after that, we can find out the gender."

Cheyenne smiled. "That's so excitin'. I'm so happy for y'all."

Charlie glowed as she grinned back. "Thank you. I just can't wait until we figure out if it's a boy or a girl. I've already been driving Ryder crazy with names."

Ryder nodded, but an equally as radiant grin sliced across his face.

Talk of potential baby names guided the line of conversation as Cheyenne and Ryder remained on the side closest to Charlie, while Cash and I made our way to the opposing horseshoe pit. We'd barely even started playing when Cason barreled over to Ryder, ruining one of my shots.

Thank God I'd not let the shoe fly or it would've hit him straight in the face as he ran across the middle of the game.

"Can I play, Uncle Ryder? Please? Please?"

Ryder cast a guilty look our way, but Cheyenne surprised me, crouching down to Cason's level. "You can throw for me, little man. I'm not that good anyway."

177

That a was a total lie. She'd held her own against Ryder—a feat in and of itself. Only one who could beat him was me.

Cason lit up, a bright smile crinkling the corners of his eyes. "Really?"

She glanced over at me. "You okay with him throwin' a few rounds?"

Well, if I wasn't attracted to her before, I sure as hell was now. Kids and animals were my weakness. I wouldn't even try to lie and say otherwise. Something about them being so small and essentially helpless made the protective side of me come out. Someone who did well with both...well, damn.

I nodded to her, giving her a thumbs up.

"Aw, come on," Cash grumbled quietly beside me. Cash had the patience of Job when it came to kids—mainly because he was one at heart—but if there was one thing he didn't do well with accommodating, it was a game of horseshoes.

I elbowed him in the ribs, pegging him with a vicious stare as I shook my head once. He could deal for one game. He glanced between me and Cheyenne, who was teaching Cason how to hold the horseshoe.

That shit-eating grin lit up his hazel eyes, making them more green than gold. "You likin' the view?" One of his eyebrows quirked up.

I rolled my eyes, but failed to bite back the smile that came to my lips.

"Mmm, that's what I thought. Girl's somethin' else. You better snatch her up before someone else does."

I gave him a hard look that I hoped said, *I'm working on it.*

CHAPTER 23

Come Home To You

CHEYENNE

Living with Maverick was easy. Astonishingly easy. Especially considering that we couldn't communicate. *Correction*—talk. We communicated easily enough even if he refused to text and make things easier. But we made it work. He was an expressive person despite his quiet nature. His eyes told a lot. They were easy to read.

I'd feared it would be hard to live with him and learn about him, but if I'd learned anything from Maverick, it was that actions spoke louder than words.

Maverick was meticulous, a complete and total perfectionist. He thrived off order and routine and familiarity. He was the type of person who could do the same thing every single day and be perfectly content. I still couldn't figure out how he didn't get bored. But I guess that's why he had his hobbies. If he wasn't working horses, mending fences or moving cattle, he was doing *something*. Working on the truck in his garage, fixing things in the barn, strumming on his old guitar on the back porch, fishing out by the pond, whittling. If it needed the use of his hands he was doing it.

Including...pleasing me. Apparently, his love language was touch, and fuck if he wasn't excellent at it. We hadn't slept together. Not yet, but I knew, just knew, he was going to wreck me when we did. It was always the quiet ones who surprised you the most. And in my short time with Maverick, I'd learned he was full of surprises.

But his favorite hobby of all, it seemed, was to cook. And my God, was he a damn good one. I'd been all across the U.S. growing up. I'd eaten lots of amazing food, but sweet baby Jesus, the boy could cook. If he didn't already have a job, I'd urge him to go to culinary school or start up a restaurant or something.

I sat on the countertop of the center island in the kitchen, sneaking fingerfuls of homemade chocolate cake batter when he wasn't looking, singing a George Strait song on the station that played through the speakers. Another thing I'd learned—he wasn't a fan of newer country music. Anything mid 2000's and later that I tried to play earned a scowl or a headshake. He liked the songs I grew up on, the ones my daddy used to listen to.

He popped the cake pans into the oven, his back turned to me, his muscles bunching and rippling beneath his impeccably ironed black shirt with every movement. I snuck another lick of leftover cake batter just as he turned around.

A scowl formed on his brutally handsome face, his scarred eyebrow quirking up.

"Oh, come on!" I cried. "This is the best part!" I swiped another fingerful for emphasis and took my time licking it off. His gaze darkened, desire brewing like storm clouds in his eyes as he watched me. His lips quirked up into a wry grin even as he shook his head and pointed at the bowl.

No more.

"Um, speak for yourself," I scoffed. "I'll eat all the cake batter I want, thank you very much. It's delicious, by the way."

Maverick's lips pulled up further, a full-fledged smile lighting up his face. Butterflies danced against my ribcage at the sight. Goddamn, he was gorgeous.

"You know, if I didn't have physical proof that you were real, I'd think you were fictional."

His face scrunched up, a question burning in his gaze.

"It's true. You clean, you cook, you *bake!* You're good with animals, with kids. You're respectful, and hot as fuck. Prince Charming ain't got nothin' on you."

He opened his mouth as if he'd respond, and my heart leapt.

Yes! Please, please talk.

I bit back the disappointment creeping into my heart as he offered me a bashful smile instead. He shook his head and pressed a kiss to my lips, a silent distraction in hopes of changing the subject, no doubt.

He did that a lot. Poor guy didn't know how to take a compliment. But I knew how to take a hint.

"Chocolate cake's always been my favorite. I don't remember a whole lot about my mama, but I remember on my fourth birthday she made this amazin' chocolate cake and homemade frosting."

He moved to the countertop beside me and pulled out a cutting board, knife, and an onion. *So, we've moved on from dessert to dinner for the moment.* He glanced up at me, interest simmering in his eyes. I didn't talk about my mama. Ever. And yet, here I was bringing her up on my own.

I sighed, a torrent of conflicting emotions welling to life within me like a tidal wave pulling back from the shore. Building. Building. Building. Emotions I hadn't let myself feel in years—sadness, anger, confusion. Tears pricked in my eyes, but I blinked them away. No. I wouldn't cry for her.

Not ever again.

I blew out a breath, one of my curls blowing up from the air. "I'm still convinced that she made it so good only so I'd be too distracted stuffing my face full of it that I wouldn't notice her leavin'."

Maverick stilled for a long moment before glancing at me, his brows knit together.

I nodded, dropping my gaze to my hands as I fidgeted with them. "Yep. She was a...a real peach, that woman."

He turned to me fully, his face a mask of concern. *Tell me?* I could practically see the words in his eyes.

The stubborn part of me wanted to rebel, to drop it, anything to not talk about the woman who'd birthed me and left me, but I'd been the one to bring it up in the first place. I couldn't just go and say that then get all defensive. No matter how much it hurt talking about her.

Maybe I needed to, though. I sure as hell wasn't gonna talk to Daddy about her.

"Like I said, I don't remember her much. She left on my fourth birthday. What kind of horrible fuckin' person does that?" I huffed a bitter laugh. "My mama, that's who. She uh…" I bit my lip. I didn't even know what to say about her. It'd been so long since I'd seen her. "She never called or sought me out. Never even sent a letter explainin' why she left. And Daddy never liked to talk about her. But I do know she was a…well, she was a whore."

Maverick rocked back, his brows rising so high they disappeared beneath his cowboy hat.

"I'm serious," I replied. "She was a hooker. Daddy swears he met her off the clock, but who the hell knows. He always told me growin' up that I looked like her…he was right." I blew out a loud breath, my head falling back as I stared unseeingly up at the ceiling. "I looked her up on Facebook a while back. Took me ten seconds and she just…popped right up. That's how easy it was to find her. She wasn't even hidin' from me… she just didn't care. In all that time she could have reached out, found me just as easily…but she. Just. Didn't. Care."

I glanced over at Maverick. He watched me intently, sadness and understanding etched plainly on his face. He reached a hand over and gripped my thigh, giving it a reassuring squeeze.

I let out a sad laugh, shaking my head back and forth. "Why did I even bring her up again?" I looked over at the oven. "Oh yeah, the cake." I nodded, meeting his gaze once more. "For a long time, I refused to eat chocolate cake. It made me think of her. Out of sight out of mind, right? But then on my eighteenth birthday I decided…fuck it. I wasn't gonna let her dictate what I would and wouldn't eat. She wasn't even in my life anymore. I wouldn't give her that control. So, I've been on the hunt ever since to find a chocolate cake better than the one she made me."

I scraped my finger along the bowl again before licking it up. "I haven't tasted your frosting yet, but if it's even half as good as this batter, I think I've found the one that'll knock her out of the number one spot."

A small smile drew on Maverick lips, the harsh lines on his face and the worried expression in his gaze softening. He leaned over and kissed me, slow, steady, soft, but no less intense. His affection was usually like that, filled with a smooth surety and quiet confidence. I pulled him to me, snaking my arms up over the planes of his hard chest and around his neck as I caged him to me with my legs.

A little hum of approval rumbled in his chest. It was the only sound he'd made at this point, but dear Lord it did something to me every time he did.

I deepened the kiss, reveling in the warmth and taste of him—hints of tobacco mixed with the sweetness of the cake batter. He'd been smoking earlier. He smelled of it too, though I didn't mind one bit. Flicking his tongue against mine, one of his hands slid up my torso before his fingers brushed against the bottom of my breast.

A rush of heat went through me, desire pooling low in my belly. My head fell back, a moan escaping me. Fuck dinner. I wanted him.

And just like that, the moment was over. He pulled away, a sadistic smirk drawing on his mouth.

"Maverick!" I growled, glaring daggers at him from my perch.

That smirk bloomed wider. He pointed to the food. Funny how *now* it was so important to cook dinner, but a moment ago he'd been teasing me with his touch and kisses. "Fuck the food. You *cannot* just start something like that with no intent on finishing it."

He shrugged, picking up the knife and pointing it toward the front door. *The others.*

Oh, yeah.

Family dinners were something I didn't know I'd ever get used to. Every day I'd been here, we'd had some sort of communal dinner. Sunday was funday dinner and cornhole. Monday was at the Mooneys. Then we had Taco Tuesday at Cash's for margaritas and tacos—Cash provided the alcohol, Maverick did everything else. Then, last night had been spaghetti at Charlie and Ryder's. Tonight, Cash had dubbed Thirsty Thursdays, and they'd be over in less than an hour for drinks and board games.

I loved how the three boys had created a family out of their friendship. It pulled at my heartstrings and it was nice having friends you could depend on, but damn...I was extroverted as hell, and even I felt burnt out from all the events, dinners, and just...everyone's constant presence.

I hopped off the counter, coming to stand behind him, wrapping my arms around him and tucking my head against the back of his right shoulder. "Come on, I bet we can get it in before they get here."

He turned to look at me, a war blazing in his eyes. Just the idea of hooking up with him in the kitchen knowing that anyone could come barging in at any moment was terrifying—and also exhilarating. I know he was thinking it too.

Please say yes. Please say yes.

He turned and kissed me, long and hard before pulling away, shaking his head and flicking me on the nose. *After.*

Another frustrated growl simmered up from within me. "Ugh, fine!" There was no use trying to change his mind. Something else I'd learned about him: he was as stubborn as a mule. Once he had his mind set, well, good luck changing it.

I hopped back on the countertop and took another fingerful of cake batter for good measure. His shoulders rose and fell in that silent chuckle of his as he continued cutting onions and scraping them into an oiled frying pan. He added in some garlic a moment later. As he pulled out the bag of chicken breasts from the butcher's, a wave of nausea assaulted me, clutching at my stomach so tightly my breath left me.

Cupping a hand over my mouth, I raced for the bathroom.

What the hell was that about? My head spun, a pounding migraine forming behind my right eye. My mouth still tasted like ash. It's like it was stuck in my lungs. I had to be sick from that.

A timid knock came on the door. After washing my mouth out with mouthwash and cleaning myself up, I opened the door to find Maverick there, a worried look on his face.

I took a breath. "I'm fine. I just think I'm sick with some lingerin' effects of the smoke."

His disbelieving look said it all, but he didn't press as we made our way back into the kitchen. He grabbed me some sweet tea to sip on while he cooked. My stomach remained queasy, but I didn't throw up as Maverick seasoned the meat and put the chicken in a pan. I started talking again, it seemed to help ease Maverick's worries, and even mine. Within a few minutes, the kitchen was filled with so many amazing smells my mouth perpetually watered, my nausea long forgotten.

I think I died and went to heaven when he let me lick the spoon of the frosting after mixing it up. "This is absolutely divine," I said, reaching for the bowl. He grinned, pulling it out of reach.

"Please? Just one more bite," I whined, a pout forming on my lips.

I'd resumed my perch on the countertop. Maverick placed the bowl on the counter opposite me for emphasis. I groaned, rolling my eyes even as my lip curled up into a playful snarl.

Maverick dipped a finger into the bowl and moved to me, holding it out before my face.

"A peace offering?" I asked begrudgingly.

He nodded, his gaze hooded, the look on his face soft, happy, amused.

I pretended to be annoyed, letting out a dramatic huff for flare before sucking his finger into my mouth.

Another hum of approval erupted from him, shooting desire straight to my core. His jade eyes swam with a need I know shone in mine as well.

The frosting tasted good, but it paled in comparison to the way his gaze made me feel.

I pulled away, making a show of licking my lips before biting the bottom one.

He liked when I did that.

His hand snaked into my hair as he crushed his lips to mine. There was an unhinged element to this kiss. It was chaotic, wild, reckless, and I welcomed it.

I tilted my head back, a soft, throaty laugh fracturing in my chest. This feeling. This passion. This wild, wanton need. I could drown in it. Die right here and now and be happy. Maverick's touch was like a damn drug. And like a junkie, I couldn't get enough.

His lips brushed against the corner of my mouth, along the curve of my jaw, before dipping down the column of my throat. He trailed feather-soft kisses to my skin, each caress shooting my desire higher and higher.

"Maverick," I breathed as one of his hands cupped my breast.

The throaty growl that rumbled through him like rolling thunder sent shivers of the best kind down my spine.

His thumb hooked in my bra, pulling it down to expose the nipple as he continued the path of kisses down my chest.

A moan escaped me as his mouth found the peaked bud. One of my hands curled around the back of his neck, holding him to me, urging him for more, more, more.

The door crashed open, so loud I thought a freight train had crashed into the living room. For a split second, I swear to God, my soul left my body.

"Well, shit. Dinner *and a show*!" Cash's crow of laughter followed. "Don't start without me. Let me get a front row seat."

I growled, legit growled, before flipping him off over my shoulder. "Fuck you, Cash!" I half-heartedly yelled.

How was I getting cockblocked again? Seriously?

Cash laughed once more. "Looks like Mav's already got that covered, Trouble."

Maverick slumped against me, his shoulders quaking. For a moment, I thought he was crying, but as he lifted his gaze to meet mine, the widest, most bashful smile I'd ever seen graced his lips. I couldn't help but return it, a soft, embarrassed laugh escaping me.

Thank God I was turned away from Cash or I'd have given him a full show. My cheeks felt warm; I could only imagine how red they were. Maverick righted my top, his intense gaze never leaving mine as if silently saying, *we'll finish this later*.

"I sure as fuck hope so," I murmured before brushing a kiss against his lips.

I was met with Cash's signature grin as I hopped off the counter and went around the island to greet him.

"Aw, why'd you stop? Things were just gettin' good."

"Don't you have some buckle bunny to shmooze over?" I grumped, even as a smile curved my lips. "I thought I remembered you bringin' home some brunette last night."

He waved a dismissive hand. "Ah, no. She's done. Already met the three-date max rule."

I frowned. "Three date max rule?" I asked, just as Charlie, Ryder, Cason, and Dutch appeared in the doorway. Play growls erupted through the house, followed by Cason's laughter, as Dutch and Brandy started to wrestle. The two—well, three including Cason, were thick as thieves already.

Ryder's smooth voice cut through the chaos, a playful glint in his eyes. "Cash's got this system. Once he's made his way through the steps, he's onto the next girl." He plopped an armful of board games onto the coffee table in the living room.

Charlie smiled at me and reached out for a hug I eagerly accepted. She smelled of lavender and vanilla, and was quite literally glowing with happiness. I knew this pregnancy was kicking her butt, but it didn't look like it. She radiated.

Cash scoffed, his hazel gaze meeting mine. "There's more to it than that. There's a whole damn art to it."

"Here we go," Ryder groaned, glancing at Maverick.

Maverick rolled his eyes and shrugged, his lips failing to hold back a grin as Cash launched into his explanation.

CHAPTER 24
Sun To Me

MAVERICK

There were some times that I wondered how Cash and I were related. This was one of those times. The brash, brazen behavior, the dumb logic. It all baffled me. But it clearly worked for him.

I shook my head as he educated Cheyenne on the CASH system.

He'd come up with it not long after Dakota left. I think it was a way for him to deal with the pain. A way to feel in control after everything he'd ever hoped and dreamed for shattered right before his eyes.

"So, it works like this," Cash said, cracking open a Coors and taking a sip. "You start out with the letter C—charm the piss outta 'em. Find out what they like and shit. It's your chance to really win 'em over." Another sip. "Next, assist them—A. Make her feel like you're useful. Capable. This leads into S—seduce them. This is my personal favorite."

Charlie groaned, rubbing a hand across her forehead. "Dear Jesus, remind me to never let Cason take dating advice from you."

Cash chortled, his obnoxious donkey bray of laughter echoing through the room. Thankfully, Cason had already run outside with

Dutch and Brandy. After another swig, Cash went on. "The last letter—H—stands for hightail it outta there."

Cheyenne moved around the island and to my side, all the while her attention still on Cash. She leaned her head against me in a silent show of affection before disappearing behind me as I worked.

As Cash explained his ridiculous system, I finished up searing all the chicken and placing it on a serving plate. It was only then I realized I wasn't the one who'd gotten the plate out in the first place. I frowned, glancing around to find Cheyenne over in the dining area setting up the table with plates and utensils.

A small smile pulled on my lips. It must have been her.

Crazy how easy things had been since she'd come here. I'd expected more of a struggle... I guess there was still time for that. It had only been a few days, but I don't know, I'd expected more problems by now.

"Oh my God," Cheyenne finally huffed, a disbelieving chuckle escaping her. "You're a sociopath, Mooney."

The whole room laughed, including Cash. Charlie's eyes glinted with playful mischief as she came up to Cheyenne's side and smirked. "I don't think he even knows what that means."

Cheyenne's lips pulled up into a matching smirk. "Bless his heart."

The two of them erupted into a fit of giggles that were drowned out by Cash's laughter.

———

As the night wore on, I noticed Cheyenne's inner light begin to dim. It was gradual, subtle, and unless you were really looking you probably wouldn't even notice.

But I did.

She still laughed and smiled and interacted, but the glimmer in her eyes had dulled. She was tired and uncomfortable, looking the way I felt most of the time.

I reached out a hand and squeezed her bare thigh—soft beneath my touch. Her gaze snapped to mine, a question brimming in her eyes.

I lifted my brow. *You okay?*

She offered me a strained smile and nodded. *So, not fine.*

I scanned the room, my eyes landing on Charlie. She gave me a knowing look, like she could see Cheyenne was done too. Patting Ryder's leg, she sighed loud enough to halt the chatter in the room. "I think we should probably get a certain little dude to bed."

"Aw, come on, Auntie Charlotte. I'm not even tired," Cason groaned from his spot on the floor. Brandy and Dutch were glued to either side of him as he stroked the coats lovingly. A yawn escaped him, as if to contradict his words.

Charlie laughed. "Oh really? Your yawn says otherwise, bud."

He whined and pouted as Charlie and Ryder rose from their spots on the couch. But it all turned to laughter when Cash scooped him up, tossing him up onto his shoulders like a sack of potatoes.

"Come on, little man," Cash said with a grin. "Have I ever told you the bed story of Goldicocks and the three whores?"

"Dear God, Cash!" Charlie hissed, before glaring at Ryder—albeit playfully.

Ryder frowned, his shoulders shooting up to his ears in a defensive shrug. "What'dya want me to do about it?"

"He's your best friend! Control him."

Ryder and I shared a knowing look, smirks crossing our faces. There was no controlling Cash. We'd tried and failed on many, *many* occasions. "I'd like to see *you* control him, darlin'," Ryder said, a brow rising in challenge.

Charlie leveled him with another glare that nobody really bought. The smirk on Ryder's face turned to one of his easy, lopsided grins, accentuating his scar, the look in his eyes saying, *you know I'm right.*

"Goodnight y'all. Thanks for the games and company," Cheyenne said, rising from her spot and hugging each of them.

I nodded goodbye as well, holding the door for them all as they filed out and headed for the Polaris to drive back to their houses. I gave a final wave and closed the door, blowing out a deep sigh as I turned the lock.

Cheyenne huffed out a laugh. "You sound exactly how I feel."

Don't get me wrong, I loved them all, loved living on the ranch with them and having such a close bond, but there was a certain point in the day where I was just done peopling.

I moved to her, grabbing her hand in mine, and pulled her toward the bedroom. She resisted a moment. "Shouldn't we clean up first?"

I wasn't the type to leave a mess usually, but I could see the weight of the day dragging her down. Waving a dismissive hand at the kitchen, I urged her on once more. She didn't resist this time, but followed along as I led her to the bathroom. I let go of her hand and turned on the water to the tub, glancing back at her.

"You wanna take a bath?" she asked, her eyes sparking with interest.

I pointed to myself and shook my head before pointing at her and nodding.

Her brows furrowed together, her nose scrunching up slightly from the motion. "You want *me* to take a bath?"

Another nod.

"But you need help. There's so much to clean up."

I pulled her to me and dipped my mouth to hers, kissing her long and slow. My fingers played with the hem of her royal blue crop top, earning a little shiver from her as they scraped against her torso.

"Maverick..." she whispered, breaking the kiss as her head fell back, a silent plea for me to kiss her neck. She did that a lot. Hell, she could keep doing it, I didn't mind one bit.

The sound of my name on her lips just about shattered any resolve I had. It was husky, smokey, seductive. She could say it a thousand times and I'd never tire of it.

I grabbed her shirt and pulled it off her, revealing her white lace bra beneath. Kissing her once more, I nodded toward the tub. A silent request to get in.

One of her manicured brows rose even as a skeptical scowl formed on her lips. With a defeated sigh, she shimmied out of her denim shorts.

God, she was beautiful. Intoxicating. All tan skin and curves... And I wanted all of her. Every inch of her. *But* when I had words. When I could tell her just how much I wanted her. Just *how* I wanted her. I couldn't even count all the ways at this point.

Right now, I just didn't have the words in me. They would come. I could feel it. I just needed a little more time.

"You sure I can't help you?" she asked, settling into the rising water. "Or at least convince you to join me?"

I gave my head a single, firm shake before kissing her once and leaving her. If I lingered any longer, I *would* be joining her.

I wasn't ready to give her all of me, but I still have plenty to offer her. Plenty to keep her happy and satisfied with. But she didn't need that right now. She needed to relax and unwind. And I needed to clean.

———

MUSIC DRIFTED THROUGH THE SPEAKERS THAT RAN through the Google Home not long later. Cheyenne's doing, no doubt. Some newer country bullshit because she knew I hated it and couldn't do anything about it. Not when I had to talk to the speaker to control it.

So, this is my punishment for leavin' her. My lips pulled up into a grin as I washed dishes.

I tuned out most of the songs while I cleaned up, though I hated to admit it, some weren't half bad. By the time I walked back into the room twenty minutes later, she stood in the bathroom wrapped in a soft, fluffy black towel, brushing her hair out as she sang along to the radio, using her brush as a microphone as she sang for Brandy at her side.

She was completely oblivious to me, so I just watched her. It was probably—no, definitely indecent of me, but I couldn't help it. She was so wild, free, full of life. And to think of what she'd gone through as a kid. For as shitty as my father was, he hadn't left. Hadn't given up on us completely, though, you could argue it would have been better if he did. But her mom just left. Left a poor, innocent child.

And unlike me, who'd withdrawn and retreated within myself, she'd embraced it, moved on from the trauma, and didn't let it affect her. She ate the cake, took back control. I wished I could be like that.

Unable to resist the magnetic pull of her any longer, I strode for the bathroom and pulled her into my arms. Her turquoise gaze settled on me as she whirled around, her cheeks blushing even as she continued to sing the last few lines of the song. I found myself swaying softly to the beat.

I don't think I'd ever like dancing, but I'd dance for her.

As it ended, a satisfied smirk tugged on her lips. "See, I told you you'd like Zach Bryan."

I shrugged. Fine. I liked him, but I liked the song more because she was singing it. Her smile widened, and she reached up on tiptoe to kiss me. Lightness filled me and, one by one, I felt the muscles in my body relax. She had a soothing touch. It was like a balm to my worries.

I cupped her face in my hands, pressing my forehead to hers. I hadn't told her just how grateful I was for her, but I hope she felt it. I hope she saw it in my eyes, and felt it in every touch, kiss, embrace.

"Thank you for forcin' me to take a bath," she said softly. "It was relaxin'."

I nodded, giving her an I-told-you look.

She smirked and rolled her eyes, her fingers playing at the pearl buttons of my shirt.

"So y'all do dinner every night?" There was a layer of guilt tangled in with the curiosity in her tone.

I shrugged. Usually. But there were some days when it was just me. Or just the boys and I. Or Charlie. I think they all felt like Cheyenne and I—well, let's be honest, I—needed the company after the fire.

"Is it worse because of what happened?" she asked, all but reading my mind.

Another shrug and a curt nod.

She blew out a breath. "Figures. Don't get me wrong, I adore them all and it's nice that y'all are so close, but... damn."

I felt that in my soul.

I huffed, a soft smile pulling on my lips as I tugged her toward the bedroom. She followed along easily, grabbing some of her things from the dresser. I'd given up a couple of my drawers to her. Without it even needing to be said, we'd both decided on her staying in here after that first night. Not gonna lie, I didn't mind. Things felt a little easier with her around. I'd always struggled with sleep, and after the fire my anxiety and insomnia were through the roof. But she helped. Her sunshine presence helped chase away the shadows and darkness.

I sat in the leather armchair by the window and pulled my boots off, my eyes glued to Cheyenne as she slipped into a pair of bright pink, lacy underwear and one of my t-shirts she'd stolen that barely covered the curve of her ass.

"You gonna shower?" she asked, coming to stand before me.

I nodded as she undid the snaps on my shirt, tugging gently downwards to pull the fabric off me.

Her eyes traveled over me, the intensity in her stare scorching. I shivered as she pulled my tank off next, all the while admiring my scars. I didn't get it. Didn't understand what she found remotely attractive about them. They were brutal and hideous and I hated them more than anything I'd ever known... I'd spent twenty years keeping them covered up. Only a handful of people had ever even seen them. Even less had touched them. Yet here she was, running a manicured fingertip up and down the mottled canyons of my flesh.

"Can I join you?" Her words were a husky whisper, holding the same sultry edge to it that her gaze did. I couldn't stop myself from grabbing her jaw and pulling her mouth down to meet mine.

A little hum of approval trickled out of her that almost shattered my resolve completely. As much as I wanted her to join me, she needed rest. Under the desire and lust burning in her gaze, exhaustion lingered. She'd been through a lot this week. What with being sick, her home burning down, and now dealing with a roommate and all of the social functions we all did on a weekly basis. Besides, we had to spend tomorrow morning getting everything loaded up and ready for the rodeo this weekend.

And I know this wasn't fair of me, was probably a bit cruel, but I picked her up in my arms, lips still pressed to hers, and carried her to the bed before setting her down.

Pegging me with a harsh, disbelieving stare, Cheyenne's bottom lip jutted out into a pout. "Ugh, seriously?"

I grinned, leaning over to kiss her once more before flicking her gently on the nose and walking toward the bathroom. She stayed on the bed, much to my surprise, though I could hear her grumbling over the music and the spray of the water as I turned the shower on. She stopped pretty quick though, and when I came out of the bathroom a few minutes later, she was curled up under the covers, her hair a wild mess on my pillows, sound asleep.

CHAPTER 25
Fix You Too

CHEYENNE

I watched Maverick as he checked his tack for what had to be the fiftieth time. He was nothing if not thorough. He wore all black —unsurprising—despite the hot July sun beating down and making everything miserable.

Him, Cash, and Ryder worked in perfect tandem. A seasoned trio who'd done this for years. Getting ready together, working around and with each other, checking each other's tack.

As if sensing me, Maverick's gaze flicked to mine, those light green eyes sparking something in me that equally exhilarated and terrified me. I brushed off the feeling, though, as he paused what he was doing and made his way towards me.

"How're ya doin', cowboy?" I asked as he came to a stop at my side. "You okay?"

He nodded before tilting his chin at me, a silent question in his eyes. Communicating was easy enough without talking now. It wasn't fool proof, but it worked...for now.

"I'm doin' good. Excited to ride," I answered.

An appreciative smile formed on his lips as he looked me up and down, gesturing at my outfit. I flashed him a smug smirk. I'd really leaned into the whole Fourth of July thing, showing up in all my star-spangled glory. A white and blue sequin show shirt, my red bootcut jeans, red, white and blue chaps with enough sparkles and crystals to blind someone. Thank God they'd been in my car during the fire, I'd paid a pretty penny for these.

Turning this way and that, I put myself on full display, reveling in the way his gaze drank me in like a cool drink of water on a hot summer's day. "You like it? Is it too much?"

Maverick shrugged even as a smile pulled wide on his lips. He waved his hand back and forth.

I laughed. "Good. That's exactly what I was goin' for."

His shoulders shook in that silent laugh of his before he pulled me against him, pressing a soft, yet no less intense kiss to my lips. I'd quickly realized that his touches, his kisses, everything about him, actually, could be summed up to that. Soft, but no less intense. It went along with that quiet surety of his that made my resolve melt when it came to him.

I leaned into him, matching his intensity touch for touch, until we both pulled away breathing heavily.

"Well, good luck to you too," I murmured, resting my forehead against his.

His lips drew up into an answering grin as he pulled back, gripping my chin. His hooded gaze sent a shiver down my spine.

I loved and hated how much of a hold he had on me. I'd never experienced something like this before. This desire. This *need*. It felt reckless and exhilarating and...real. And that scared the hell out of me. I'd never needed anyone in my life. I could take care of myself. But something about Maverick called to my soul.

The shiver of desire turned to one of fear, my stupid thoughts ruining the moment as quickly as it started. I tried to play it off, dropping my gaze and tucking a stray curl behind my ear. Hopefully he thought I was just being shy or something. If he noticed a change in me, he didn't let on. For which I was grateful.

"Rodeo now, fuck later, you two! Come on! They're about to release everyone's picks!" Cash hollered, raring to go at the back of the trailer.

I rolled my eyes, even as a grin pulled on my cheeks. Maverick looked at me as if to say, *after you.*

"I'll catch up." I pointed to the Mooneys' RV. "Gotta grab my hat."

Despite the fact we weren't far from home and wouldn't be staying on the rodeo grounds for the two-day event, Mrs. Mooney did nothing half-assed. She'd forced Bad to get the RV ready so we all had a place to stay out of the heat and get ready for our events.

Maverick gave me a questioning look, his brow arching up. *Are you okay?*

I nodded, pushing up on tiptoe to give him a quick, reassuring kiss. "I'm fine, cowboy. I'll be there soon."

He looked like he wanted to argue, but he didn't press. Not that he would. Not with him still not talking. For once, I was grateful for that.

I needed a moment. To focus. Center myself. It's not like I needed to be there for the picks anyway for my event.

With a final look, he hurried off toward the rest of the group. Sighing, I made a beeline for the RV. I spied my hat box the minute I opened the door—right on the armchair Mrs. Mooney claimed as mine to put my things. Taking a few deep breaths, I focused on settling my heartbeat as I opened up the box.

Mrs. Mooney's voice in the trailer damn near scared the piss out of me. "That was some good luck kiss."

Holy hell, she was quiet. I hadn't even realized she was in here. I'd figured she'd gone with the rest of the group. My heart thumped a wild dance against my ribcage as I whirled to face her. "Jesus Christ!" I clapped a hand over my mouth. "Oops, sorry. You scared me!"

A hint of a smirk drew on her lips, mischief and mirth swirling in her gaze. She glanced between me and the door, almost like she was watching Maverick walk away, something in her entire demeanor shifting, softening.

"How's he doin'?" she asked, before turning to take me in once more.

I shrugged. "He's doin' better, I think. I just wish he'd talk, though, you know?" I bit my lip a moment before blowing out a loud exhale. "There's just some conversations and questions I have that require a little more than a nod or a head-shake."

Like what was going on between us? What did he want? What did I want?

Mrs. Mooney offered me a sympathetic look as she moved to the ironing board she'd set up in the center of the RV aisle. She placed the American flag show shirt—Cash's I assumed—on the board and began ironing. "Time and patience, honey," she offered. "I know it's hard, but push him more than that and he'll just dig his heels in. Boy may not seem like it, but he's stubborn. More stubborn than Cash, even."

"More stubborn than Cash?" I balked at that. Sure, Maverick could be unwavering and relentless, but Cash was the epitome of stubborn.

Mrs. Mooney glanced up at me for a second before returning to her work. "Oh yeah. You see, Cash is difficult about ninety-nine percent of the time, which makes it pretty predictable that he's gonna be stubborn. I always have a backup to my backup plans when it comes to dealin' with him." She smiled softly, setting down the iron so she could adjust the shirt before starting the process again. "Now, Maverick is the exact opposite. Most of the time you don't have to worry about him pitchin' a fit or puttin' up a fight, but that one percent of the time always comes durin' the least expected moment and over the least expected thing. It catches you off guard."

I let out a little huff. "That actually makes a lot of sense."

Mrs. Mooney grinned. "You learn a few things raisin' up three very different kids. None of them are the same, and the way you deal with one, you may not be able to do with the other."

"I can't even imagine." I could hardly take care of myself, I couldn't even begin to comprehend what all it took to raise a kid. "I don't think I've ever met—"

Mrs. Mooney cut me off. "You *haven't* met True. He doesn't come around much." I wouldn't quite call the words cold, but there was certainly an unwelcome edge to her tone. I didn't know what to say, so I just nodded.

She glanced at me, her gaze drifting up and down my body, taking me in. She had this intensity about her that made me fidget. She'd been nice enough to me, and I *think* she liked me, but I wasn't ever quite sure.

"Enough talk about them boys, how're you doin', honey?" Her words held a layer of concern I wasn't expecting. It tugged on my heartstrings. This week had been such a whirlwind of activity and drama, what with the fire and Maverick's silence, me moving in, and now the rodeo. It didn't leave much time to worry about myself.

"Me? I'm fine, Mrs. Mooney."

Her brow rose, the frown on her face saying exactly what she thought of that. "Girl, if you're gonna lie, at least be convincin'."

I don't know why, but tears pricked in my eyes then. It's like she saw right through the bullshit and down to the sadness and confusion I tried to bury deep down. I took a breath, fighting back the tears swimming in my eyes. *Please, don't let me cry.*

"I'm a little stressed," I admitted on a sigh. "The insurance company called this mornin'. They're only gonna give me thirty-five hundred dollars for the trailer and the product I lost for my business."

"That ain't much," Mrs. Mooney said as she placed the ironed shirt on a hanger and hung it up on one of the cupboard knobs. She moved to a hat box sitting on the kitchen dinette next and grabbed out a cream felt cowboy hat and a brush.

I shook my head. "No, it ain't, but I ain't surprised. That trailer was almost as old as me. It ain't worth anythin' really."

It had been full of memories, though.

Daddy bought it after the last time Mama left. We'd lived in that thing, traveling all across the country, from the time I was four-years-old. Then when I turned eighteen, Daddy gave it to me. That trailer had more memories than money could ever buy off, but try telling that to an insurance company.

I loosed another sigh and fidgeted with my own hat, picking a piece of hair off it. "I can make it work, though. A thousand bucks and I can at least start up my online shop again, and the rest I can use as a down on a new trailer. If I get a job and can make some money winnin'in the next few rodeos, I can afford monthly payments on it."

She paused in her brushing, her gaze flicking to mine. Something swirled and sparked to life in them. Not anger, not worry. I couldn't quite explain it. Trepidation maybe?

"Things not workin' out at Maverick's?" Her tone held a steely edge to it.

I frowned, shaking my head. "No, it ain't that. I just...I've always taken care of myself. I don't like bein' a burden."

She sat the brush down and returned the hat to its box with a quiet intensity that made me shiver. "So, this arrangement with Maverick, it's just outta convenience?" The cold accusation in her tone said everything. She thought I was using him.

"I ain't usin' him, if that's what you're thinkin'."

She continued on as if I hadn't said anything. "That boy's been through hell and back. Been through far more than any person should have to go through. If you wanna leave, leave now. Before you break his heart."

Guilt and frustration ate at me, clawing at my chest and forming a lump in my throat. I wasn't trying to take advantage of his kindness. I wasn't trying to use him. But even upset and angry, I could see why she would see it that way. She'd raised him. Of course, she'd be protective.

Tears swam in my eyes once more, a single one slipping down my cheek. I didn't brush it away as I met her fierce stare, even though every fiber of my being hated showing the slip in emotion. I wanted her to see it. Wanted her to know how I felt.

"Look, I don't know what the future holds with us. It's partly why I need him to talk. I don't know what we are. What he wants. What he expects of this situation. But I do know that I care about him. I care... and I don't wanna hurt him. I know you're worried about him, but I can tell you right now, I ain't no Ashleigh. I ain't gonna take advantage of him and leave him. You don't have to worry about that."

Her face softened, the scowl that had formed smoothing out. "You know about Ashleigh?"

I finally wiped my cheek, giving her a gentle nod. "Yeah. Cash told me about her. I can't tell you what all is gonna happen between Maverick and I, but I can promise you right now I ain't ever gonna treat him the way she did."

Mrs. Mooney's head cocked slightly to the side, her scrutinizing gaze holding my own for a long moment. A slow smile blossomed on her lips, lighting up her pretty face. "I hope that boy talks soon, because it'd be a shame if he lost you."

My heart squeezed, all of the air leaving my lungs in a whoosh. I hadn't even realized I'd wanted her approval, but hearing her all but give it to me right now... My eyes watered again.

Dear God, I was a damn mess. *Get yourself together, Chey.*

"Thank you, Mrs. Mooney," I croaked out, hating that I sounded so emotional.

She offered me a smile. "Go take a moment and get yourself sorted out. You got an event to win."

I smiled and dipped my head in a nod.

———

My hair blew in the wind as I sat in the passenger seat of my truck, the Texas stars twinkling in the sky like a thousand diamonds, Maverick driving beside me. I'd fought to drive—I was plenty capable of it—but Maverick was nothing if not polite. Not gonna lie, being a passenger princess wasn't half bad.

I still rode the high of winning the first round of barrels, qualifying for the final round tomorrow night. I needed this win, and now I was one step closer. Maverick, Cash, and Ryder had qualified for their events as well.

"Wouldn't it be crazy if we all won in our events tomorrow?" I mused, glancing over at him. He smiled and squeezed my hand in his, his eyes twinkling with amusement.

Brandy panted happily at my feet, her tongue lolling out of her mouth. I gave her a couple pets with my free hand. Everything about that moment felt so good. So nice. So...right.

Maverick's phone buzzed on the center console, his home screen lighting up to show a text message with a familiar name.

Ashleigh.

My stomach clenched, my heart squeezing tighter and tighter, cutting off the air in my lungs.

Another one with her name. And another. And another.

I couldn't see any of the text beyond that, not that I cared or wanted to. Anger and fear boiled in my chest.

"Seems like this Ashleigh person really wants to talk to you." I didn't hold back the venom in my voice.

Maverick's throat bobbed, his hand slipping from mine as he fidgeted with his hat. Worry danced in his eyes as he met my stare. His silence made my anger boil hotter and hotter, until my emotions came spilling over the top. My words were full of fury and hurt when I spoke next. "Who is she to you, Maverick?"

I needed to know what he thought of her. What threat she posed. What problems I was looking at because of her.

He shook his head, his gaze pleading.

I clenched my fists, my jaw tightening for a moment.

"No. I need more than that, Maverick." I needed more than a head shake or nod. "Your aunt and Cash have both told me *plenty* about her. I know what she did to you last Christmas. I know that y'all had been talkin' again and she screwed you over and that's why you went out last Saturday." Tears pricked in my eyes, and damn it, but my voice quivered as I asked, "Is she gonna cause problems between us?"

Pain shone in his gaze, hung in every nook and cranny of his entire being. It radiated from him as his lips parted and he blew out a breath.

"Please," I breathed, tears blurring my vision. "Please, talk to me. Or just...I don't know write it down. Text it to me. Fuck, for all I care, pull off to the side of the road and write it in the fuckin' dirt. I just—I need to know."

I needed him to reassure me that she wouldn't be a problem.

His brow furrowed, the scowl on his lips causing deep, angry grooves on his harsh, handsome face. His jaw clenched and unclenched as we sat in deafening silence.

"Look... I don't need you to talk today. Or tomorrow. Or even a month from now. If you never talk again, well, I'm sure we can make it work. But I need to know what that girl means to you, Mav. I need to know that what I feel for you is worth fightin' for. I need some reassurance."

I guess this was the defining moment. The deal breaker.

Had someone told me last Saturday that in a week from now I'd be wanting to dive into a relationship after barely dating someone, I'd have laughed in their face. Yet here I was, very much standing on the precipice of that decision. Trying to decide to jump all in or walk away.

I *needed* an answer.

Was I being irrational? Insensitive? Was I being unfair and selfish? Maybe. Probably. But I couldn't back down now. *No*—I wouldn't.

I know he'd been through a lot this last week. And I couldn't even begin to fathom the toll it had taken on his past trauma, but I couldn't be with someone if they couldn't give me all of them. And if he couldn't reassure me in some way or form of my fears, well, then he couldn't give me that.

He reached a hand out, brushing his thumb across my cheek to wipe away one of my tears. I watched the silent battle play out on his face. Anger. Frustration. Fear. Determination. Pain. He opened his mouth. Closed it. Opened it once more. My heart clamored in my chest, beating so wildly against my rib cage I thought I might crack a rib.

"Please," I whispered, gripping his wrist and leaning into his soothing touch.

But the longer we drove, the louder that silence got. He remained closed off to me. Distracted.

This was what I got for putting myself out there. For taking a risk. This was why hookups were so much easier.

No more. No more relationships. No more letting my stupid, weak heart get in the way.

Maverick tapped my leg, urging me to look at him. I whirled his way, ready to snap out some nasty, mean response, but it died on my lips as I saw the sorrow on his face. Sadness swelled within me, washing away the anger and leaving nothing but desolation in its place, fizzling out in the aftermath.

I knew he wanted to talk. I knew he was trying. And I'd told him the truth earlier, if he never talked again that would be okay. I wasn't upset that he wasn't speaking. I was upset that even though he held my hand, even though his touch made me burn with need, I didn't know how he felt about me. I knew that actions spoke louder than words, and I knew it might be selfish of me, but right now I needed more than actions. More than what he could give.

CHAPTER 26
Cowboys Never Cry

MAVERICK

I fucked up. Every second, every mile we drove in silence towards the ranch I felt Cheyenne withdrawing more and more. I'd lost her, before she was even really mine.

Fuck.

It's like all the light had left her. Like when storm clouds swallowed up the sun.

The worst part about this was it was my own damn fault.

Rage trembled through my veins, coiling tight in my limbs. Why couldn't I *just. Fucking. Talk*? Why did my very actions to deal with my grief negatively affect those I cared about most?

Aunt Violet, Bad, and Cash hadn't given up on me. But they didn't really have a choice now, did they? Would any of them have stuck around with me not talking if I wasn't their family, their charge?

I didn't blame Cheyenne. It hurt, but I understood.

She knew about Ashleigh. Knew at least partly about the bullshit I'd gone through with her, or else this wouldn't even be an issue...and I hadn't done a damn thing to ease her concerns.

Truth was, she didn't have to worry about Ashleigh anymore. I was done with her. Frankly, I should have been a long time ago. But I also understood the need for more than a pleading head shake.

I glared at my phone as we pulled into the drive and headed toward the barn. Of course, Ashleigh would try to worm her way back in at the most inopportune moment. She had a habit of doing that. A habit, I realized, I'd perpetuated and allowed for just about twenty damn years.

I hadn't even fully put the truck in park before Cheyenne hopped out, Brandy hot on her heels.

I was losing her. *Do something. Say something.* I opened my mouth, hoping, praying, willing words to come out...but nothing.

Still. Fucking. Nothing.

I slammed the flat of my palm against the steering wheel. Once. Twice. Three times.

She was already unlocking the back of the trailer to get out Country Road by the time I made it back there. Everything about her warm, inviting demeanor had changed, shifting to something cold and dark. She looked at me with eyes that used to remind me of summer lakes and streams, but were now as frigid and hard as glaciers.

I opened my mouth to say something again. *Please...please.*

But nothing.

I didn't miss the flicker of disappointment ripple through her. Pursing her lips, she muscled open the trailer.

In silence, we unloaded the horses. In silence, we walked them back to their stalls. In silence still, we made our way toward the truck, so I could park and unhitch the trailer. I'd never been a stranger to silence, and during this last week, I'd gotten used to it between us. It hadn't been awkward or stilted. It felt natural.

But this... I hated this.

She pulled her hair back into a messy ponytail, stray pieces framing her sad, beautiful face.

"Can I have my keys?" Her words sounded hollow. Dead. Lifeless.

I made her feel that way. Guilt crashed through me. I'd done this. I'd pushed her to this point. I'd driven her to leave. Damn it.

My brow rose, the silent question lingering in my confused expression. *Where are you going?*

She looked at Brandy by her side as she spoke. "I gotta go into town. Get some stuff. Don't worry about makin' dinner for me or waitin' up."

I shook my head, a new question burning in my throat. *Why?*

"Thank you for all you've done for me...truly. I appreciate it. But I think—" Her words wobbled, her bottom lip quivering ever so slightly. "I think it's time I-I moved on."

Her last words felt like a sledgehammer straight to the heart. Pain blossomed in my chest, my breath leaving me in a whoosh of air.

Leave? She couldn't leave. She'd come to mean a lot to me, and I was no good at letting go.

Cheyenne gripped her right elbow with her left hand, a defensive gesture if I'd ever seen one. I reached for her—if I could just make her see how much I wanted her. Needed her here. Emotion swirled in her gaze, a myriad of anger, want, sadness, and finally, nothing. I dropped my hand as she spoke next.

"I just... I need more, Maverick. And I realize that might be selfish and unfair of me...but I-I gotta be fair to myself too. I can't be with someone who can't–" Tears streamed down her cheeks as she met my gaze. "Can't give me what I need. I can't do this anymore."

I found myself nodding. I understood. She didn't deserve this. Didn't deserve broken, used parts. And that's all I was. But she'd seemed the type to look at the ugly and find something beautiful.

"I'm sorry, Maverick." Pain resounded in her voice; I watched it harden her soft, pretty features. Dipping her head so her gaze didn't meet mine, she grabbed the keys from my hand, nodded at Brandy, and turned away.

I didn't even remember grabbing them out of my pocket.

Say something!

Every muscle in my body, every nerve ending, even my blood sang, bellowed, and roared to chase after her. But I didn't. I just stood there. Watching. Waiting... *For what?*

For her to turn around and change her mind?

Why would she? Better yet, why *should* she?

My heart thumped to the beat of a ticking time bomb. If I let her leave, she was gone. There would be no getting her back.

She'd taken care of me that night of the fire. She'd cleaned me, clothed me, sang me to sleep. She'd been a light in the darkness. The sun to my shadows.

Her truck rumbled to life as she slid into the driver's seat and slammed the door. The gears shifted. And then she was rolling away, her truck gaining speed with each turn of her tires.

"Wait!" The sound out of my mouth was foreign to my ears. Like I'd forgotten how to form words. But the attempt shattered whatever spell —or curse—had kept my words at bay.

My feet started moving. First one step. Two steps...then I was running. Sprinting to catch up with her truck.

She wasn't going that fast, thankfully. I smacked a hand against the door as I sprinted beside it. Cheyenne's tear-filled gaze met mine, her face turning into a mask of surprise. She damn near took me out with the driver-side mirror as she skidded to a stop.

"Maverick?" she cried as I wrenched open the door. "What the hell?"

"S-stay," I whispered, my breath sawing in and out of me. I wasn't sure if it was from the run or the pent-up anxiety thrumming through my veins.

A gasp fell from her lips, more tears welling in her bright blue eyes. She cupped a hand over her mouth, a sob escaping her. "You just... You tal—"

I didn't let her finish. Leaning over, I dragged her mouth to mine. "Stay with me," I breathed, resting my forehead to hers and cupping her face. The words felt raw, weird coming out of my throat. "Please, don't go. I want you here. I want you with me. I'm sorry I didn't say anything earlier. I...I wanted to...god, I wanted to."

Cheyenne's soft, warm hands cupped my own, her bottom lip trembling as more tears slipped down her cheeks. But a smile brighter than any sunrise bloomed on her lips.

"Well, damn, cowboy. All you had to do was say somethin'."

A laugh rumbled out of me. One with actual sound, and I'd never felt such happiness than in that moment. I leaned back and flicked her nose gently.

"Hey!" She batted away my hand, and I used the moment as an excuse to unfasten her seatbelt and urge her out of the truck. She let me, her mouth finding mine the moment she was out. Her arms wrapped around my neck, her kisses deep and wild. I lifted her up, savoring the feel as her legs snaked around my waist.

Cheyenne broke the kiss first, drawing back to look at me. "You talked," she breathed, smoothing her fingers over my brow. It still hurt a bit from last weekend, though it'd started to close. "What made you?"

I cupped the back of her neck, drawing her in close so I could kiss her once more. Slow. Unhurried. I felt every muscle in her body melt into my embrace. Desire swirled to life in my chest. Dear Lord, I wanted her.

"You," I said, pulling away. "The thought of you leavin' and not knowin' how much I need you."

She placed a whisper-soft kiss to my lips, a mischievous glint twinkling in her eyes. "How much, cowboy?"

A grin tugged on my mouth. "Want me show you?"

She smirked, and when she spoke her words were low, smokey. "I want you to tell me...and *then* show me."

I kissed her once more. "I think I can do that."

CHAPTER 27
The Devil Wears Lace

CHEYENNE

"You... The thought of you leavin' and not knowin' how much I need you."

Need. Not want.

I didn't think my heart could take anymore today. He didn't just want me. He *needed* me. And as much as I hated to admit it, I think I needed him too. That was the only thing that could explain the pain I felt driving away.

Maverick set me down on my feet slowly, though he made no move to pull out of my embrace. "How 'bout I drive us back to the house and I tell you all the ways I want you as we wash up?"

I tucked a stray curl behind my ear. "I like the sound of that."

Desire sparked in his gaze, his grip on me tightening ever so slightly. Without another word, he whisked me up, carried me to my truck—where Brandy still waited—and drove us to the house.

Every second, every inch closer to the house we went, the more the tension in the car grew. It was like a wildfire, growing, spreading, rising. By the time he shifted the truck in park and opened the driver's side door, I all but shook with anticipation.

He came around to the passenger-side, pulling me out of the truck before I could say a word. Then I was in his arms again as he carried me toward the front door. His lips found mine, one of his hands holding me up, while the other slithered along the curve of my waist and towards one of my breasts.

God, he made me burn. Brighter than any fire. The sun, even.

I vaguely heard Brandy's toenails on the concrete floor, before nothing. She must have curled up on the carpet in the living room. I glanced back and grinned. *Good girl.*

Maverick's hands sparked desire through my veins as he carried me to his room. Once in the bathroom, he relinquished his hold on me long enough to turn on the water.

Not even a heartbeat later he was there again, towering over me with his lean, chiseled frame. Most of his face lurked in shadow from his cowboy hat. His hands trembled as he held my waist.

I shivered and reached up, pulling his hat off.

"Caref—" he said before nodding as I sat it upside down on the countertop.

I grinned. "Don't worry, cowboy. I know the rules."

He chuckled, his breath fanning against my cheeks, as he slowly—painfully slowly—began undoing the snap pearl buttons of my shirt.

My gaze flicked to his. "So, you finally gonna tell me what all you wanna do to me?"

His lips tugged upward as he pulled the last button free. He trailed a finger from the hemline of my jeans all the way up my stomach, and to my bra. "I want to kiss every single inch of you," he murmured, pulling my shirt off and discarding it on the ground.

I followed suit—albeit much quicker—all but ripping his shirt off before working on the tank he always wore beneath. "Mmm," I murmured as he traced lazy patterns along my shoulders and chest. "That sounds nice, but I think you can do better."

He worked at my jeans next. First the buckle, then my zipper, before I shuffled out of them. One of his hands toyed at the lacy fabric of my underwear as he held me against him. Maverick's mouth found the corner of mine before dipping to the curve of my jaw. He kissed a path up along it before nipping at my earlobe. "I want to taste that sweet pussy of yours again." His voice was a deep, sexy rumble in my ear.

My knees went weak, a gasp escaping me. "Maverick." I never expected him to say something like that.

His eyes glinted, almost wickedly. God, he was fucking hot. "It's true," he breathed, his lips moving on to the column of my neck. "I want to fuck you on the counter. Like I should've done the other night. And the dining room table. I want to take you in that armchair in my room, and have you sit on my cock and ride me 'til you're a screamin', wild mess."

I shivered, my breath hitching in my throat as one of his hands dipped to the curve of my ass and squeezed.

"You got quite the mouth on you, cowboy," I whispered.

One of the corners of his lips pulled up into the ghost of a smirk, a huff of laughter escaping him. "But what I wanna do right now, is take you in that shower, kiss you breathless, and fuck you from behind."

A laugh bubbled out of me. He couldn't possibly know just how much I loved a foul mouth. I trailed my fingers over the plains of his stomach, undoing his buckle and mirroring his actions from earlier.

"Well," I said, dipping a hand beneath the hem of his boxer briefs and settling over his hard cock. "What're you waitin' for?"

It was the invitation he needed.

One minute, we were standing there, the next, we were both fully unclothed and dipping beneath the spray of steaming water. He dragged his mouth to mine, one of his hands going for my breasts, while the other slid to my core. His fingers teased it in soft strokes that sent desire rippling through me and making my knees go weak.

His mouth clashed with mine, a war of tongues, teeth. I reveled in the flames of pleasure that stoked higher, hotter, and brighter with every touch of his. My hand drifted over the planes of his chiseled stomach, along the V of his hips, before resting on his hard cock. A groan went through him, making his chest rumble. I don't think I'd ever heard a sexier sound. My body answered on instinct, a shiver of desire shooting straight to my core.

"Easy," he murmured, breaking our kiss to whisper in my ear. "You keep doin' that and I won't be able to do all the things I wanna do to you."

A wicked smirk pulled on my lips. "Is that so? Well, then..." I grabbed his cock and slid my hand up and down the hard length.

He pulled back enough to peg me with his burning green gaze. There was so much heat, so much wicked desire lurking in that stare, that my breath escaped me in a gasp.

God, I wanted him. Wanted him inside me. His touch, his kisses, they were nice, but I needed more. I needed to feel him, every hard inch of him as he slammed his cock inside me.

A low chuckle came from Maverick, challenge sparking in his gaze. "Oh, so you wanna play that way?"

I tilted my chin up at him, a defiant gesture, meeting his heated stare. I picked up the pace as I stroked him, watching the war play out on his features. Challenge and pleasure battled, and for a moment, I thought he'd give in and let me win. But then he lifted me, pressing me firmly against the wall of the shower, one hand wrapped around my neck with his cock poised at my entrance.

My eyes widened even as my body reacted to him—caging my legs around his waist. Surprise pumped through me. I hadn't expected this raw emotion from him. This dominance. This darkness. But I loved it. I loved everything about it.

And I wanted more.

His hand at my throat lingered, waited, his gaze holding a question in it. "This too much?"

I kissed him, pulling him closer, a silent plea to continue. He matched me—unrestrained, like up until this point he'd never fully given all of himself. When I pulled away, water dripping down every inch of us, I bit his lip, earning a hiss from him.

"That all you got, cowboy?"

Dark desire exploded like a supernova in his eyes. He slid into me—one fast, fluid motion. I cried out, my head falling back against the tile. Maverick set up a slow pace. We rose and fell to a rhythm all our own, ebbing and swelling with each stroke, each thrust, each brush of our bodies. His grip on my throat tightened. Not enough to block off the air, but a delicious pressure that sent my desire blazing through me.

Maverick's intense stare met mine. "You like that?"

I nodded, sucking my bottom lip between my teeth. His gaze flicked to it, hunger washing over his features. He thrust into me, his hand still on my throat as I held his gaze.

"But I want more."

His scarred brow rose and he stilled inside me. No. No, I didn't want him to stop. I wanted the exact opposite. I moved against him, urging him to continue.

He exhaled a low huff of laughter and eased me to the floor.

A spark of anger surged to life. "Maverick, wha—" But my words left me in a rush as he spun me around, his cock brushing against my backside and his hot breath in my ear. "Bend over." The words were low, gravelly, and filled with so much domineering intensity that I didn't hesitate to obey.

I braced my hands against the tile, bending over for him. He gripped my hips, poising himself at my entrance, but he didn't slide in. No, it seemed he was proving a point. That he was in control. At least, for the moment. He leaned forward, pressing a kiss right between my shoulder blades. A shiver shot through me as I arched into him. "Maverick," I breathed. "Please."

A hum of satisfaction escaped him, vibrating in his chest like thunder rolling in before a storm. A precursor to what was coming. "I like when you say my name."

He teased me once more, his cock *right. Fucking. There*. I tried to lean back into him—something, anything to have him in me once more—but he held my hips firm. Wrapping an arm around me and forcing me upright just a bit, one of his hands went to my breast, squeezing, kneading, before teasing my nipple. Desire sparked in my core.

I moaned. God, I was close. I'd be closer if he'd actually fuck me again.

"Maverick," I repeated as he rained kisses up and down the column of my neck.

But still, he didn't make a move to enter me.

That's it. I couldn't take it anymore. Glancing back at him, defiance and challenge coating my words, I bit out, "Fuck me. Now."

His lips drew up into the sexiest goddamn smirk I'd ever seen. "Who's got the mouth now, darlin?"

But my words spurred him into action. With a thrust, he slid his cock into me, picking up a quick, steady pace. Easing me down a bit—my hands fighting for purchase on the wet walls—he palmed my breast, working me closer to the edge with each wild touch and thrust of his hips. All the while, he rained kisses down my shoulder, my neck, even along the curve of my spine. There was something possessive about each movement. Like he wasn't just fucking me, but worshiping me. Worshiping my body with his.

Just that thought alone made me teeter on the edge of an orgasm. I was poised on the precipice, my desire burning so hot through my veins that I trembled.

It hurt. Hurt so fucking good.

I think he understood that somehow. Just from my body language, from the little cries that fell from my lips. Upping the tempo, his movements turned faster, wilder. And then he grabbed my ponytail, gripping it tight, and tilted my head up. He kissed along my neck, down to the base of my throat, his teeth scraping against my skin as he nipped and caressed me along the way.

I gasped as heat scorched through me, starting in my toes and working its way up, up, up. My nerve endings were on fire, sparking and sizzling as my orgasm loomed just before me.

And then he bit me.

Not hard enough to draw blood. Not hard at all, really, just the right amount of pressure along the muscle of my neck.

That was all it took. One bite. One thrust. And I was shattering apart atop his cock, my cries drowning out the sound of the shower. Maverick didn't slow, in fact, he thrust into me harder, faster with a delicious, brutal intensity I'd never felt before.

He all but roared his release as he slipped out of me just at the last second, though he held me close as we both rode the waves of our orgasm. I lost track of how long we stayed like that, our breaths and heartbeats syncing up as we came down from the high of what we'd just done. The water rained down on us still, the warmth of the droplets almost cold compared to the heat still pumping through my veins.

"That was..." I turned to face him, wrapping my arms around his waist and resting my chin on his chest. "Can we do that again?"

His lips curled up into a satisfied smirk as he pushed some of my wet curls back off my face. "Give me a few minutes, and gladly," he murmured, leaning down to kiss me softly.

My stomach decided at that moment to rumble to life—a pang of hunger stirring within me. *Of fucking course.*

Maverick's hooded gaze turned to one of mild concern. "You hungry?"

I waved him off, reaching up on tiptoe to kiss him once more. "I'd rather fuck you."

He smirked, but the concern didn't leave his gaze. "Food first," he said, "fuck later." His words held a finality to it that I didn't bother fighting.

I knew a losing battle when I saw one. With a dramatic huff, I rolled my eyes. "*Fiiine.*"

His gaze warmed, his smirk widening as he flicked my nose and urged me from the shower. As we made our way into the bedroom, I noticed the MRC brand on his back. Right on his left shoulder. *They must all have one.*

I'd always wanted a tattoo or a brand, but never could decide on having something on me permanently. Charlie and Ryder both had their tattoos, and I absolutely loved them, but I just couldn't think of something I'd want forever.

Maverick tossed me one of his t-shirts, which I slipped on happily. "So," he asked, sliding into a pair of pajama pants. "What'dya want?"

I pulled my sopping wet hair out of the ponytail, and ran my fingers through it. "No, I wanna cook."

"You sure? I don't mind."

"I know you don't. But you always cook."

He shrugged as we made our way to the kitchen. "I like to cook."

I stopped him, wrapping my arms around his waist. "Please, Maverick. Let me do this for you."

I don't know why, but I wanted, no, needed to do this. To show him just how much this moment meant to me. He'd talked. I don't know the how or the why of it, but the fact he'd talked for me meant more than I could ever explain.

He gripped my chin, holding my stare. Whatever he saw there softened the harsh lines of his face. He nodded, leaning down to brush his lips against mine once more. "Okay. So, what're you makin' me?"

CHAPTER 28
Mine

MAVERICK

Cheyenne rummaged through my cupboards, a look of fierce determination on her face. I stood back, letting her flit about, reminding me of a bird. I could watch her all day. She had this inner glow about her, this magnetism that drew me in. I was little more than a moth to her bright, unwavering flame.

Her lips pulled up into a satisfied grin as she stood before the countertop, hands on her hips while she looked over her findings. "Perfect, you have everything for it."

"For what?" I asked, eyeing the half dozen cans sitting before a metal bowl she'd grabbed. Canned corn, green chiles, enchilada sauce, black beans, an unopened jar of salsa, canned chicken, and a box of rice.

She turned on the oven, washed her hands, and rifled through the utensil drawer before pulling out my can opener. "This is what I like to call my southwest bake." She went to work, grabbing for the canned chicken, draining the water, and plopping it in the bowl before adding some taco seasoning and spices to it. Then she started opening the cans and added them in. "I know it doesn't look like much, but I promise you it tastes better than it looks...It's my three favorite things when it comes to a meal. Quick, easy, and delicious."

My brow rose. It didn't look like much. Just a mish mash of different ingredients. But some of the best things I'd cooked didn't look all that great.

She scoffed. "Don't judge. We can't all be the next Gordon Ramsey like you."

I rolled my eyes, a grin drawing on my lips as I took a seat at one of the island chairs, watching her mix everything together. "Hardly."

She paused, pegging me with an are-you-kidding look. "Maverick, you're the best damn cook I've ever known... and I've had Mrs. Mooney's cooking."

My eyes widened, my grin pulling wider. "Don't let her hear you say that."

Cheyenne found a 13x9 pan and began dumping all the ingredients in. "I'm serious."

I fidgeted, deciding to change the subject. "So, what's next?"

"Well, you put it in the oven for twenty-five minutes, then voila! Add a little sour cream, a little hot sauce, and some cheese, and boom, you got yourself a southwest bake."

I nodded. Sounded easy enough. "What made you choose this meal?"

She shrugged as she moved to the oven, loaded in the pan, and set a timer. "It's my favorite...and it's the first recipe my daddy taught me. When I was growin' up, we traveled a lot." She came to my side, leaning against the countertop beside me.

I couldn't help but notice the curve of her ass peeking out from beneath my shirt. I bit back a shot of desire. I wanted her, but I wanted to talk to her more right now.

"Daddy was a lineman, and after my mama left, he decided to sell our house, buy a trailer and we started travelin'. He could work from wherever, so we'd stay in a town for a job or two and then move on."

She talked about her mom leaving so casually, it still shocked me. I knew that if she was anything like me, deep down, it still haunted her. But she didn't let it show. I applauded that kind of strength.

"This was a quick, easy dinner that we could make on the road. It's limited ingredients. As you can tell, super-fast prep time, and minimal clean up. Daddy was always findin' recipes like this to try, but this one will always be my favorite."

I wrapped an arm around her waist and dragged her against my side. Even sitting in the bar-top chair I was a little taller than her. With my free hand, I tilted her chin up to me. "Well, I can't wait to try it," I murmured against her lips.

She leaned into the kiss a moment, before pulling away, an incredulous look in her eyes. "You're just sayin' that."

I shook my head. "No. The best meals are ones that are cooked from the heart."

She scrunched up her nose, that incredulous look turning to complete disbelief as a laugh bubbled out of her. God, she was gorgeous when she laughed. She did it so freely and easily, but it was always genuine. She was pure sunshine bottled up, and even though I didn't drink, I'd get drunk on her any day.

"That is the biggest crock of shit," she giggled.

I chuckled even as I shook my head. "It's true. Aunt Violet always used to say cooking is a work of the heart. It ain't just about the ingredients, but the love and passion you put into it."

Cheyenne's laughter sobered, but the smile remained on her face. "Whatever you say, cowboy."

I flicked her nose, a little habit, I'd come to realize. She scrunched up her face once more, accentuating the freckles, before leveling me with a playful glare. I leaned over and kissed her, halting any more argument from her. She didn't resist as I pulled her more firmly into me once more.

"So," I whispered against her lips. "What'dya wanna do now?"

She pulled away and chewed her bottom lip, a mischievous sparkle entering her turquoise gaze. "Well, we've got twenty some minutes, and I *do* happen to recall you mentionin' somethin' about that dinin' room table."

Even as she spoke, her hand drifted up my thigh before settling on my cock. A sharp hiss left me in a rush, desire zinging to life within me. Well, fuck.

My grip on her waist tightened, a rumble of approval escaping me. "What're we waitin' for, then," I replied.

Her little gasp made my cock hard. I picked her up before she could do or say anything else, her legs caging around my torso on instinct. I relished the feel of her in my arms, one of my hands gripping her ass, while the other knotted in her long, wild curls. Laughter trickled out of her when I bumped into the head of the table, tilting her head back, exposing the elegant curve of her neck. I trailed a gentle path of kisses along her jaw and all the way down to the base of her throat. Her little sighs and moans were kindling to the fire burning inside me.

I hadn't lied, I wanted her on this table. Ever since Thursday night when we'd been interrupted.

I set her down on the tabletop, her legs still firmly wrapped around me. Her hands roamed over my stomach, my chest, before snaking up along the curves of my shoulders and finally hooking around my neck. Her touch was electric, turning every nerve ending in my body into a livewire.

The feel of her in my arms, the taste of her on my lips, it was all-consuming, intoxicating. She was everything I didn't know I needed. I'd been so wrapped up in Ashleigh for so long, that I hadn't realized the smoke-show right in front of me. How different things could be right now, had I noticed Cheyenne sooner.

The connection we shared... I'd never felt anything like this. It terrified me as much as it exhilarated me. But one thing was for certain...I wanted more of Cheyenne. All of her. Whatever she was willing to give me.

As if my touch melted her, she laid back, her blonde curls splaying in a beautiful mess around her as her back met the wooden tabletop. She looked like a streak of sunlight against the dark wood. I leaned over, my lips finding hers once more as one of my hands drifted up along the inside of her thigh, teasing, taunting in their lazy pursuit.

She wriggled and writhed beneath me, urging me for more. More touching, more kisses. Just...*more*. And I'd happily oblige.

Her little moan as my fingers stroked her core was a damn symphony. I leaned back to take her in even as I worked her, stoked her higher and higher. Her eyes were closed, her lip sucked between her teeth, my shirt riding up over the plains of her stomach, exposing tan skin and delicious curves.

As I slipped a finger inside her, starting up a slow, steady rhythm, her eyes shot open, locking with mine. My desire blazed, like the flames of a fire. Dear Lord, I wanted her.

With my free hand, I pushed up her t-shirt and kissed a path up to the swell of one of her breasts before finding the nipple and teasing it. She arched beneath my touch on instinct. A breathless whisper of, "more," falling from her lips.

Damn, she was fucking sexy.

I inserted a second finger, picking up the pace and earning more sweet sounds from her. Curses and hisses and moans. Her eyes rolled shut, her hands splayed flat on either side of the table, her manicured fingernails curling and whitening as they tried and failed to grip something.

I loved that I could do this for her. Loved that my touch sent her shuddering. That my kisses made her melt. That my hand made her beg for more. She made me feel wanted, needed in a way I'd never known before. I wanted to give her more. My time, my attention. Whatever she wanted.

A sound akin to a shotgun boomed through my living room as the front door burst open, with none other than Cash lingering in the doorway. I startled, my hands ceasing their movement, my eyes settling on him across the way.

"Who's ready to celebrate? I know Cheyenne's ready for a—oh shit!"

Cash's gaze clashed with mine, surprise written all over his face. Before he could say anything, I pointed toward the door. "Get the hell out, Cash."

He recovered quicker than I expected, a mischievous smirk drawing on his lips. "Where the hell was my invi—" His head cocked to the side, realization dawning on his features. Pure, innocent excitement shone in his hazel gaze. He all but bounced up and down with exuberance. "You...you fuckin did it. You talked!"

"Yes, he can talk again, idiot, can you shut up?" Cheyenne snapped, speaking for the first time since this whole thing started. Her cheeks blazed red, but there was no embarrassment in the tone of her voice. "We're busy. So, get the hell out of here."

"He's..." Cash's gaze met mine once more. "Your're...you're fuckin talkin'."

"Cash," I replied, "Get out."

He made no move to leave, even went so far as to lean against the doorway, crossing his arms over his chest and one foot over the other. "She really fucked the words right outta ya, didn't she?"

"Cash!" Cheyenne half shrieked, half growled. "Get the fuck out. Now!" She reached for one of the candles on the dining room table and hurled it at him. He caught it easily, that shit-eating grin pulling somehow wider on his lips. *Bastard.*

"You sure you don't need my help, I can give a few—"

"Get the hell out!" Cheyenne and I shouted at the same time. With a final chuckle, Cash closed the door behind him. She sagged back onto the wooden tabletop, her hands shooting up to cover her face. She shook beneath me, and for a moment I thought she was crying until soft muffled laughter bubbled out of her.

"You really need to start lockin' the damn door," she said, wiping her hands down her face to look up at me.

It was only then I realized I still had two fingers inside her. Ignoring her words, I leaned down, pressing a long, slow kiss to her lips, working up a steady rhythm once more. She melted into my touch, any remnants of shock or annoyance vanishing.

"He'd just find another way in," I murmured, pulling back to look at her.

She dragged me back down, her lips finding mine once more as she murmured, "less talking, more fucking."

It was the only invitation I needed.

Her hands clawed at my pajama pants, tugging them down and exposing my cock—hard and ready once more.

She let me fuck her on the table. Let me hook her ankles up around my neck and fuck her till she came apart on my cock. And when I bent her over the table, plowing into her from behind until the oven timer went off, she didn't even bat an eye.

"Let it burn," she murmured, as I rained kisses and nips down her neck as I veered closer the edge.

The food did burn...but I ate every damn bite gladly in the end.

———

CASH HAD WAY TOO MUCH FUN TELLING EVERYONE ABOUT mine and Cheyenne's little hook up the next day. Thankfully, the fact that I was talking again was more of a shock than my actual actions, so that was the main gossip at the rodeo.

"You ready?" I asked, coming up behind Cheyenne and hooking my arms around her middle. She leaned into the embrace, even as she continued to check on Country Road's tack.

She nodded and spun around to face me. "I feel a little dizzy today, and I have this crazy migraine, but I'm ready."

I frowned. "You sure you're okay?"

She nodded, reaching up on tiptoe to plant a soft kiss on my lips. "I'll be fine, cowboy."

"You take anything for the headache?"

A nod.

"If it keeps up, maybe you should go to the doctor's," I offered. She'd been sick quite a bit this past week. Between the headaches and the queasiness, something wasn't right.

Another kiss to my lips. "You worry too much, it's not good for you. It causes frown lines."

I rolled my eyes, flicking her nose gently. She scrunched it up and batted away my hand, but it served as the distraction I think she intended.

"One more good luck kiss?" she asked.

I was helpless but to oblige her.

———

I HADN'T DATED MANY GIRLS WHO RODE. I HADN'T DATED very many girls in general, to be honest. Not when I was so hooked on Ashleigh. Ashleigh never cared for riding. She could if she needed to and was comfortable enough around horses, but she never had a passion for it.

Funny, since horses were how we'd met.

Her mom was the therapist Aunt Violet and Bad hired to come help me talk. Her mom ran a mobile equine therapy program, and brought Ashleigh with her to almost every single one of our sessions.

And while Ashleigh could ride a horse—make it go, spin it around, stop it—she couldn't ride like Cheyenne.

And boy, did she sure ride. Country Road was small and fast. Faster than a streak of lightning. She tore across the starting line and shot for the right barrel, her and Cheyenne moving so quick it was almost like they were soaring through the air. The way they moved, it was effortless as she rounded the barrel and headed for the next.

The clock ticked away. The seconds feeling like minutes. With each passing moment, my excitement grew.

"Come on, come on, come on," I murmured beside Cash and the rest of our group, who all cheered and hollered for Cheyenne. She rounded the final barrel, but took it too sharp. Country Road knocked into it, making it wobble before righting itself. But that little bump was all it took for the two of them to lose their stride.

They crossed the finish line with a 14.169. Not bad at all. But not the 13.9 she needed to win. Reserve Champion was still great, though.

I stood, waiting for her against the pipe-stall as she cooled down Country Road in the warmup arena. Nothing on her face showed even a flicker of anger, but I could see it in the tension in her body. In the way her hands and legs flexed and clenched.

"You okay?" I asked.

"I took that fuckin' barrel too sharp."

I nodded. "Yeah. But it is what it is. Second is still pretty good."

She came to a stop on the other side of the pipe-stall. "It's still not first, though."

"But it ain't last," I replied with a shrug.

She rolled her eyes but a small, closed-lipped smile quivered to life on her face. "True."

I nodded, gesturing for her move toward the gate. She met me there and dismounted before the two of us walked Country Road back toward the trailer. "You can't win 'em all, Chey."

She sighed and leaned into me, any of the remaining fight leaving her, so I wrapped an arm around her waist as we walked, enjoying the feel of her warmth at my side. The trailer came into view when she froze in place, a groan escaping her. "Oh god, I feel..."

I glanced over at her, finding her all but swaying on her feet. Her face was white as a ghost, a sheen of sweat coating her brow.

"...I feel dizzy." Even her voice sounded off. Weak.

I steadied her. Worry shot through me. "You okay? What's goin' on?"

She shook her head as if to clear it. "I...I don't know. I'm probably just overheated. This weather ain't helpin'."

I nodded. She wasn't wrong. Even with it almost being dusk, it was still nearly a hundred out, then add the humidity to it. "Come on, let's get you some water."

I let her lean on me as we walked the rest of the way to the trailer before forcing her to sit in one of the lawn chairs. I stole the reins from her and tied up Country Road, leaving her tacked up for the moment as I grabbed a water out of the cooler, and thrust it into Cheyenne's hands. "Here, have some of this."

She drank a few sips before cupping her hand and pouring some into her hand to slather along the back of her neck. She'd already taken her hat off, leaving it discarded upside down in the chair beside her.

What was going on with her? The headaches. The vomiting. Now, the dizziness. I remember being sick for a bit after the fire, but she hadn't even been in the thick of it like I was either time. And even now, I felt perfectly fine. Could it really be that? Or was it something else entirely?

"You okay?" I asked, wiping a hand across her brow and pushing her curls back off her face.

She blew out a breath and nodded. "I'm okay. A little nauseous, but the water helped. I think I was just dehydrated."

I pursed my lips. There was more to it than that, but it was beyond me for the moment.

She laughed, pressing her free hand to my chest. "I'm fine, cowboy. I promise."

Not gonna lie, hearing her say that, the smokey warmth of her voice, the bubbling sound of her laughter, it eased some of my fears. The knot in my chest loosened a bit. Not completely, but a bit.

"Seriously, Maverick..." She leaned in, tilting her head so as not to bump my hat still on my head as she kissed me reassuringly. "I'm okay. Now come on, we gotta get back for the bull riding."

CHAPTER 29
There Goes My Life

CHEYENNE

I woke up to rays of sunlight streaming in through the window in Maverick's bedroom. My head spun, and my tongue felt like it had been glued to roof of my mouth. I needed water and some ibuprofen.

We'd gone out last night celebrating our wins. Maverick and Cash snagged first in team roping. Cash had gotten Reserve Champion in bareback bronc riding, and Ryder had gotten another first in bull riding. I'd drank way too much. Especially, considering we'd be drinking today for the Fourth.

The smell of food let me know Maverick was already getting things ready for that. What time was it, even? I wiped the sleep from my eyes and grabbed my phone off the charger. 9 AM. Of course, he'd let me sleep in. I'm sure all the chores were done. He'd probably cleaned the house, and gotten at least half the dishes ready for today.

I smiled at that. *Perfect man.*

A wave of desire sparked to life, trying to push away the nausea cloying for dominance in my body. Maybe a shower would help. I walked into the bathroom and froze. Sitting right there on the counter was a box of pregnancy tests. A frown tugged on my mouth. Why were there pregnancy tests on the countertop? Better yet, why would Maverick put them there?

You're really askin' that? The little voice of reason whispered in my mind.

I thought of the past week. The couple of vomiting episodes. The headaches. The dizziness. The fact that my damn show jeans were tight as hell trying to put them on this past weekend.

Knots formed in my stomach, accompanied by an overwhelming wave of nausea.

"Oh, for fuck's sake."

No. No, I couldn't be pregnant. There were about a hundred different reasons for all that. Pregnancy symptoms and period symptoms were almost identical. I blew out a breath and ignored the pregnancy tests, grabbing for my toothbrush out of the vanity, the boxes all but mocking me in the corner of my eye. The taste of mint in my mouth brought on another wave of nausea and a growl escaped me.

"God damn it," I groaned, spitting the toothpaste out and reaching for the box.

What could taking a test hurt? Better to be safe than sorry, right?

My hands trembled as I opened the box and tore open the sealed test. It was one of those fancy ones that would say 'pregnant' or 'not pregnant'. Dear God, I hoped like hell it said the latter.

It didn't even take the full two minutes like it stated on the box. Nope. Ten. Fucking. Seconds.

One little word appeared on that small screen and then the whole world shifted beneath my feet. My heart lodged in my throat, my stomach clenching so tightly I actually wished I could throw up just to relieve the pressure. I took in a deep breath. Well, tried. It's like my lungs didn't work anymore. It reminded me of the fire, when no matter how hard I tried to get in a deep breath I just couldn't.

My legs buckled and I curled my knees up to my chest, trying and failing to control my breathing.

Fuck... Fuck. Fuck. Fuck. Fuck. Fuck.

How? How the hell could I be pregnant?

You know how.

I'd always been horrible at remembering to take my birth control pills, but I'd also always been so irregular that it made me forget about my time of the month completely until it decided to rear its ugly head when I was least expecting it. I'd gone so many months without a period that I'd honestly stopped thinking getting pregnant was even a possibility.

But that would mean... Oh God. Nate would be the father. Which, what a fucking shame.

My vision tunneled, my breaths becoming shallow, labored. I buried my face in my hands, only then realizing my cheeks were wet with tears. Oh my God. What the hell was I going to do? How far along was I?

I pulled my phone out of my back pocket, blinking away the tears in my eyes as I tried to focus on my screen. I fumbled my way through the pages of apps, trying and failing at least a couple times to click on the period tracker I hardly ever even needed to use. My heart raced as I tracked the weeks.

A broken sob escaped me.

Ten. Ten damn weeks.

I was ten weeks pregnant and didn't even have a clue. Probably still wouldn't have had it not been from Maverick. Speaking of—a knock sounded on the door, his deep voice accompanying it. "You okay, Chey?"

I sniffled, trying and failing to get ahold of myself as I choked out, "N-no."

The handle turned a moment later, Maverick's tall frame taking up the doorway. His gaze landed on me, wide-eyed and filled with worry.

"H-how?" I bit back another sob, my bottom lip trembling as I tried to keep it together enough to finish my sentence. "H-how did y-you know?"

He knelt down and picked me up like I weighed nothing more than a feather before leading me out of the bathroom and onto the private back porch. He sat in the rocking swing, holding me in his arms as we swayed back and forth. He was so quiet for so long I thought he might not have heard me, but when I opened my mouth to finally respond he managed to speak.

"You've been complainin' of headaches from the first day you got here...and you've gotten sick a few times." He didn't look at me as he spoke, but out toward the little pond where a couple ducks swam around. "I've seen you gag at least three times this week from different smells. And well, I don't know, maybe it's cuz Charlie's pregnant too. It just seemed logical."

"Well, you were right." I huffed, shaking my head in disbelief.

I couldn't believe that he'd been able to tell before me. *I* was the one pregnant. How could I have not seen the signs? How could I have been that blind to it? But the symptoms had been mild, and I didn't even really know what to expect. I hadn't had any reason to really be looking for signs in the first place.

My eyes blurred with tears once more as sob after sob wracked me.

I was pregnant. With a capital fucking P.

Maverick cupped my face in his big hands, his calluses scraping against my skin as he wiped my tears away and forced me to meet his gaze. "What're ya gonna do?"

I chewed on my bottom lip, lifting my shoulders up into a weak shrug. "I...I don't know," I murmured. "I–I really have no business raisin' a kid. I mean, hell, I didn't even know I was pregnant until you pointed it out." I slipped off of his lap, the overwhelming urge to move, to walk, to...*something* taking over.

Walking to the end of the porch, I leaned against the wooden column, aware of Maverick's stare. How the hell had I wound up in this situation? Pregnant with some other guy's baby while living and sleeping with Maverick.

I wondered what he thought of me. He probably thought I was a whore, and what was worse, is I couldn't even blame him.

My heart hurt.

What all was going to change now? Would he kick me out? End things completely?

No, Maverick wouldn't do that. He wasn't an asshole. He was too kind to do something like that. But I couldn't imagine this boded well for us as a...well, whatever the hell we were.

My bottom lip trembled as my eyes fluttered closed, a loud exhale escaping me as I tried to get a hold of myself. Fresh tears leaked down my face, but I didn't have the strength to wipe them away.

Unable to ignore the weight of his stare any longer, I turned slowly to face him. My words were hushed, broken, small as I spoke. "I can't be a mom... I'm—I'm not ready. I have no home, no job. I'm a hot fucking mess, Mav. I just...I can barely even take care of myself."

Maverick stopped swinging, planting his feet firmly on the ground while placing his elbows onto the tops of his thighs. He rubbed his palms back and forth—the only sound for a moment. His silence was killing me. Considering we'd gone basically a week without talking but still being able to communicate, he was more closed off than ever. The look on his face, in his eyes, gave nothing away.

"You gotta do what you gotta do."

I frowned. "I don't know *what* to do."

He stood up, his boots scuffing against the wooden deck as he came to stand before me. "If you're lookin' for me to tell you what to do, I can't do that for ya. This is somethin' you gotta decide for yourself."

A weight settled on my chest, so heavy I felt like I was drowning. "Will you think less of me if I..." I swallowed, nausea slamming into me at the thought of my next words. I blew out a breath, more tears falling from my eyes. "If I get rid of it?"

Something flickered in Maverick's stare. Not anger, or judgment, or anything like that, but something sad, wistful. He cupped my cheeks and wiped the tears away gently, his deep voice soft and smooth as he spoke. "Who the hell am I to judge you for what you decide to do with your body? It ain't my place. For the record, though, I think you'd be a great mom."

A sob escaped me, my knees all but buckling under the weight of his kind words. They just made me feel worse. Worse, because I didn't agree and I didn't really think I wanted to take the risk in finding out.

Maverick was there to catch me. As always. Funny how in less than a week, I'd become entirely too dependent on him picking up the broken pieces of my soul. I was too selfish to stop him right now, though. Maybe I'd always be.

"The dad..." Maverick asked, "Is it the guy you told me about? The one you chased off with a cattle prod?"

I nodded.

"You gonna tell him before you make a decision?"

I blew out a shaky breath. "I wasn't plannin' on it. Especially since I'm not plannin' on k-keepin' it."

Saying the words aloud seemed even more awful than when they'd formed in my mind. But I couldn't have a baby. Maverick may be right. Maybe I could be a good mom, but not right now. I just... This wasn't how I wanted to bring a new life into the world.

It didn't stop the guilt from gnawing at me, though.

Maverick nodded, running a hand back into my hair as he cupped my head. "Tell him. Even if you ain't plannin' on keepin' it, you should still tell him. I'd wanna know if I were in his position."

"Even if he's a piece of shit?" I sniffled.

He nodded, that same emotion swirling in his eyes that I couldn't quite pin down. I pursed my lips, patting my back pocket for my phone only to remember it was still in the bathroom. "I'll go call him."

He dipped his head once more, his lips parting like he wanted to say something before closing. He blew out a breath and pressed a gentle kiss to my forehead. "I'll be right here."

CHAPTER 30
Red Rag Top

MAVERICK

I'd figured she was pregnant, but knowing for sure now... Fuck.
Did this change things? Of course, it did. But how much?
She's gettin' rid of it.

My stomach clenched at the thought. I hadn't lied to Chey when I'd told her I wouldn't judge her for her decision. It was her body, her life. But the idea of giving up such a precious gift—*Stop. It ain't like it's yours.*

What would people think of us if she were to keep it? I could only imagine what they'd say. I'd never much cared what others thought, and while I knew Cheyenne didn't either, dealing with that would be a whole other level of hell I don't think either of us were prepared to deal with.

Especially with us being so new—whatever "us" was. I still wasn't quite sure.

She'd gotten me to talk. She'd pulled me out of the darkness. She'd seen me at my lowest, my worst, and she hadn't run. She'd planted wild-flowers in the darkest parts of my soul and brought me back to life.

I cared about her, that's for sure. Deeply. Truly. And I wanted to explore whatever connection we had more. Regardless of what she decided. Hell, I'd take care of her and the baby too. I wanted to tell her that, but how did I say that without making her feel like I was pressuring her to keep it? A baby that wasn't even mine.

It's not my place.

I paced the deck. I wondered what her ex would say. She'd not mentioned much about him other than the cattle prod incident. Would he want her to keep it? Would he convince her to take him back?

My heart clenched at that and I bit back a curse. An ember of possessive rage bloomed in my chest. I didn't want to let her go. I would if I had to, but—fuck. I clenched my fists at my sides.

"I called him."

Cheyenne's weak voice stopped my heart for a moment. I whirled to face her, taking her in. She leaned against the doorframe, like she was too weak to hold herself up. Tears shone in her turquoise eyes, her bottom lip trembling as she tried to hold in the brunt of her sobs.

I moved to her, reaching out a hand to pull her to me, but I let it fall. What if she changed her mind and didn't want me touching her?

"What'd he say?" I asked, fear clawing at my chest, my throat. My voice trembled as I spoke. I wondered if she heard it.

The strength she held herself together with crumbled right before my eyes, her face falling, her eyes dimming to dull pits of despair. "He…" Her words dissolved into cries as she curled into herself, burying her face in her hands.

Fuck it. I pulled her into my arms, running a hand softly through her hair. I soothed her, gently rocking her back and forth. I don't know how long we stood there like that. It could have been a minute or a few hours. All that mattered, all I cared about was her. I'd stay there all damn night if I needed to. If she wanted me to.

"He…uh…" she looked up at me, tears pooling in her eyes before slipping down her cheeks. "He threatened me…if I…if I k-keep it."

Rage bubbled up in me. Who the hell did he think he was threatening her? "Fuck him." Any man who had the fucking nerve to tell a woman to get rid of their unborn child wasn't a fucking man at all. They were a coward. I tilted her face up, forcing her to meet my stare.

"Don't let his words affect your decision. You do what you think is best. For you. For that baby. Not him. Fuck him."

Another broken sob escaped her. "He... all b-b-but adm-mitted burning d-down the trailer. I'm...I'm scared, Maverick."

I sighed, pulling her tighter into my arms. "I won't let him touch you or that baby."

"Maverick."

"I won't," I said, resolve hardening in my chest.

She looked up at me, sadness swimming in her gaze. "I know, Mav. But I...I can't do it. I can't deal with this fear. I just...I can't—" Her shoulders shook as a new wave of sobs took over. I held her through it all, even as defeat settled like a weight in my stomach.

It wasn't fair. I had no right to feel this way. To feel like I had any claim to this unborn baby. I can't even explain *why* I felt like that. Maybe because I knew just how horrible it was to lose something precious. It wasn't the same, but losing Ellie Mae, having her sweet, innocent life ripped away and ended... well, it just wasn't fair.

And that baby didn't do no wrong. Wouldn't even get the chance to. Just like Ellie Mae.

I held her there until her sobs turned quiet. Until her shoulders stilled and her sniffles ceased. "I'll take you," I said quietly, my voice sounding hoarse as it cut through the silence. "If this is what you want, I'll take you."

She looked up at me, a frown on her face. "I couldn't possibly ask that of you."

"You ain't. I'm offerin'. Ain't no way in hell I'm lettin' you do this alone."

"Mav, I—"

I clutched her chin between my thumb and forefinger. "Let me do this for you, Chey."

Her eyes watered, tears brewing as her bottom lip trembled. But after a moment she nodded, the next word coming out as little more than a broken, lifeless whisper. "Okay."

CHAPTER 31
Two Pink Lines

CHEYENNE

"*Let me do this for you, Chey.*"

Maverick's kindness nearly broke me. I didn't deserve it, but I sure appreciated it. It was only after I choked out an "okay" that I realized the clinic would likely be closed for the holiday, not to mention it was a Sunday morning and Maverick would be getting ready to head to church. Not that he wouldn't skip out on it for this, I had no doubt in my mind, but still, I didn't want him to. Then there was the fact I'd have to explain our absence for Cash's Fourth of July Bash, as well as I'd have to come up with a reason for why I wasn't drinking... Not like I hadn't drank my fair share last night, and it's not like I was planning on keeping it, but still. The thought of drinking knowing I was pregnant just seemed so absolutely wrong.

I voiced all my concerns aloud to him.

"Don't worry about me...and I can find somewhere to take you. There's plenty of places open today."

I exhaled slowly, wiping at my eyes even though it was no use. It was like I was perpetually crying at this point. "I can wait til tomorrow."

"You sure?" His brow rose. "We can skip out on Cash's party."

I pegged him with a hard stare. "We can't just skip your best friend's party...on your own damn property."

Maverick shrugged. "I'd do it if that's what you wanted."

Tears pricked in my eyes. Dear Lord, he was so sweet. And kind. And selfless.

"Thank you, but we aren't skippin' Cash's party. He'd just bother us until we gave in and went. It's fine if we go tomorrow."

He wiped the tears from my cheeks. "Okay. I was gonna head to church in a bit, but I can stay if you want me to."

I shook my head. "No. You go ahead. I'll stay here. I need to work with the filly today anyway."

"You sure you wanna do that today?"

"Might as well. It'll give me something to do other than cry."

His brow furrowed, his gaze serious. "You're not makin' a convincin' argument, Chey."

I appreciated the concern, but I needed this time alone. I needed time to think. To breathe. To come to terms with this. "I'll be fine. I promise."

His eyes searched mine for a long moment before he sighed. "Okay. Charlie'll be home. Cash recruited her to get all the decorations set up... Maybe you could talk to her? I mean, since she's, you know...in the same boat as you."

"No." I pulled out of his grip. "I don't want her to know. I don't want anyone to know."

It was bad enough he knew. Yes, he was being absolutely sweet and accommodating and amazing, but what would this change between us?

I honestly was too afraid to ask.

He lifted his hands up in a placating gesture, concern washing over his face. "Okay. Sorry."

More tears welled in my eyes before slipping down my cheeks. Dear God, I hated this crying bullshit. And here I was, a blubbering mess. I hated being pregnant. I wiped angrily at my tears and sniffled. "No, I'm sorry. I'll be fine, okay. Please don't worry."

Maverick nodded, the concern still lingering in his eyes, in every inch of him really. I could tell he wanted to plead his case for staying— ever the protector. But I needed some time alone.

I offered him what I hoped was a reassuring smile. "I'll see you in a bit."

His frown deepened, a muscle in his jaw ticking. So, he clearly wasn't convinced. I don't think I'd be either if the tables were turned. But I didn't have it in me to do anything more. A part of me just wanted to curl back up under the blankets and cry myself to sleep. Another part of me wanted to run away. Hop in my truck with Brandy and Country Road and just drive, drive, drive until we ended up in a new town, new county, a new state, even.

But I didn't have a trailer. I mean, the winnings I'd made from the rodeo yesterday, combined with the insurance money were hardly enough to make a decent down, but I could make it work.

A longing stirred in my chest, that wandering, drifting part of my soul calling. I glanced at Maverick. Could I leave right now? He'd welcomed me into his home. He'd taken care of me. He'd saved me and Brandy despite nearly breaking himself in the process. Could I really just run away?

The drifter part of me stilled. Its whispers dying on the wind.

I couldn't leave. I couldn't fathom saying goodbye. But I knew that if I stood here any longer, he'd find a reason not to go to church and stay here to mother hen me. So, I mustered up my brightest smile and leaned up to kiss him. "Thank you, Mav... For everything," I whispered, before walking back into the room.

———

THE LITTLE RED FILLY SNORTED AND PACED THE MINUTE I grabbed a lead rope. She pinned her ears as I placed a hand on the latch to her gate. Well, great. This was gonna be fun.

I glanced down at Brandy. "Stay." She laid down, settling in for the shit show that was likely to ensue.

I rested against the gate, the sun beating down on me despite it only being 10 AM. Maybe choosing to work with her right now was a bad idea. A thin sheen of sweat already coated just about every inch of my skin.

"Sh," I soothed, opening the gate slowly and walking into the stall, latching the gate behind me. The horse pranced, a wild panic in her eyes.

She looked about as terrified as I felt.

Tears welled in my eyes, blurring my vision. Great. Just what I needed right now. But I couldn't help it. The helplessness and confusion and just complete and utter shock shattered the floodgates holding back my tears. And I knew it was completely stupid, not to mention so incredibly dangerous, but I buried my face in my hands, sob after sob wracking my body like waves against a cliff.

How had I ended up pregnant? How could I have been so careless? So...irresponsible. I could still hear Nate's threats in my head. The way he'd all but gloated about my tailer. He'd burnt down my home. What would he do if I had his baby and he found out?

I should call the Sheriffs and tell them he'd basically admitted burning it. But it was my word against his. The stupid trailer park's video cameras were broken and hadn't recorded anything in months so there was no way of proving it was him. No one had seen him. Plus, I didn't want to see what he tried to do to me if I pressed charges.

I couldn't have this baby.

I was terrified. Just as terrified as this poor filly.

Something brushed against my arm, and I jumped. My watery gaze flew to the horse, who spooked and shuffled back a few steps, a snort escaping her as she pinned her ears.

Shit, I'd forgotten where the hell I was, what I was even supposed to be doing. What a great fucking horseman I was. I needed to get out of here. What I was doing was dangerous on a good day, but in this state of mind, it was nothing more than a goddamn accident waiting to happen.

To my surprise, the filly took a step toward me. And then another. And another... Until she stood right before me. And then she nuzzled my stomach.

Could she possibly know I was pregnant?

Great, so apparently even the damn horse knew but I hadn't. Just more proof that I had no business having a child. And then I was crying again, because you know, why not?

She rested her head against me, and slowly one of my hands found the side of her cheek. I ran a tentative hand across it, careful to go slow and not spook her. I don't know how long we stayed like that, but when she finally pulled away, I wasn't crying anymore. The fear had left her gaze, a softness there I hadn't expected to find.

"You're a good girl, aren't ya?" I kept my voice low, whisper-soft.

She didn't answer, because of course she didn't, but I'd take her calm as a sign we were making progress. I didn't do much else with her aside from run my hands along her neck and back, getting her used to my touch, my presence. Despite doing a whole bunch of nothing, sweat dripped off of me in buckets. My hair felt like a mop on my head as I exited her stall. Gross. Pulling my trucker hat off for a moment, I tied my hair up into a bun before plopping my hat back on. I needed a shower. I felt emotionally and physically drained, but at least I hadn't thrown up today. There was still time, though.

I latched her stall, intent to go back and shower and prepare myself mentally for Cash's party later on, only to find Charlie making her way toward me.

"Hey!" She waved at me before shielding her eyes from the hot sun.

"Hey. Maverick said you got conned into decoration duty?"

She snorted. "Yeah, but honestly it beats goin' to church with the boys."

"Not religious?" I asked.

"It's not that, really..." Charlie's shoulders rose and fell. "Church just never really has been my scene. Too much gossip for my taste."

"I get it." Church hadn't really been my thing either. But more so because Daddy and I moved around so much. Daddy hadn't been too religious to begin with, though, so church hadn't been much of a priority before.

Charlie smiled, but something in her gaze held a level of concern in the grey depths. Or maybe I was just projecting. "You okay?"

I frowned. "Yeah. Just hot and tired."

"You sure?" Charlie's brow rose.

So, I wasn't projecting. Was I that easy to read or had Maverick said something?

"What did Maverick tell you?" I grumbled out, defeat ringing in my words.

"Nothing. You just have tear stains on your cheeks. And... I don't know—" She rubbed at her tattooed arm. "You look sad." The softness and sincerity of her words, the worry in her gaze written plainly on her pretty face, broke me. Shattered the walls of my composure, leaving nothing but rubble.

Then I was crying. No, not crying. *Sobbing.* Body-wracking, gut-wrenching sobs that made me cave in on myself. I was a fucking mess, but I couldn't stop it.

"Oh my God, girl... what's goin' on?" Charlie's warm hands gripped my shoulders, gently forcing me upright.

I looked at her through my tears, her silhouette blurred. "I'm...p-pregnant."

Charlie rocked back at that, surprise shining in her gaze. "Really? Is it with that asshole ex of yours?"

Another sob tore from my chest, the pain of it shooting though me and bowing me inward. The only thing keeping me upright at this point was Charlie. I couldn't speak, so I just nodded.

"Oh, Chey..." She pulled me into her, enveloping me in a hug. I held onto her for what felt like forever, riding the waves of my emotions, until my tears didn't run like rivers, and my sobs didn't feel like punches to the gut.

She pulled away as I wiped my cheeks. "So, I'm guessing you told Mav?"

I huffed. "Are you kiddin'? He knew before I did. I woke up this mornin' to a box of pregnancy tests sittin' on the counter."

Charlie's gaze widened before a soft, knowing smile settled on her lips. "Figures. Maverick is the most observant person I've ever met. He guessed when I was pregnant too."

"Really?" I sniffled.

She nodded, taking a seat on one of the mounting blocks in the shade. "Oh, yeah. He knew before I even had a chance to tell Ryder. Thank God it was him and not Cash, or there would've been no way to keep that secret until Ryder got back."

My mouth twitched into the ghost of a grin, but it died just as quickly as Charlie asked, "How far along are you?"

I took a slow, deep breath. "Ten weeks."

I didn't miss the surprise that washed over her face, but to her credit, she tried to hide it well. "You don't want to keep it, do you?" There was sadness in her voice, but no judgment. Same as Maverick.

A lump lodged in my throat, holding the air in my lungs hostage. I lifted my shoulders as I tried and failed to come up with what to say. How could I make her understand that it wasn't even so much a question of want. I simply *couldn't*. I couldn't keep this baby. I had no business keeping this baby. But if I tried to explain, would she understand that? She was pregnant herself, and keeping it.

"I'm scared," I finally managed to admit, the sound little more than a hushed squeak.

She reached a hand out, gesturing for me to sit down beside her. I did, and for a long moment we just stayed there, shoulder to shoulder in silence.

"You know, when I found out I was pregnant, I cried for like a solid five hours." She huffed a laugh, playing with her engagement ring. "Thank God, Cason was still in school, because there was no way in hell I would have been able to keep my shit together if he were there."

"You were upset?" I asked, turning to look at her.

She met my gaze. "It's not that. I was. I *am*...happy but there was a part of me—there still is, really—that was absolutely fucking petrified."

"But you and Ryder are together. You're gettin' married."

"Yeah, and I absolutely want to start a family with him, but I wasn't anticipating it being quite so quickly. I mean, we're still trying to figure out how to parent Cason, and now we're just throwing another kid into the mix. Not to mention, the fact we *aren't* married yet, and I am not giving up my dream wedding to have some courthouse ceremony because I'm scared of what these old Karens at church have to say about Ryder and I having this baby out of wedlock."

Charlie blew out a breath, causing the wispy bangs framing her face to blow up in the makeshift breeze as she rolled her eyes. "I'm also terrified of how my body's gonna change. I've grown up with a mother whose been hounding me about my weight all my life, and I can't wait to hear the bullshit she has to say when I start showing..." When she looked at me, her stormy eyes swirled with emotion.

I hadn't even thought of any of that. She seemed so ecstatic about the whole thing. She was glowing. Happy. Even though she didn't have a bump yet, there was just something...*different* about her. The way she held herself, she was changed and confident. I never would have thought she was terrified...then again, I'd never thought to ask.

It's like she read my thoughts. "I'm allowed to be scared, but also ridiculously happy to be having this baby. Is it ideal timing? No. Am I prepared at all? Hell no...but as long as I have Ryder, I know we'll make it work."

"I wish I had that," I admitted. I just had a baby daddy who literally threatened me.

Charlie's gaze turned sympathetic...but also a bit hopeful. "You have Mav...if you want him."

A deep, shuddering breath went through me. "It's not the same. I'm having someone else's baby. What if he gets tired of taking responsibility for someone who isn't even his? What if he resents me? What if he doesn't even want me anymore?" Hot tears rolled down my cheeks.

"Have you asked him any of this?"

I shook my head.

"Talk to him." She placed a reassuring hand on my leg. "Maverick is probably the kindest, most loyal, most good man I know. He's also not an idiot, and he'd be an idiot to let you slip through his fingers because of this." She pegged me in place with her pleading stare.

"It's not just Maverick," I admitted, my voice faltering.

"Then what is it?"

I told her about Nate. About the threat. About what he'd done to my trailer. "If he finds out, Charlie... I don't know what he'll do."

Charlie pursed her lips, concern, understanding, and sympathy washing over her. She blew out a deep breath. "I'm sorry. I can't even imagine being in that position."

I met her gaze. "What would you do?"

"Me?" She shook her head, her mouth falling open only to shut once more before opening back up again. "I'd like to say that I wouldn't let that dickhead have any say in my decision. But..." She shrugged. "I honestly don't know."

I nodded. Not the answer I wanted, but then again, I couldn't expect her to answer that.

"But I do know one thing..." She glanced down at my stomach.

"*That* baby is yours. No one else gets to decide what you do with your body but you. Not your asshole ex. Not Maverick. Not me. Not any stupid Karen that tries to make you feel guilty or worthless. You decide what's best for you. And if you're not ready to be a mom, well that's no one's damn business but yours."

Tears pricked in my eyes. I hadn't wanted Charlie to know about me being pregnant, but I'm glad she'd found out anyway. It felt nice to be seen. To be understood. To have someone in a similar boat—well, minus the bullshit drama. It felt nice not to be so alone.

"Thank you," I said, offering her a soft, genuine smile.

She bumped shoulders with me, a warm grin lighting up her face. "You're welcome. Also...totally not pressuring you at all, but it would be pretty cool to get to raise babies with you."

I snorted, rolling my eyes, but my smile pulled wider. The idea was intriguing. But fear still rode my thought process right now. "Need help with decoration duty?" I asked.

She nodded, understanding the need for a distraction. "Boy, do I ever."

She stood up, grabbing my arm and hauling me up after her before launching into a tirade of all the things we needed to get done. I welcomed the distraction with open arms. It gave me something to do other than worry. Because as comforting as this little chat had been, it also filled me with concern.

Concern about what decision I would make.

Now, more than ever, I didn't know what to do.

———

MAVERICK AND I PULLED INTO THE ROUNDABOUT BEFORE Cash's house. He glanced over at me, his gaze blocked by his sunglasses.

"You sure you wanna do this? We can go back home. I don't mind."

I appreciated the concern, but honestly, the distraction of this party would be a welcome reprieve from the shift that forged between us since he'd gotten back from church.

Sure, he was courteous, and kind, and caring as ever, making sure to tend to my every need, but he hadn't touched me since he'd gotten back.

And if I'd learned one thing about Maverick Holstrom since moving in with him, it was that touch was his love language—a brush of our fingers, shoulder nudges, chin tilts and warm embraces, hell, even a forehead kisses. But since he'd gotten home...nothing. I'd never thought myself one who craved or even needed physical touch. But it's like he had magic in those fingertips. Every inch of me longed to reach out and touch him, but I didn't.

Something had changed between us. That much was clear.

I thought of Charlie's words. *"Talk to him."*

But sometimes actions spoke louder than words...especially with Maverick.

And not gonna lie, I was afraid to. Afraid of finding out exactly what he thought of this situation. What he thought of me. Would he regret sleeping with me? Would he want me to leave? Would he want to end things romantically?

I wasn't ready to hear those answers yet. So instead of asking him, I braved a smile, hoping, praying he didn't press any further as I said, "I'm sure, Maverick. Thank you, though."

Something flickered in his eyes. A flash of emotion there and gone so quickly I couldn't place it. But I felt it like a crack forming between the two of us. Making that shift, that chasm wider.

And I didn't know what to do to stop it.

CHAPTER 32
Cowboys Ride Away

MAVERICK

"**M**averick."

I'd grown used to her calling me Mav or cowboy in casual conversation, so when she used my name like that...it felt odd. Almost like a rift had forged between us.

She'd been closed off, guarded, unreadable since I'd gotten back from church. Understandable. I couldn't even begin to imagine what she was going through. What she was feeling.

I didn't want to add to her worries, her stress. As much as I longed to touch her, hold her, and offer her whatever comfort I could, I didn't want to push. She had so much to worry about, I didn't want her to have to worry about us either. I'd be here for her. Waiting. For as long as she needed.

Cheyenne got out of the truck before I could stop her, making a beeline for Cash's front door. It's like she was trying to avoid me. My chest tightened, worry burrowing deeper and deeper.

What had changed? Well, aside from the obvious. Did she not want to be with me anymore? Or worse, did she think I didn't want her anymore? The fact she was pregnant changed nothing for how I felt about her. It might for some people, but it didn't for me. Hell, if she changed her mind and told me she wanted to keep it, I'd be okay with that. And if she was worried what other people would say, well, I'd come up with a solution for that too.

I needed to talk to her, but not here. Not with so many people around. Tonight. Tonight, I'd talk to her.

I'd barely made it to her side before Cash opened the door, dazzling in all his star-spangled glory. His board shorts were red white and blue with a red solo cup and ping pong ball pattern. He wore no shirt, but a myriad of shiny mardi gras-styled beads in red, white, and blue. His large, polarized sunglasses even had an American flag design on their plastic frames.

"Well, look at you, Mooney," Cheyenne chuckled, sounding so much like herself it gave me pause. Her smile pulled wide on her cheeks, that familiar glow that had been all but absent a few moments ago shining brightly once more.

Cash grinned, pulling his glasses down to glance between us. "Y'all are late. Had to get a quickie in, didn't ya?"

I clenched my jaw, but Cheyenne laughed, smacking Cash lightly on the chest before pushing past him. "You're an idiot."

I made to follow her, but Cash stopped me with a hand to the shoulder. Sunglasses still lowered he regarded me for a long moment, the usual mirth gone but replaced by a seriousness he almost never showed. "You okay?" he asked.

I nodded. From the way Chey had reacted earlier to me mentioning her talking to Charlie, I knew she didn't want anyone else knowing. "I'm fine. Just mentally preparin' myself for takin' care of your sorry ass tonight."

Cash's crow of laughter was a welcome sound. It seemed to break whatever seriousness he'd possessed a moment ago. Clapping me on the back, he urged me inside. I followed him through the house—a true bachelor pad with a pool table, bar, indoor gym, and a walk-in pantry filled with enough alcohol to start up a liquor store. It was spotless—not because of him, but because Aunt Violet came over twice a week to clean it for him. The entire place was bedecked in American flag decorations. Balloons, streamers, signs.

Charlie and Cheyenne had really outdone themselves.

People milled about in the fenced off backyard as we walked outside. A group played cornhole on the grassy area to the left of the large above-ground pool Cash, Ryder and I had spent most of Wednesday and Thursday setting up and filling with water. More people swam or lounged around the bar we'd built off the side of one end. Friends from back in school, church, others whom we'd met rodeoing. Cason ran around with a couple of his friends from school in tow.

I spied Charlie and Ryder on the opposite side of the swim up bar, making drinks. They both waved hello before making their way over.

"Who's ready for a shot?" Cash asked, wrapping an arm around Cheyenne.

Her gaze met mine—panic shining in the turquoise depths for a moment. "I'm uh...not drinkin' tonight," she replied. I doubted Cash noticed the quaver in her voice—he'd had a few drinks in him—but I didn't miss it.

"What?" He turned to her, disbelief shining in his eyes as he pulled his sunglasses down to regard her. "You promised last night you'd be my drinkin' buddy. Don't tell me you're chickenin' out!"

Cheyenne offered him a guilty shrug.

Cash scoffed. "Come on... What are you, pregnant or somethin'?"

The color drained from Cheyenne's face, her body going stiff. Even from a few steps away, I noticed the tears brewing in her gaze.

I opened my mouth, to make an excuse, to change the subject, but how? I didn't drink so she couldn't use the excuse that she was going to take care of me. And it's not like we lived far enough away to say she was going to be the designated driver. If we said she was sick, Cash would just call bullshit.

Charlie's warm, buttery voice drew my attention. "Cash you're an idiot. I asked her not to drink so I had more than just Maverick and I here to make sure none of you dumbasses get drunk and drown in the pool."

That seemed to appease him, for now. Fuck, it was gonna be a long day.

———

"YOU READY?" I ASKED THE NEXT MORNING, MEETING Cheyenne's gaze.

I shouldn't even have asked. From the way she hovered by the door, a look of resignation in her eyes, I already knew the answer.

I hated this. Hated that she felt this way, and despite my best efforts, nothing I seemed to do helped. I'd tried talking to her last night after we'd gotten home from Cash's, but she'd shut it down quickly enough. She'd not gone to sleep with me, but instead chose to sleep in the guest room—if she even slept at all. The dark bags under her eyes led me to believe she hadn't.

It's like she'd withdrawn into herself, and nothing I did got through to her. Was this how I'd been last week when I wouldn't talk? Guilt materialized in my chest, constricting and tightening around my heart.

Cheyenne didn't respond to my question. At least not verbally. The only answer was her opening the door and walking out to my old Chevy.

Say something. That little voice in my head begged, pleaded to do something, *anything* to fix this. I'd done nothing wrong, but I was losing her regardless, and I didn't know what the hell to do to stop it. This decision...it was killing her. I could see it. But who was I to tell her what to do? I had no say in this. No leg to stand on. All I could do was be there to support her and pick up the broken pieces. Which I'd do. I just wished I could do more than that.

We drove in silence, each mile more and more painful.

Say something... Say something.

I glanced over at her. She leaned against the door, her legs tucked up against her chest. She wore one of my oversized t-shirts and a pair of ripped denim shorts, a trucker hat and bun hiding her wild curls. Her gaze was fixed on the terrain outside—nothing but golden rolling hills and cows. Lots of cows.

There wasn't a single drop of sunlight left in her. No warmth. No hope. She looked lifeless. Cold.

It broke my damn heart.

"Chey."

Her gaze snapped to mine, a silent question on her face. Tears welled in the blue depths of her eyes.

I glanced at the road as I spoke, unable to meet her sad stare. "Look, I know I'm the last person who should be askin' this of you, but..." I blew out a breath and finally braved her gaze. "I need you to talk. Please."

Tears streamed down her cheeks, her mouth bobbing open and closed multiple times. Exhaling shakily, she said on a broken whisper, "I...I don't know what to s-say."

With a tentative hand, I reached for hers. "Say somethin', anythin'... I just...I need to know what you're thinkin'. I hate seein' you like this. It–it scares me."

Some of the tension, however small, melted from her as she gripped my hand back. "It scares me too. I don't know what to do. A part of me thinks maybe I should keep it. But then I think of Nate. And his threats. And what everyone else will have to say. And then there's this...thing goin' on between us. And what if you grow to resent me? What if this changes how you feel?" Her words became quicker and more frantic the longer she talked, her chest rising and falling rapidly.

My heart cracked. She was worried about me? About me resenting her? Dear Lord, I should have talked to her. Should have reassured her.

I pulled off on the side of road, the dirt crunching beneath my tires the only sound to break the silence. Placing the truck in park, I turned to face her more fully. "You don't gotta worry about me."

Her bottom lip trembled, her gaze falling to the floor as she spoke. "You say that, but—"

"No. No buts." I shook my head, leaning over to tilt her chin up. Despite the worry and concern riding my emotions, I spoke calm, even. "I can promise you right now, Cheyenne, you never gotta worry about me regrettin' or resentin' you. Never."

A choked sob escaped her, but I continued on before she could protest. "As for the other concerns...I won't let Nate do anything to you. And if you're worried about what other people might think if you decide to keep the baby—" I shrugged. "Tell 'em it's mine. I don't care. I'll even go so far as to buy you a ring, if that's what you want."

She shook her head, disbelief mingling with the tears in her eyes. "Why?" she sobbed. "Why would you do all this for me?"

I slid the hand holding her chin along her jaw, before cupping the side of her face. "You took care of me...now, let me take care of you."

She scoffed. "Maverick, I would hardly compare singing you to sleep to you literally ruinin' your life for me. A girl you don't even know."

And there it was, I realized. The root of her worries, her fears.

"Is that it? You're worried if you keep it, it'll ruin your life?" I wasn't judging, just curious. I'd wondered if it was this.

Her eyes fluttered closed, her lashes dark and spiky from her tears. Fresh ones streaked down her cheeks. Her composure broke, her face falling into her hands that rested on her knees as her shoulders shook. Muffled cries escaped her.

Fuck. I'd only made things worse.

"Cheyenne," I soothed. "It's okay."

Her head whipped up, her devastated gaze meeting mine. "No, it's not!" she croaked out. "It's not okay. What person could possibly think that their life was ruined because of their unborn child?" She tilted her head toward the ceiling of the car. "It's selfish and horrible, I know. That baby is the product of *my* irresponsibility, and yet here I am ready to get rid of it because it's inconvenient. That baby doesn't deserve that. It deserves a mom who's gonna love it. Take care of it. Be selfless for them. Someone like Charlie." She wiped at her tears, resignation ringing in her words. "I'm no better than my mama."

"It ain't the same, Chey—"

"Isn't it?" she snapped, self-loathing and anger and hatred written plainly on her face, burning in her eyes, and echoing in her words. "My mama could've stayed, but she left. Same as I could have this baby, but I...I can't. That baby deserves better than me."

I blew out a slow breath, sadness welling in me, pricking tears of my own. I blinked them away. The fact she could think so low of herself broke my heart, but I realized there was nothing I could do to convince her otherwise. And nothing I said would stop her today. Not that I had any right to. This was her decision.

I needed to respect that.

"You sure this is what you want?" I cupped her face.

Pursing her lips as more tears fell, she nodded.

"Okay." I shifted in my seat, turning myself forward once more. Putting the truck in drive, I hopped back on the road.

CHAPTER 33
Ticking

CHEYENNE

Every second was a constant battle between my heart and mind. The conflict in me so intense it hurt to breathe. To think.

Maverick's words rattled through my head and echoed in my heart. He was willing to do all of that for me. But why? There was being kind, there was being caring, and then there was this.

He'd make an excellent husband. A phenomenal father. A part of me—a large part— wanted to take him up on his offer. Raising the baby as his, marrying him, all of it.

I may not be in love with him yet, but God, everything he did seemed to lead me in that direction. I cared for him. Deeply. Deeply enough that it scared me. I was falling. Faster than I ever had before.

But going along with Maverick's plan meant settling down. I was twenty-five. I didn't want to settle down. Not yet. I had so many places I still wanted to go. Things I wanted to see. Maverick didn't seem like the spontaneous, adventurous type. He was the same routine every single day for the rest of his life kind of guy.

And I liked that about him, but would I like it after a few months? A few years?

I couldn't keep this baby, raise it with him, and then what...leave when I got bored of being in the same place for too long? That wouldn't be fair to any of us.

And it made me no better than my piece of shit mother.

Getting rid of this baby...it would destroy me—it *was* destroying me, but it would be better this way.

It has to.

Maverick pulled into the clinic parking lot and put the truck in park in one of the spots near the entrance. He turned to regard me. Those jade eyes swirling with emotion. "Want me to come with you?"

I bit back tears and shook my head. As much as I didn't want to be alone right now, I didn't want him to be there with me for that either. It was bad enough I had to go through it. I didn't want him to see that.

I faked a smile through my tears and grabbed for the door.

He stopped me with a hand on my arm. I turned, and he cupped my face in his familiar, calloused hands. "Hey. I want you to know I don't think anything different of you. I'm always gonna be here for you."

His words broke me, shattering the guard I had around my heart like glass. He may not think differently of me, but I already did.

I already hated myself for the decision I was making.

It's crazy how you always speculate what you'd do in a situation, but then when that situation actually happens, you find you were completely and totally wrong.

I would hate myself for this for the rest of my life, and yet, I couldn't manage to stop myself from sliding out of Maverick's grip and opening the door. I didn't look back at him as I grabbed my purse. As I shut the door. As I placed one foot in front of the other and forced myself toward the clinic.

My heart thundered in my chest, tears falling so steadily I couldn't even see. I was like a living, raging storm of emotion.

It's almost over.

But was it? This was just the beginning. Getting rid of the baby was only one of the steps. What lasting trauma would this cause me?

I'd been irresponsible and now was faced with the consequence of my actions, and instead of bucking up and dealing with those consequences, I was backing out. Giving up. Daddy would be so disappointed.

I hadn't called him and told him. Same reason I didn't want anyone else knowing. I was embarrassed. Scared. Scared to know what he thought of me. He'd stayed with my mama even after all the shit she'd done. He'd fought for her until the last night she left. And instead of letting his life go to shambles, he'd stayed. He'd showed up...for me.

Nausea washed through me, making my throat clench on instinct. *Oh, dear Lord, please don't let me be sick.*

My breaths sawed in and out of my lungs, yet somehow, I still couldn't breathe.

Was I really doing this?

I have to.

I placed a hand on the door handle, peered through the foggy glass at the empty waiting room. I wiped at my tears with my free hand, steeling myself for what was to come next when the strangest thought overwhelmed me. It was like getting slammed by a wave in a storm.

An image of me looking down at my stomach. Of a rough, calloused hand pressed to it. An image of Maverick holding a little blanketed bundle, rocking it and showing it the horses. And then the ghost of a song drifting on the wind of "You Are My Sunshine".

My breath left me in a whoosh, some new emotion swelling and bursting to life in my chest.

I dropped my hand from the door handle, turned on my heel, and made my way back to the truck. Sliding into the passenger seat, I shut the door behind me and whispered, "Drive."

Maverick didn't speak as he nodded and backed up, but he didn't need to. The warmth in his gaze, the welcome feel of his touch as he pulled me across the seat to sit in the middle one said it all.

And as I curled up beside him, his arm wrapped around my shoulders, I focused on that new emotion in my chest...

Hope.

———

By some miracle, I was able to get a same day appointment with an OBGYN, so after a couple hours of hanging out in San Antonio, Maverick and I pulled into the parking lot. He left the car idling, making no attempt to get out as I grabbed my purse.

"Will you come with me?" I asked, placing a hand on his arm still gripped on the steering wheel.

A look of disbelief flickered in his gaze as he met mine. "You want me to?" His deep voice was thick with emotion.

Of course, I wanted him to go. He was my...well, we hadn't really figured that out yet. But I cared about him, and I wanted him there with me.

I nodded. "I do."

He turned the car off, pocketing his keys, and grabbed his hat off the dash before placing it on his head. Taking a deep breath, he nodded. "Okay. Let's go."

———

I don't think I'd ever felt so nervous in my life. Who knew that sitting in a room full of pregnant women and mothers could be so intimidating. Maverick sat beside me, his hand resting on my leg that wouldn't seem to stop shaking, his light gaze scanning the room as we waited for them to call my name.

"This your first?"

I glanced to my left, acknowledging the pregnant woman who'd just spoken. She looked to be around my age, with a little toddler sitting beside her, playing with some toy. He couldn't be any older than two, and by the looks of it, she was ready to pop at any minute.

Two under two... Just the idea was terrifying. I couldn't imagine one, let alone another that close in age.

"I'm sorry, what?"

She smiled and nodded at the two of us. "Is this your first baby?"

I frowned. Was it that obvious? Also, who just asked that? She laughed before I could manage an answer. "Sorry, y'all just look like I felt the first time around."

"Oh." I blew out a breath, glancing at Maverick. He wore a

guarded expression, so I couldn't really tell what he was thinking or feeling. But he was touching me again, so there was that comfort. I met the woman's stare once more. "Yeah. I'm pretty terrified, to be honest."

She offered a sympathetic smile. "It's gonna be okay. I ain't gonna lie and say it's a cakewalk, but—" She glanced down at her little boy, her smile pulling wider. I wondered if she realized one of her hands drifted to her stomach as she spoke. "It's worth it."

I returned her smile, looking to Maverick for...I don't know what. Reassurance. Comfort. His grip tightened on my leg gently before releasing the pressure.

"Cheyenne Harris?"

Relief and terror vied for dominance in my stomach at hearing my name. I shot up out of my seat, so quickly that a wave of dizziness settled over me for a moment, making me sway on my feet. Maverick's hands were there to steady me. I turned to regard him. He sat on the edge of his seat, watching, waiting, but not moving. Not until he got the go ahead.

I looked between him and the nurse. "Can he come too?"

"Of course," the nurse said brightly.

After getting settled into a room, giving a urine sample, and given a paper blanket with instructions to undress from the waist down and cover myself, I sat on the exam table, Maverick beside me in a small chair. He was so tall that it looked like it fit a kid and not an adult. If I wasn't worried that I'd throw up from nerves the moment I opened my mouth, I might have made fun of him. As it was, I just watched the clock in silence, every tick of it deafening in the quiet room.

A knock came on the door a moment later, followed by a woman in a white doctor's coat. She looked more like a middle-aged rodeo queen and less like a doctor, in my opinion. With her Farah Faucet waves, picture-perfect smile, and western garb on beneath the coat.

"Well, hello, y'all. Looks like we're havin' a baby," she said cheerily, as if she was announcing the finalists for a short go and not confirming my pregnancy. And while it could easily come off as disingenuous, I could tell she really loved what she did. That joy and lightness was a bit infectious, easing some of the fear knotted in my chest. "Pregnancy test came back positive, so congratulations! Now, let's figure out how far along you are, Miss Cheyenne."

After explaining the timeline to her, she urged me to lay down and grabbed out the portable ultrasound resting in the corner. My heart beat louder than a damn jackhammer as I pulled my shirt up enough to expose my stomach and she squirted the cold ultrasound jelly onto my torso.

"Alright, now let's see just how far along this baby's measurin'." She glanced between Maverick and I. "Y'all excited?"

We met each other's gazes. I still couldn't read him. His face was a mask of calm, his eyes giving nothing away. I hated that I couldn't figure out what he was thinking right now. Now when it had become so easy.

I offered him a soft smile and reached for his hand and murmured, "As I'll ever be."

His answering squeeze eased more of the fear in my chest.

The doctor shifted the little handheld device attached to the machine and pressed some buttons on the keypad. She spouted off something as she roved the thing over my stomach, but honestly, I didn't comprehend anything, not as I watched the dark screen, trying and failing to understand what I was seeing.

"And there it is." The doctor pointed with her free hand at a little blob on the screen. It sure as hell didn't look like a baby, but there it was, I guess.

My heart constricted, a loud roar dulling all the sound in the room.

"Chey?" A deep, familiar voice cut through the blood rushing through my ears.

I let out a shaky breath, my gaze darting to him. "Huh?"

He nodded at the doctor. "She asked if you wanted to hear the heartbeat."

"Oh..." I chewed my lip, my body trembling with... Fear? Excitement? Both? I met the doctor's light brown gaze. "Um...sure."

She smiled, pressed a couple more buttons, and then...

Beneath the white noise of the ultrasound machine was this thu-thump, thu-thump, thu-thump.

My free hand came to my mouth, a breathless gasp falling from my lips. Tears blurred my vision. "Oh...oh my God."

That was a heartbeat. My baby's heartbeat.

How could I have even thought of getting rid of that? I turned my watery gaze to Maverick. Emotion shone in his eyes and was drawn plainly on his face. Awe and excitement and wonder...and love.

There was no doubt about it. Love blazed in his light stare. And when he met my gaze, unshed tears of his own lining his eyes, that love was aimed at me too.

CHAPTER 34
Wondering

MAVERICK

How was this possible? How could I care so much about something that wasn't even more than a heartbeat yet?

That baby wasn't mine, and yet the minute I heard that thumping, happiness—pure, undiluted happiness I had never felt before—filled me, warmed me to my core.

One thing was for sure, though. No matter what happened, no matter what became of Cheyenne and I, I would always love that baby. And I would take care of it, die for it, do anything I could to keep it safe.

After a few more minutes of listening to the heartbeat and the doctor taking down measurements, Cheyenne was cleared to get dressed, and an appointment was made for a couple weeks later for her twelve-week checkup. The baby was measuring at ten weeks and three days, with a due date of February second.

Nearly seven more months. It seemed so far away, but I had a feeling it would be here quicker than we were expecting.

I already was coming up with a mental blueprint for nursery furniture. Maybe oak? Or pine? Dark or light stain? I wondered if it was a girl or boy. Would Cheyenne want to find out or wait and have it be a surprise?

It's not yours.

I tried to ignore the voice of doubt in my mind. There was still a really good chance Cheyenne decided to up and leave. We still hadn't talked about what we were. What the plan was. If she wanted my help raising it. If she wanted everyone to think it was mine.

I wanted to ask her. I'd looked over at her almost a dozen times now as we drove home to voice my thoughts, but she was closed off. Impossible to read.

She wasn't lifeless anymore, but there was a wall up around her right now. One I didn't want to knock down. She'd been through so much today. So many decisions weighing solely on her shoulders. I didn't want her to have to worry about what we were on top of that. I would be right here, waiting.

It wasn't a lie—I was the one thing she didn't need to worry about. I could be patient. Bide my time. I was in no rush.

"So," she asked, her tone lighter than it had been all day. "When do you think we should tell everyone?"

"Depends. Do we wanna do an announcement or just tell them?" I glanced at her.

We. Dear Lord, I'd just gone and assumed. "I'm sorry, I meant, you. Not we."

She smiled despite my floundering. "I don't know. I figure Cash will likely find out sooner or later. Maybe we should tell them before he guesses and tells the whole town about it."

I nodded, but I was still in my own head. *Ask her what we are.* It was the perfect time. But it's like my mouth and brain had stopped working. The line of communication being severed between the two.

"Any ideas on how to tell them?" Her smokey voice drew my gaze.

I shrugged. I had about a million ideas, but I also didn't want to overstep. This was her announcement. Her baby. I needed to remember that. "You should do what you want." I instantly regretted the words the minute they left my mouth. "I'm sorry, I meant this is a big moment for you. You should do whatever you like best."

"Oh." Her smile faltered a bit, and my heart sank. But just as quick as it faltered, she went on like nothing happened. "I'm sure I can figure something out."

Say something. Clear this up. Fix this.

But I didn't want to be a burden. I didn't want to pressure her. If she wanted to talk about what we were, she'd ask...right? She'd always been assertive, sure of what she wanted up until now. She had no problems with asking or telling me what she was thinking. The fact she wasn't now had to mean something.

———

It was late afternoon by the time we got home. Cheyenne had fallen asleep on the way, giving me plenty of time to think of what I wanted—no, needed to say. I had it all planned out. I needed to work horses first, but I'd make her dinner, and then we could talk about it then. Just the two of us. No Cash, no Charlie and Ryder, no Bad and Aunt Violet.

No distractions. No interruptions.

I studied her for a moment. She looked so peaceful, so calm. None of the worry or uncertainty from earlier lined her features. She was beautiful. For a moment, I debated just leaving her there, not wanting to wake her, but she deserved to sleep somewhere more comfortable than my truck.

She stirred in my arms as I carried her into the house. "When did I fall asleep?"

"Somewhere around Hondo." I placed her on the bed. "I gotta go work horses, but feel free to stay in and rest."

She wiped the sleep from her eyes and stretched, reminding me of a cat waking up from a nap. "I can come help. I just gotta get changed."

I shrugged. I'd never turn down her company.

She nodded, but something lingered between us as she got dressed, reminding me of the rift from earlier, only not so noticeable or large. Hoping to bridge that gap, I said, "I was thinkin' I could convert the guest room into a nursery, if you wanted. I can keep the bed in there for you, though, that way you've got somewhere to sleep."

She stilled as she put on her boots, a frown forming on her face as she leveled me with a narrowed look. "Do you not wanna be with me?" Anger and accusation rang in her words.

I rocked back, a matching frown tugging on my own mouth. "What're you talkin' about?"

"You just basically said you don't want me in your room anymore."

"I never said that." Worry and confusion rose in me. What the hell was she talking about?

She crossed her arms over her chest, her turquoise gaze blazing with defiance. "Yeah, you did. You said you'd leave the bed in there so I had somewhere to sleep." She pursed her lips, pegging me with a challenging look. "Not to mention, you seemed less than thrilled when I asked you about being involved in the announcement. You acted like you couldn't care less, especially considering you essentially told me you'd marry me earlier today. So, once again...do you not wanna be with me?"

There was so much anger, so much defiance and fire coming off of her. It was the first time I'd really seen her temper, and boy, she got hot quicker than I'd expected.

Guilt ate at me. Looking back on our conversations, the way I'd phrased things, I could see her misinterpreting what I said. Blowing out a breath, I took a step toward her.

Time to put out the fire.

CHAPTER 35
Tell Me Like It Is

CHEYENNE

"I was thinkin' I could convert the guest room into a nursery, if you wanted. I can keep the bed in there for you though, that way you've got somewhere to sleep."

His words were innocent enough, but they hit me like a freight train straight to the gut. He was going to leave the bed in there so I had somewhere to sleep? What the fuck did that even mean? Was he kicking me out of his room? Did he not want to be with me?

He'd been weird since we'd left the doctor's appointment. I get that we hadn't really defined the relationship, but I'd taken him into the exam room with me, for fuck's sake. We'd seen the ultrasound together, listened to the heartbeat...from our conversation earlier, I'd just assumed that meant he wanted to be with me.

Was I completely wrong?

Anger bristled to life in my chest, my thoughts like kindling to a fire, making me hotter and hotter with each passing second.

I stilled as I slid on my boots, my angry, hurt gaze flicking to him. "Do you not wanna be with me?" I hadn't meant for the words to sound so accusatory, but honestly, at the moment, I didn't really care. I was confused and scared and frustrated.

My emotions were shot to shit, and I had no more patience left in me. None. Not after the rollercoaster of a day I'd had.

He frowned, rocking back at my words. "What're you talkin' about?"

"You just basically said you don't want me in your room anymore."

"I never said that," he replied, shaking his head.

"Yeah, you did." I crossed my arms over my chest. "You said you'd leave the bed in there so I had somewhere to sleep..." I thought of the car ride. How he'd corrected himself when he'd said *we* then floundered. How he'd basically shut down when I'd asked about telling his family about the baby. "Not to mention, you seemed less than thrilled when I asked you about being involved in the announcement. You acted like you couldn't care less, especially considering you essentially told me you'd marry me earlier today. So, once again...do you not wanna be with me?"

A part of me knew I was being snarky and a bit petty—okay, maybe a lot petty. But I was scared. Scared that I'd just gotten myself into a situation with a guy who didn't actually want to be with me.

You know that's not true.

Maybe he wasn't in love with me, but Maverick wasn't the type of person to string me along. Not when he knew first-hand what that was like.

He blew out a breath, pulling his cowboy hat off to run a hand over his short hair before righting it atop his head once more. Guilt shone in his gaze as he said quietly, "Of course, I wanna be with you. I just... sometimes I ain't no good at findin' the right words."

I huffed. "Well, no fuckin' shit. You proved that last week." The words were out before I could even think.

He stilled, sadness and hurt blooming in his gaze, flickering to life along the harsh, handsome lines of his face. Shame welled up inside me, so intense and brutal that I thought I might throw up. How could I say something so horrible? So unkind? God, I was terrible. Absolutely terrible.

I cupped a hand over my mouth, a broken gasp tearing from my throat. "I...I'm so sorry. That was horrible of me."

I expected anger. I *deserved* anger. His wrath. His fury. I deserved for him to kick me out. To call things off completely. But instead, he took a step forward and pressed a hand to my cheek, his pained gaze settling on me. What was worse... There in the depths of those light jade eyes was also understanding. "It's okay. You ain't gotta apologize, Chey. You've been through—"

No. No, there was no way he could possibly be making excuses for me. Sadness, guilt, and anger clawed for dominance in my chest. Sadness that he just took those hurtful words, guilt that I'd even said them in the first place, and unjustified anger because here I was completely out of control emotionally, yet, as always, he held himself together with such ease.

"Goddamn it, Maverick! It's not okay. You shouldn't be justifyin' my actions. That was inconsiderate and horrible of me. I'm upset and I lashed out, but that ain't okay."

He shrugged. And that broke my heart. The fact he could so easily brush it off. Like he was used to people lashing out and taking their insults.

"So, tell me why you're upset," he said softly, not a hint of anger or judgment lurking in his gaze.

I took a breath, trying to push back the anger that still burned unproportionally bright in me. It's like my heart hadn't gotten the same memo my brain had. So, while I understood I was being irrational and bitchy, I couldn't quell the fire inside me that looked to destroy anything and anyone in its blazing path. "I feel like I'm drowning and my fuckin' life preserver is broken. I feel like it's just one wave of bullshit poundin' into me after another, and every time I come up to breathe, somethin' else happens. I'm scared and I feel out of control..." My words fell out of my mouth like vomit, my breaths rasping in and out of my chest faster and faster as my voice became more rushed and high-pitched.

Maverick cupped my face, his gaze unreadable as emotion after emotion flickered in the depths, as well as passed over his face. His mouth tugged into a contemplative scowl, not necessarily aimed at me

—at least, I hoped—but the situation likely. His eyes narrowed ever-so-slightly, and a moment later he said, "Come with me."

I frowned. "Where?"

"Just come with me." His voice held both a pleading and final note to it. He wasn't going to tell me where we were going, but he also wasn't going to force me there. This was a choice. My choice.

And while it annoyed the hell out of me that he was being so cryptic, I tossed my hands up into the air and shrugged. "Alright, let's go."

He led me out to the truck, whistled for Brandy, and the three of us started off down the road. He'd mentioned riding horses, but I was in no mood for that. Annoyance rippled through me as I said, "I don't think me ridin' is the best idea right now, Maverick."

He stiffened in the seat beside me, but his words were soft, his gaze knowing as he met my harsh stare. "I ain't gonna have you ride."

"Then what are you gonna have me do?" I asked, crossing my arms over my chest. Worry and frustration and that damn anger that wouldn't go away simmered in my soul. This was why I liked being alone. Why I liked to go off when I was annoyed or mad. I knew I had a temper, and sometimes, most times, it was best to just leave me until I'd burnt up all the frustration on my own. Right now, every cryptic response, every unspoken emotion that went across Maverick's face, set me more and more on edge.

Maverick placed a hand on mine and gave it a reassuring squeeze. "Have a little patience, Chey. Please."

I rolled my eyes and huffed. "In case it ain't obvious, I don't got a lotta that."

His lips pulled up into the barest ghost of a smirk, the look in his eyes warming, as if he wanted to say, *I can see that.*

But he didn't. Which was almost more infuriating than him saying it.

We pulled up to the barn and he cut the engine, nodding for me to get out and follow him. By the time I reached his side, he had a rope in hand and pointed at the dummy cow already set up about ten feet away. "You ever roped?" he asked, glancing at me.

I scoffed. "Yeah."

He nodded once more, holding out the rope. "Alright then, rope the dummy."

I didn't take it, my hands finding their way to my hips defiantly. Annoyance bristled within me. "Why?"

If he was bothered by my attitude, he didn't let on. Even I knew I was being unreasonable and bitchy, but it's like I couldn't stop it. I couldn't pull back or control my anger anymore. It just had to fizzle out.

"Just rope the dummy, Chey," he said, his deep voice remaining calm, even.

I blew out a breath through my nose and rolled my eyes. "Fine." I took the rope, built a loop, and tossed it at the dummy. The rope clacked against the plastic before sliding around the horns.

Casting an expectant glance his way, I raised a brow, my hands going to my hips once more. "Okay. Done. What was the point of that?"

A muscle feathered in the corner of his lip, almost like he was fighting the urge to smile. "Do it again."

"What? Why?" I scoffed.

He leveled me with a heavy gaze that made me feel like he was looking through to my very soul. "Will you trust me?"

And there was so much sincerity, so much earnest vulnerability in that pleading tone, that I found myself nodding and releasing the rope from the horns and building a loop again.

Another toss. Another, "Again."

On my third throw, I asked, "So what's the lesson, oh, wise one?"

He settled himself against the barn, propping one foot against the wall, while crossing his hands over his chest. "There ain't no lesson." He nodded at me. "Again."

But there was a lesson there. Because at some point, my muscles began to loosen and relax. My anger dissipated like smoke on a strong breeze. The rhythmic clack of the rope hitting the dummy became a calming melody that soothed my soul. Even as my fingers started to blister from the rope, I kept throwing. Again and again and again.

It was like every toss got rid of some of the tension.

I thought of last week when Cash had thrown till his hand bled. I'd thought him crazy then, but something about the repetitive motion, the sound...it soothed me.

Maverick didn't do much more than offer a few pointers here and there. *"Make a bigger loop,"* and *"You didn't follow through with your hand"*. He didn't try to talk to me beyond that. It's like he knew what I'd needed before I even did.

"Alright. That's enough." Maverick's deep voice cut through the quiet of my mind.

I rolled up the rope as he walked to my side. He grabbed it from me and set it down on the dummy before reaching for my hand to examine it. "How're you feelin'?" he asked, though he kept his gaze on my blistered fingers.

I took a deep breath and exhaled slowly, my chest feeling lighter than it had all day. "How'd you know I needed this?"

He shrugged, finally meeting my gaze.

"So, we're back to the shruggin'?" I asked, thinking of that first night a little over a week ago. Dear Lord, it'd only been a week, but so much had happened.

Maverick dropped my hands, and my heart squeezed, my body aching for his touch. I hadn't lied, it was like a drug. And I was addicted.

To my complete and utter surprise, he gripped my chin and tilted it up to fully meet his gaze. "Now, let me try this again. I want you. All of you. Whatever you're willin' to give. I meant every word I said this mornin'—all of it. But I didn't want to just assume you wanted that too. You've got so much on your plate and I was just tryin' to give you space and be respectful."

Tears burned in my eyes, but I didn't try to wipe them away. As much as I hated people seeing my tears, hated how they made me feel weak, I wanted him to see them. I wanted him to know how much this moment meant to me.

"I want you too," I breathed. "I want to be with you. As far as I'm concerned, Nate isn't the father. You've been far more of a father to this baby already than he's been."

A soft smile blossomed on his lips, like the first rays of a sunrise. There was so much love and hope and happiness shining in his gaze it made my heart hurt.

"Why?" I asked softly. "Why are you willin' to do all this for me?"

His hand slid down to cup the side of my neck while he wrapped an arm around me and pulled me against his strong, hard body. "Because... I...well, I love you."

The breath left me, my knees going weak. Thank God he held me because I didn't have the strength in me to stand upright. He loved me? How? Why?

"How could you possibly love me? You don't even know me."

He ran his thumb over my bottom lip, his voice low and husky as he spoke. His eyes held a warmth and depth to them I'd never seen before. "I know plenty about you, Chey... I know you like chocolate chips on your pancakes, and licking cake batter out of the bowl. Your favorite song is "Me Against the Mountain" by Ian Munsick, and you love the color blue. But not light blue or navy, royal blue. You just might be able to outdrink Cash—" His lips pulled up a bit more. "And don't tell him this, but you rope better than him too. Also, contrary to what he might think, you're prettier."

I couldn't help the smile tugging on my lips even as tears slipped down my cheeks.

He wiped them away with his thumb as he continued on. "I know you like to sleep on your left side every night, and you scrunch your nose up when you're being flirty. You like bein' around people, but you also have your limits. You're the friendliest person I've ever met, but you are also stubborn as hell when you wanna be. Charlie and Ryder adore you, you and Cash may as well be twins, Bad likes you, and Aunt Violet approves..."

My heart could burst in that moment. He'd figured out all of this in just one week. All this time I'd thought his silence meant he'd been withdrawn into himself, and yet he'd been silently observing and learning about me.

"Time means nothin' to me, Cheyenne. Life's too short to wait for the perfect moment. Now, I ain't expectin' you to love me too. But I think you could, given time."

I shook my head, soft laughter falling from my lips as I smiled up at him. "You really are perfect, cowboy."

"Nah." He shook his head. "But I promise to be good to you." He moved back a half step, glancing down at my stomach, one of his hands hovering just above it. He looked to me, his gaze holding a silent question.

My head dipped in the smallest nod, my breath hitching in my chest, heart pounding so loudly, so wildly I didn't know how he didn't hear it. And as he placed his warm hand against my stomach, something in me just...shifted.

It's like the world had been off its axis, and in that moment, everything had been righted.

His deep voice reverberated through my bones, my veins, my very soul. "I promise to take care of you. To love you and this baby with all that I have...if that's what you want."

A pathetic sob escaped me as I placed a hand over his on my stomach, and as he pulled me in and kissed the breath from my lungs, that feeling of hope returned.

It blossomed in my stomach, in my heart, like wildflowers in the spring.

CHAPTER 36
Blue

MAVERICK

Six weeks.

Six weeks had come and gone. Cheyenne was officially out of her first trimester and well into the second. Though the only other person besides me who knew was Charlie still. As far as I could tell, Ryder didn't have a clue, for which I was ever grateful to Charlie.

She and Ryder had just made an official announcement the week before—a little baby boy due mid-February—and even though Cheyenne wouldn't admit it, I think a part of her longed for the ability to do that too.

She didn't want Nate finding out. I'd tried to tell her that there wasn't anything he could do. That being he was a part of the horse world as well, we'd likely run into him at some point, so why did it matter if he found out now or later.

But she was adamant on not doing an announcement. At least not right now.

But let me tell you, it was hard as hell keeping this a secret from Cash, Ryder, and Bad and Aunt Violet. I had no right to feel the level of happiness and excitement I did, but I wanted to share that with them anyway. And each day I had to keep it a secret from them grew harder and harder. Not to mention, it was getting more difficult for her to conceal with each passing week.

I think a part of her was scared. Scared to know how everyone would take it. Cash and Ryder would be thrilled. I honestly think Bad would be fine with it as well. The only wild card was Aunt Violet. I honestly didn't know how she'd react.

"Breakfast's ready," I called over the music playing through the house's speakers as I made her a plate of bacon and pancakes with chocolate chips on them. She wanted them damn near every morning, and Lord help me if I didn't have the stuff to make them. I'd known pregnancy hormones were a thing, but they could switch on and off at the most random things.

I'd learned real quick to keep an extra bag of chocolate chips in the pantry.

Cheyenne didn't answer. Though with the music on, I wasn't surprised. I placed her plate on the island and walked to our bedroom, halting in the doorway.

She stood almost diagonal to me, her profile on display as she turned this way and that, examining herself in the mirror. She wore a cobalt blue bra and matching underwear—my new favorite color—and her long, light blonde curls fell almost all the way down to her hips. She was absolutely stunning as the mid-morning sun shone in on her from the window, making her look like some sort of angel sent down to earth. But the most beautiful thing about the picture, the thing that took my breath away, was the swell of her stomach.

She'd started to show a few weeks ago, not to the point she couldn't hide it, but right now was the first time she really *looked* pregnant.

It knocked the breath from me. I can't even begin to describe just how fucking beautiful she was or what seeing her like that did to me. Like a moth to a flame, I found myself making my way up behind her. I pulled her back against me, placing a hand over her stomach, while trailing a path of kisses up along the curve of her neck.

"You're absolutely gorgeous," I murmured in her ear.

"Really?" I wondered if she even realized the nervousness in her voice. She met my gaze in the mirror for a moment before glancing at her stomach. "Even like this?"

I couldn't believe she was asking me that. She was absolutely gorgeous. "Especially like this," I replied, holding her gaze.

Her eyes sparked with surprise, her smile soft and full. She leaned back into me, her eyelids fluttering closed as we swayed to the music coming from the speakers.

"We should probably tell everyone," she said softly, breaking the quiet as she turned to face me. "At least your family."

My brow rose.

"I'm sick of tryin' to hide it. I don't know how Cash hasn't figured it out by now, and I'm tired of comin' up with lies for why I can't drink with him."

I nodded, trailing my fingertips up and down her back. "Okay, how do you wanna tell them?"

She shrugged. "Well, it's Thursday, which means game night. Might as well tell 'em then."

"Want me to invite Bad and Aunt Violet? Or should I wait?"

She chewed her lip. "How do you think they'll take it in person?"

I pursed my lips. "Bad'll be fine, I think. Shocked, but he'll deal with it well. Aunt Violet may be a bit prickly at first, but she'll come around quickly enough." My lips pulled up into what I hoped was a reassuring smile. "She's been all but beggin' Cash and I for grandbabies for years now."

Cheyenne's gaze still held a hint of worry, but she blew out a breath and nodded. "Okay. Let's set it up then."

CHAPTER 37
She's Alright

CHEYENNE

Cash's loud laughter echoed through the entire house. Dear Lord, how was he so damn loud? Ryder and Charlie's voices drifted into the room at a much lower rate. Aunt Violet and Bad were here by the sound of it as well.

I took a deep breath and fussed with my shirt in the mirror for the umpteenth time. It was weird, I typically wore tighter fitting clothes, but had been wearing more flowy, looser fabrics the past two weeks, not wanting to risk anyone noticing my bump, and now that I was wearing a fitted tank top and denim shorts, I felt almost paranoid. Like any second I was going to ruin this massive secret. But that was the whole point of tonight. Not having to hide this anymore. I knew it was killing Maverick, and not gonna lie, it sucked for me too. His friends and family had become a vital part of my life, and keeping this from them hurt.

I wasn't worried about Cash or Ryder finding out so much, but Mav's aunt and uncle were a completely different story.

They were the closest thing he had to parents. While Maverick's undying resolution and kindness literally knew no bounds and was admirable, to say the least, would they see this pregnancy as the great thing he seemed to think it was? Or would they hate me?

Might as well go and find out.

I walked into the living area, finding them all hanging out in the kitchen and connected dining room. Maverick hovered over the stove—typical. Cash already had a beer in hand. Also, typical. Ryder sat in one of the barstools at the island with his arm wrapped around Charlie who leaned against him, his hand protectively resting on her stomach.

I couldn't help but admire the two of them for a moment. They were such a gorgeous, striking couple. With his scar, her tattoos, and their blend and clash of fashion that just worked.

Aunt Violet fiddled around at Maverick's side while Bad hung back, leaning against one of the countertops while trying to get Cash's attention to sneak him a beer.

But Cash wasn't paying attention to his dad. Not as his hazel gaze flicked to mine, then my stomach, then back up again once more. "Now wait just a damn minute! When the fuck did you get pregnant? I just saw you earlier!"

It was like someone turned the volume off in the room. I swear to God, you could hear a pin drop as everyone turned to me.

A nervous laugh bubbled up my throat as I tucked a stray curl behind my ear. "Um...yeah. So...surprise."

Charlie flashed me a bright smile. Ryder's gaze was a bit more confused—almost like he was trying to figure out the math, but the math wasn't mathing with the size of my stomach—but overall, he looked genuinely happy despite that. Bad and Aunt Violet shared in their astonishment. But Cash's expression was the most noteworthy. If I didn't feel like my stomach was in my throat and I'd throw up at any minute, I might have laughed.

He made his way to me, his free hand immediately going to my belly as he prodded it like he needed to make sure it was actually real.

I smacked his hand away, letting out a disbelieving laugh. "What the hell, Mooney? You don't just touch people's stomachs!"

The thought of anyone touching my stomach aside from Maverick was so weird and foreign to me, but it wasn't surprising. Cash had no sense of boundaries. He bestowed a shit-eating smirk at me before glancing toward Maverick, who wore a possessive scowl on his face as he dried his hands off with a dish towel.

Cash's lips somehow pulled wider on his stupidly handsome face. "Y'all have been busy, I see."

That hit like a ton of bricks to the chest, bringing me right back down to reality. I couldn't meet anyone's gaze as I spoke—not even Maverick's. "Um...it's not his."

Well, if the silence in the room had been quiet enough to hear a pin drop, Aunt Violet's surprised gasp was louder than a train horn. "What do you mean?" Her words were fine enough, but there was an angry layer to her tone, mingled with the shock.

A warm hand wrapped around my waist before resting on the side of my stomach. I glanced up to meet Maverick's fierce gaze. I hadn't even noticed him make his way over. My chest constricted, fear and frustration and anxiety snaking around my heart like boa constrictors. It hurt to breathe. I opened my mouth to respond but it's like words failed me, leaving me floundering like a damn fish out of water.

Maverick's deep voice was like a balm to my soul. "Cheyenne's ex got her pregnant. She's gonna keep it, and we're gonna raise it up together."

We.

My heart fluttered at the thought. Out of both excitement and a hint of terror. If I was being completely honest, a part of me—one that grew smaller more rapidly by the day—still worried about the "we" part. Still worried whether or not I'd be able to stay settled in one place for the rest of my life. But Maverick proved nothing if not tenacious. He'd given me countless reasons to stay. Each and every day proving more and more what an amazing boyfriend and father he was already shaping up to be.

I think the only thing stopping Maverick's aunt from going absolutely ballistic was the fact Charlie and Ryder were there. Anger burned like hot coals in her eyes, her scowl saying everything she hadn't said aloud. Bad's usual easy grin—so similar to his son's—was drawn into a thin, straight line.

Well, that's just fuckin' great. I wasn't really surprised, though. I'd expected this.

Cash's low whistle drew my gaze. "Well, shit, man. You're gonna be a dad." He grinned at Maverick and held out a hand for his cousin to shake. Maverick hesitated only a moment before shaking it back. Cash's hazel stare flicked to me then. "Congratulations, Trouble. Kid's gonna have one kickass mom."

Tears lined my eyes, a broken little laugh escaping me. I hadn't expected Cash's approval to mean so much, but hearing it—without a trace of accusation—made my heart swell so much it hurt.

Charlie and Ryder came up to us next. "I'm so excited you decided to keep it!" she squealed as she wrapped me in a hug.

I grinned. "Well, you made a pretty convincin' argument with gettin' to raise up our babies together."

"Wait...you knew?" Ryder whirled to Charlie, shock ringing in his words. "And you didn't tell me?"

Charlie placed a hand on Ryder's chest. "Baby, it wasn't my place to say anything." She pressed a soft, apologetic kiss to his lips, stopping any argument from him.

Ryder offered her a soft look before turning back to me. "Congratulations. Kid's lucky to have parents as cool as y'all."

I grinned. "Not as cool as havin' a professional bull rider for a daddy, but thanks."

Charlie grinned, leaning into Ryder, whose hand tightened around her instinctively. "When're you due?" he asked.

"February second."

"Well shit, you're farther along than Charlie!" He laughed, shaking his head in disbelief.

I smiled and shrugged. "Only by a couple weeks."

Cash came up to my other side, cracking open a beer. I swear, it's like he pulled them out of thin air. "Aw, come on now... Y'all are makin' me feel left out. Maybe it's time Big Daddy becomes a daddy too."

"Cash Ulysses Mooney!" Aunt Violet's stern voice cut through the room like a whip. Murder shone in her gaze as she pegged him with a harsh glare. "You bite your tongue."

Cash's lips pulled up into an impish grin. "What? You're always talkin' bout how you want grand babies. I'd be doin' y'all a service."

I bit back a laugh at his name. Of course, he'd have some crazy middle name. But then I thought of the initials. "Wait..." *c...u...m*. No. *No fuckin' way.* "Your initials are C.U.M?"

Maverick groaned at my side while a hushed chuckle escaped Ryder. Charlie shook her head, even as a smile graced her lips. Cash's infamous grin shone brighter than a star exploding.

But Bad's answering smirk was the best. "It's what he started out as."

"Clint Mooney!" Aunt Violet gasped, placing a hand to her chest, horror marring her pretty features.

Bad answered with a chuckle and a shrug. "What? It's true."

———

THE ROOM DISSOLVED INTO THE USUAL CHAOS THAT consisted of any family gathering. I'd gotten used to their constant presence—for the most part.

Overall, the tension that accompanied my announcement vanished. But then I'd meet Aunt Violet's stare and my nerves would skyrocket. From the heated look in her gaze, she'd be pulling me aside at some point. I didn't know when, but I knew it was coming. I could feel it.

After asking at least a dozen times if I could help Maverick wash dishes and hearing about a dozen different excuses of why I couldn't, I finally made my way out onto the front porch. But not before hearing Aunt Violet's voice cut through the chaos. "Maverick, honey. You sure about this? This ain't like bringin' in some stray animal."

Anger sparked to life in my chest, like fire to a match. I wasn't looking for handouts. In fact, I'd already gotten my store back up and running and was trying as much as I could to contribute in any way I could with horse feed or groceries. But she was just being protective. I didn't blame her—not really.

I closed my eyes and tilted my head up at the dying sun, letting the weak rays tickle my cheeks with warmth.

July and August had been hot as hell, and if the weather kept up like this, September would turn out just the same. But the evenings brought the promise of cooler weather.

Leave. The whisper went through my mind and soul like a soft breeze. Wyoming or Montana would be nice right now. I looked back toward the door, my heart constricting in my chest. Blowing out a breath, I let the idea drift away.

I'd show Aunt Violet I wasn't going anywhere.

CHAPTER 38
Wonderin' Bout the Wind

MAVERICK

"**M**averick, honey. You sure about this? This ain't like bringin' in some stray animal."

Annoyance bristled in my chest. "Aunt Violet," I warned. I noticed movement in the corner of my eye. Looking up, I caught a glimpse of blonde curls disappearing through the front door.

Shit.

I wondered if Cheyenne going out had been a coincidence or because she'd heard Aunt Violet. She wasn't the quietest person. An overwhelming urge to go check in on Cheyenne rippled through my entire being. I was half tempted to turn off the water and leave the dishes in the sink so I could go to her.

"What?" Aunt Violet asked defensively. "I'm just concerned. What you're doin' is admirable...but I just...I'm worried for you."

I kept my gaze on the plate I washed and said, "you don't gotta."

"Maverick." Her tone held a pleading note to it that sparked both anger and guilt in me. They never worried about Cash, and we all knew he could use someone caring a bit more about the reckless decisions he made. Even still, I felt sick to my stomach knowing I worried her. But my temper won out in the end. I rinsed the plate and let it clatter onto the countertop. Rage bubbled within me, like boiling water in a pot. Silence settled through the house like a shroud, making me painfully aware of everyone's attention.

I met Aunt Violet's stare as I said, "I'm the one who urged her to keep it, okay? This was largely my idea."

"I know." Her gaze turned sad. "That's why I'm concerned."

"What're you sayin'?" I fought to keep my voice calm as rage pummeled into me like waves on the shoreline.

Aunt Violet's eyes begged for me to see reason. "You've clothed her, fed her, housed her. Now, you're gonna raise her baby? What if she leaves? You'll have no right to it. No claim to that child."

Her words stung—cutting deep and twisting like a dagger straight to the heart. I narrowed my gaze on her, the muscle in my jaw clenching. "It ain't gonna happen."

"Maverick—" Aunt Violet began.

"Leave it alone, Violet." Bad's voice held a warning note to it. He rarely used that tone—least of all with her—but when he did, you knew you were verging into hot water.

I met my uncle's stare for a long moment, but didn't find anger or worry or judgment shining in it like with Aunt Violet's. No, in the light depths, understanding flickered like a soft, warm fire.

Aunt Violet's voice drew my gaze. "Clint, stay out of this."

I nearly rocked back at the challenge in her voice. She never fought with Bad in front of us. Behind closed doors, yes. I'd heard the fights. But in public, they usually appeared as a unified front, for the most part.

Aunt Violet met my stare once more. "Look, I try not to get involved in you boys' affairs—"

Bad huffed, another warning in his gravelly tone. "So, don't."

She ignored him, continuing on as if he said nothing. "I like Cheyenne. I really do. She's funny, kind, beautiful." Aunt Violet's shoulder rose and fell in a guilty shrug. "But that girl's as wild as the wind. She may be smooth and steady right now, but she may be gone in the next minute, leavin' you in a cloud of dust."

I gritted my teeth as I clenched my fists at my sides, my fingernails digging into the meaty flesh of my palms. "I know."

"Do you?" She pegged me with a sad, yet stern stare. "Are you prepared for that very likely possibility, Maverick?"

Her words broke open the dam holding back the fears I fought so hard to keep at bay every day. They roared to the surface, breaking through the cracked infrastructure.

Of course, I knew how fragile this situation was. Of course, I knew that I could wake up one day and she'd be gone without a trace. All I could do now was hope and pray that she had enough reason to stay.

That *I* could be enough reason to stay.

Drawing on every ounce of dwindling calm I possessed, I sucked in a breath. Returning my aunt's stare, I made sure my voice, my words didn't hold a shred of doubt. "I understand your fears, Aunt Violet... and I know you're just tryin' to look out for me. But this is my life, my choice. I love her and that baby, and I'll do whatever it takes to make them happy. I need you to respect my decision."

We stared at each other in silence for a long moment. Everyone in the room looked at us to see who would break first. Aunt Violet may be strong and stubborn and fierce like the waves, but I was the cliff she crashed against—unmovable. There was no way in hell I'd break first.

She breathed deeply, her gaze softening as a chink formed in her protective armor. With a sigh, she opened her arms to me and pulled me into a hug. "My sweet boy," she murmured as she held me.

Most of my anger melted away as I hugged her back.

She pulled away and cupped one of my cheeks as she looked up at me. With a sad smile, she whispered, "I hope she deserves you."

But Aunt Violet had it all wrong. It wasn't about who deserved the other more. This was a team, a partnership. We were only as strong as the other. Cheyenne and I might not have been together long, but we worked well together. We played to each other's strengths. We made each other better.

CHAPTER 39
Giving Up On That

CHEYENNE

The front door opened and shut, the scent of magnolias filling the air. Aunt Violet.

I turned to meet her gaze as she came to my left side. I wouldn't say it was as hot as coals, like it had been earlier, but it definitely lacked the usual warmth I'd grown accustomed to. She sucked in a breath, no doubt readying herself for the tirade I knew was coming, so I spoke before she could.

"Look, with all due respect, Mrs. Mooney, if you've come out here to scold me, you can save your breath. I already know what you're gonna say." I said on a sigh.

I just wanted to get this over with. I was exhausted, both physically and emotionally. Hopefully everyone would leave soon so that I could soak in the tub—preferably with Maverick—and then snuggle in bed while he ran his fingers through my hair until I fell asleep. It had become almost a nightly ritual, and the thought of it now brought a sense of longing to my chest.

Aunt Violet scowled, one of her brows rising in challenge. "Oh, and what exactly do think that is?"

I blew out a breath, letting my eyes flutter closed for a moment before replying, "You think I'm using Maverick. Taking advantage of his kindness for my own personal gain. You think I'm no better than Ashleigh." I finally leveled her with my gaze—far calmer than I actually felt.

She pursed her lips, her head tilting to the side ever so slightly.

I nodded. "Yeah, that's what I thought... Look, I don't blame you for thinkin' that. I would think the exact same thing if I were in your shoes. But believe me when I tell you, I have no plans on hurtin' your nephew."

She let out a sigh. "I know you have no plans to, but that don't mean he ain't gonna get hurt."

I didn't know what to say. We were at an impasse. A crossroads with a dead-end on either side. Nothing I said would change her mind. Only actions. So, I just lifted my shoulders in a shrug and said, "I'm gonna make this work with him, whether you believe it or not."

"I hope so," she replied softly, coming to lean against the railing beside me. Crossing her arms over her chest she continued, "I like you, Cheyenne. I really do. But I know your kind."

"My kind?" I scoffed.

She didn't know me. She hardly knew anything about me.

"You gotta gypsy soul, and it takes you wherever the winds may roam. Tryin' to tie you down and keep you in one place is like ropin' in the wind. Damn near impossible."

I opened my mouth...to say what actually? She wasn't entirely wrong. My whole life had been on the go, Texas had been the first state I'd stayed in more than a couple months. But even still, in the past couple years, I'd lived all over the state.

"I'm not gonna leave him," I finally settled on saying.

Her disbelieving look spoke volumes.

"I mean it," I continued. "I'm stayin'."

"Even in a few months from now? Or a year? Maybe five years? Are you gonna stay with him for the long haul?"

I thought of Maverick. Of our blossoming relationship. We worked well together, and living with him was far easier than I'd ever expected. And he meant the world to me.

"Yes."

A flicker of surprise flashed in her gaze, some of the anger melting away. "Do you love him?"

I thought of his admission to me six weeks ago now. He proved each and every day how much he loved me and this baby. And I loved him. Though, I'd been too scared to admit it.

I'd never told a boyfriend I loved them. Never. Honestly, I hardly ever stayed in a relationship long enough to get to that point. I think deep down, some part of me was scared to be that vulnerable, to open myself up *that* much to another person.

Keeping my chin up, my head held high, I said with certainty, "I do."

Some of the harsh lines in the corners of her eyes softened. "Then tell him. Tell him every day. As much as you can. Maverick's the strongest man I've ever known, but it's the strong ones who need the most remindin'."

"I will," I said with a nod.

I don't know what she saw or heard in my eyes or voice, but it seemed enough to satisfy her. With a nod of her own, she turned and left me alone on the front porch.

Well, that was fun.

My heart fluttered anxiously against my ribcage still, trying and failing to calm after that stressful conversation. I tried to focus on my breathing, taking slow, deep inhales in before blowing them out.

Why was this harder than it had been telling my own dad? He'd congratulated me, told me he'd be making a trip out from Mexico or Hawaii or wherever the hell warm tropical place he'd decided to vacation at, and that was that. No judgment. No questioning. It'd been so much easier.

The door creaked open once more and my hopes rose like the swell of an ocean wave thinking it was Maverick, only for my dismay to plummet down once more as Bad came out instead.

His hazel gaze landed on me, his lips pulling up into a hint of a smirk. "Easy girl. I ain't comin' out here to scold ya."

"Your wife already did that," I huffed, the words falling from my lips before I could stop them. I clamped a hand over my mouth at the admission.

Bad chuckled and waved me off before making his way off the front porch and onto the gravel driveway. He gestured with a nod for me to follow. I did. Not only was I probably one of his biggest fans and just the thought of being in his presence was the coolest thing ever, but also, when Bad said something, you listened.

He didn't talk for a few moments, the only sounds that of the gravel crunching beneath our feet and the cicadas screeching in the trees. "You know what the baby is?"

I shook my head, examining my cow print slip-ons as I walked. "No. Maverick and I went to this place to have an ultrasound that tells you the gender, but we've been waitin' to open the envelope."

"How come you haven't opened it yet?" No accusation, no confusion, just pure curiosity.

I glanced over at him. "I don't know, honestly. I think I'm scared."

"Why?"

"I don't know. Maybe because then it just makes it even more real."

He huffed a laugh, jerking his chin toward my stomach. "That's as real as it gets there, girl. It don't make no difference what that baby comes out as."

"So, you weren't scared of havin' one over the other?" I'd been stressing about what the baby was. A girl hopefully meant cute outfits and hairstyles and adorable sassiness, but it also meant boy drama and girl problems, and periods, and catty friends and sassiness aimed at me. Boys had their whole slew of issues as well, though.

"Oh, I was scared as hell at the idea of both, but in the end, it don't matter. You got no control, so why bother worryin' about it? You get what you get, and you raise 'em up with the same morals, respect, and kindness you would if it was a boy of girl."

A soft smile toyed on my lips. "Wise words."

Another huff from him. Silence fell over us for another moment or so before he spoke again. "I ain't the type to put my two cents in to places where it ain't asked for, but I'm gonna offer you some now. Take it, leave it. I don't care."

I watched him as we walked, a silent request for him to continue.

"A lot of people are gonna have a lotta shit to say about you, Maverick, and that baby. They're gonna tell you all sorts of things, and try to make you do what they say..." He met my gaze. "You don't listen to a damn word of it unless you and Maverick feel it's right. Ain't nobody gonna be an expert on that baby the way you are. Not me. Not Charlie or Ryder. Not even Violet. And for the love of God, not Cash." I chuckled at that. "That's your baby and you do what's best for it."

I nodded. There was something so oddly soothing about his gruff, gravelly voice. In the last few moments, all the tension I'd been carrying around melted like snow in the spring sun.

"Your parents know?" he asked.

"I told my daddy. He's happy. I haven't talked to my mama since she left when I was four."

He nodded, but didn't press. For which I was grateful. Talking to him reminded me a lot of talking to Maverick. Neither man pressed and prodded for information, but they had a way of making you *want* to talk to them.

"Give Violet a few days and she'll cool down. She might blaze bright and hot at the beginning, but the good thing about her is she simmers down real quick."

"You sure about that?" I asked in disbelief.

He chuckled as we came to a stop by the pond's edge. I hadn't even noticed we'd moved from the gravel to the grass. The last rays of the dying sunlight cast a weak reflection on the pond's relatively smooth surface. Bending over, he grabbed a stray rock and bounced it off the water, causing it to skip three times before making a splash. "I've been with that woman for damn near forty years. Trust me. Give it a few days and you'll be wishin' she was still mad at you. She'll be talkin' baby names and plannin' your shower by the end of the week, I guarantee it."

I watched as he picked up another rock and wound his arm back before letting it fly. This was my hero, my idol growing up. I'd spent so many years as a child imagining what I'd ever do if I ever met him, and here I was not only talking to him, but talking about me and my baby, no less.

He'd managed to somehow replace all of the anxious energy within me and turn it to calm just by his presence. Picking up a rock as well, I mirrored his actions. For a while, him and I just stood there, neither of us talking, just throwing rocks.

It was dark by the time I finally said, "Thank you."

He paused mid-throw, meeting my stare. "For what?"

I didn't even have the words really. For calming me down, for taking me away from the party to have a moment, for being as awesome of a person as I'd always imagined him to be. "For everythin', I guess."

His brow rose.

I huffed a nervous laugh, tucking a curl behind my ear and shrugged. "They always it's never good to meet your heroes, cuz you always end up disappointed, but I'm glad to have met you, Mr. Mooney. I'm even more glad that I get to date and have this baby with your nephew."

His features softened, even as his eyes sparked with amusement. "Hero? Girl, you need to find yourself some better heroes."

I laughed. "Nope. You'll do just fine. I don't think I'd get as lucky a second time."

He chuckled as we started back for the house. His voice reminded me of the gravel we walked on as he said, "So, I was really your hero?"

"I knew all of your stats for years. Went to every rodeo you were competin' in that I could get to. I forced my daddy to take me to NFR your final year."

He laughed. "You were just a little thing then, weren't you?"

"I may have been little, but Daddy knew there was no changin' my mind once I got an idea."

He laughed. "Tenacious... I like it."

I smiled, pride swelling in me that Clint "Bad" Mooney called me tenacious with a smile on his face.

———

EVERYONE LEFT SHORTLY AFTER BAD AND I GOT BACK FROM our little walk. My heart didn't feel so heavy, and even though the tension remained thick between Aunt Violet and I, Bad's words echoed through my mind. *"Give Violet a few days and she'll cool down."*

Charlie and Ryder left quickly after Cash's parents. They'd had to pick up Cason from his friend's house. Getting rid of Cash had been a bit harder, but after Maverick threatened to wake him up at the ass-crack of dawn to do chores, Cash let Maverick drive him back down the road to his house. He'd drank half a twelve pack in the course of the night.

There were no dishes to wash—thanks to Maverick and his aunt—so, with nothing else to do and a house to myself...well, aside from Brandy, I made my way to the bathroom to soak in the tub.

The hot water soothed my muscles, as the essential oil bath bomb and Epsom salts soothed my soul. Listening to my favorite country station on the house speakers, I closed my eyes and settled deeper into the tub.

Brandy's toenails clicking against the tile floor in excitement were the only indicator Maverick had returned. It still amazed me how someone as strong and powerful could move so quietly.

"Well, aren't you a sight for sore eyes?" His deep voice sent shivers shuttering down my spine. I opened heavy lids to take him in. Dear Lord, he was sexy as hell in his usual getup—black on black on black.

I smiled. "You gonna join me?"

His eyes burned with want and need, his lips curving up into a sensual grin, but he shook his head and nodded at the plate in his hands. "Not yet. I made you somethin'."

I sat up in the tub, examining what he'd brought. A cake. Probably vanilla or buttercream, maybe even cream cheese from the light frosting—my favorite. "You cannot keep spoilin' me like this, Mav. I'm gonna end up bein' the size of a house," I teased, even as I gestured for him to come closer.

He obliged, much to my delight, offering me a fork as well. "You could eat a million cakes and you still wouldn't be the size of a house."

God, he was so perfect and sweet. I grabbed the utensil from him and looked at the cake he offered me.

"You sure you don't want to cut me off a piece? I feel bad just diggin' in with a fork."

He shrugged. "I made it just for you anyways."

One of my eyebrows quirked up. Okay, super sweet. But... "Why?"

Another shrug. "I just wanted to." *A man of many words.*

I eyed him and the cake for a moment longer. "You're sure it's okay to just take a bite?"

"Chey, eat the damn cake." His tone held a warm, playful note to it, but beneath that there was a layer of finality. I didn't argue as I stuck my fork in and cut out a chunk. My heart froze mid bite as I noticed the color of the cake itself...

My chest tightened. Excitement and fear and disbelief and so many other emotions I couldn't even begin to comprehend or explain swelling and rising in my chest like a tsunami. I swallowed the bite in my mouth. "Oh my God..."

Pink. The cake was pink.

"Is this...did you make me a gender reveal cake?" My heart beat faster than hummingbird wings.

His lips pulled up into a soft, bashful grin, his eyes holding a mixture of hope and worry in them. "I made it just in case you wanted to do it tonight...but with how the night went, I figured you wouldn't want to make it a big deal."

Oh my God. A girl. Both elation and fear danced along with my thumping heart in my ribcage. I was having a girl.

"Maverick..." I breathed.

I had no words. Nothing to explain just what this man's actions did to me. Tears brewed in my eyes like summer storms, my throat tightening with emotion.

This man...this perfect, wonderful man who managed to keep the gender from me for over two weeks. Who managed to bake me a cake without me even realizing it. Who managed to give me the sweetest most intimate and meaningful gender reveal I could ever imagine...

I didn't deserve him.

His face fell, his shoulders sagging as he placed the plate on the countertop, mistaking my inability to speak as unhappiness, no doubt. "I'm sorry. I shoulda asked before I went and did somethin'. I didn't think you'd wanna do a big ol' party for the reveal. I—I'm sorry."

I shook my head, wiping the tears that slipped down my cheeks before reaching for him. "Come here," I choked out, my voice failing me.

But actions always were easier for us.

Like a magnet, he gravitated toward me, clutching my hand in his.

"Get in," I whispered, pleaded.

He undressed slowly. First, his cowboy hat that he placed upside down on the countertop beside the pink-filled cake. Then his long-sleeve button up and his undershirt, putting his beautiful scars on full display. He'd stopped hesitating when he bared them to me. I still couldn't fathom why he'd be ashamed of them at all. One day, I'd make him feel comfortable enough to not wear a long-sleeve all together. But for now...baby steps.

He settled into the tub opposite me, but he wouldn't meet my gaze, not completely. Situating myself onto my knees, I leaned forward and tilted his chin up. "Thank you," I murmured, pressing a whisper-soft kiss to his lips.

His hands came up to rest against my cheeks, the familiarness doing something to my body, my very soul. "You ain't mad?" There was so much worry and fear in his words, in his frown and the furrow of his dark brows.

I offered him a warm smile, situating myself in his lap more comfortably as I held his bright jade gaze. "How could I ever be at you for that?"

"I didn't ask first. Was what I did okay?"

I shook my head, a disbelieving chuckle escaping me. "You somehow managed to bake an entire cake without me noticin', and the reveal couldn't be more intimate and perfect and exactly what I wanted. I don't care if other people find out, but I wanted this moment to be special for you and I." I glanced at the pink cake for only a moment before rising from the tub.

"What're you—" But his words trailed off as I grabbed the plate and climbed back into the tub. Straddling him once more, I cut off a piece of cake and held it out to him.

"You're gonna be a girl dad," I said, smiling.

I swear, tears welled in his eyes, a small, disbelieving smile curving his lips. He opened his mouth, closed it. Opened it again. A soft smile of my own tugged on my mouth at seeing him so at a loss for words. "I love you, Maverick Holstrom, and I sure as hell don't deserve you. But I'm glad me and this little girl have you."

Some emotion I couldn't quite place rippled across his face—

elation, fear, awe, unworthiness...they bled so seamlessly together, I wasn't really sure. It's almost like he didn't believe this could possibly be happening to him. So, the moment he took the bite I offered him and met my stare was like a moment of acceptance that caused a shift in me.

My life would be forever changed. Not just because I was pregnant. Not just because I was choosing to have this baby with him. I had never known what anyone meant when they said things like "home is where the heart is", but I was starting to now.

It was with him.

It should have terrified me. Made me run for the hills. I think with any other man it would have. But with him... For the first time, the thought of settling down, of spending the rest of my life with one person didn't make that part of my soul that longed to be free grow wary. In this moment, none of the fears or worries or frustrations of life could bring me down.

I rode the high of happiness as we fed each other cake, as we fucked in the tub to my favorite country songs, as he pulled me into his arms once we'd gotten in bed and he ran his fingers through my hair until we'd fallen asleep. And the whole time I couldn't help but thinking that this just might be my own personal heaven.

CHAPTER 40
Break My Bones

MAVERICK

Aunt Violet came around quicker than even I'd expected.

Not even two days passed before she was blowing up my phone with baby names and ideas for a shower. Almost a week later and I was convinced Cheyenne would go crazy from all the attention.

"God, your aunt's relentless," Cheyenne said, walking into the barn while sliding her phone into the side of her bra. Her spurs clinked against the dirt as she grabbed a halter and headed for the little red filly's stall.

"What happened?" I asked.

Cheyenne tossed her hands up in the air in frustration, blowing out a loud breath. The filly snorted, pacing at the back of her stall. I eyed her for a long moment. Hopefully she calmed down. The thought of Cheyenne working the baby still was admirable, but unnecessary, and it made me uneasy. So much could happen, none of it good.

Cheyenne didn't have anything to prove. She didn't need the money; I was more than capable of providing for all three of us. But she was set on doing this still, and some battles just weren't worth fighting with her, I'd quickly come to realize.

"She really, really, really likes the name Hyacinth or however the fuck you say it, and no matter how many times I try to explain that I am absolutely not naming my child that, she just doesn't get it."

I grimaced as I brushed down my project colt, Blue Zeus. "That is a god-awful name."

"Right?" Cheyenne pulled the latch on the stall door and slipped inside before closing it behind her. "And it's not like she has horrible taste because there's nothing wrong with Cash's name. And what's his brother's name again?"

"True," I replied, my hand stilling on Zeus's back as I watched the filly pace some more.

"True. An interesting, unique name...not Hyacinth. And what's worse?" She glanced at me. "She wants to call her Cinthy for short."

Cheyenne made her way to the stall, struggling for only a moment to catch the nameless filly. And while the horse didn't spook or rear or do anything wild and crazy, I didn't like the tension in her muscles, the position of her ears.

If Cheyenne noticed the filly's uneasiness, she didn't let on. Which worried me. She had a way with animals, she really did. She was smart and intuitive and she and the horse seemed to do really well together. But something didn't feel right.

"She seems a little flighty today. You sure you wanna work her?" I asked.

Cheyenne shrugged. "She seems fine to me."

I frowned, but Cheyenne knew the horse more than I did at this point. She came out religiously every mid-morning and early evening to work with her. Saddling her, desensitizing her to sounds, materials, environments.

Maybe I was just being overprotective. I felt like I had good reason to, though. Another week gone and her bump was becoming more pronounced. I'd never been more attracted to her. But seeing how far along she was and knowing that what she was doing had the potential for disastrous consequences scared the hell out of me.

I bit my tongue. *She's gonna do what she wants to do.*

She led the filly outside, disappearing through the barn doors. I heard the hinges creak open on the round pen before creaking closed once more.

I continued brushing Blue Zeus down, telling myself I wouldn't go out and hover. This was her deal, her horse. I wanted—no, needed to respect that. But each moment I spent inside with the blue roan colt sent my heart rate pumping faster and faster. By the time I put him in his stall, hung his halter, and walked out of the barn, I was pretty sure I might have a damn heart attack.

The dying sun cast the round pen in a sea of burning orange light, bright enough that I still had to shield my eyes even with my sunglasses on. The filly loped around the arena, snorting and breathing heavily. Her tail was erect, ears in a position I still wasn't entirely too happy with, but I didn't say anything as I took a seat on one of the mounting blocks and watched them.

the filly settled into her warm up, and some of the worry knotted tight in my chest loosened a bit. Maybe I was just being paranoid. I noticed Cash rolling up the road in the old piece of shit ranch truck he demanded we bring from his parents' house. As much as I hated the thing, it had come in handy on numerous occasions—if you could get the thing running.

He seemed to notice us as well, angling the truck over toward the barn.

"Hey! Think you can help me with this damn thing. It's makin' some weird ass noises," he called, leaning damn near half way out of the truck. As he lumbered to a stop, a loud popping noise erupted from it, echoing off the barn and making the plague of Grackles resting in the trees fly away.

The filly's squeal drew my attention. She galloped around the pen, tossing her head, pinning her ears. Terror clenched me like a vice as she tore straight at Cheyenne. Fuck. Fuck. Fuck.

Cheyenne dodged the horse, climbing up the pipe-stall with swift speed, but it was too close of a call for my taste.

"Get the hell out of the arena!" I bellowed, my heart a panicked staccato reverberating through my ears, my veins, my bones.

I felt the heat of her glare from where I stood. "Excuse me?"

"Get out," I repeated, my tone unyielding.

To my surprise, she did. "What the fuck is the issue?" she spat, coming to stand before me with a hand on her hip, a defiant look shining in her turquoise gaze.

I couldn't let her get hurt. I'd never forgive myself if something happened to her. "You ain't workin' that filly anymore," I replied, hoping she wouldn't question the decision.

But that wasn't the girl I was dating. She was wild and reckless, fury and flame. She was gasoline and the lighter. "Like fuckin' hell I'm not."

"Cheyenne, you damn near got trampled just now." I whirled a hand toward the round pen where the horse still trotted around, snorting and swishing her tail.

She rolled her eyes. "I was fine. It was Cash's stupid truck. If you're gonna be mad at anyone, be mad at him."

I wasn't mad at either of them, but at the whole situation. At the lack of control I felt over the events that had just unfolded. With a sigh, I said, "I don't want you workin' with that horse." It wasn't that I didn't trust Cheyenne, but the filly was a completely different story.

Her lips drew into a scowl, her brows furrowing together. "Why? She's been fine up until just now."

I shook my head. So, she hadn't noticed the horse's tension earlier. It told me all I needed to know. "The minute you grabbed that horse's halter, she started actin' funny. Why'd you think I mentioned somethin' in the barn?"

"Okay, so I missed that. I would hardly say that justifies takin' my damn horse away."

"It does when it's my horse and your actions put you and *that* baby in danger."

Her gaze on me narrowed, her eyes blue infernos that held the heat of a thousand suns. Well, shit. If I wanted to piss her off, I'd definitely accomplished that.

"Hey, now y'all. Let's not fight." Cash came between us, his voice holding a mocking calmness to it. I knew what he was trying to do, what he so often did with great success, but I wasn't in the mood for his antics.

"Cash, not now."

His hazel gaze widened a moment, a look of shock settling around him. With a nod, he walked back to the truck and sat himself in the driver's seat. Thank fuck, I'd expected more of a fight.

"That's bullshit," she snarled at me. "I've been workin' my ass off makin' progress with this horse and you want me to just stop workin' her?"

"It's my horse, Chey."

Even as I said the words, a part of me knew I was going too far. But I didn't know what to do to make her see how foolish this was. If she was going to be careful, attentive, and smart then fine. But she'd proven tonight she wasn't paying enough attention, and all it took was one wrong move, one tiny, little misstep and she and the baby could end up hurt. It wasn't a risk I was willing to take.

Downright fury blazed from her. "Fine, I'll buy her from you," she countered, crossing her arms over her chest.

"She ain't for sale."

Cheyenne growled in frustration, throwing her hands down at her sides. "Fuckin' hell, Maverick! You're such a goddamn control freak!" With that she stomped away. I took a step to follow. "Don't you fuckin' dare come after me right now. If you know what's good for you, you'll leave me the hell alone for a while," she shouted, not even bothering to look back.

I watched her stalk towards the road to our place, her footfalls becoming quieter and quieter the further she got. With each step, my guilt grew, replacing the fear and anger.

"What the hell happened?" Cash asked.

I whirled to him. When had he gotten out of the truck? I hadn't even heard him close the door. Ripping my cowboy hat off to rub at my brow, I grumbled out, "I fucked up."

"How?"

I recounted the events to him. Cheyenne's inattention, the horse's nerves. All of it. It still sounded bad, but maybe I'd overreacted a bit.

Cash shrugged when I finally finished. "So, she fucked up. She's human, you can't let her not ride cuz of one mistake."

"But she's pregnant. What if she gets hurt?"

"What if she falls in the shower? What if she trips over that damn dog of hers that's always on her heel? You gonna not let her bathe or get rid of the dog because of a *what if*?"

"That's the..." My words drifted off as I looked at him, shaking my head in disbelief. "Smartest thing I think I've heard you say in years."

Cash chuckled. "I was due for a word of wisdom. You're welcome."

I rolled my eyes but I couldn't hide the small grin on my lips as I righted my hat on my head once more. "I should probably go apologize."

Cash placed a hand on my shoulder. "Give her some time to cool down a bit."

"You just want my help with your damn truck."

He grinned and shrugged, not even bothering to hide his intentions. "Might as well kill two birds with one stone."

I shook my head but waved a hand in the truck's direction. "Alright, let's see what the hell's wrong with this piece of shit."

"Hey now, don't talk about her that way... She's sensitive," Cash said defensively, going so far as to stroke the truck's rusted hood as we came to its side.

I may not be able to fix or control the situation with Cheyenne at the moment, but I sure as hell knew I could fix this problem.

When Cash and I got back to my house, Cheyenne wasn't there, though Brandy was. Cash mentioned something about noticing Charlie's Tacoma heading toward my place earlier, so they must have gone off somewhere. I pulled out my phone to check in with Cheyenne when I noticed a message.

Chey: Went to dinner with Charlie. Be back later.

Well, that answered that.

As much as I wanted to talk to her and make things right, I was glad she could spend this time with Charlie. It was good they had each other through this. Lord knows, I didn't have all the answers, and she needed time with her friends.

I turned to Cash. "Well, Cheyenne's out at dinner with Charlie, so what do you wanna do?"

Cash's face lit up. "How 'bout a boy's night?"

"First," I said, grabbing a Coke out of the fridge, "Ryder ain't here and I'm in no mood to deal with your antics alone. And second, it's a Wednesday night."

"So? Everyday's a party if you want it to be."

I huffed a laugh, taking a long sip of my drink. "Wanna practice?"

"We rode earlier," Cash groaned, reminding me more of a child than a twenty-seven-year-old man.

"Yeah, and we looked like shit. We got a rodeo comin' up in a week, and if we rope anythin' like how we did today, we're fucked."

Cash rolled his eyes, making his way to the fridge to grab himself a beer. Just like Chey's chocolate chips, I always made sure to keep at least a six pack in the fridge. "Fine...but I'm hungry."

"How 'bout I cook up some steaks and you call your dad and see if him and Goodie wanna come over and work the chute?"

"Well, it ain't as good as bangin' buckle bunnies, but it'll do. Make sure not to burn mine like last time."

I narrowed my gaze on him. "I don't burn things...ever."

Cash's shit-eating grin lit up the room.

It'd been a while since it was just him and I. Since Chey had moved in, she and I were together a lot. Not that I minded. I enjoyed her company, but even if Cash was obnoxious and annoying as hell, he was my brother in all the ways that mattered. And I could always count on him for a good laugh or a distraction. After the little spat with Cheyenne, I needed both.

CHAPTER 41
Found Your Love

CHEYENNE

The arena lights were on when we got back to Mercenary Ranch.

"They must be practicin'."

I'm sure that was all Maverick's doing. Cash was one of those annoyingly talented people who could fuck off all day long, then kick ass the minute he set his mind on it. Then there was Maverick.

Maverick, who didn't strive for good. Didn't strive for great...but perfection. Maverick was the kind of person who mastered every single thing he did. I wish I had the patience for that, but my mind just got tired after a while.

"Wanna watch Uncle Mav and Funcle Cash ride, Cason?" Charlie called over her shoulder.

I watched Cason bob his head up and down excitedly in the rear-view mirror. "Can we get Dutch and Brandy first?"

If Cason was home, it was more than likely the three of them were together. So, after swinging by the houses to grab the dogs, we made our way to the barn and parked beside the old ranch truck.

A familiar, harsh and gravelly tone sliced through the warm night like a blade as he spewed a whole string of curses, bringing a smile to my face. Looked like Bad was here. An answering chuckle, and a voice completely opposite—smooth and suave, with an undercurrent of arrogance. Goodie.

I always enjoyed any time Goodie and Bad were together. They're dynamic was so intriguing, so amusing. Bad was brash, unapologetic, and rough around the edges, while Goodie was tempered, diplomatic, a true businessman.

"Well, look who decided to join us. Or are you too cool for us now, Mister Cason?" Bad turned from his spot atop the pipe-stall. Cash and Maverick were herding a steer through one of the gates on the far end of the arena.

Cason's cheeks blazed red, and he dipped his head, a muffled, "Sorry," escaping him.

"Hey, it was your son's bright idea to sign him up for flag football," Charlie said, wrapping a reassuring arm around her nephew's shoulders. She'd made him get rid of the mullet—correction, his school had made him get rid of the mullet—so Cash and Ryder decided, stupidly, to cut his hair for him.

They'd absolutely butchered it, to the point Charlie ended up taking a set of clippers and just buzzing it short. It was still a bit of a shock not seeing his head of dark, chocolatey colored hair, but it did make his blue eyes pop.

Bad's harsh features warmed into a smile. "I'm just messin', kid. You ready for your game this weekend?"

Cason nodded, finally meeting Bad's gaze.

"Good. How 'bout you go on and get ol' Peckerhead out of his stall and tack him up? You wanna ride a bit?"

Cason was already sprinting toward the barn before Bad even finished.

I smiled at his retreating figure. He was a cute kid. A *good* kid. So good it made me worry that I wouldn't get so lucky. Would my little girl be a sweet little thing like Cason, or a little hell raiser?

Knowing how I was as a child, I'd bet on the latter.

"How's that little filly comin'?" Bad asked, looking down at me as I settled beside him against the pipe-stall.

I cast a glance at Maverick. If he heard, he made no indication. But he was setting up in the box for the steer Goodie loaded into the chute. A look of pure determination made up his brutally handsome features. I doubted he heard.

I was still annoyed about our little argument earlier, but after having some time to calm down and Charlie to talk some sense into me, I wasn't bubbling with anger. Maybe just a low simmer.

The truth is, I could have handled the situation better, but I was angry and embarrassed and frustrated. And worse, I hated that Maverick called me out. Because I *should* have noticed her behavior. I *should* have gotten my emotions under control before dealing with her. I'd been frustrated and emotional about Aunt Violet's damn near constant barrage of phone calls—since she refused to text—about baby names. And it's not that I wasn't grateful, since I didn't have a mother to share in all of this excitement with, but not gonna lie, it was a bit—okay, a lot —overwhelming.

I glanced at Bad, noting the questioning look on his face. What had he asked me? Oh, yeah...

"The filly's comin' along well," I replied.

"I'm surprised Mav's even lettin' you anywhere near her."

Had Maverick not told him? I was honestly a bit surprised he hadn't. Maverick and Bad talked. A lot. Far more than I'd expect for someone as quiet as Maverick. But either Bad was just playing dumb, or he genuinely didn't know about the argument his nephew and I had just gotten into.

"Maverick doesn't *let* me do anythin'. I'm breakin' that filly and I don't need his permission."

Bad's green-gold gaze swirled with amusement. He whistled low before it broke off into a chuckle. "Well, aren't you fiery, tonight?"

Some of the annoyance from earlier returned, though I didn't burn as bright as before. I settled my gaze on the arena and watched Cash and Maverick do a few runs. They worked together in perfect unison. I'd seen plenty of family members rope together, but there was something almost surreal about how well they complimented each other.

"What's different about Maverick?" Charlie's soft, lilting voice gave me pause.

I looked at him with a more assessing eye.

That's when I noticed it.

My heart stopped. Skipped a whole damn beat, or maybe even three.

He wasn't wearing a long-sleeve. Nope, it was nothing more than a simple black cotton t-shirt, his muscled arms on full display. I couldn't make out the scars from the distance, but I could imagine them in my mind, like I'd memorized every beautiful ridge and canyon.

Pride and happiness surged to life in my heart.

What had made him change? When I left, he'd been wearing a long-sleeve. But it *was* hot out still. Maybe he'd decided to stop being self-conscious and change into something more comfortable. Even if it was only in front of his family.

But the fact he was even wearing a t-shirt at all chased away any lingering annoyance I felt. I wanted to run out into the arena, pull him down from Black Betty, and kiss him stupid.

My cheeks hurt from how wide my smile pulled on my face as I said, "He's not wearin' a long-sleeve."

"That's it?" Charlie asked, before nodding to herself. "I guess you're right. I don't think I've ever seen him in anything but long-sleeves."

I didn't look at her as I spoke. No, my gaze was glued to Maverick. "It's because of the scars."

"Oh, from the accident." It wasn't so much a question as a statement.

Bad's gravelly voice managed to pull my gaze from my hot as hell boyfriend. "I think I can count on one hand the number of times I've even seen a glimpse of 'em." He looked at me, wonder and a bit of awe in his gaze. "I don't know what you've done to that boy, but I like it."

Charlie smiled and nudged me. "Look at you working your magic on him."

I laughed and rolled my eyes. "It ain't magic, just confidence."

The truth is, I wasn't doing anything to Maverick other than loving him, appreciating him, showing him with my words and my body how truly amazing he was.

He was the one with the magic in him, I just gave him a reason to shine.

———

CHARLIE AND I HUNG AROUND AS THE ROPING PRACTICE turned into a lesson for Cason. All four men took turns offering him bits of advice, though the most vocal by far were Bad and Maverick. While they both had different methods—Bad was more concerned about the overall experience, whereas Maverick was zoned in on tweaking the small details—the two taught well together, complementing one another's strengths and weaknesses. Bad had a short temper and attention span; Maverick was calmer, but tended to get a little too hyper fixated on individual issues. I knew they were related, not by blood... But it still surprised me how similar they were.

By the time Cason's lesson ended, it was nearly nine.

"Alight, bud. I think we should call it a night," Charlie called from my side. "You still got school tomorrow."

Cason had just slid out of the saddle when a car with blinding headlights tore up the dirt road toward the barn.

"Who the fuck is that this late at night?" Bad grumbled, his brow furrowing.

I glanced at Cash. "One of yours?"

He clutched a hand to his chest, mock horror coating his features. "You act like I have so many."

"You do," Maverick, Charlie and I managed to all say at once. *Nice.*

"Y'all are assholes." Cash feigned indignation.

Maverick nudged him with his shoulder as the two walked their horses out of the arena. "Takes one to know one."

Cash's bray of laughter was enough to make Black Betty snort and toss her head. But his laughter died as quickly as it started, his usually light, warm gaze, turning dark and cold. I followed his stare, confusion gnawing at me, to fix on the person stepping out of the car.

Maverick stood ramrod straight, a look of disbelief flashing in his eyes. My heart stopped beating all together for a long moment, my lungs seizing.

I didn't need an introduction.

This was Ashleigh.

I don't know what exactly I was expecting, but my vision of the infa-

333

mous Ashleigh wasn't this. She was tall—very tall—with long, willowy arms and legs. Her hair was as black as a starless sky, and stick straight as it brushed against her hips. She was pale, a stark contrast to her dark, grunge-inspired outfit. I'd never expected Maverick with anyone but a cowgirl.

"Well, if it isn't Smashleigh... I see you crawled back out of hell." Cash recovered the quickest of everyone as he sauntered toward her. A mean, malicious spark flickered in his gaze, revealing an angry, hateful side of him I honestly hadn't expected. Didn't even think he was capable of.

But he'd told me enough about Ashleigh to let me know he hated her with every fiber of his being. And as fun-loving and easy going as he was, this was the same guy who'd gotten in a fight as a kid for some idiot making fun of Maverick. A darker side to Cash lurked just beneath the surface. I wondered just how dark it was. Wondered if even he knew how dark it was.

Ashleigh's hooded gaze scanned each and every one of us, disdain written plainly in the sneer on her lips as she settled on Charlie and I. "Looks like you've been busy, Cash. Not one, but two buckle bunnies, and both pregnant. Your parents must be so proud of you."

Her sickly-sweet voice caught me by surprise. I'd expect it to be sensual and raspy from the look of her. But even the surprise didn't do much to dim the blast of anger that bristled to life in my chest. Who the fuck did she think she was calling a buckle bunny? I earned my buckles, and not on my knees—the dumb bitch.

Though Charlie didn't say anything, I knew she felt the same. The stiffness in her shoulders, the silent fury blazing in her storm cloud gaze said it all.

I sucked in a breath to reply, but Cash beat me to it. "Actually, neither one of them are mine. In fact—" His lips pulled up into a sadistic smirk as he nodded at me. "Maverick's the buckle bunny in this case. He's hers."

I fought back a smile. Cash might be a dumbass about ninety-nine percent of the time, but right now, I was so proud of him I could kiss him. Okay, maybe not that far. But still.

Ashleigh's gaze was sharper than a knife as it snapped between me and Maverick, but some of her bravado faltered, her voice wobbling as she asked, "Is that true?"

I settled my gaze on Maverick, my breath hitching in my throat as I waited for him to reply. What if he said no? What if her coming back here changed things and he decided he wanted her instead? I wasn't typically so self-conscious, but damn, between these stupid hormones and the fact that despite how absolutely awful I could tell Ashleigh was... Well, he'd been in love with her for a very, *very* long time. What if her coming back was enough to change everything?

I knew the answer before he even replied. It shone brightly in his eyes—complete and utter certainty. And most of all...love. He didn't even look at her as he held my gaze and nodded.

My heart danced against my ribcage. Tears—of relief or happiness, I didn't really know at this point—brewed in my eyes like a fluke summer storm. Good God, he just couldn't get any more perfect, could he?

I wish I would've had my phone out to catch her reaction, her gasp of sheer disbelief and barely restrained fury. Well, if she'd looked at me with disdain before, her fierce gaze held nothing but white-hot hatred now.

I bit back a smug smile as Ashleigh's mouth opened and closed repeatedly, trying and failing to come up with a response. She finally settled on growling, her fists curling at her sides as she turned to Maverick. "Can we talk?"

Bad and Goodie took that as a chance to excuse themselves, both of them heading to Goodie's truck. Cash made no attempt to leave, his attention fixed on Ashleigh, watching her with the same level of intensity as he did when he was in the box readying for a ride. He was watching, waiting for her to make a move.

I strode to his side and nudged him gently, glancing over at Charlie and Cason as I said, "Come on, let's go untack the horses."

Cash resisted only a moment longer before a malicious sneer pulled on his lips. "I'd say it was nice talkin' to ya, but it wasn't so...bye."

"Oh, fuck you, Cash," she hissed.

His sneer turned wolfish. "I'm sorry, I don't speak bitch." With that, he led Playboy into the barn, followed by Charlie and Cason, along with Peckerhead in tow. I moved to Maverick, who still held

Black Betty. She eyed me as I approached—the mare was possessive as hell of him. But I was too, so I guess we both had that in common. So many emotions swirled and danced across Maverick's features. Anger, worry, frustration, fear—each passing and shifting so quickly it was impossible to pinpoint just one. I could only imagine how shitty of a situation this was for him. I didn't envy him at all right now.

"I'll untack her for you," I said, pressing a hand to his bare arm, my fingers caressing the canyons of mottled flesh before coming to rest on his reins. He shivered beneath my touch, something in his light gaze flaring.

"You sure?"

I nodded, holding his unwavering stare.

He blew out a breath and released the reins. I didn't kiss him, even though every possessive part of me wanted to just rub it in this bitch's face. Somehow, I didn't think Maverick would like that. He wasn't the type to gloat or boast. So, I wouldn't either. Ashleigh could have this last moment with him. It sure as hell would be the last.

Even though I didn't kiss him, I did make sure to plaster on my fakest, brightest smile as I turned to her and said, "I'm Cheyenne, by the way. I've heard a lot about you."

I couldn't tell the exact color of her eyes in the dim evening light, but I recognized the anger and hatred burning in the depths. Oh well, after tonight, I'd never have to deal with her again—hopefully.

A sneer pulled on her lips. "Well, I've heard nothing about you."

I shrugged, completely unfazed. Casting one long, final look at Maverick, I led a less than thrilled Black Betty to the barn.

For a split second, I feared she might trample me or run me down, but aside from snorting, tossing her head, and glancing back periodically at Maverick, she followed along.

The barn lights were glaringly bright compared to how dim it was outside. My gaze flicked to Playboy, still tied up just outside of his stall, Cash was nowhere to be seen. Cason stood just outside Peckerhead's stall as Charlie hurriedly pulled off his saddle and saddle pad before all but tossing them onto one of the racks. I frowned as she made her way to the barn doors.

That's when I noticed Cash. I'd walked right by him. The sneaky bastard.

"Well, you gonna hurry your ass up and join us, or what?" Cash whispered as Charlie settled at his side.

I frowned at the two of them. "Are y'all really gonna snoop?"

Charlie gave me a sheepish grin. "Don't tell me you don't want to hear what happens."

I did. Dear Lord, I really did. But that was horrible of me, right? I shouldn't care. I'd won whatever little war Ashleigh was in with me. Maverick was mine. Shouldn't that be enough?

I glanced between Black Betty and my two friends. Well, there was the chance that Black Betty might kill me for trying to untack her. I'd only handled her a few times, and it hadn't ever been more than this. Maybe I should leave that for Maverick. He'd understand, right?

"Hold on. Let me tie her up," I said, hurrying to put her in the cross ties in front of her stall.

I settled between Cash and Charlie, Cason completely ignoring us as he brushed down Peckerhead and told him about his football practice like he was an old friend and not a horse.

The three of us peeked out around the barn door. From where Maverick and Ashleigh stood, neither could see us—hopefully—but we could hear them clear as day.

"I don't know what the hell he sees in her," Cash grumbled, his gaze narrowed on the brunette.

"Okay, seriously though," Charlie scoffed. "I was expecting her to be more..." I turned to meet her gaze. Her shoulders lifted into a guilty shrug. "I just expected her to be prettier. I know that sounds awful, but well...he's been obsessed with her for almost two decades...I was expecting...more."

"Right?" I was so glad I wasn't the only one who'd thought that. I could understand her having a shitty personality but him putting up with it because she was a complete knockout. As shallow as that was, I'd be the first to admit I'd done that before. Case and point...Nate. But Ashleigh was a bit, well, plain. It's not that she wasn't pretty. She was... in a *plain* way. There was nothing seemingly special about her. Not that I was trying to toot my own horn, but if she was so god-awful to

Maverick *and* not drop-dead gorgeous, then what about her had kept him under her spell for so long?

Cash seemed to understand without me saying anything. "Maverick is loyal. To a fault. It's one of his greatest strengths, but with her...his greatest weakness." He glanced at his cousin and back at me. "Also, she was his first."

"Ah." Charlie and I both nodded, understanding dawning on us at the same time.

"That explains so much," Charlie replied.

Cash shushed us, nodding toward Maverick and Ashleigh. "They're talkin'."

So, settling in, the three of us let relative silence fall in the barn as we huddled together and listened like a bunch of eavesdropping teens and not grown-ass adults.

CHAPTER 42
Angel Wings

MAVERICK

I cast one last worried glance toward the barn Cheyenne disappeared into. I hoped Betty behaved. She seemed okay enough with Chey, but still. I didn't trust her with anyone but me, really.

"So…" Ashleigh's soft, accusatory tone drew my attention. "Who is *she*?"

I turned to face her fully. Anger permeated from her; I could practically feel it. She'd never reacted well when I'd tried to move on. Never been good at letting me go. To be fair, I wasn't any good at it either…

Until now. Until Cheyenne.

The two of them couldn't be more different. They were night and day. Ashleigh was like the moon on a cloudy night. Cheyenne was the sun.

"She's my girlfriend," I replied, though she was so much more than that.

My own resolve surprised me. Ashleigh had always had a way of making me feel like I needed to tread carefully, or walk on eggshells. But none of the usual worry accompanied me as I met her heated glare.

"How long have you been with her?" She crossed her arms over her chest, one of her hips jutting out into a defiant stance.

I shrugged and blew out a sigh. I didn't see why this mattered. "Couple months now."

Her eyes narrowed, almost like she was doing the math in her head, before her lips drew down into a furious scowl. "You were talking to her and I at the same time?" Her words dripped with accusation.

Funny, she'd get so mad and accuse me of that when she did it all the time. She'd been the one who'd slept with another man in my own bed. On the night I proposed. Anger and sadness and those old devastating feelings fought to rear their ugly heads, but I pushed them down. No. I was done with letting those emotions control me.

"Her and I hit it off the night you were supposed to come work things out with me," I finally settled on saying, making sure to keep my tone calm and even despite the anger brewing inside me like a storm.

"I told you I had work!" Her words, her stance, everything about her turned defensive, her sweet voice holding a desperate, shrill note to it.

I leveled her with a knowing look. "Ashleigh...you and I both know you didn't have work."

It hurt saying the words out loud. Acknowledging the fact that I'd been second best. That I *always* was second best for her. Always the back up. I was the safe harbor when her love life went to shit. The one who picked up the broken pieces from every guy who fucked her over, only for her to use me up, bleed me dry, and then leave before things got too serious. And then when things inevitably went south, she'd come crawling back again.

I think it hurt more, though, that I let it happen for so long.

Why had I done this?

I was the voice of reason when it came to Cash and Ryder's love lives. I'd spouted off a whole bunch of shit to Charlie a few months ago about not letting a love like theirs go to waste. And yet, when it came to my own love life, I was as much of a mess as Cash... Okay, *almost* as much of a mess.

Ashleigh's gaze welled with angry tears as she choked out, "So, I fuck up, and you go and get some girl pregnant?"

Her words hit like a sledgehammer to the chest. If only she knew the baby wasn't mine. But she didn't need to know that. Besides, I intended to raise that baby as mine. To love it as *mine*.

I opened my mouth to respond but she continued on. "I'm sorry, okay? I was scared. Scared of jumping back into things and..." Her words dissolved into sobs as she launched into my arms.

For a moment I just stood there. I didn't know what to say, what to do to make her stop. I didn't want her to feel this way. I didn't want to be the reason for her tears. As much as she'd hurt me over the last almost twenty years, I didn't want to see her hurt. But I also couldn't keep doing this for her. Being her punching bag, her shoulder to cry on.

I placed my hands on her shoulders and slowly, gently created space between us.

"Maverick I'm so—" she sobbed, her hands coming up to grasp my arms. But the minute her hands met my flesh, she pulled back, a look of pure, undiluted horror spreading across her face. Her gaze landed on my scars. "Oh my god, they're so much worse than I remembered."

Well, if her words had felt like a sledgehammer a few moments earlier, these were like a damn dagger straight through the heart.

For a moment I'd forgotten about them. Cheyenne seemed to like them, made sure to mention how beautiful they were every chance she got. And tonight, despite every ounce of my mind screaming at me to keep myself covered up, I'd opted to defy the odds and let them show. No one seemed to mind or notice.

Until now.

I swallowed past the lump in my throat, my arms crossing protectively over my chest—like that could somehow hide them.

"Sorry," I mumbled.

She leaned into me once more. "Maverick. I'm sorry. For last Christmas. For two months ago. For everything. I just...I want to start over. I want you." Her words, her eyes, her touch were pleading. "Are you really gonna have a baby with some random girl you don't even know? You know me. You love me." She pressed a hand to my chest, tears slipping down her pale cheeks. "Is that what you want? A baby? Marriage? I can give you that. I can be everything she is and more for you, Mav. Please. Just give me a chance. I love you. I really do."

343

I pursed my lips, my head falling back to rest on the night sky above. I let my eyelids flutter closed for a long moment as her words rolled over me.

"Mav..." Ashleigh's voice was weak, pleading. "Say something."

I sucked in a deep breath and met her brown gaze. It was crazy to think this was the same girl who'd come to one of her mother's therapy sessions at the Mooneys. Who'd talked to me so animatedly and innocently about the new emo band she'd discovered. Who'd all but shoved one of her headphones into my hands and urged me to listen. It was I Caught Fire by The Used. I think I'd fallen in love with her right then and there. She'd been the first person to treat me normal besides Cash and the rest of the family.

Was there even a shred of that girl still in the woman standing before me? Or had she disappeared along time ago, and I'd just been trying to convince myself she was still there?

"You know how long I've wanted to hear you say those things? How long I wanted to marry you. Start a family with you..."

Something shifted in her gaze, lightening the dark depths. Hope.

I went on before she could speak. "I wanted forever with you, Ashleigh...but not now. Not anymore."

Tears welled in her eyes before falling down her cheeks. A broken, choked sob escaped her. "Wh-what? But...but... You're gonna throw this all away? Throw *us* away after all this time?"

I wiped at her tears. I couldn't help it. I didn't love her anymore. I realized that the moment Cheyenne touched my arm and walked into the barn. But I still cared about Ashleigh, and I hated seeing her hurt, especially at my expense.

"Ash..." I sighed. "You and I both know we're never gonna work. Our story's been over for quite some time now. Both of us were just too stubborn to let go."

Anger sparked in her gaze like the flame to a match. She batted my hand away from her cheek, her words filled with venom as she spat, "Couple months with this bitch and suddenly you're in love? No. I don't believe that."

I shrugged. "Believe it or don't... but she's my story now."

She seethed, her jaw clenching tight, her entire demeanor changing from pleading to pissed in a heartbeat. "I drove all the way fucking down here for this?"

"I'm sorry," I said, meaning every word. I was sorry for everything. For the years of back and forth between us. For holding on so tightly when I should have just let her go. "I can give you money for gas if you need." She glared at me but said nothing so I continued on. "I hope you find someone who makes you happy, Ashleigh. Lord knows it's never been me."

"Go to hell, Maverick." She stomped back to her car, opening and slamming her door shut, before peeling out as she reversed and turned around on the gravel road.

Just like that, she was gone.

"Goodbye, Ashleigh."

I watched her taillights dwindle down the road before disappearing all together. All the while, waiting for the sadness, the devastation to grip me like it did every time she left.

But there was none of that. Only anger. Anger that swelled and raged within me like a hurricane. Twenty years. Damn near twenty years I'd wasted on her. Twenty years of letting her use me, letting her hurt me, all just to feel a shrivel of her love. And when I was finally done, when I finally decided to move on, she was ready to give it—give that love I had wanted so badly for so long.

But her and I both knew she didn't mean anything she'd just said.

She didn't want a marriage. She didn't want a baby. She didn't want horses or a ranch or any of that. She just didn't want anyone else to have me.

I sucked in a deep breath and looked skyward, counting stars as I tried to calm my angry heart. But it did nothing. Releasing the breath slowly, I settled my sights on the barn.

Charlie, Cash, Cason, and Cheyenne were all there working in quiet silence. They'd been listening; I wasn't an idiot. It didn't take Cash anywhere near this long to untack and brush down Playboy. I would give it to Cheyenne that it *may* take her this long, only because Black Betty was cinchy and temperamental.

But the tell-tale sign they all knew, beyond how slow they were, was the fact no one would look me in the eye, save Cason, who barreled up and asked, "Who was that lady? She owes me money for the swear jar."

Even sweet Cason couldn't quell the anger bubbling up inside me. I shouldn't have come in here. Seeing all their faces, their worried glances cast my way—I hated it.

I put on my best fake grin, and tousled what was left of Cason's hair. "She's no one, bud." Pulling my wallet out of my back pocket, I grabbed a twenty and held it out to him. "Here. Tonight's payment for the swear jar."

Cason's eyes lit up as he snatched the cash out of my hand. "Auntie Charlotte. Look!"

Charlie finally met my gaze as she came to his side, offering me a soft, knowing smile. She'd had a shitty ex too. She understood the hold and toll they had. "Wow. Look at that, bud!" Wrapping an arm around his shoulder, she said, "We gotta get you cleaned up and in bed."

"Bu—"

Charlie wasn't having it, though. After saying goodbye to everyone and giving me one final, sympathetic smile, she led Cason out of the barn.

Cheyenne approached me slowly, her hands slightly splayed out at her sides, almost like she was trying to soothe me, but anticipating me spooking and running away like some wild animal. I didn't blame her. I *felt* wild and out of control right now, but the sight spiked my anger.

"Mav." Her bright gaze held me in place, worry and sadness and something else lurking there. "I'm so sorry about earlier, I—"

"Not right now." I shook my head.

I didn't want to talk about earlier. I didn't want to be around her at all, in fact. Not because I was angry with her—I wasn't—but because I had years of pent-up rage roaring within me to be let out, and I didn't want her to see it or get caught in the crossfire.

"We'll talk later."

A line of worry appeared between her brows as they knit together, her lips pursing. I could tell she wanted to argue—from her stance, to the stubborn set of her jaw—but after looking to Cash for silent reassurance, who gave her a single shake of his head, she finally sighed. "Alright. I'll be at the house."

She walked out of the barn without another word.

My gaze met Cash. "Thank you for that," I murmured. There were so many times when I was grateful we were so close, this being a prime example.

Cash nodded, oddly quiet for someone who should be jumping for joy right now with what just went down.

"Take Chey home for me, please?" I asked.

Another nod as he started off for the barn doors, but not before stopping at my side, placing a hand on my shoulder, and meeting my gaze. "I'm proud of you."

You'd think I'd won a championship buckle, not ended a toxic relationship. But his approval meant the world to me. I dipped my head in a nod.

I walked through the barn aisle to the opposite side and up the stairs leading to the workout room. My gaze fell on the punching bag, its mere presence a welcome sight. Settling before it, I finally unleashed my rage. Let it pour out of me and into my hands as I punched and punched and punched 'til my knuckles bled.

CHAPTER 43
Put Me In My Place

CHEYENNE

Maverick didn't get back until nearly midnight. I'd given up pacing on the front porch to raid the fridge in hopes of finding something to stress-eat, but it didn't help. When that failed, I moved on to sulking in the tub until the water turned cold, to sitting on the front porch, to finally contemplating going out and finding him.

I heard the crunch of his boots on the gravel before his dark silhouette emerged from the foggy night like a wraith. Even from a distance, I could feel the weight of his stare.

Every inch of me went on alert as I took him in. There was something...different about him. Not wild. No, there wasn't anything wild about Maverick, but there was something *free* about him. Like a part of him had been locked up and caged, and now that cage had been opened.

I shivered.

He didn't speak as he walked past the trucks and onto the pavement. He didn't speak as he stopped before me, hooking a finger beneath my chin and forcing me to meet his gaze. Desire and want and need blazed in his eyes as his mouth hovered just inches from mine. My body reacted

349

on instinct, my heart fluttering in my chest and desire igniting low in my belly—I was helpless against him.

But then the sharp tang of blood filled my nose, and I pulled out of his grip, my gaze going to his hands. Blood coated his knuckles.

"What happened?" I asked, gently grabbing his hand and examining the broken skin.

He shrugged but made no attempt to move his hand out of my grasp. "I was workin' out."

My mind went to the punching bag in the gym above the hay loft. I reached for his other hand, unsurprised to find the flesh ripped open there too. Shaking my head, I looked up at him.

He offered me another shrug, finally pulling his hands away. "I'm fine."

Grabbing one of his hands once more, I drew him to me, needing the comfort of his familiar touch. "Maverick, I wanted to apologize for earl—"

"Chey, you don't gotta."

Annoyance bristled in my chest. "No, goddamn it! Stop." His brow rose before I continued. "Stop justifyin' my actions. You were right, I wasn't payin' attention. I wasn't in a good mindset, and if you hadn't noticed yet, I don't do well with people tellin' me what I can and can't do." I inhaled deeply and blew out my breath. "I shouldn't have stormed off like that. I just—when I get upset, I run away."

Maverick brushed his fingers against the back of my hand before grabbing it and pulling me closer. "Can I talk now?" he asked, the barest whisper of a teasing smirk tugging on the corner of his lips, even though his words were innocent and earnest.

I rolled my eyes, biting back a grin as I pressed my hands to his chest, reveling in the feel of his strong, steady heartbeat. "Yes, go ahead and say what you gotta say."

"Truth is, I coulda handled things a bit better myself as well. I got scared the minute I saw that filly charge you and I just...reacted. I'm sorry for talkin' to you like that."

I offered him a soft, reassuring smile. "All's forgiven, cowboy."

"I'm even more sorry for what happened after. The Ashleigh situation, sendin' you away like that. All of it." His hold on me tightened—almost like he was afraid to let me go.

"You meant everythin' you said to her earlier? You're sure this is what you want?"

As much as I wanted him and as happy as I was that he chose me over that bitch, a part of me was terrified he'd change his mind. And what was worse was I wouldn't really blame him. I couldn't even imagine what raising someone's baby who wasn't mine would be like. To be honest, I couldn't even begin to fathom how I was going to raise my own baby.

I wasn't the motherly type.

Not like Charlie, who'd stepped into the role of mom to Cason with such ease. She wore pregnancy so well in spite of the constant sickness she still went through even though she'd entered the second trimester.

Maverick didn't seem in the least bit worried about that though. He'd be the most amazing father, and I had no doubt he would love my baby like it was his very own.

His gaze burned with love as he tucked a stray curl behind my ear. "I've never been more sure of anythin' in my life, Chey. I want you..." He settled his other hand on my stomach, his gaze flicking down to my bump and back up again. "I want this baby. I want to raise her up on this ranch with you."

Tears pricked in my eyes even as a smile played on my lips. "I love you."

The desire and need in his gaze sparked brighter. I shivered in anticipation. He dipped his mouth toward mine, hovering just a breath away. "I love you too," he whispered, before kissing me. Slowly. Deeply.

My arms slid up around his neck, and I leaned into him as I rode the high of his kisses, his intoxicating touch. I'd never felt something so intense, so...raw. For someone as even-keeled and calm as Maverick was, when he loved...fuck, he loved hard.

It was nothing but fierce passion. Burning desire. Scorching touches and searing kisses.

I kissed him until my lungs screamed for air, only pulling away long enough to take a breath before pressing my lips to his once more. I wanted him. All of him. Every day for the rest of forever.

Forever.

The realization should have given me pause. I'd never wanted forever with someone. But as he kissed me breathless...as he knotted his fingers in my hair and ground his body against mine, I realized I wanted forever with him.

I broke the kiss, my chest rising and falling in fast, shallow breaths. "More," I whispered.

It was his undoing.

———

IT WAS NEARLY TWO IN THE MORNING WHEN WE FINALLY collapsed into our bed, curling up against one another underneath the blankets. Maverick wrapped an arm around me, and my fingers found the familiar mottled flesh of his scars, stroking them gently, lovingly.

I thought of Ashleigh's words earlier, an ember of anger flickering to life in my chest.

How could she have said something so incredibly awful about them? How could she find them repulsive when they were a testament to his strength? A reminder that he'd danced with death and won.

His scars were beautiful, and the fact that dumb bitch made him feel like they were anything but made tears line my eyes.

Pressing my lips to the scarred flesh, I kissed him. Again, and again. Over and over. Inch by inch. I poured every bit of love in me into those soft caresses, hoping he understood what I was so desperately trying to show him.

That I loved every bit of him. Scars and all.

When I turned over to face him, intent to kiss the ones marring his chest, unshed tears shone in his eyes.

"You are beautiful, Maverick," I whispered, continuing my trail of kisses.

He kissed me. Softly. Whisper-soft, and when he pulled away, I watched twin tears slide down his cheeks.

"She made you cover them up, didn't she?" I asked, settling myself closer as I laid on my side and faced him, all the while making sure to continue stroking his scars.

He heaved a deep, shaky sigh. "Not exactly," he murmured, his fingers finding the side of my belly and drawing lazy patterns on my skin. "I was already self-conscious of them before her, but...well, I think they scared her."

I fought back an eye roll. She'd never deserved him. *Dumb bitch.*

"I want you to promise me somethin'."

He nodded, a silent request to go on.

"I never want you to hide them from me. Ever."

Another nod.

"I mean it, Maverick. The strength you showed today barin' your scars for us all..." Tears stung in my eyes. I pressed a kiss to his lips, pulling back enough to look him in the eyes and whisper, "I am so fuckin' proud of you."

His lips pulled up into the faintest ghost of a smile. "I promise."

———

THE NEXT FEW MONTHS PASSED BY IN A COMPLETE BLUR— along with Thanksgiving, Christmas, and New Years. Everything changing so swiftly I hardly had a chance to get used to anything. Pregnancy was weird in that way. It felt both so short and so long at the same time. I was closing in on thirty-four weeks. Thirty-four weeks pregnant. And they'd flown for me. Granted, I didn't know for ten of those weeks that I was in fact pregnant. But still...

What was even crazier was for the most part, it had been easy. Like surprisingly easy. Which was completely opposite of poor Charlie.

That was another weird thing about pregnancy. How different it was for each person. Charlie was only a couple weeks behind me, but the morning sickness never left. In fact, it only seemed to get worse. She was tired all the time, constantly getting headaches or feeling nauseous. Then here I was, riding horses, breaking babies, and going about my day like it was just any other Thursday.

But through all the sickness and lethargy, she smiled and laughed like it was no big deal. I doubted I'd be quite as optimistic if I were in her position. And to be honest, I'd probably resent me for having such an easy pregnancy in comparison.

"How could I hate you?" Charlie asked, grabbing a fresh baked sweet roll off the baking sheet. They were one of the only things that didn't make her sick, and it gave Maverick the excuse of working on his bread making skills.

I swear...I'd never met a man who enjoyed learning and trying new things as much as Maverick. He was always—I mean, always—doing something. Working on the truck, cleaning or messing around with tack and bits and bridles, learning how to shoe horses, fixing repairs around the barn, working on the nursery, learning new recipes to cook and bake. The list was endless. All the while, ensuring he paid attention to me, to Cash, as well as practicing for rodeos and jackpots, and giving Cason lessons, and helping Charlie whenever Ryder was gone.

It was insane.

He truly was a jack of all trades. Always giving and giving and giving. He was my safe space, my soft place to land when the weight of the world got too heavy, the haven from the worries of life and pregnancy, and I was so grateful for him.

I reluctantly dragged my gaze from Maverick who hovered over the stove making something that smelled absolutely delicious, and plucked a hot roll off the baking sheet as well. "I don't know, because it's been so hard for you and so opposite for me," I replied with a shrug.

Charlie laughed, not a single hint of bitterness or annoyance lingering there. "So? That isn't your fault. I'm just glad one of us is having an easy time."

Cason appeared from out of nowhere—I swear, the kid had the sneaking skills of a ghost—and snatched a roll off the plate. By the time Charlie noticed, he was already darting back toward the front door where Dutch and Brandy waited patiently for him. "Hey, only one. Save room for dinner!"

He waved her off, disappearing outside as quickly as he came.

I offered her a sympathetic smile. She was always so positive through this whole thing, so flexible and fluid. When life gave her lemons, she made lemonade. "So," I asked, changing the subject, "any more headway on baby names?"

Charlie tried and failed to bite back a smile, tucking her long bangs behind an ear. "We *may* have come up with one."

Maverick's voice nearly startled me out of my seat. "Ryder didn't mention anythin' about y'all settlin on one."

"We've been goin back and forth on whether to keep it a secret 'til he's born or not."

"How come?" I asked.

She took a bite full of roll before chewing and swallowing. With an eyeroll, she answered, "Mostly because of my mom. She's been so fucking fussy this whole pregnancy, and I just know that if we tell her the name we're intending she'll throw a fit."

"So, y'all are keepin' up with the Wright family tradition then?" Maverick asked, a hint of a smirk curving his lips upward.

Charlie's smile held the same mischief that danced in her eyes. "How could we break that?"

I grinned. "Ah, come on! I wanna know what name y'all chose! Please, tell us."

She stuffed the rest of the roll into her mouth, a distraction no doubt, conflict swirling in her gaze. "I want to," she finally said, "but Ryder will throw a fit if I go back on the deal *I enforced*. Not to mention, if Cash finds out, then the whole town might as well know too."

"That's fair," Maverick said, pausing in his cooking to stand before me where I sat on the countertop. He situated himself between my legs, one of his hands brushing my thigh in a soft, reassuring gesture. I don't know how it was possible to relax with such a simple touch, but I let out a breath I hadn't even realized I'd been holding in. That's what him coming around felt like, the impact he had on my anxiety and worries. The calm to my storm.

Mav might be okay with not knowing, but *I* wanted to know what epic name Charlie and Ryder came up with. It had to be if they were keeping up with the innuendos. "What if we guess?" I asked.

Charlie laughed and reached for another roll. Mav batted her hand away, shaking his head. "Dinner's almost ready."

She rolled her eyes but sighed, a grin on her lips. "I highly doubt you'll guess it, but sure. I'm interested to see what names you guys come up with."

A trill of excitement shot through me as I racked my brain for potential names. By the downward tilt of Maverick's lips and the line furrowed between his brows, he was thinking too.

"Okay, I've got one," I finally said after a few moments. "Striker. Like Strike her right. It's also a mix of both his and his daddy's names."

Charlie's grin pulled wider but she shook her head. "Clever, but no."

Maverick's voice drew our attention. "What about Slater?"

I bit back a laugh. *Slayed her right.*

"Another excellent one, but still no."

I blew out a breath, tapping a finger to my lips. "What about..." even the thought of the name had me grinning. "Wrecker. Wrecker Wright."

Charlie's stunned silence sent fireworks of excitement exploding in my chest.

"It's that, isn't it? No fuckin' way. I can just see it now, Cash having some little onesie made that says somethin' like *get wrecked* on it."

Laughter bubbled out of Charlie. "That was my exact thought, but it's still not it. We *almost* went with Wrecker, though."

"What? It isn't that?"

"No." She shook her head. "But I'm loving hearing your ideas, so keep them coming."

After a few more minutes of guessing, Maverick and I both gave up. Dinner was ready, and I was out of innuendos.

Charlie sat down in a chair opposite me. Cason sat diagonal to us both, his hair mussed up and streaked with sweat from playing outside. Brandy and Dutch panted from the dog bed in the corner of the living room.

"What about y'all?" Charlie asked. "Any contenders for little miss?" It was funny, she didn't have an accent really, despite growing up here, but now that she was back, every now and then a 'y'all' or 'bless your heart' would escape her with the barest hint of a twang. Looked like you could take the girl out of the country, but couldn't take the country out of the girl.

I glanced at Maverick, who sat diagonal to me. His gaze flicked to my swollen belly, his hand reaching out to brush it in reassurance.

"Apparently naming babies is far harder than naming animals." I glanced back at Charlie.

She laughed before taking a sip of her sweet tea. "How so?"

I shrugged. "I don't know. I just... What if we pick the wrong name? What if we fall in love with one and she comes out and the name just doesn't fit her?"

"Well, what names were you thinkin'?" Charlie asked.

I looked at Maverick once more. "Might as well tell her. Maybe she's got some ideas."

"We liked Kinleigh at first, but it's kinda popular. I liked Winter, but Chey ain't a fan. We both like Oakley...like Annie Oakley, but spelled with a l-e-i-g-h at the end," Maverick replied.

She smiled. "Ooh, Oakleigh is super cute. What about a middle name?"

Maverick huffed before muttering, "We barely got the first name down, now you want a second?"

I chimed in, "I was thinkin', actually the other day about middle names. What about Mae?"

A muscle in Maverick's hand flexed, his grip on my belly tightening almost imperceptibly, and when I looked at him, his jade eyes swam with a current of emotions I couldn't quite place. I frowned. "Do you not like that?"

"N-no, I..." I didn't miss the way his voice dipped and cracked. "My...uh...my sister's name was Ellie Mae."

My breath hitched, tightening in my chest. "I'm sorry. I...I didn't know." Cash had mentioned his sister's name before, once or twice, but I didn't recall that her middle name was Mae. It had been so long since we'd talked about Maverick's past though that I could have maybe just forgotten. I wouldn't forget something like that though. Not something as important as that.

Families were still a soft subject for Mav and I—well, mostly him. Dredging up those dark memories, reliving the past was hard...on both of us really. And as long as he didn't force me to bring them up, I wouldn't do that to him either.

Blowing out a breath, I pressed a reassuring hand over his. "I'm sorry. I get if that's too hard for you. We can think of somethin' else. We got ti—"

"No." Maverick's tone held a desperate, yet final note to it that made my heart crack. He met my stare. "Ain't much good came out of my family, but I'd be honored to have this little girl share the same name as my sister."

My heart shattered entirely at the fierce love written so plainly on his face. I leaned in and pressed a soft kiss to his lips, trying to assure him with my touch when words seemed to fail me. I didn't know what to say to that, but I'd be damned if I didn't give him this after he'd given me so much.

Maverick remained quiet throughout dinner and excused himself as quickly as he could to retreat to the barn with Cason for a lesson while Charlie and I offered to stay and clean up. I'd noted the shift in him immediately, but hadn't wanted to say anything until it was just the two of us. He did this from time to time—withdrew into himself and got really quiet. Well, okay, quieter than usual. He was always quiet, sometimes almost painfully so, but then there were times like this where the silence was so cold and hollow that I feared he might slip into one of his silent episodes again.

I wondered if it was the mention of his sister that did it this time, or if there was more to it than that. Worry niggled at me, but I pushed it down. One thing I'd learned about Mav was that he'd talk when he was ready. Push him too much and it would only take longer. He'd dig his heels in and get really stubborn.

I understood that all too well.

———

By the time Charlie and I finished and made our way to the barn to get Maverick and Cason, it was late. Cold had finally won out against the relentless Texas heat, the evening air bringing a sharp, chill crispness to it that I appreciated. But too much colder and I'd be an unhappy camper. I liked the warmth—like a little cactus, I thrived in heat. Not cold, harsh temperatures.

I pulled my jacket around me tighter and glanced at Charlie. "Ryder comes home this weekend, right?"

Her smile lit up the dark, the excitement written in every inch of her. "Yes, thank God." My brows knit together in question and a sheepish look replaced the excitement on her face. "Sorry, I know that sounded bad. I've just missed him, and with being so far along I haven't wanted to travel that far. I mean, I know we still have about a month left, but... I don't know. I still get so sick and I don't want him to have to worry about that as well as competing."

I met her gaze, offering her a soft, reassuring smile. "That makes sense. He's home from here on out till the baby comes, right?"

She nodded, running a hand through her hair as a broad smile lit up her face once more. "Yes. I'm excited for him to be home for more than just a few days here and there. There's so much to do and so little time. I can't believe they're almost here."

I blew out a breath, mist forming in the air. A mixture of unease and excitement sprung to life in my chest. "I know. It's crazy."

"You ready?"

I barked out a laugh. "Fuck, no. Are you?"

She let out a chuckle. "Not at all. Some days I just want this pregnancy to be over and I'm like, okay, I'm ready, but then I think of things like feeding schedules and diaper changes and percentiles and I start freaking out. Not to mention the actual labor."

The uneasy feeling in my chest roiled, before settling a bit at the realization that Charlie, for as put together as she seemed, also felt the same. At least I wasn't alone in this. I couldn't imagine being in this position by myself.

"Same, girl. Same."

CHAPTER 44

West Texas Weather

MAVERICK

I was halfway through Cason's lesson when a black Lexus pulled up by the barn. Deja vu hit me for a moment, and I imagined Ashleigh's tall frame sliding out of the vehicle, but it wasn't her. Thank the Lord.

Though, I wasn't necessarily in the mood to deal with the person who slid out of this car either. Cash hopped out, leaning over to kiss whoever drove, before closing the door and sauntering my way. So that's why he hadn't been home for dinner. My nerves coiled and writhed within me. I wasn't really in the mood for any of his antics. Which wasn't fair. He hadn't said a word and I was already annoyed.

I wasn't even mad at him though, or really mad in general for that matter. I was just...I don't know. In my own head, I guess. I felt like I was a soda can that'd gotten all shaken up, and was just sitting, waiting to either flatten out or explode.

Right now, I wasn't sure which way it would go. And I didn't want Cason to see how I acted when I got angry.

Flickers of ugly memories struggled to rear their heads. I fought them, pushing them deep, deep down, but a few trickled through. *Dad's yelling. The sound of beer bottles shattering. The boom of my father's fists against the wall.* I shuddered, trying to shake out of my mind.

I'd never laid a hand on anyone like my dad did, but his anger ran through my veins. It was a part of me. One I hated, and tried as hard as I could to keep at bay.

Cason's voice echoed off the barn and across the arena, pulling me fully from my dark thoughts. The smile he aimed Cash's way shone brighter than any of the arena lights. "Funcle Cash!" he called from atop Peckerhead, urging the gelding toward us.

"Hi'ya, little man," Cash called back, waving animatedly before coming to my side and leaning against the pipe-stall. "You almost done?" he asked, glancing my way.

"Just about. Though I'm sure the kid would love if you gave him a few pointers." I caught a glimpse of red tail lights before they disappeared completely. "What part of the Cash system we at with this one?"

Cash's gaze flicked to mine, concern dulling his usually bright, happy features. I almost never commented or asked about his conquests. I didn't care, because I knew *he didn't care* about them. Not really. They were only there to fill a void. A hole that'd been there since the summer he graduated high school. A hole that he seemed set to dig himself further and further into. Before he could get a word out, Cason came to a stop before us.

"How's your lesson goin', bud?" Cash recovered quicker than me, a dazzling smile lighting up his face.

"Good!" Cason beamed right back. "Uncle Mav said he thinks I'm ready to start ropin' on the horse!"

"Now, hold your roll there, kid," I replied, pegging Cason with a pointed look. "There were two parts to that. What was the first?"

Cason's cheeks reddened as he offered me a sheepish grin and replied, "He said I gotta rope the dummy cow fifty times in a row—"

"And *then* you can start ropin' off him," I finished, crossing my arms —covered, mainly because of the cold—over my chest.

Cash clapped his hands together, a warm grin on his lips. "Well, you heard Uncle Mav. How 'bout you go tie up ol' Peckerhead over by the barn and grab out the ropin' dummy and get started?"

"But fifty's a lot!" Cason whined, albeit halfheartedly.

I bit back a chuckle at that. "How 'bout this? You do half tonight, and half tomorrow before our lesson."

Cason's whoop of excitement was answer enough.

"But—" I cut in, before he could get too excited. "No misses. You mess up, you miss, well, then you start back at zero."

That seemed to take the wind out of his sails a bit, but he still held that level of enthusiasm only he and Cash seemed to have about mundane things. He nodded, a grin on his face. "Deal, Uncle Mav."

I nodded. "Well, go on then. Tie him up and get started."

Cash and I remained in relative silence as Cason rode the old gelding out of the arena and toward the barn to tie him up. When he was finally out of ear shot, Cash whirled on me.

"What's goin' on?" His brows knit together, a rare frown on his face.

He reminded me of Cheyenne in that way. Not much seemed to get them down for too long. You could always expect them to be laughing, smiling. But where Cheyenne reminded me of the sun, Cash reminded me of summer nights. Warm, wild, and full of mischief.

I didn't lie. I didn't try to make excuses. With a sigh, I leaned my arms against the pipe-stall, staring unseeingly toward the arena. "Cheyenne's thinkin' of includin' Mae in the baby's name."

Cash stiffened at my side. Talk of Ellie—or my family at all, for that matter—wasn't somethin' we did often. Cash didn't really remember her too much, only that her, him and True had played together a few times when Dad was gone or too drunk to bother fighting Mom about taking us to visit the Mooneys. But those occasions had been rare. Mom had always tried to hide the damage Dad did from Uncle Bad and Goodie. I had no doubt if they'd known what all he'd done to us, they'd have killed him.

It sure as hell made Cash uncomfortable. To him, we were brothers, we took care of each other, and the infrequent reminder of my dark past upset him. Not that he'd have been able to do anything, but he'd always taken upon himself to look out for me. And he always had.

Cash's stare was heavier than a semi-truck as I turned to meet his gaze. "You okay with that?" he asked.

I nodded. "Yeah...I'm honored, actually. Deserves to be somethin' good that comes outta my family."

"She ain't the only good," Cash said, his voice soft yet determined. "*You* came outta that family."

My chest tightened, a mixture of emotions fighting for dominance in my heart—pride and love, but also guilt and disbelief. Throw them all together and I didn't know what to think, let alone what to say even. So, I did what I did best: I didn't say a damn thing. Blowing out a breath, I reached for my hat, removing it to run a hand through my close-cropped hair.

My heart went out to my cousin. He'd always been my biggest supporter, my fiercest friend. My brother. He might be a pain in the ass, but he had a good heart. A far better one than he let people think he had.

I didn't look at him as I picked at the felt of my hat, ensuring that nothing was out of place. A lump lodged in my throat as my mouth bobbed open and closed once. Twice. "I'm..." I cleared my throat. "I'm afraid I'm gonna turn out like him."

This entire time, from the moment Cheyenne decided she wanted to keep the baby and stay with me—giving me the honor and chance to raise her as my own—this dark thought had hung around, lurking in the shadows, growing, festering. What if I ended up like my dad? I didn't have many good memories with him, but he couldn't always have been bad. Mom wouldn't have been with him if he'd always been that way, right?

Cash scoffed, disbelief coating his features. "What the hell makes you think that?"

"I'm his blood. That anger runs in me. What if..." My words drifted off into nothingness. I couldn't even say them aloud.

A memory sparked to life. I hadn't always been quiet like this. Hadn't always taken the road less traveled, been the bigger person. Once I was hot and angry and let my emotions rule me. Dad had beaten most of that fight out of me. Most, but not all. Every now and then it rose to the surface, bubbling over and exploding.

What if I hurt them?

"Mav...Mav!" Cash's hands gripped my shoulders, gently shaking me. I slowly lifted my gaze to lock with his.

Concern and sadness swirled on my cousin's face. "You ain't him. You ain't ever gonna be him. You're better. Always have been, and you always will."

I didn't know where all this anxiety and self-doubt was coming from. It always lurked there, I guess, but I was usually a bit better at hiding it. But so much had happened, so much had changed in such a short time. My entire world had been flipped upside down, ripped inside out, and finally righted, and I was still trying to get my bearings. I thought I'd known what I wanted in life, but then Cheyenne came in like some wild, west Texas storm and now I couldn't imagine—didn't want—a life without her in it.

And I was terrified, completely and utterly terrified, that I would somehow fuck it all up.

Cash squeezed my shoulder once more, dragging me back to the present.

"I'm scared I ain't gonna be good enough for them," I finally admitted aloud.

Cash just shook his head, a small, soft smile coming to his lips as he huffed a laugh. "Mav, you're the best man I know...You're good at just about every damn thing, and I don't think there's a more perfect job for you than bein' a dad."

The lump in my chest grew larger, moisture pricking in my eyes. I cleared my throat, but Cash went on before I could get any words out. "You might get angry. You might yell every now and then, but who doesn't? I mean look at Dad. He fucked up every once in a while. He raised his voice and got on us, but he apologized when he was wrong and taught us how to focus that anger."

I nodded. Those first few months with Uncle Bad and Aunt Violet were hard for me. I'd never been in a loving household, and while Bad seemed rough around the edges, he was like leather, give him some time, and he'd soften right up. He was firm but fair, and wiser than any man I knew.

He'd taught me it ain't about suppressing the anger, but channeling it. I channeled it into learning new things.

Cash clapped me on the shoulder. "You're kind, patient, under-standin'. You were always there to defend me, protect me, encourage me, push me. I have no doubt you're gonna do that for that little girl."

My lip quivered up into the barest hint of a smile, hope and pride winning out against the war of emotions within me. "You think?" I asked earnestly.

Cash grinned. "I fuckin' know so. Now, do me a favor...channel all that anger and frustration into winnin' the Hill Country Jackpot next weekend."

I grinned, happy for the change in subject. "I can do that," I replied with a nod, glancing over toward the barn. Cason stood about five feet behind the dummy, situating the rope in his hands. "Come on," I said, "let's go give him some pointers."

Cash nudged me in the shoulder as we started off that way. "I don't know, man. I think pretty soon that kid's gonna rope better than you or I even."

I chuckled. "Speak for yourself."

But he wasn't entirely wrong. Cason had all the makings of being a great cowboy. Then again, when you lived with three professionals and had the infamous Bad Mooney training you almost daily, you weren't destined for anything but greatness.

———

CHEYENNE WAS QUIET AS HER AND CHARLIE CAME TO CHECK on Cason, giving me space until everyone had left. A pang of guilt shot through my heart. So, she'd noticed. I'd hoped I'd hidden my anxiety well enough, but guess I hadn't been fooling anyone.

"Wanna drive back to the house?" I asked, nodding at the old ranch truck.

Cheyenne huffed a laugh. "That piece of shit is one drive away from breakin' down. I'd rather just get a move on and walk."

With a nod, we started off for the house, the crunch of dirt and gravel under our feet the only sound for a few long, tense moments as I gathered my thoughts and tried to figure out what to say. "I'm sorry," I finally managed to get out. "I've been in my head a lot tonight, but I don't want you thinkin' you'd done somethin' wrong."

She pulled her jacket around her tighter as she nodded and met my gaze. "Wanna talk about it?"

No. I'd rather get kicked in the ribs than talk about my problems and insecurities, but she deserved the truth. We were a team after all. And a team was only as strong as its weakest player. So, with a nod, I said, "Mentionin' my sister brought up some...well, some not great emotions about my family."

"I'm sorry." She reached out a hand, grasping for mine. It was cold despite being tucked into her jacket pocket. I pulled her closer to me, trying to give any extra warmth I could.

"It ain't your fault. I don't talk about my family much, because, well, I didn't have the greatest upbringin'."

"Cash and Bad mentioned a bit when you weren't talkin'," she said softly, blue eyes flicking to mine as she tried to gauge my reaction.

I blew out a breath. "I'm sure whatever they told you was mild in comparison to what all I remember."

She squeezed my hand, leaning into me a bit more as the porch light from our house sprung to life in the distance—a shining beacon promising warmth. "You can tell me. You know about my mama."

I blew out a breath. "Thank you, I appreciate that, and I do wanna tell you, but..." I couldn't look at her as I choked out, "I ain't quite ready to share that ugly part of me yet. With anyone. It's too dark. Too raw. I..." I shook my head, finally meeting her gaze. "I'm sorry."

I expected annoyance, maybe even anger from her. I mean, she *had* told me about her past. What I'd gone through—it was bad enough to be plagued with the memories. But talking about them? Dredging them up, reliving them, speaking about them aloud. I didn't have the strength to tell her yet. As I looked into her eyes, I didn't find a shred of anything other than affection. Love.

"That's okay," she said softly. "When you're ready, I'm here. There ain't no rush."

CHAPTER 45
Hold My Halo

CHEYENNE

The bathroom of Cowboy's was dim, the music slightly muffled and drowned out by the near constant chatter of women talking and laughing and gossiping as they came and went. Charlie fussed over her outfit in the wall of mirrors, every inch of her exuding worry and self-consciousness as she kept her gaze down anytime someone looked her way.

"I can't believe Cash convinced everyone to come out to a bar," she huffed, tucking her bangs behind her ear. "They have a jackpot roping tomorrow. They should be home getting rest."

A part of me agreed, but everyone could use a little fun to let loose. Things had been so tense with mine and Charlie's looming due dates. I think this was Cash's odd way of showing us a fun time before the babies came and we couldn't just go out any Friday night and dance the night away.

I chuckled as I came to stand beside her. "It's a dance hall," I clarified, nudging her hip with mine. "There just happens to be like four bars in it."

She rolled her eyes even as a smile graced her lips. "Semantics." Her gaze flicked to a random girl who glanced at both of us, her curious stare going to our stomachs. There wasn't any possible way to hide it now. The moment the girl disappeared into a stall, Charlie turned to me, shame lingering in the furrow of her brow, the downward pull of her lips. "This is so awkward. Literally everyone is staring at us."

I turned to her, forcing her to meet my gaze. "First off, fuck everyone who's starin' at you. They're all just jealous they don't look as drop-dead gorgeous as you, *even* being eight months pregnant."

I wasn't lying. Charlie looked stunning in the black long-sleeved dress that hugged her curves. I was more of a color girl, myself, but Charlie wore the hell out of black, looking all sleek and edgy and sexy. Her copper hair always stood out so well against it.

Charlie's mouth tugged upwards slightly, but she pegged me with a pointed glance.

I went on before she could protest. "And secondly, who cares? We have just as much right to be here as them. It's a *dance hall,* we came here to dance. It ain't like you or I are drinkin'."

The smile she fought so hard to suppress finally broke through, like the sun peeking through a sky of clouds. "We do look pretty good, don't we?" she said with a smirk.

I grinned, turning back to look at our reflections once more. "We look fuckin' fantastic."

Charlie laughed. "How are you always so confident?"

I shrugged. "I just know my worth, girl. Time you learn yours as well."

"Have you met my mom?" Charlie asked, her stormy eyes meeting mine in the mirror.

"Ah, to hell with whatever bullshit she says. Don't give her the satisfaction of tearin' you down." I grabbed one of her hands and squeezed.

With a smile, she squeezed it back before sighing. "Alright, let's go back out there."

We walked out together, the loud music replacing the chatter in the bathroom. People moved and mingled all around us, the neon signs and blue lights of the dancehall casting everything in a cool tinted glow. I spied our table across the way. Ryder and Maverick stood there talking to a couple of their friends. Bad and Violet surprisingly enough had joined us, and hadn't come off the dancefloor since we'd gotten here an hour ago. Cash hung out at the other side of the table, closest to the dance floor, charming the pants off an entire group of girls, while keeping his arms wrapped around the waists of two more.

God, he was such a man-whore, but at least he was upfront and honest about it. There were no games with him. You knew exactly what you were getting. A wild night, a great story. A one-night stand. Maybe that's why I didn't hate him for what he did. The women who gravitated toward him knew exactly what he was all about, and they wanted him anyway.

My gaze went back to Maverick, who watched me now, a hungry, possessive look in his eyes. I shivered at that look. At what it meant.

A wide grin blossomed on my lips as I tossed my hair over my shoulder and made my way towards him—

Before my right arm was wrenched backwards, my entire world spinning as I was whipped around, coming face to face with none other than...

"Nate?" Disbelief coated my words, unease thrumming to life in my chest.

He towered over me, anger brewing in his eyes like a summer storm. "I thought I made it fuckin' clear you weren't keepin' it." His tone was sharp, deep, his grasp on my arm biting as he squeezed tighter.

This man had burned down my trailer for making a fool of him. Fear gripped me, squeezing the air from my lungs. Fuck. This was exactly what I had been afraid of in the beginning. I thought of the fire. Of the threat he'd made over the phone when I'd told him about the baby. His fingers dug into my arm, tighter, tighter, tighter.

No, I wasn't going to let some piece of shit playboy scare me. Anger sparked to life in my chest, chasing away the fear. How dare he touch me. Threaten me. Threaten my child.

Glaring up at him, I managed to say with a calm I didn't feel, "Get your fuckin' hand off me."

I felt the weight of Charlie's gaze. Of Ryder's. Of Cash's, even. But I felt none other more than, Maverick's.

Nate's grip only tightened, pain blooming under his touch. "What're you gonna do about it?"

"I think she just told you to get your hands off her." Maverick's deep, stern voice boomed like thundering, soothing the knot in my chest. His familiar scent filled my nose as I felt him come to a stop at my side. I glanced up at him, and my breath hitched in my throat.

I'd seen Maverick calm. I'd seen him in pain. I'd seen him protective and upset. But I'd never seen him like this. Those usually light jade depths had darkened, hardened. Pure, unapologetic rage danced in his eyes and etched along the severe lines of his brutal, handsome face.

He towered over me, over Nate even, looking like some angel of death come to my aid.

Nate, to his credit, didn't back down, but some of his confidence faltered, his words nowhere near as sure as they'd been with me a moment before. "This doesn't concern you, *friend*. I suggest you stay out of it."

His grip on me had loosened, and I wrenched my arm back toward me, but he readjusted and gripped tighter, a flash of pain shooting through the limb as he pulled me closer to him.

"You and I need to settle some shit," Nate growled, pegging me in place with his heated glare. His hot breath fanned my cheeks, reeking of beer. I cringed, repulsion rippling through me. What had I ever seen in him?

I met his glare, my anger burning brighter, hotter. "Fuck you, Nate," I snarled, before spitting in his face.

It was enough for him to let me go as he swiped at his cheek before pulling his hand back, a look of dark intent in his eyes.

That was all it took...The final chord of Maverick's self-control shredding apart entirely.

He moved then—quicker than a cottonmouth. Faster than a flash of lightning. As swift and sure as a fierce flowing river.

CHAPTER 46
Take It Outside

MAVERICK

I know there was no such thing as soulmates—at least not like the ones in Cheyenne's books where their fates were written in the stars or premeditated by a god or goddess...but you couldn't convince me that there wasn't something pulling Cheyenne and I together.

She was the missing puzzle piece I'd spent damn near my whole life searching for. The way she'd come into it, the way she fit with me so seamlessly, well you couldn't convince me that that wasn't fate.

So, when I say I felt her gaze from all the way across the dancehall, I wasn't lying. I forgot what I was talking about, where I was, because in that moment, all I could think about, all I could see was her.

Her long blonde curls were wild as usual, brushing her waist as she moved. The yellow long-sleeve and white suede fringe skirt she wore were a bold choice, but she wore the hell out of it—like she wore the hell out of everything. I know I sounded like a broken record, but she was gorgeous. Absolutely gorgeous... The fact she was pregnant made her even more so.

Her gaze met mine, and even from across the room, I felt the heat in her stare. The silent promise in the mischievous upward tilt of her lips. Adrenaline and desire pumped through me at the unspoken promise written plainly on her face.

Until dread crashed through me at the sight of some stranger grabbing her arm.

"—Mav... Mav?" Ryder's voice sounded far away, drowned out like I was underwater.

My vision went red, fury boiling through my veins. I didn't know who that man was or what the hell he wanted, but the way he touched her—

Then I was moving, my boots eating up the distance between Cheyenne and I. I knew she could hold her own. Knew she was plenty capable of taking care of herself, but I wouldn't let her deal with this all by herself.

"What the *fuck*?" Cash's voice sounded just a step to my right, while Ryder came up on my left.

"Who the hell is that?" Ryder added.

My gaze narrowed, anger roiling around in my chest, demanding to be let out. "I don't know." But I sure as hell was going to find out.

The music drowned out to white-noise as I made my way through the sea of bodies leading toward Cheyenne.

"Get your fuckin' hand off me." Her voice was laced with venom, her stance promising violence.

The man's grip tightened as I came upon them, but he didn't notice me, not as he growled out, "What're you gonna do about it?"

"I think she just told you to get your hands off her." I don't know how I even managed to get the words out. My jaw was clenched so tightly I was surprised it hadn't broken, shattered. My heart thundered in my chest, hard enough to crack ribs.

Cheyenne glanced up at me, her gaze meeting mine as I came to a stop beside her. A mixture of panic and rage blazed in the bright depths, and I knew right then and there who this was. I'd never seen the asshole, but I didn't need an introduction, the way he interacted with her said it all. The unexplainable fury. The way his eyes dropped to her stomach, a look of pure disgust coating his features.

Nate.

He wasn't what I'd expected with long, shoulder-length dark hair, dark, angry eyes, a five o' clock shadow beard. He wore a black tank top and jeans, no doubt to show off his half sleeve and bulging biceps. But it didn't matter how much he could lift if he didn't get his goddamn hand of Cheyenne.

I'd fucking kill him.

The thought alone should have given me pause, but I didn't care. I'd spent most of my childhood being bruised and beaten by a piece of shit just like him. I wasn't a kid anymore, and I'd be damned if I stood by. No one would threaten her. Especially not him.

Nate looked at me, some of his bravado faltering for a moment until he recovered enough to say, "This doesn't concern you, *friend*. I suggest you stay out of it."

Friend. I always hated when people used that word as a threat. It took everything in me not to throw a punch at him right then and there. But I wanted to at least give Cheyenne the chance to handle this herself. Maybe the night didn't need to end in violence.

A part of me—a deep, dark, forbidden part of me—found that a shame.

Cheyenne used the moment as a distraction, wrenching her arm toward her, but Nate's hold held firm. He yanked her back toward him, gripping her tight enough to wrench a pain-laced gasp from her lips. His attention snapped back to Cheyenne as he lowered his face dangerously close to hers, growling, "You and I need to settle some shit."

I shook, fists clenched to the point my nails dug into the meat of my palms. The mild pain did little to quell the tide of anger that rose and rose and rose with each passing moment.

No more. This conversation was over.

Every muscle in my body tensed as I made to move forward and rip his hand from her. No more standing by idly. I wouldn't let him hurt her. But before I could move, Cheyenne's entire demeanor changed. Hardened.

"Fuck you, Nate," she snarled, before spitting in his face.

He let her go, an annoyed growl escaping him as he swiped at his cheek. If I'd thought he was pissed before, it didn't compare to the shift in him right now. Dark, malicious intent flickered to life in his gaze, his hand rising.

I knew that look. That stance. I'd grown up with all my life.

Memories and nightmares of my father fueled my anger like kindling on a fire.

He didn't even draw his hand back fully before I moved.

I stepped forward, my hand gripping his forearm and wrenching it back while turning him away from me. He struggled in my grip, bucking and thrashing, grunts of anger and curses ringing through the air. People stopped to watch, curious expressions on their faces, but I paid them no heed as I pushed Nate toward the closest exit.

"Get the fuck off me, man!" Nate growled even as I put more pressure on his arm. "This has nothin' to do with you."

"You wanna hit someone?" I grumbled in his ear, "You can try and hit me."

He struggled against me, but I continued to hold firm. Each step sent a surge of adrenaline pumping through my veins. I sensed Ryder and Cash on either side of me, always there. Always having my back.

Cash slipped by me to push open the door, the cold night a welcome reprieve from the heat of the dancehall. The scent of cigarettes and tobacco filled my nose, the chatter of the small group of people outside nothing compared to a few moments ago.

I shoved Nate with enough force to make him stumble to his knees in the middle of the parking lot. Rolling my shoulders, I unbuttoned my sleeves and pushed them up over my forearms, allowing for more movement.

"Looks like this dickhead's got friends," Cash warned, low and close to my ear.

My gaze settled on the two men making their way over to Nate and helping him up. "Should be easy for you two, yeah?" I asked, glancing between Cash and Ryder.

Cash's usually easy-going grin was positively feral, the glint in his hazel eyes promising trouble. He'd always been a hot-head, and he loved nothing more than the thrill of a fight...well, aside from maybe a good lay. Ryder's demeanor was more serious, his dark eyes glinting with the same level of intensity as when he was about to get on a bull. He cracked his neck, stretching it one way and then the other.

I didn't need to turn around to know Cheyenne was there. I could feel her. Sparing her a glance, I turned and met her gaze. Worry lurked in the turquoise depths, but also stone-cold resolution.

I hoped she was okay with I was about to do. I knew violence wasn't always the answer, but then again, sometimes it was. I'd never been much of a talker. Actions spoke far louder than words. Something like this though, you didn't talk through this. If you had the audacity to put your hands on someone you better be prepared to back that action up. Nate had already done enough to Cheyenne. I couldn't—*wouldn't* stand by and let him threaten or touch her.

I'd fight Nate, whether she approved or not, but deep down I wanted to know she was okay with it. As if sensing the struggle within me, she offered a single, firm nod. Silent permission for what I was about to do.

Nate's angry voice drew my attention forward. "I'm gonna fuck you up," he shouted, spitting at the ground.

I took that as invitation enough. Curling my hand into a fist, I stepped forward.

•

CHAPTER 47
Wait In The Truck

CHEYENNE

Maverick moved with a lethal grace and ferocity I'd never seen before. He still possessed that same level of quiet confidence, that surety, but it was more than that. He didn't move just like a guy who knew how to brawl. He knew how to *fight*. How to punch, how to duck and deflect. In fact, all the boys did.

And, goddamn, that right hook of his...

Charlie squeezed my hand tightly, a gasp falling from her lips as Ryder took a nasty hit to the ribs, but he didn't even bat an eye as he dove back into the fray, swinging.

My gaze snapped back to Maverick. I couldn't take my eyes off him. I was no stranger to scrapping every now and then—courtesy of my big mouth and not always knowing when to quit—but this wasn't a scrap.

To Nate's credit, he hung in longer than I'd expected. I'd thought he'd have gone down after that first right hook. He was hurting, that much was apparent. Barely hanging in there, but he hadn't given up yet. Blood flowed from his nose, his mouth, one of his eyes already puffy and swelling shut. He spit at Maverick, spraying spittle and blood through the air. Maverick swiped at his face, a growl of frustration escaping him.

But that's all it took.

Nate used that moment to take a cheap shot at him, hitting Maverick square in the jaw, rocking him back. My breath caught in my chest, my heart skipping entirely.

Please be okay. Please be okay. I squeezed Charlie's hand as panic settled around me like a cloud of smoke. It seeped into my lungs, stealing whatever little bit of breath I had left. But then a warm hand settled on my shoulder, and I glanced up long enough to find Bad at my side. He didn't meet my gaze, but it's like he knew I needed the silent support all the same.

His gaze was glued to the fight. I'd hoped him and Violet wouldn't have noticed the altercation.

Would he step in? Would he stop the fight? A part of me wanted him to. Wanted him to stop this before it went any further and someone got seriously hurt. But Bad had been known for his temper in his rodeoing days, and he didn't seem the type of man to break up a fight. He was the type to see it through and finished.

Something shifted in Maverick. Something dark and angry and vicious—the tension in his shoulders, the harsh, brutal lines of his face, the severe look in his gaze...

Nate didn't have a chance.

Maverick struck. Hard enough to send Nate staggering back before hitting him once more. Nate's legs gave out and he toppled to the floor. But Maverick didn't stop as he knelt over him and struck again. And again. And again.

I cringed at the sound of those punches. At the force in his hits. Nate's head lolled, but Maverick kept going. All the while, a mixture of awe and horror swelled up inside me. Awe, because I'd only ever seen a fight that intense in a damn movie, but horror, because it was so much worse in real life.

He was taking it too far. Losing himself in the fight. It's like a light switch had gone off in him. Maverick—the voice of reason, the one with the level head, the one who never lost his temper—was gone. This...this was the beast that lurked beneath the surface. The monster his father's violence and abuse created.

I didn't give a damn what happened to Nate, but I could only imagine what damage it would do to Maverick if he went too far.

Cash was there all of a sudden. Had he dealt with the guy he'd been fighting? I honestly hadn't even noticed. He grabbed Maverick by the shoulder, muttering something I couldn't hear over the commotion from the onlookers, but it's like Maverick was gone. He shoved at Cash, swinging a fist his way. Cash caught it in the shoulder, a loud curse escaping him.

Maverick didn't even miss a beat as he turned his wild gaze back on a barely struggling Nate.

A tear slipped down my cheek.

He couldn't keep going. As much of a piece of shit Nate was, I didn't want his blood on Maverick's hands. His death. That's where we were headed. I could feel it, the dread of it all coiling in me tighter and tighter, turning my stomach into a roiling sea of despair.

Maverick wasn't the type to let something like this slide. He wouldn't stop until he'd finished.

I grabbed Bad's arm. "Stop him. Please."

If anyone could do it, it was him.

Bad's hazel gaze met mine for a moment before he stepped forward. It's almost like time stopped. Ryder and the guy he fought came to a standstill, both of them backing off to watch Bad storm for Maverick. Cash rubbed at his shoulder, watching his dad with an intensity he rarely showed.

CHAPTER 48
Ride The Lightning

MAVERICK

I was like a man possessed. All reason, all mercy, all rational thought left me as I pummeled the man's face with my fists. I saw red. I saw black. I saw nothing but memories, echoes. My own fears and insecurities flashed before my eyes in nonsensical images that drove me to punch, crush, destroy.

Another hand on my shoulder. Another echoing voice calling my name. But the beast inside of me, fighting for purchase over my sanity, sank its claws in deeper. *Hurt. Fight.* That's all it wanted.

I lashed out, struck—the beast inside me winning. My gaze settled on Bad as my fist sailed through the air.

Only he caught my hand easily and dragged me into an embrace. Not so much a hug as a smothering hold meant to starve the flames of my rage of the oxygen that sent them burning out of control.

"You got him, boy. He's done." Bad's deep, gravelly voice grated in my ears, cutting through the haze of rage blazing within me.

But it wouldn't break. Not completely. Not quite. "Ain't done yet." I ground out. My voice. It sounded different. Almost like someone else was talking.

Bad's voice was soft in my ear, yet stern, hard. "You keep goin', he's gonna die."

"Good," I grunted, the wild, feral part of me still struggling for a hold. I needed to kill that man. The reason for the beast inside me. The reason for a lifetime of torment. A lifetime of pain.

"If he dies, you gotta one way ticket to prison. Who's gonna take care of Cheyenne? The baby?" Bad shoved me back enough to look at me, his hazel eyes boring into my own.

Cheyenne... The baby.

Something shifted in me then. Broke. Tore loose. I looked down at what I'd done. At *Nate.* At the bleeding, sobbing, broken man that I had almost killed. Not the one with eyes the same color as mine.

"It ain't him, son," Bad said softly, his hand on my shoulder. "It ain't him."

The air left my lungs in an explosive whoosh, chased out by sobs of grief as I realized what had driven me to nearly commit murder.

Oh, God.

I backed away from Bad, shaking as my gaze dipped to my hands. My knuckles were already swelling up, my fingers caked in blood. Tears flooded and blurred my vision as I inhaled a shaky breath and looked up slowly to meet my uncle's unrelenting stare.

"That ain't him, and you ain't either." Bad pulled me in once more, pressing his forehead to mine. "It's over Maverick. Just let it go. It's over."

Shame and guilt filled me, wrenching the air from my lungs and making my knees weak.

What had I done?

CHAPTER 49
Heart Like A Truck

CHEYENNE

Bad gripped Maverick's shoulder, similar to the way Cash had when he'd tried to get him off Nate. And just like with Cash, Maverick swung, wild and furious. Bad caught the punch easily, and pulled him into a hard, unrelenting embrace. Maverick struggled for a moment, reminding me of that little red filly the first time I'd watched him work with her—all anger and fire and brimstone.

Bad spoke to him, his hold on Maverick unyielding. Bit by bit, inch by inch, the anger slowly dissipated from Maverick—the tension in his muscles, the anger lingering in every fiber of his being melting away like ice in a glass on a warm day.

I watched in stunned silence, tears slipping down my cheeks as Bad moved back a step. All the fight was gone from Maverick, a hollow shell of despair in its place as he glanced down at his hands. He looked pained, haunted, tortured. And then Bad's hands gripped Maverick's shoulders as he pressed his head to his nephew's.

Bad spoke to him, even from the distance I could see his lips moving, though I didn't know what he said—I probably never would. But it seemed to bring Maverick back to himself.

389

Cash came up to them then, and Maverick let go long enough to pull his cousin in for a tight hug.

Ryder joined the fray, even as Nate struggled and moaned on the ground. His friends tended to him, casting worried glances Maverick's way. Almost like they were scared something might set him off again and he'd come at them next.

What would happen now? The unease still hadn't left me; I still felt like a ticking time bomb was about to go off inside my heart. Would the cops come? Would Nate press charges? Would Maverick go to jail?

My breath sawed in and out of my chest, a strangled cry falling from my lips. It was all too much. Too. Too. Much. A warm set of arms was there to catch me as I felt the world start to tilt, the smell of magnolias filling my nose. Violet held me in her arms, as sob after sob wracked me.

I don't know how long I stood there like that, but my entire body went still as I felt Maverick's stare on me. Slowly, I peeled myself out of Violet's grip and turned to face him fully. He looked every bit the dark angel as he picked up his discarded hat off the ground, examining it a moment before replacing it on his head and striding toward me.

I wiped at my tears.

There wasn't a trace of the monster in him. Almost like it had been purged in the fight. Another woman might have been afraid of him.... worried that that monster would poke back through at some point down the line. But I wasn't.

He'd never hurt me. Never lay a hand on me. He wasn't his father. He was the same man who'd run into a burning trailer to save my dog, the man who'd picked up all the shattered pieces of me when I'd fallen apart the first few days we'd been together. He was the same man who'd driven me damn near two hours away to an abortion clinic when every fiber of his being fought that notion. He was the same man who loved me, and loved this little girl like she was his own.

Maverick's face, his eyes, shone with worry. Without him saying a word, I knew just how terrified he was. Terrified that I'd seen this side of him and would leave.

So, as he came to a stop before me, as his guilty gaze met mine, unshed tears hanging like drops of starlight in his eyes, I pulled him to me and let him fall apart.

———

Maverick paced back and forth, so fiercely it was a damn miracle he hadn't carved a path into the concrete. He'd removed his hat a while ago, leaving it in the back of Ryder's truck. As he paced, he speared his fingers through his close-cropped hair.

I watched in silence, not knowing what to do. He wouldn't talk to anyone, save Bad, and only enough to mutter, "I can't go to jail, Bad. What am I gonna do?" Or some variation along those lines.

I was honestly more than a bit surprised the cops hadn't showed up yet. It was crazy though, within a few minutes of the fight breaking up, the crowd dispersed, people going back to their night as if Maverick hadn't just smashed Nate's face in.

To them it was probably just two guys getting in a fight over me. If only they knew how much deeper and darker it was than that.

I shivered at the thought of seeing Nate's broken, bloodied face. He looked almost unrecognizable as his friends all but dragged him away. At least he was alive and breathing. It was more than he deserved, but I didn't have to worry about Maverick having murdered someone.

"Ouch! Mama, it's fine. I'm *fine,*" Cash grumbled a few feet to my left. Violet dabbed at his bloodied eyebrow. He was fine for the most part, aside from a blooming black eye that was halfway swollen shut. Ryder was better off appearance wise, but he'd injured his ribs from the looks of the way he held them—the same ones he'd broken back in March.

Guilt welled in me. I knew it wasn't my fault. I'd literally done nothing wrong, but Maverick had gotten involved because of me. Okay, that was a lie. Maverick struck me as the type to defend a woman's honor regardless of their relationship to him. But still, this had all started because Nate had found out about the baby.

I glanced down at my stomach, a hand going to my belly as I tried to feel her. I'd not felt any kicks or somersaults or any of the usual movement I'd grown so used to, but then again this was the first time I'd thought of it after finally coming down from the craziness of the fight.

Worry knotted in my chest, but I didn't say anything. I didn't want to add more problems to the bunch. I'd keep an eye and start worrying when I needed to.

My gaze drifted to Maverick once more, who continued his pacing while Bad reassured Maverick to the best of his ability—a near impossible feat it seemed.

Maverick's eyes shone with unshed tears as he choked out to no one in particular, "What am I gonna do?"

"Cheyenne." Bad's voice sent my heart racing.

"Yes, sir?" I asked, hopping off the tailgate and making a beeline for him.

Bad appraised me for a long moment. "How're you doin'?"

I blew out a breath. "As good as I can right now."

He nodded. "You two are ridin' with me. Violet's gonna drive the others."

I glanced at Maverick before turning back to Bad. I was glad he was the one taking us home. I didn't know what to do with Mav. How to break through the paranoid episode he was going through. Truth was, I was trying to navigate my way through a sea of emotions as well. I still couldn't quite comprehend all that had transpired. "Yes, sir."

I turned to Maverick, holding out a hand before him. "Hey... hey, Mav. Come on. Let's go home."

His gaze lifted to meet my own, the worry exuding from him making my heart squeeze painfully in my chest. "What about the cops? Don't we need to wait?"

Bad moved before Maverick, gripping his shoulders firmly while leaning in close. "Don't worry, boy. Everythin's gonna be okay."

"But—"

"Maverick. Listen to me." Bad spoke quietly, but no less stern. "Nothin's gonna happen to you. Everythin's gonna be alright. Just get in the damn truck."

His harsh voice seemed to finally cut through some of the cloud of worry that hovered over Maverick. He blew out a deep breath and nodded, silently moving to me and offering me a hand. "I'm sorry," he whispered, as he led me toward Bad's truck.

Everyone else was piling into their designated vehicles. After a quick

goodbye to Cash, Ryder, and Charlie, I helped Maverick into the backseat, before climbing in myself...

CHAPTER 50
Concrete Angel

MAVERICK

Hollow.

I felt hollow. Cold. Empty.

Even holding Cheyenne's hand, gripping it like it was a life preserver and I was lost at sea, I still didn't feel anything. It's like I was breathing, but not alive.

I don't remember the drive back to the ranch. I think Bad and Cheyenne talked a bit, but I couldn't be sure.

How had I let myself go like that? I'd never lost control before. Not like that. Never on a person. The punching bag, sure. But what I'd done... It's like my control snapped.

Thank the Lord Bad stopped me. Had he not, well, I don't think anyone could have.

"We're home," Cheyenne said softly, squeezing my hand. Her blue eyes swam with worry, her cheeks stained with tears.

Did she think differently of me? Did she think me a monster? Would she leave now that she'd seen this side of me? I wouldn't blame her if she did.

A little trickle of fear ignited in my chest...and honestly, I welcomed it. It was better than feeling nothing at all. But I still couldn't bring myself to speak as she helped me out of the truck and we headed for the house.

Brandy was there to greet us as Cheyenne opened the front door. She made sure to say hi to Chey first before coming to my side, sitting right at my feet as if she sensed my unease.

Bad shuffled just inside the doorway. "Want me to stay?" he asked, looking at Cheyenne, but it felt like the words were meant for me.

I couldn't even bring myself to shake my head. To look at him, even. Shame and guilt joined the fear in my heart. I couldn't begin to think what he thought of me now. He'd spent the last twenty years teaching me how to control my anger, my rage. He'd taught me to harness it, embrace it, and use it for good. In the course of five minutes, I'd taken all those lessons and shoved them back in his face.

Cheyenne's voice was surprisingly calm as it floated through the room. "I got it...but thank you, Bad."

I noticed him nod once in my peripheral vision. "Okay. Call me if you need anythin'. I'll be back in the mornin'." I felt the weight of his stare for a long moment. My eyes almost betrayed me.

I tried to not let the opinions of others define me, but I'd be lying if I said I didn't care what others thought. Maybe it was the fact that nothing I ever did growing up with my father ever seemed to be good enough, but I craved acceptance. I needed it.

And Bad was one of those people that I sought it from most. I'd always strove to be the best version of myself—I owed him that after all he'd done.

I'd sure gone and failed him, hadn't I?

He moved forward and pressed a hand to my shoulder. "Look at me, boy."

Slowly, hesitantly, I raised my gaze to meet his. Those hazel eyes, so much like Cash's, bored into me. My throat tightened, my heart seizing in my chest. It hurt to breathe. I opened my mouth, but no words came out. I had so much to say, so much to apologize for. But nothing seemed like enough.

Something shifted in his eyes, softening the severe scowl that seemed ever-present on his face. He pulled me into an embrace. A real hug this time. One meant to soothe, not to subdue. I could count on one hand how many times he'd hugged me. He wasn't the type to show emotion like that. We'd always been better with words than feelings, and that was saying a lot, since both of us were shit with words.

I clung to him, my shoulders quaking, the weight of what had happened becoming too much. He pulled back to look at me, something warm lingering in his gaze. "You're alright, kid. It's okay now."

I rocked back at his words, breaking the hold of our embrace. "I nearly killed him."

Bad's lips pulled up into the whisper of a smile. "But you didn't."

"Only because of you."

Bad simply shrugged, like beating men's faces to a pulp wasn't horrible. He adjusted his hat atop his head, gripped my shoulder and squeezed reassuringly before letting go of me... And then, without another word, he was gone.

I dropped my gaze once more, my chin all but resting against my chest. The shame still hung around me like a shroud that wouldn't come off.

Cheyenne's familiar citrusy scent filled my nose as she came to stand before me. "Hey...hey look at me, Mav."

I couldn't. Couldn't bear to see what emotions lurked in the turquoise pools of her eyes.

"Maverick... Hey..." Her warm fingers hooked under my chin and forced me to meet her stare. There was no fear there, worry still shone, but resolve swam in there as well. And love. So much love.

I'd thought I felt inadequate with Bad. But I'd never felt more inadequate, more undeserving until now.

Cheyenne let out a choked sound, tears brewing in her eyes. She moved her fingers from under my chin to my cheek, wiping at the moisture there. I hadn't even realized I was crying. She dropped her hand, making sure to take mine in her own, and led me through the house to the bathroom. In silence, she turned on the tub before coming to stand before me.

"Come on, let's get you cleaned up."

It was so reminiscent of the night of the fire it gave me pause. How could she be so calm? She'd been assaulted tonight. Threatened. Had watched me beat up her ex.

Then she started to sing...and it broke everything in me.

I bit back tears as she slowly undressed me and then herself, before situating us in the tub. She grabbed a washcloth and soap, singing softly the whole time, and proceeded to gently clean the blood from my hands and caked under my fingernails. She took her time, easing her strokes around my torn open and bruising knuckles.

As the song ended, dying on her lips, she finally glanced up at me. "Thank you," she whispered.

"For what?"

She pressed a soft kiss to my knuckles—light as a feather. "For protectin' me." Taking my hand and placing it on her belly, she continued, "For protectin' her."

That damn near broke me.

How could she not see how problematic this was? I'd gone too far. I'd lost control.

"Don't," I ground out through clenched teeth, pulling my hand away. "Don't paint me as the hero."

Her brows knit together, her head tilting to the side in question. "What're you talkin' about?"

"You and Bad, you're just tryin' to make me feel better 'bout what I've done. I beat a man senseless...I could—no, should have to deal with serious repercussions, and y'all are actin' like it's no big deal."

"Maverick, had you not stepped in, he *would* have hit me. He deserved everything you gave him."

I shook my head, burying my face in my hands. I couldn't breathe, the tightness in my chest painful and heavy. Her hands on mine were soft, gentle as she peeled them away, forcing me to meet her stare once more.

"I don't understand," she whispered. "What's really goin' on?"

My eyelids fluttered closed, a deep, painful breath whooshing from my lungs. Just the thought of admitting this to myself hurt...but trying to say it out loud. I couldn't look at her as I spoke, my head falling back as I struggled to finally say, "At some point...when I was hittin' Nate...I

398

wasn't hittin' him no more. I—" I swallowed past the lump in my throat. "It was my dad."

Silence. So loud it was deafening.

I went on, still not looking at her, just to fill the quiet. "I've spent my whole life tryin' to be everythin' he wasn't. Calm, where he was angry. Quiet, instead of loud. Patient when he was hasty... But, all that...everythin' I worked so hard for went down the drain in a minute. I became no better than him. All of the hurt and pain and anger I've kept inside all this time rose up... and just like that, I was out of control. All I could see was red. All I could hear was the sound of my blood boilin'. All I wanted... Well, I wanted to kill him."

The sound of the water's movement drew my attention; Cheyenne poised herself before me, cupping my face in her hands. "I'm so sorry... but it's okay."

A spark of anger blossomed in my chest. "Damn it, Chey...it ain't okay! What I did ain't okay!" I rose from the tub, sending water sloshing over the sides as I got out. "What if I—" I fisted a hand and pressed it to my mouth, biting at the knuckle. Pain surged from the bruises but it was a pain I welcomed. A pain I deserved.

"What if you what, Maverick?" There was a steely edge to her voice. Not anger... I couldn't quite tell what it was.

I shook my head once, tears swimming in my eyes. "What if I hurt you or the baby?" I choked out, the words broken, weak.

Resolve shone in her gaze as she stood up and followed suit. "You won't."

"You don't know that," I replied, grabbing a towel. "And that ain't a risk I'm willin' to take." I didn't give her a chance to respond, but instead turned on my heel and headed for the room.

I know it was cowardly, I know it was wrong of me to do, but I couldn't look her in the eye any longer. I felt so much guilt and shame and disappointment. And fear. So much damn fear it made me tremble. How did she not see how dangerous I was? The damage I could do? That man—that horrible, violent, angry man—was in my blood, coursing through my veins. And so long as that anger festered in my soul, I was a danger to her.

"So, what?" she asked, a deathly calm note in her words as she came out of the bathroom wrapped in a towel before stopping a few feet opposite of me and the dresser. "You wanna break up?"

The thought of her leavin' terrified me. But I didn't know what to do. I didn't know how to stop this feeling of dread choking me to death.

I slammed a fist down on the dresser, shaking the contents and making Cheyenne's perfume bottle wobble atop it. A wave of helplessness pummeled into me. "You don't understand, Chey. I don't want to hurt you!"

She didn't flinch, didn't blink. I expected anger or at least annoyance from her, confusion maybe, but not a wink of any of those emotions hung in her gaze as she slowly made her way toward me and pressed a gentle, yet firm hand to my chest. "Then make me understand. Let me in. Tell me what happened to you. Let it out... I promise I won't run. You don't have to fight this demon all alone."

My bottom lip trembled as I bit back tears. I couldn't tell her. Couldn't open up that cupboard I'd kept locked up for so long. No one else needed to see the pain and suffering and hurt. It was my burden to bear. I couldn't put that on her.

I managed a weak shake of my head, my throat squeezing shut, cutting off the air to my lungs.

Her gaze dipped to my chest, her hand sliding up to rest over my heart. "Please, Mav. Don't you see? It's eating you up alive. Festering and growing here until it gets out of control. It won't matter how patient or slow to anger or calm you try to be. If you don't let it out, if you don't purge it from your soul and address it, it's always gonna have power over you." Her gaze came back up to mine, and the love and hope and understanding in her eyes nearly shattered my resolve. She reached up on tiptoe and pressed a soft kiss to the corner of my jaw before whispering, "You don't have to talk to me. But talk to someone. Cash or Ryder. Better yet, Bad. Hell, maybe even a therapist. They could help."

I exhaled a slow, shaky breath, fighting the tears swimming in my eyes. I hated how weak I felt. Hated how her words resonated so deep in me. *Growing. Festering. It's always gonna have power over you.*

Her hand fell from my chest as she turned away, grabbing something quickly from the top drawer of the dresser. In silence, she padded to the door to our room, but she stopped in the doorway. "You know, you're terrified of turnin' out to be like your daddy. But you're already far better than he ever was. It takes strength to be good, Maverick. It takes strength to see the ugly inside of you and want to be better. I've never seen such strength in someone until I met you."

And with that, she walked out of the room.

The tears I'd fought so valiantly moments before finally fell, the loss brewing in me something I can't even adequately describe. I heard the door to the guest room shut, and even though I knew she hadn't left, her absence felt like a gaping hole in my chest.

I don't remember getting dressed. Don't remember even leaving the room. But in less than a minute, I'd pulled on a pair of pants and found myself heading toward the nursery.

She stood there, still wrapped in her towel, a hand clasped over her mouth looking around the room. I'd painted it, a soft, warm yellow with white trim that went nicely against the greyish stain I'd used for the furniture. The mural I'd begun painting on the main wall wasn't done yet.

Shit. I forgot to lock it after working in there the other day.

"It's uh...it's not all finished, but I wanted to surprise you with this."

Cheyenne pressed a hand to the smooth, gray wood of the crib, her tear-filled eyes meeting mine as she turned to face me. A soft, sad smile played on her lips. "You are so good and so kind and so strong, Maverick...I wish you could see you the way I do."

The dam holding back my fears cracked then. I couldn't keep them in any longer, I needed to tell her. Everything.

I moved to her, picking her up in my arms and taking her to the bed I'd kept in here. I didn't speak as I pulled the t-shirt she'd taken from my room over her head, or as I drew back the covers and urged her to lie down. Curiosity lined the slight furrow of her brows, the questioning frown on her lips, but she did as I silently asked. Sliding into the bed beside her, I leaned back against the headboard, the fluffy pillows propping me upright. Cheyenne settled at my side, resting her chin on my chest.

And then I told her my story. Every dark, ugly, terrifying bit.

CHAPTER 51
Save Me

CHEYENNE

Oh my God...

Rage, sadness, anger, and disgust pulsed through me so thoroughly it made me sick. What Maverick had gone through—no, *endured*—what he'd endured was nothing short of horrifying. Every time he'd paused and I'd thought it was over, he'd tell me another story. Another instance of his dad being an absolute shit human being. He made my mother look like a fucking saint.

There was so much hurt and anger and fury beaten into Maverick it was no wonder he damn near bashed Nate's face in...and I'd let it happen. I'd given the fucking go ahead.

Guilt ate at me. Had I known I'd have maybe rethought letting him fight Nate. He didn't need any more bloodshed, more violence.

I glanced over at the alarm clock on the bedside table. Quarter to two. Maverick still slumbered beside me. I hadn't slept at all. Every time I closed my eyes, images of him suffering at the hands of his father plagued me.

And all of this... it was my fault.

First the fire, forcing him to fall into that silent episode... Now this

403

fight, bringing up the horrors of his childhood and the toxicity of his father. Not to mention, he'd taken on raising the baby of the very man whose face he'd bashed in... they all had one thing in common.

Me.

And you could say that it's not like I'd caused any of this intentionally—which was true—but it didn't change the fact that I was the source of all of his recent trauma. I'm sure he'd argue that wasn't the case, but facts were facts.

My gaze fell on Maverick. I could see him clearly despite the dark; my eyes had all night to adjust. All of the usual tension was absent. The familiar furrow of his brow, the usual downward curve of his lips had vanished. He looked so peaceful, boyish almost. How I wished he could always look so carefree. How I wished he hadn't been plagued with such a dark past.

I should leave. Give him the opportunity to find someone new, someone better. Someone deserving of him. Because Lord fucking knew I wasn't. I never had been. He'd be upset for a while, but he'd move on.

My heart squeezed, sadness so crushing washing over me that it stole the breath from my lungs. Who was I kidding? He wouldn't move on. Hell, he'd let Ashleigh dangle him along for damn near twenty years. He didn't quit things. He didn't give up.

I couldn't leave him... But I couldn't be in this room right now either.

I needed some air, and thanks to this pregnancy, I needed to pee. The joys of having a baby pressing constantly on your bladder. I rose from the bed quietly, so as not to disturb him, and padded through the house from the nursery to our room. I thought of the barn, this wild urge sparking in my chest to go see the red filly. It was stupid to go out this early and work her, not to mention freezing cold, but Maverick would be awake in an hour or so and I wasn't planning to get on her. Just spend some time with her. These last few months I found myself going out to her stall when I was frustrated or stressed out. This seemed as good a time as any.

After going to the bathroom and pulling on some clothes, I made to grab my phone. Just in case Maverick woke up and I was still out there. The home screen lit up, a text message notification showing on the front. My stomach dropped, my throat lodging in my throat as my eyes scanned and scanned and scanned the words. It was from a random number. Not even one from Texas...but I had no doubt who this was from.

This isn't over... tell him I'm comin'.

I couldn't breathe. My lungs just wouldn't fucking work. Those two sentences hit like a sledgehammer to the chest. Fear gripped me like a vice. Oh my God. It was Nate. Of course, it was. He was stupid and stubborn and now he wanted revenge after being humiliated.

Fuck.

I should tell Maverick, but the thought alone stopped me in my tracks. Hadn't I brought enough trouble into his life? Enough worry and heartache and suffering. This text—this threat—would only add to the pile of the mess I'd made in Maverick's life.

Tears pricked in my eyes as the realization became painfully, horribly clear.

I *had* to leave. I had to let him go.

I couldn't be the reason for his suffering. I couldn't be the reason for something happening to him because of Nate. He'd find out easily enough I was no longer with Maverick. I'd make it known. That way, when he came after me—which I knew he would—he'd leave Maverick out of it. He'd be an idiot to go after him after what Mav had done to him.

I bit back sobs as I scrambled to grab my things, packing whatever I could take easily and quickly into a bag. I could buy more stuff later. It's not like I'd had much since I was still replenishing even months after the fire.

Within five minutes, I'd gotten what I needed, every sane, logical inch of me screaming to stop, to think, to *stay*.

But Daddy always said I'd thought with my heart and not my head. I let my emotions get the best of me. Couple that with a mean stubborn streak that just wouldn't quit once I had my mind set...well, there wasn't really much that could change my mind now.

With a bag of my belongings strapped over my shoulder, I took one last look around, my gaze falling to the note I'd left on the dresser as I tried and failed to shut all the memories down of the man I loved more than anything I'd ever known.

But sometimes if you loved something, you had to let it go. Had to let it be free. Let it grow and flourish. I was the thing holding Maverick back. I was the one who wasn't good enough for him.

I hoped he'd find someone who made him happy. Who made him smile freely and laugh often. Who made him feel loved and beautiful. Scars and all.

I had hoped that person could be me.

But I was wrong.

CHAPTER 52
White Buffalo

MAVERICK

I woke up to sunshine streaming in through the window. *Sunshine?* Peeling my eyelids open, which were heavy from exhaustion and tears, I glanced around the room. My heart raced, pattering in my chest.

Where the hell am—

The baby crib came into view, the familiar gray wood easing some of my worry. *The nursery.* But why was the sun up?

I glanced to the alarm clock and cursed. 6:57 AM.

What the hell? How had I slept in so long? My body was so used to 3 AM that I hadn't needed an alarm in years.

I thought of everything that'd happened last night. The adrenaline. The fury. The guilt. The pain of reliving my past. I guess if you looked at it like that, it made sense I'd slept in. But still... Wiping the sleep from my eyes, I made my way through the house.

I wouldn't let myself dwell on what had happened last night. I wished I could say that my talk with Chey made me feel lighter, happier, but truth was, it hadn't. My past didn't justify my actions. What I'd done wasn't okay. It never would be. And I'd have to live with that now... But at least now someone knew all of the broken, cracked, and ugly parts of me. Maybe now, I could start to heal.

I wondered where Cheyenne was. Maybe she'd fed and cleaned? A wave of guilt trickled to life in my chest. She shouldn't have to do that. Not with how pregnant she was. I swear, any day she was gonna pop.

She must've still been out in the barn, because she and Brandy weren't anywhere in the house. I pressed the button on the coffee maker, wondering why she hadn't started it yet. She was always making a pot of decaf first thing in the morning—leaving all the remnants on the counter because she'd forgotten to put all the stuff away. Frowning, I made my way into the room. I needed to hurry. We had a jackpot roping today. The Hill Country Classic to be exact. The bane of my existence, more like. It was the one fuckin' event in Texas Cash and I hadn't won at least once.

Today would be the day... unless I didn't get a move on.

Coming to a stop before the dresser, I noticed a piece of paper with my name scrawled across the front in pretty, neat handwriting. Fear skittered down my spine, the crushing weight settling over me making my limbs heavy. My lungs felt tight, labored, as I slowly reached for the note.

My fingers fumbled with trying to unfold it once. Twice. My eyes scanned over the words with the third try.

MAVERICK,

I want to start off by telling you that I am so sorry. I'm so sorry that you have gone through countless traumas...so much hurt and pain and horror. I am in awe of your strength, your courage, and your fierce ability to do good. You are such an amazing man who deserves nothing but happiness.

Which is why I have to leave...

Nate's coming after me. He threatened me again, and I don't want to cause you more pain by dragging you into the mix. Last night... The Fire. They're all my fault. I keep hurting you, and even though it isn't intentional, the damage can't be undone.

I love you, Maverick. I've never felt this way before. I've never cared enough about a person to want to settle down, to stay in one place. I wanted that with you, but Nate isn't going to stop, and I can't stand by and let you fight my battles for me.

You deserve... Well, you deserve to have someone who only brings you happiness. Who makes you smile and adds light to your world. Someone better than me. You deserve someone as good and kind and wonderful as you, and we both know I am not that, nor have I ever been.

I wish this letter could make you angry enough to hate me, but you aren't built like that, Mav. Maybe time and distance will ease the hurt. I know that this is shitty and cowardly of me, but it was the only way.

Please don't come after me. Please move on.

-Cheyenne

My legs gave out, my kneecaps cracking against the polished concrete floors. But I didn't feel it, not as the crushing weight of despair filled my lungs and drowned me.

Which is why I have to leave.

Gone? She was gone?

No. No...she couldn't. I'd bared my soul to her. I'd told her all the deepest darkest parts of me and she'd kissed my tears away. She'd held me. She'd loved me. She couldn't be gone.

I needed her. I needed her to bring the light she'd talked about in her letter back. She was the sun to me. She was it. Did she realize all she'd done for me? How much she'd helped me these past months? How could she think she wasn't enough?

I should never have told her about my past. Not right after the whole fight with Nate. I'd scared her. Pushed her too far. Spooked her like if you moved too quickly with one of the babies. I'd been so focused on the progress we'd made that I forgot her flighty nature.

And now she was gone... because of me.

Despite the crushing weight of my sorrow, I stood, opening the drawers of my dresser. All of her clothes were gone. Racing through the house, I wrenched open the front door. Her truck was gone too.

No. No. No. No. No. No.

My lungs seared as I tried and failed to get air down my throat. Rage

411

—pure, undiluted, unrelenting rage trembled to life in me, so violently my limbs vibrated from it. Fisting my hands so hard that I cracked open the scabs forming from the night before, I turned and punched the wooden column on the front porch. Pain bloomed, spiderwebbing up through my knuckles and into my wrist. The crunch of broken bone filled my ears. But the physical pain was a welcome reprieve from what I felt in my heart.

Please don't come after me.

Another punch.

Please move on.

Another. And another and another...until my knuckles were bloody, my breath was gone, and I had no strength left in my legs to stand. And when I couldn't stand, when the anger retreated, a fierce cold, hollowness took its place in my soul. I roared out to the sky above me.

She was gone. Her and the baby... they were gone.

And they'd stolen my heart with it.

———

"MAV...MAVERICK!"

I wasn't sure who was speaking, and honestly, I didn't really care. A heavy emptiness had settled around me, and it was all I could do to force air into my lungs. Not even the sun shining down could warm the cold I felt in my heart. In my soul.

I laid curled up on the front porch, pain thrumming from the tips of my fingers and snaking up my hand and wrist. I'd broken something. Multiple somethings, if I were being honest, but the pain was nothing. Physical pain I could deal with. The thing about being beaten is it makes you tough. Makes pain just a part of the process. Bones mend. Cuts heal. Bruises disappear. But a broken heart. That didn't heal. You kept that hurt with you forever.

"Shit. What the hell happened?" That sounded like Cash.

Two sets of hands grabbed me up by the shoulders, and after blinking a few times against the sunlight, Ryder and Cash's features swam into focus.

"What the fuck happened?" Ryder asked, his dark gaze filled with worry, the scowl on his face pulling on his scar.

"She's gone." It didn't even sound like me. There was no life. Nothing to it. It was just...hollow.

Cash scowled and pulled off his sunglasses as he asked, "What do you mean gone?"

I waved a hand toward the tire marks on the gravel leading away from her spot by my truck. "I mean she's gone. Left a letter and shit. She ain't comin' back." Pain shot through my fingers like lightning and I winced before letting out a curse.

"Fuck," Ryder breathed, looking at my hand. "Is that from the fight?"

I shook my head, taking in the damage, before glancing at the splintered wood of the column. It hadn't even cracked it in two. But that's what I got for going up against a four by four. Both Cash's and Ryder's gazes fell on me.

"Well, damn." Cash met my stare, a determined set to his jaw. "Let's clean you up and go after her."

I shook my head, though every bit of me wanted to nod. "No."

Cash rocked back at the words, confusion washing over him. "What? What do you mean?"

"She told me not to come after her."

Ryder pulled his ball-cap off his head, raking a hand through his hair as he let out a loud sigh. "Goddamn it, Mav. Just cuz she says that, don't mean she don't want it."

"You're wrong, Ryder. That piece of shit threatened her again. I don't know how or what he said, but she's gone. She don't want to involve me in any more of that, so I have to respect her wishes."

I expected Cash to argue—him and I usually disagreed on how to go about things—but I didn't expect the anger or argument from Ryder. "You're really gonna let her go? Why? Why're you givin' up on her?"

I opened my mouth, but no words came out. I didn't know what to say. There wasn't a reason that would convince him. But it didn't matter what Ryder thought, Cheyenne didn't want me chasing after her. And I loved her enough to respect that. He didn't have to understand or agree. But it's how it was.

Ryder shook his head, chewing on his bottom lip like he was ready to scold me. It was weird having the roles turned. I was typically the one talking sense into him and Cash.

"Come on," Cash cut in, breaking the tension brewing between Ryder and I. "Let's get you to Charlie and Ryder's place. Mama and Dad just got there. Mama'll take a look at it."

I didn't want to go. Every fiber of my being urged me to stay here. Right in this place, lest Cheyenne somehow, some way miraculously came back.

But she wouldn't.

I knew that in my heart of hearts. So, blowing out a deep breath, trying to block out the pulsing in my hand, I gave him a stiff nod.

———

"MY HEAVEN, WHAT ON EARTH HAPPENED TO YOU, MAVERICK James?" Aunt Violet's voice held a shrill note to it as she shot from the kitchen to examine me. Bad's closed off expression gave nothing away, but there was a sad, knowing look in his eyes if you knew what to look for.

"She gone?" he asked, as if he already knew. Maybe Cash had already told him, though I doubted it. Bad was the most astute man I'd ever known.

I thought of her. Thought of the baby. They both were gone. And I had no claim to that child, no right to feel this way, but it was like having my soul ripped from me. I'd tried to play it cool, to not get my hopes up, but getting the opportunity to raise that child as mine was going to be an absolute honor that I looked forward to more than anything.

My chest tightened. Swallowing past the lump in my throat, I gave a single, stiff nod.

For a few minutes, the room erupted into chaos, everyone arguing about what to do. Ryder and Aunt Violet were in fierce agreement to go after her, while Cash and Bad held strong in favor against it. Charlie surprisingly didn't say much, but there was a strange look in her eyes. Not anger, but sharper than sadness.

My heart thumped in my chest, the beat pulsating, quickening as the pace turned faster and faster. Sound turned muffled, almost like I'd jumped underwater. The blood in my veins felt hot, and the pain in my hand became a living, breathing thing. My limbs locked up, paralyzing me in place, my feet feeling like they were stuck in cement. Anxiety ate at me as each second that passed felt like my hold on my temper was waning. I fisted my hands at my side, a wave of pain so strong snaking its way up my arm that my vision blurred in the corners for a moment.

Fuck. I needed to wrap it so I couldn't do that again.

"Enough!" My voice still didn't feel like my own. It was cracked, raw, broken. I leveled a stern look at everyone in the room. "She's gone and don't wanna be chased. Now, can someone help me clean up my damn hand so I can rope today."

"Maverick James Holstrom, you are *not* ridin' in that jackpot." Aunt Violet took a step toward me, defiance blazing in her gaze. "You and I are goin' to the hospital right now to get that hand checked out."

"Aunt Violet, with all due respect, I ain't goin' to the hospital. We haven't missed this jackpot since we were kids, and I'll be damned if I scratch."

I looked at Cash for...for I don't know what. Reassurance, or to just gauge his reaction. I knew it was stupid riding with a broken hand—something in there was broken, of that I was sure—but I needed to keep my mind on something.

I needed this. If I couldn't go after Chey, if I couldn't have her, then I needed this win.

Cash pulled his sunglasses off and ran a hand through his light brown hair. With a nod, he righted his glasses and said, "Big Daddy feels a win comin' on."

"Cash Ulysses Mooney!" Aunt Violet warned. "You will—"

Bad stepped forward. "Let 'em go, Violet." His voice was calm, gravelly, and held a sense of finality that even Violet didn't fight.

Anger brewed like a storm in her eyes, but she waved a flippant hand in the air and moved toward me. "Well, get on over here. Let's see what we can do with this mess of a hand."

Ryder blew out a frustrated growl. "I'll go get the fuckin' trailer hooked up," he snapped at no one in particular before storming through the kitchen and to the back door.

Charlie offered us all an apologetic look. "He's just worried. He'll be fine."

"Why?" I didn't understand the anger from him, not really. I mean, they were friends first but... Cash I could understand, he and Chey had gotten really close over the past few months, reminding me of long-lost twins or something.

"He knows what it's like, losin' someone you love because they're scared to communicate their fears... He knows what's worth fighting for. You and Chey worked really well together." Charlie blew out a breath and sighed. "And she means something to all of us. She may have been your girlfriend, but she was our friend too. We're worried about her. I get that she doesn't want anyone coming after her, but..." She shook her head, glancing down at her pregnant belly. "I get why he wants to go after her."

I hadn't even thought of the impact her leaving would have on the others. Her and Charlie had gotten close too, sharing a bond none of us could even know with their journeys into motherhood.

I nodded, still not really knowing what to say.

She was gone.

Charlie excused herself from the room shortly after, going to find Ryder so they could get something to wrap up my hand while Aunt Violet urged me toward the kitchen peninsula to get to work cleaning the wound. Bad and Cash whispered quietly amongst themselves, but I couldn't make out what. My mind had settled into a catatonic state—all the fight, all the rage, all the worry leaving me. In its place was that cold, familiar hollowness.

I didn't even feel the pain as Aunt Violet wiped and cleaned my bloodied knuckles, or as she wrapped my hand with gauze and Coban once Charlie got back. Movement to my right caught my eye as Cash left out the front door without a word. Bad mentioned they'd be back in a bit, but I didn't reply. I couldn't find words...words were too much again. Not quite like the time in the fire. I *could* talk...if I wanted to.

But I didn't want to anymore. Not when the little bit of sunshine in my life was gone, leaving nothing but memories and darkness in her wake.

CHAPTER 53

On My Way To You

CHEYENNE

I drove through the night—a minor miracle since it was raining. But more than that, the tears flowing freely down my cheeks blurred my vision. I couldn't stop crying. Couldn't stop thinking of him. Of every moment since that night in Cowboy's months ago that changed my life forever.

Him being all nervous, talking about horses. Kissing me outside. Asking me to read him one of my books. *Lord of the Rings...but with porn in it.* The fire, but the connection that we formed after that. The bond we shared. That first night in his home, and then falling for him a little bit more each and every day so that by the time he started talking again I didn't stand a chance. Then there was finding out I was pregnant and through all of that, through all the fear and anguish and worry, he held me, he loved me, he supported me. And when we heard baby girl's heartbeat...

There were so many memories, each moment more beautiful and magical and heart wrenching than the last. Maverick was kind and good and everything that was right in the world. He was a prime example of

not letting your past define you. The bravest, strongest man I knew...
And I'd left him.

Left him in the middle of the night, like a fucking coward.

A wave of disgust and self-loathing surged through me, strong
enough to choke the air from my lungs. My vision was blurring, my
nerves growing all tingly. Fuck. What was happening to me? I pulled off
to the side of the highway and slammed the car in park as sound
morphed and wobbled, a loud ringing filling the silence.

"Fuck. Fuck." My breath sawed in and out of my lungs, my chest
heaving from the effort. I looked to Brandy in the passenger's seat as she
let out a whine. I tried and failed to focus my breathing as I reached out
a hand to pet her. The ringing wouldn't stop, and I felt hot and cold all
at once. What the hell was happening? She crawled over the center
console and placed her head on my stomach. I ran a hand over her fur,
over and over again, forcing slow, deep breaths down my lungs.

Tears welled and blurred my vision once more as I pressed my head
to the steering wheel and let out a gut-wrenching sob. God, it hurt. It
hurt so fucking bad.

Why did it have to be like this?

Go back. The words were like a caress from my subconscious.

I wanted nothing more than to listen, but...but going back wouldn't
change anything. I was a danger to Maverick and his family. Nate
wouldn't stop. The stupid texts I kept getting from random numbers
were proof enough.

I thought of Maverick, my heart breaking just a bit more. Had he
read the letter yet? I bet he had. I glanced at the clock on my car. 9:36
AM. There was no doubt in my mind he was already awake. He'd had to
have read it by now.

I wondered how he was handling it. Guilt racked through me,
pummeling the air from my lungs so thoroughly that I saw stars for a
moment and thought I might pass out. He probably hated me. I
honestly hoped he did. I deserved it.

My cell phone buzzed somewhere in the cup holder. Probably
another threat from Nate. But the buzz was different. *A call, then.* A
whirlwind of emotions stirred in my chest. Hope and dread, curiosity
and fear. Was it Nate? Maverick?

Curiosity got the best of me in the end, and I reached for my phone, my head still resting against the steering wheel. I couldn't lift it; my limbs had turned to mush. The will to move, to do anything more than just merely exist was too much.

I frowned at the familiar name on my phone. *Charlie.* I shouldn't answer. I didn't want to deal with her questions, her anger. She'd no doubt be furious. But it's like my brain and mind weren't in agreement.

My thumb hit the green answer button.

"I'm not comin' home, Charlie," I sobbed out by way of greeting.

"I know. I wanted to make sure you were okay. How's baby girl?" Charlie's voice was soft, understanding on the other line. And that was somehow worse. I didn't deserve her sympathy, her kindness.

"We're f-f-fine," I replied, struggling through the words.

"Breathe, Chey. It's okay. Just breathe."

I wiped uselessly at the tears leaking down my face. It's like my tear ducts had broken and liquid just flowed from them endlessly now. "It's n-n-not o-k-kay. I fuckin' left him!"

"I know." Her voice was sad. "He told us. He said Nate threatened you?"

I huffed a bitter laugh, sniffling as I said, "Oh, yeah. About a dozen fuckin' times." My phone buzzed and I glanced down to see yet another random number show up as a text notification across the top banner of my phone. "Make that thirteen now."

"Chey..." Charlie loosed a sigh. "I'm so sorry."

"I didn't want to leave," I whispered, leaning back against the seat and closing my eyes. Brandy's head on my stomach helped soothe some of the ache inside me. "I love him...but I'm scared."

"I can't even imagine."

I sucked in a deep breath. "H-how is he doin'?"

I had to know. I knew it was torture. I knew it would do me no good, but I...well, I needed to know.

Another sigh. "About as good as you'd think."

Which meant fucking horrible. Worry and guilt swirled in my chest, filling my lungs like smoke. I let out a sob. And through it all, Charlie just listened, the other end of the line remaining quiet. She didn't push me or try to pry. Before I knew it, my sobs turned to whispers, then whispers to words. "...He bared his scars to me, Charlie. He told me everythin'...and I just left."

"You can come back..." Her voice was soft, hesitant, as if she wasn't quite sure she should say the words aloud, but couldn't help it.

I scoffed. "Everyone would hate me. *He* would hate me."

"He doesn't hate you and you know it. None of us do."

"You don't?" I sniffled.

Charlie blew out a breath. "I understand you better than you think... I know what it's like to run away from your problems. I know it's not the same, but...when I saw the banamine in Ryder's truck, I was so angry and scared that he'd fallen back into that behavior again. But then he'd explained and I just felt stupid and angrier, because he called me out on my fears and forced me to make a choice...them or him. I let my fears win out, and it just about killed me. I'd never felt so broken or lost as I did that night."

I huffed in agreement. "I get that. It's like this knot of pain in my chest that just won't quit."

"It doesn't get better," Charlie admitted softly. "It was literally only a week...but I felt like I was dying."

Another wave of tears sprung to life in my eyes. I didn't even try to wipe them away as I choked out, "You and Ryder are perfect together though. Me...fuck... I'm no good for Maverick. Just ask Aunt Violet."

"Number one, who gives a shit what anyone else thinks? Who gets to say if you're right for him or not? And second, Aunt Violet was actually one of the loudest ones in favor of coming to find you."

I frowned, the realization more than a bit of a surprise. "Really?"

"Yes. But that doesn't matter. What matters is that regardless of what *you* think of yourself, what anyone thinks of you really, all that matters is that Maverick thinks you're enough."

"To be fair, he also thought Ashleigh was."

"Stop being a smart ass," Charlie chastised, though there was a hint of warmth to her words. Tears still flowed down my face, but the sobs didn't make me feel like I'd keel over and die anymore, so small wins, I guess. "Look, point is, you are good for him. Everyone can see that."

"How? I've just brought up endless amounts of trauma for him, and—"

"*And,*" Charlie cut in. "You helped him find his voice. He's more talkative now than he ever has been, which is saying a lot because he hardly talked at all before. You've made him more confident, more open with others, fuck, Chey...you got him to show his scars."

I pursed my lips, wiping uselessly at my face once more. I couldn't get the words out as a wave of emotion washed over me, drowning me in its intensity.

Charlie went on before I could. "What's so fascinating about you and Maverick, is that logically, you two don't work. You're wild and reckless, where he is calm, unchanging. You're bright and fiery, while he is cool and closed off. You're spontaneous, always living by the spur of the moment, and let's face it, Mav is a creature of habit. But despite that, despite all those differences, he tempers your flame, and you light him up. And if that isn't something worth fighting for, then I don't know what is."

My heart swelled as I thought of Maverick. Of the perfect man who held my heart. I wanted to believe her. I really truly did, but that stupid, scared, little voice in my head continued whispering, *run... Get away.*

"It's not that easy," I choked out.

"Oh, knock that shit off, Chey. I've been where you are. Is it easy? No...but love ain't easy. It's hard and messy and there's times when it gets so muddied and frustrating and dire that you don't know how you can go on, but you do. You push through. You ride the storm. You tell the stupid fears in your mind to shut the hell up, and you love that man until the fear disappears, until the storm passes. It ain't easy...but it's worth it. I promise."

I wondered if she realized how she'd grown from the time I'd first met her. She'd really come into her own, found strength in her relationship with Ryder and her journey into motherhood. She was brave, strong, and kind.

"Do you love him?" Charlie asked.

"Of course I do," I choked out on a sob.

"Then listen closely. I'm going to tell you the same thing this really smart now six-year-old told me when I broke up with Ryder. He asked me, if I left Texas, who would be there to love and watch out for Ryder the only way I could... So, I ask you this... If you leave, who's going to love Maverick? Who's going to light up the darkness inside him like only you can?"

I couldn't answer. I couldn't speak. I couldn't breathe. Not as the weight of her words hit me dead in the chest.

"I know you think this is better for him in the long run, that you only bring him hurt, but you're gone and he's still hurting. And he's gonna, until you come home."

A sob fell from my lips.

"Come home, Chey...please."

I struggled to get air down my lungs, that ringing filling my ears once more. I needed to think. To figure out everything. I just...I needed a moment to compose myself. "I-I gotta go." Hanging up before Charlie could argue, I gripped the steering wheel with both hands, trying to ride out the fear and worry and pain raging within me.

Brandy whined at my side, nudging me with her nose, but I ignored it.

What was I doing? Was Charlie right? It was hard to think I was good for Maverick, like she said. Yeah, he'd opened up, but that wasn't just because of me. But then I thought of that night he'd bared his scars, showing us all quite possibly the darkest moment of his life, and hope and love and pride swirled in my chest.

I took a deep breath and glanced at Brandy. "What am I doin', girl?"

She didn't answer, because, of course, she didn't.

The dark, angry clouds in the sky were pierced by shafts of sunlight at that moment, and I found myself mesmerized as I watched the sun chase away the storm. And as I watched the sky turn from black to a pale blue bathed in pinks and purples and gold, I felt a flutter of motion in my stomach.

My heart leapt, a wave of relief soothing the fear inside of me. She was okay. And by the string of the following kicks and familiar movements, she was happy.

I couldn't run away. Not this time.

Not just for Maverick, but for this little girl. This little girl who deserved to have a Daddy who loved her, cherished her, worshiped her. No one could do that better than Maverick. No one could love her more fiercely, or raise her better.

I pressed a hand to my stomach and looked down at Brandy. "No more runnin', girl. I ain't my mama."

I'd let my fear turn me into the very woman I hated more than anything. Running away when things got hard. Letting my fears win.

But I wasn't my mother, and I wouldn't give up on Maverick. Not now. Not ever again.

CHAPTER 54
Keep The Wolves Away

NATE

The day after the fight...
12:49 PM

I roused from sleep, pain pounding through me—behind my swollen eyelids, in my goddamn ears. The sound was deafening, wrenching a groan from my lips.

Wait...

The pounding wasn't just in my ears. That was the door. Gritting my teeth and forcing myself to sit up from my spot on the couch—I hadn't had the strength or energy to make it to the bed—I trudged toward the noise.

My head felt like it was filled with cobwebs, partially from the pain, but also from the half-drank fifth of whiskey and the bottle of painkillers sitting scattered across the coffee table. They'd only done so much. At least part of my face was still numb.

As I padded across the wood floors, I caught a glimpse of myself in the small entryway mirror.

Holy shit. I looked awful. Almost unrecognizable with all the swelling and bruising. Both eyes were black and purple, my lip cracked open. The air shifting around my face as I turned it this way and that was almost enough to make my eyes blur.

Fury pulsed through my veins. Fuck that dude...and fuck Cheyenne. *That bitch*. Of course, she'd kept the baby. That girl was always more trouble than she was worth.

A scowl formed on my lips before falling into a grimace as another wave of pain flooded through me. Something was broken. Had to be.

I should go to the ER...

But there would be too many questions. I'd already been trying to lay low since the whole trailer park fire. There was no need to draw more attention to myself. But the idea of pressing charges on that prick and getting him arrested, leaving that little slut all alone did sound pretty damn nice.

A knock sounded on the front door once more, and I bit back a groan as I moved forward and turned the knob, yanking the door open.

Two cowboys stood on the front porch. No, not just two cowboys. I recognized the younger one from the night before—that prick's friend who'd knocked out Jesse. He looked all suave and soft, but the kid had a mean right hook. I recognized the man beside him a moment later.

Clint "Bad" Mooney. Rodeo Champion, wannabe cattle baron. Man had a temper...and an influence in the horse world. *A lot* of influence.

Well, shit.

"What the fuck do you want?" I spat out, ignoring the aching in my face. Blinking alone hurt, talking was pure agony.

"We wanna talk," the younger cowboy said. Must be his son. They looked similar enough.

I glared at them, spitting at their feet. The movement took more effort than I'd intended and I instantly regretted it. "Ain't in the talkin' mood," I grunted, before slamming the door closed.

A part of me wondered what they wanted. Couldn't be anything good, though. Likely to find out what I planned to do. Maybe threaten me a bit. But I didn't really care enough to find out.

I locked the door and turned to walk back to the living room. A chill skittered through me and I froze, my feet becoming nothing more than cement blocks. Someone was in the house with me. I could feel the shift in the air. It was like it was charged. Energized. An unfamiliar scent floated around the room.

I nearly jumped out of my skin when I saw him. Waiting in the darkness of the living room. As if conjured from the shadows themselves, a man stepped before me.

Some guys were really good at football. Some guys were good at talkin'. I was good at knowing when I was out of my fucking league.

This guy...

He was tall, built and held a dark, savage look in his eyes. He wore a kutte with motorcycle patches all over it. My eyes stuck on one in particular, though. A flaming Viking skull flanked by axes. Battle Borne MC. One percenters—real bad guys. Big timers. You didn't fuck with them... ever. Those that did were often found in pieces in the desert. If they were found at all.

A shiver went through me. I hated him on instinct.

He didn't speak as he moved toward me. Fear swelled in my chest, forcing my breathing to shallow. I couldn't move. Couldn't think. Couldn't even properly breathe. How the hell had he gotten in? Was Bad Mooney involved with the Battle Borne? Fuck...were they going to have me killed?

My pulse hammered through my veins as the biker reached out, slowly, so fucking slowly that I swear my entire damn life passed before my eyes...

But he didn't touch me. Nope. He just reached past me and unlocked the door, his hardened, hazel gaze never leaving mine.

"Who the fuck are you?" I choked out as I tried and failed to keep my voice from quavering.

Bad Mooney's voice boomed like thunder behind me as he stepped through the doorway. "True's my friend. He ain't yours. You don't wanna piss him off. So, I suggest you invite us in, listen closely, and we won't have a problem."

My gaze flicked between the three of them. They all shared similar features, those same golden-green eyes. Well, fuck. This was a whole family affair.

"Fuck it, yeah sure...come in." I limped my way back to the couch and sat, grabbing the bottle of whiskey for what...comfort? Protection? Not that it would do much against these three. Bad Mooney was known for his temper, his redneck son knew how to scrap, and the other was a fuckin' Battle Borne.

A bottle wouldn't do shit against them. I wished I had my gun on me.

The biker snatched the whiskey out of my hand and set it down on the table, gentle-like, as if it were a wine glass with a delicate stem. Then he got down in my face and looked into my eyes.

"I want you..." He paused and held my gaze hostage. "To listen. And understand what you hear. You can't listen if you're drunk. That can wait until after we're gone. This won't take long, unless you piss me off."

His voice was far smoother than I'd have guessed, but heavy with unspoken violence. Like a fine whiskey, the smoother it went down the more trouble you could get into.

Unable to speak, I nodded.

I watched in pained silence as Bad Mooney came to a stop before me and reached into his back pocket. Oh fuck...was this it? Was he gonna shoot me? I swallowed back the fear snaking around my lungs.

A wad of cash fell with a resounding thud on the coffee table, causing the pills to disperse. Not just a wad. A *big* wad of cash. So big I'd be afraid walking around with that amount of money.

"Look," he said, his voice rough like sandpaper or gravel. "You gotta problem, and I gotta problem. My nephew bashed your face in. And *you* burnt down his girlfriend's trailer and threatened to hit her in public. Now way I see it, there's two ways to go about it... One, we get the cops involved. It'll be messy and stressful on everyone and I don't really got time for that." He cleared his throat. "Or two, you keep quiet, and leave Cheyenne Harris alone." He nodded at the money. "You do that, and this here's yours."

I snorted, a bitter laugh escaping me. Rage and reason warred for dominance in my chest. There was nothing I wanted more than to get back at the bitch. Ruin her life before she tried to ruin mine with that damn kid of ours. But...

Despite the pain, I reached forward and fingered through the stack of bills. Five grand. Well, damn.

I chewed on my bottom lip, anger bubbling through me. Must be fucking nice to have enough money to just buy your way out of things. I glared up at Bad Mooney and then his sons, my gaze falling lastly to the Battle Borne biker.

They were no joke. And if Cheyenne was under their protection because of this...well, fucking with her was basically a death sentence.

Bad Mooney's lips pulled up ever so slightly in the corners. "We gotta deal? You leave Cheyenne alone. You don't involve the law, and we're good?"

I bristled as he repeated the terms one more time, like I was some idiot kid who didn't know my right from my left. But I didn't really have much say in this, did I? Not unless I wanted beef with one of the most dangerous biker gangs in the southwest.

"Yeah, whatever," I grumbled, nodding at the cash.

The biker stepped forward, his eyes holding a dark, dangerous glint to them. "Yes, *sir*," he growled out. The frigid coldness in his words froze my blood. He hadn't raised his voice, but my ears rang all the same.

"What the fuck are you talkin' about?" I fought to keep a tremor out of my tone. Failed.

"I think—" The man put a tattooed hand on the table top, his gaze pegging me in place. Another shiver went up my spine. Kid couldn't be older than twenty-five, but everything about him exuded power. I saw the threat in just his stance alone. "—you meant to say, '*yes, sir*'."

Fuck him and his manners.

But despite my annoyance, I grumbled out a quiet, "Yes, sir."

That seemed to appease Bad and his other son, and with nothing more than a tilt of their hats, they all made to leave. I glanced down at the money all but burning a hole in my hands. Five thousand dollars was a good chunk of change. One I could use right now. But rage still flickered within me at the thought of that bitch and her pregnant belly. I reclaimed my bottle of whiskey and took a long pull. I wouldn't call the cops. Wouldn't go after her.

The liquor burned a path down my throat—a pleasant reprieve from the pain still throbbing across my face.

But...accidents do happen.

And I don't know if I was paranoid, or if that biker fucker had some sort of sixth sense, but his lips pulled up into the barest hint of a smirk as he knocked his knuckles against my table once. Twice. "Gotta feelin' I'll be seein' you again soon."

"I don't think I will." I pulled what courage I could from the alcohol. Some of these biker punks were pussies playing at being gangsters. If I showed him I wasn't rattled, he might fuck off.

"You misunderstand." He crouched down to my level again. Face inches from mine. His voice was still cold and dangerous, but his eyes burned like hellfire. And I understood in that moment, that while Bad and his other kid didn't want any trouble. *This* one did. "You won't see me. But I'll see you."

CHAPTER 55
Something In The Orange

MAVERICK

I paced and paced and paced, silently cursing myself for not asking Cash where the hell he was going before he left. With a final ring, his voicemail came on, and I growled, fumbling to turn off my phone. Doing things with my left hand sucked...but if there was any hope of me using my right for our run, I needed to save what tiny shred of strength I still had in it. It throbbed and pulsed beneath the makeshift splint; the Norco had done nothing for it. Though, I didn't suspect it would.

Aunt Violet was right. I needed to get it checked out. But my hand would still be broken tomorrow. My shot at winning wouldn't.

Black Betty snorted from where she stood tied up to the trailer, her tail raised high in the air, making her look like a damn Arabian. Playboy stood completely unbothered beside her.

"You get a hold of him?" Ryder asked, coming out of the trailer with Playboy's saddle pad to place on his back. Cason sat quietly watching us in one of the camper chairs by the trailer.

"No." I stalked for the saddle rack and followed Ryder's lead, grabbing Black Betty's gear. "I've called him a dozen times."

Charlie came around from the front of the truck. "He didn't answer my calls either, and Aunt Violet hasn't heard from Bad."

"Well, fuck." Nothing seemed to be going right today. I blew out a steadying breath, trying to keep a hold on my temper.

Ryder came to stand at my side. "Maybe you should scratch," he offered, the look in his eyes soft, sincere.

I scowled. "No. I ain't scratchin'."

He should understand more than anyone.

I needed this. The thought of—No. No, I wasn't thinking about her. Not right now. After my run, after the rodeo, hell, even on the entire truck-ride home, I could think about her. I could fall apart inside. But not right now.

"Well, you got fifteen minutes 'til they start callin' names. If he ain't here by then, it won't matter what you want."

"You could rope in his place."

Ryder barked out a laugh, genuine mirth gleaming in his gaze for a moment. "You know I'm shit at ropin'."

"You ain't that bad. Besides, you can head, I'll heel. You can at least get the rope around the horns."

Ryder sighed, placing his hands on his waist. Almost like he was thinking about it. He shook his head before meeting my gaze. "I think you'd be just as likely to win with Charlie as you would with me."

"Hey!" Charlie frowned beside him. Ryder drew her into his side, kissing her lightly on the forehead. "Sorry, darlin'. I meant no offense to you."

She offered him a small smile and leaned into the touch.

"So, you really won't do it?" I asked.

Both of them cast glances my way. Ryder's mouth popped open to reply but words never came. An odd look came over his face, almost like disbelief.

"Big Daddy's in the house!" A familiar, cocky voice called from behind me.

Annoyance and relief sprung to life, chasing away the worry. I turned and scowled at my cousin. "What the fuck, Cash? Where the hell were you?"

Bad seemed to materialize out of nowhere, a determined look in his eyes as he clapped me on the shoulder. "Don't matter. He's here now. And y'all have a jackpot to win."

———

BLACK BETTY TWITCHED AND TENSED BENEATH ME AS I held her back in the box. Mare was old, but man, put her in a box and she'd run down any steer faster than a yearling. I forced deep breaths down my lungs as they got a cow ready for our run. Cash readied himself on Playboy to the left of the chute, flipping his coils and rolling his shoulders. I took in the familiar sights and sounds of the arena, letting the adrenaline pumping through my veins do its work on my pain. Even though my hand still pulsed, I could drown it out, ignore it to a point. The fucking makeshift splint made it impossible to move my wrist, though. I struggled with flipping my coils for a third time.

"My fuckin' hand," I growled.

Cash cast a worried glance my way.

"Y'all ready?" the cowboy working the chute asked.

A wave of frustration went through me as I tried and failed to grip my rope properly. Fuck it. I couldn't wear the damn thing.

"Hold on," I bit out as I laid my rope over the horn and pulled out my pocket knife from my back pocket. Betty continued her anxious twitching beneath me as I struggled, pain ricocheting through my bones with each movement. But I couldn't throw with this fucking shit of a wrap on.

"You got thirty seconds," the cowboy at the chute called out.

"Got it, Mav?" Cash called from my left.

"I'm fine," I snapped, ripping the cast free and grabbing for the rope. "Just be ready." Flexing my fingers, a wave of white-hot agony shot through my knuckles and wrist. But at least I could hold the rope. The scabs and cuts were broken open once more; I didn't particularly care though.

"Ten seconds."

I flipped my coils hurriedly, forcing slow, deep breaths down my lungs to quiet the roar of agony in my mind. But as Cash looked across

437

the way at me, nodding to ask if I was ready, a blessed wave of adrenaline crashed into me, drowning out the pain.

Sound and sight peeled away, leaving the world quiet. So wonderfully quiet. Another slow, centering breath as I braced myself for the surge of power coiling tighter and tighter in Black Betty. She had a knack for hurling herself out of the box, like a tidal wave tearing for the shore.

I nodded...and the chute shot open.

The steer darted out, and I drew my hand up and back to lift the lasso. Pain, so dizzying and intense it made me nauseous, jolted through my limb. My vision blurred and blackened, my nerves growing white hot and tingly.

I—I couldn't.

My fingers wouldn't loosen up enough to toss the rope. It was already almost too much trying to stay upright as wave after wave of pure agony pummeled into me.

The steer was already halfway down the arena and my fingers were locked around the rope. A crushing weight of failure joined the pain—I never missed, let alone missed a damn throw. But my *fucking hand*.

I couldn't even focus on whatever the hell Cash was saying to me as I slowed Black Betty and turned her toward the exit. It's like he was speaking another language. I just rode past him out of the arena and hopped off Betty so I could walk her back to the trailer. I didn't need to die trying to cool her down when she was amped up like this. The walk back to the truck would be fine enough.

And as I stalked toward the trailer, as I did everything in my power not to pass out from the pain, I thought of Cheyenne kissing my knuckles, cleaning my wounds.

Fuck, I missed her. I missed her laugh. Her smile. I missed the way she almost always held a look of mischief on her face, in her eyes. I missed how she had concerts in our—my—bathroom almost every night, singing into her brush to Brandy like she was belting into a microphone. I missed how most nights she would read her books aloud to me, while I laid my head against her stomach, feeling our ba—

My vision blurred, and I didn't know if it was from the pain or my tears at this point.

Fuck. I just *missed* her.

But she wasn't coming back.

A slow, lazy clap pierced through the haze of my thoughts. I frowned as I paused in unsaddling Betty and glanced over my shoulder. Bad walked over, his lips curving upward into the barest hint of a smirk. Though his hazel eyes hid behind his sunglasses' stare, I had no doubt they swam with mirth.

"Well, feel good about yourself?" he asked, coming to stand a few feet behind me and crossing his arms over his chest.

I chewed on my lower lip, frustration mingling with the pain radiating from my hand. I didn't realize how much having it wrapped had helped manage the pain, but, fuck, it hurt now. "Oh, don't act so high and mighty. I know you've done shit just as dumb, if not dumber."

He snorted, a huff of laughter falling from those lips drawn up into a smirk. "Yeah, well, you're smarter than me."

And I don't know why—maybe it was because of everything I'd gone through in the last day—but the anger brewing in my chest spewed forth like a geyser.

"That ain't fair. Why am I always held to this higher standard? If Cash had done somethin' like that, no one woulda batted an eye. But I do somethin' stupid once and everyone's got somethin' to say." My fists curled at my sides, and I instantly regretted it as another answering shot of pain lanced through my knuckles and hand. "Fuck," I growled, before letting out a whole string of curses.

I knew it was an overreaction. I knew on any other day, any other time I wouldn't have reacted the way I did. But today was not that day.

Bad's hand on my shoulder was warm, heavy, just the same as the look on his face. "You ain't Cash, boy... Thank God. I don't know what the hell I'd do with two of ya."

A reluctant huff of laughter escaped me, and just like that my anger vanished, leaving me hollow and empty once more. I looked down at my swollen, broken hand, at the cuts and bruises. "I thought the physical pain would help, you know?" I asked, unable to meet his stare. "Like somethin' to distract me now that she's gone."

"Did it?" There was no judgement, no condescension in his tone.

I shook my head. "Not even a bit," I choked out, finally forcing myself to look at him.

He nodded slowly, a sad, knowing look on his face. He blew out a breath and nodded at one of the camping chairs set up by the trailer. "Sit your ass down and start bandaging up that hand of yours. I'll untack her."

"She might kill you," I said, quirking an eyebrow. For Bad to offer to do anything with Betty meant that the situation was dire. He'd always hated her, and she'd hated him. She hated everyone but me... and Chey —mostly.

"Not if that nag knows what's good for her," Bad answered with a grumble.

A soft chuckle fell from my lips as I rifled through the trailer for some more bandages and Coban. After finding all the supplies, I plopped myself into a chair and started wrapping. Bad joined me a few moments later, pulling out a leather pouch from his back pocket. We sat in silence for a few moments while I struggled with my hand and he methodically filled and rolled his cigarette. Finishing, he pressed one to his lips and grabbed his lighter.

That first puff of sweet tobacco smoke on the air settled my nerves a bit. I'd stopped smoking since finding out Chey was pregnant—not that she'd asked or would have minded— but now that she was gone...

Bad noticed my gaze and offered me the cigarette. I didn't even think twice as I reached across the way and took it.

"You know, I wouldn't be so hasty to call her gone." Bad's voice was soft yet sure as he rolled himself another.

A flood of images sloshed though my mind, rocking me so thoroughly tears sprouted in my eyes. I bit them back as I met his gaze. "Don't. Don't give me hope when there ain't none."

"Remember that ranch horse we got... what was his name, Fucker?"

I chuckled in spite of myself. "Tucker."

"Right, Fucker. Took us, what, almost three weeks of havin' to rope him in his stall just to get him out? Another two to get him to let us put a damn halter on him—"

"—another couple weeks 'til he'd walk up to the gate and let you pet him," I cut in.

Bad puffed on his cigarette and nodded. "You and I had put a ton of work into him at that point, the fucker had come a long way...but your dumbass cousin had to go into his stall bein' his loud, obnoxious-ass self, spooking the sonovabitch, and went and pissed away all that we'd done."

I nodded, remembering that horse, that moment, clearly. Tucker had been my first project horse Bad had let me call the shots with. I'd been so proud of how far he'd come only for Cash to ruin it. But I hadn't given up on the horse. I'd just started the whole thing again. Building up that trust bit by bit, day by day, until I could all but hang on him without him spooking.

"That girl and that horse are the same. She's got a past you ain't gonna ever understand or know fully. Trigger responses you're gonna be figurin' out your whole damn life. And things will be goin' good, great even, then the littlest thing sets you back. Don't be so quick to give up on her. If she's anythin' like that horse, she'll be back."

I didn't speak, didn't respond. I couldn't. Not as my heart fluttered with hope in my chest, choking the air from my lungs.

Hope was a dangerous, powerful thing... but God, I hoped he was right.

———

A WAVE OF DISAPPOINTMENT SETTLED AROUND ME AS WE pulled up to the barn at the ranch and I didn't see Cheyenne's truck. I didn't know why I even expected to. She hadn't called or texted—not that I thought she would. Bad's words were like a curse I couldn't get rid of in my mind.

Damn him for giving me hope.

Ryder had driven Charlie, Cason, Cash, and I back so that Bad and Violet could just go straight home. No use making an extra trip here. A thick tension brewed the entire truck-ride home. I applauded their efforts to make sure I was okay, but right now, all I wanted was to be left alone.

They'd all tried to encourage me to come over to Ryder and Charlie's for an impromptu dinner and movie night, but I just wasn't in the mood. Everything reminded me of her now. Every place on this ranch. The barn. Ryder and Charlie's. My house. Her presence still lingered around here. I wondered how long that would last.

A pang of sadness shot through my soul, but I struggled to ignore it. An impossible feat.

Cash still lingered outside the barn as I walked out from getting Betty put away. Annoyance mingled with the sadness as I pegged him with a fierce glare. "Where the hell were you today?"

Cash feigned a shrug, but I saw right through the easy-going facade. Something dark lurked in his hazel eyes. Something I probably should be more worried about, but was too annoyed to press further at the moment. "Dad told you don't worry 'bout it."

I blew out a breath through my nose, but didn't press. In the end, it didn't matter. If Bad had told him not to say anything then he wouldn't budge. But a knot of worry welled to life in me all the same. Whatever they'd done, they'd done on my behalf, of that I was certain.

"You sure you don't wanna come to Charlie and Ryder's?" he asked.

I shook my head, some of the annoyance leaving me, a deep hollowness replacing it. I was tired. Soul tired. The type of tired that no amount of rest or sleep could fix. I wished I knew what could stop it.

Something told me that whatever it was had wild blonde curls and eyes the color of gemstones.

"I just need some time alone," I finally managed to say.

Cash nodded, lacking any of his usual flare. "I can drive you home."

"Nah... I wanna walk. The fresh air helps clear my head."

Another nod from him, followed by a sigh. "I'll come check on you later."

I didn't bother arguing. It would do no good. Cash did what Cash wanted. So, with a loud exhale, I nodded and waved him off as I started my slow, lonely trudge back to the house.

I walked in silence, the night sky covered in a thick layer of clouds. A storm was rolling in, I could feel it. Even the air seemed like it was holding its breath. The chill, winter wind bit at my skin, but I welcomed it. Anything to replace the hurt in my heart. A heavy mist started falling down halfway to the house, soaking through my clothes within a moment. I couldn't even bring myself to care about my felt hat getting wet.

I didn't care much about anything.

How had I lost her? How could I have let her go? Maybe I could still go after her? But where the hell did I even start looking?

A single, sharp bark pierced the night, causing my steps to falter. I frowned, glancing up at the sound of footsteps. A red cattle dog raced toward me, another bark escaping it—this one bordering on a happy yip.

I frowned, pausing fully as I took in the dog. "Brandy?"

My heart leapt as she barreled into my legs, rubbing herself up against me, her tongue lolling out of her mouth as she begged for pets. How was she—

My gaze snapped up toward the house. A familiar truck sat beside mine in the driveway. And hopping down off the tailgate, looking like some angel from the glare of the porchlight silhouetting her appearance, was Cheyenne.

I tore off down the road toward her, gravel and dirt flying around me. Each step sent a jolt of answering pain reverberating through my fingers and up through my hand and wrist but I ignored it easily, hope and adrenaline driving my feet forward.

She was here. She was back.

I skidded to a stop just before her, my arms pulling her in and drawing her close. I clung to her like my life depended on it, while my heart beat like hummingbird wings against my ribcage.

"You came back." The words left my lips in a broken whisper. I could barely speak, let alone breathe as I pulled back, gazing down into those beautiful turquoise eyes.

God, she was gorgeous.

Tears welled in her gaze, a single droplet slipping down her cheek, but she smiled through it, a choked laugh escaping her. "I sure did, cowboy."

Cradling her face in my hands, my pain all but forgotten, I pressed the softest kiss to her lips. Tentative, hesitant—so as not to scare her away again. She leaned into the touch, kissing me back.

"What made you change your mind?" I asked, pulling back just enough to rest my forehead against her own.

She pressed her hands to my chest. "You...and Charlie. She called and talked some sense into me. But the thought of leavin' you... The thought of givin' up on us..." She glanced down at her belly before looking at me once more, her gemstone eyes shining brightly. "The thought of our baby not gettin' to grow up with her daddy...well, I just couldn't give up on that."

My breath hitched in my chest, tears pricking in my eyes.

Our baby.

I smiled, pressing a soft kiss to her forehead. "I love you."

A broken sob escaped her. "And I love you," she replied, bringing her hands up to cup my wrists.

Pain shot through my hand at the pressure, and despite my best efforts, I pulled away, wincing.

Worry knotted her brows. "What happened? Is that from last night?"

I blew out a breath and glanced beyond her to the porch column for a moment. "No... I uh...I went up against the column on the porch, and...well, I lost."

She shook her head, a disbelieving chuckle escaping her as she gently grabbed my arm to inspect the makeshift splint. "Oh my God, Maverick. And you roped like this?"

I shrugged. "Well, yeah. I wasn't gonna scratch."

She huffed. "Stubborn cowboy."

"Now, that's a bit hypocritical, don't you think?" I asked, but there was warmth in my words as I drew her against me.

She tilted her head back to meet my gaze, a vulnerability I rarely saw shining in her bright eyes. "I'm sorry for leavin' like that. I was just... well, I was scared. I know that don't make it right. But...that's what I've always done. It's second-nature to me." She blew out a deep, shaky breath. "I'm sorry that I hurt you in the process, though. You didn't deserve that." She pressed a hand to my chest, her gaze dipping down for a moment. "I don't want you to think that I left because of what you told me last night. It was never because of that. You don't know how much it means to me that you shared that piece of you with me. That you found me worthy enough to bare your soul like that." Her gaze traveled up my body once more, the intensity in her gaze paralyzing me in place. "I *need* you to know that it wasn't that."

My good hand traveled up her curves, between her shoulder blades, and knotted in her long, wild curls at the nape of her neck. Leaning in, I murmured softly against her lips, "I know."

She resisted a moment, putting pressure on my chest so we remained but a breath away from each other as she spoke. "I can't promise that I'm never gonna get scared and run off again. It's been a part of me for so long, it's a habit that's gonna take a while to break. Like with the red filly, you know..." Her shoulders lifted in a shrug. "It don't matter how many times I go into her stall, I can't just go grab her or else she runs. I gotta be patient... Just like with her, sometimes, I spook myself, and I need some time to come to terms with what's happenin'. So, I can't in good faith tell you somethin' like this ain't ever gonna happen again, but I *can* tell you that I will always, always come back to you. I ain't givin' up on this. On you. On us."

Bad's words rang in my mind from earlier. He'd been right. I'd been so dead set on the idea that I'd lost her, that I hadn't seen reason. Seen the signs. She was like every wild or abused horse I'd ever dealt with. Having her say that aloud though...I understood now. Understood and knew exactly how to deal with it.

Patience and love. Both of which I looked forward to showing her for the rest of my life.

I pulled her to me fully and claimed her mouth in mine. She opened to me, deepening the kiss, matching my intensity with a hunger, a want, a need of her own.

I loved that about her. How wild and open she was with her passion. She loved so deeply, so intensely.

Need and love thrummed to life in my chest as I got lost in her. The familiar feel of her lips on mine. Her tantalizing scent. The way she fit so perfectly in my arms.

She was here. She was home. And I'd never let her go again.

CHAPTER 56
Scared to Live Without You

CHEYENNE

Maverick's touch was like fire, and I wanted nothing more than to be burned.

I'd expected... Well, honestly, I didn't know. A part of me had thought he'd shrug me off, push me away, tell me to leave. But I preferred this much more.

I would have understood had he done any of those things. But that wasn't the way Maverick worked. He was resilient, stubborn, and patient. So, so patient. He had a fierce understanding for hurt and broken things. Because he was broken himself.

I think that's why we worked so well together. We were both broken. Both suffering from childhood traumas that shaped us into who we were. How we interacted with the world around us. Individually, we were wrecks in our own right, but together...well, together we had the patience and understanding to recognize and heal the cracks in one another.

I didn't know what would happen with Nate. I hadn't gotten anymore texts since about midday. Something told me he wasn't done, though. But for now...for now I wouldn't worry about that or bring it up to Maverick.

Not when the most amazing man I had ever had the pleasure of knowing kissed me breathless.

Tomorrow we could deal with it.

Thank God he'd come back when he did. A part of me was afraid he'd have been gone all night, and I'd have sat here waiting until he got back. I'd almost left five times, to be honest—my worries and fears creeping into my chest and sowing seeds of doubt. But for the first time in my life, I ignored them. I pushed them away and *stayed*.

It was hard as hell, but I did it. Because he was worth it. He would always be worth it.

I broke Maverick's kiss, pulling away just enough to look up into his jade eyes as rain started to pour down from the sky. Fat droplets soaking me to the bone. "Come on, cowboy. Let's get you cleaned up and out of this rain."

He kissed me once more, releasing his hold on me, but making sure to keep my hand in his. Almost like he couldn't bear the thought of letting me go, in case I ran away again. He didn't have to worry about that, though. I wasn't running.

He led me in silence into the house, through the bedroom, then finally stopped before the tub. It was like last night, but with the roles reversed. He turned the tub on, taking his time peeling off my clothes—pausing to pepper kisses along my neck, my jaw, my lips. He even sang—well, hummed along to the Randy Travis song he told the house speaker system to play.

It both broke my heart while simultaneously mending all the shattered pieces.

As Maverick made love to me in the tub, as he toweled me off, led me to bed and started the entire seductive, torturous process all over again, I realized no one would ever compare to him. Not ever again.

He was perfect and kind and fierce and passionate. He was good and just and selfless. And I wanted the rest of forever with him.

———

THE BABY'S DUE DATE CAME AND WENT UNEVENTFULLY. FIVE days had passed—leaving me feeling more and more anxious. Not for the labor and birth so much, but for the after. For being a mom. For having to take care of a newborn and all its wants and needs. I could hardly take care of myself and now I was going to take care of a tiny version of me. What if I sucked?

I had no doubt Maverick would be amazing. He was amazing at everything. He would take on the role of being a father the same way he did with everything else—with dedication and ease and patience. So much fucking patience.

I brushed down the red filly in one of the cross-ties just outside the barn. I still hadn't named her. Bad warned me not to. That once I did there was no getting rid of her. Not going to lie, a part of me—a large part of me—wanted to keep her. She'd come such a long way, was turning into such a good horse. But number one, she wasn't mine, and number two, even though I loved her, I wasn't about to back out of the bet I'd finagled my way into all those months ago. If the red filly sold, then it wasn't meant to be.

That didn't mean I couldn't enjoy every minute I spent with her. "You're a pretty girl, you know that?" I crooned, coming to stand before her and pet her forehead. She nudged my stomach in silent agreement, forcing a smile to my lips.

A flash of lightning streaked across the sky, followed closely by the crack of thunder. The filly startled and snorted a moment, but I shushed her, stroking her forehead gently and whispering soft words of assurance. "It's alright, you're okay."

I glanced at the sky—an angry gray with black thunderheads looming like giants on the horizon. A storm was coming.

"Come on," I said, grabbing her lead rope and taking her out of the cross-ties. "Let's get you put away."

It wasn't much later that Maverick came stalking into the barn, Ryder hot on his heels. They both looked equally as pissed as worried.

"What's wrong?" I frowned as I closed the door to the red filly's stall.

"There's a whole section of fence in the far pasture that broke, somehow," Ryder huffed from his spot beside Maverick.

Maverick let out a frustrated sigh. "We lost a couple cows already. We gotta go fix it before the storm hits and we lose more."

I nodded. "Alright. I'll saddle up Country Rose and we can all go."

He scoffed. "You ain't goin' nowhere."

A scowl formed on my lips. "And why the hell not?"

He rocked back at that, a look of disbelief marring his handsome features. "You're due any day now, Chey. I ain't deliverin' our baby in a goddamn pasture."

I wanted to argue. I opened my mouth *to argue*, before blowing a deep breath and rolling my eyes. "Ugh, fine." A huff escaped me.

A small, tight smile started to bloom on his lips, but worry still coated his brow.

"What's wrong?" I asked. "It shouldn't take too long, should it? Not if y'all go together."

He chewed his lip. "We don't want to leave y'all."

Ah, there it was. The real problem. I understood the concern, but—

I moved closer to him, pressing a soft, reassuring hand to his chest. "Mav, I feel exactly the same as I did yesterday. And the day before then. And the day before then. I highly doubt the baby is coming. And Charlie isn't due for another week."

The look on their faces told me they weren't convinced.

I glanced at Ryder, then back at him. "Look, why don't y'all take the ranch truck? It'll be quicker than ridin', and y'all can carry everythin' you need. Fixin' that pasture should take no longer than, what, three hours tops with both of y'all? I ain't gonna have a baby in that little time. Charlie says that most first time moms are in labor for hours. *Hours*, Mav."

His light eyes flickered with uncertainty.

"You'll be there and back before I can even miss you. Ain't no use losin' the whole damn herd over this. Go while the storm ain't here. I'll be fine."

"I don't want you here all alone…" But the fight had left him. I'd won, he was just drawing it out now.

"Charlie should be back soon from droppin' Cason off at school. And Cash and Bad will be back in a few hours from that stupid futurity event or whatever the hell thing it was they went to this weekend." I leaned up on tiptoe and pressed a kiss to his lips. "Go do this before you worry yourself to death, Maverick."

He wrapped an arm around me, drawing me in close. "Fine," he murmured against my lips. "But if you need anythin'... If you start to feel anythin', you call me. Immediately."

"Yes, cowboy," I murmured, pressing another kiss to his lips.

He pulled back, gripping my chin between his thumb and forefinger. "I mean it, Chey."

I offered him a soft smile. "I know."

———

MAVERICK LEFT SHORTLY AFTER WITH RYDER, THOUGH they'd opted to take Ryder's truck instead of the ranch one. Ryder claimed they might as well walk, with how shitty and unreliable Cash's was. Not to mention, the windows didn't roll up on one side, and it had started raining.

Well, looks like I'll be spending the day inside.

I had a couple orders to make, and maybe I'd spend the time trying new candle scents since Mav was gone. He loved when I came up with new ones, but hated the process. Claimed it was too hard on his nose. Well, he wasn't here to complain now, was he?

I headed out to the garage to grab all my things. It didn't take long to set up and pretty soon the whole house smelled like lavender, vanilla, and a touch of lemon. I was so over this stupid, cold weather, and the smell reminded me of the sun and springtime and warmer days. God, I missed the warmth, and it hadn't even been that cold this year.

I found a baggie of dried wildflowers and began sprinkling them atop the melted wax when a string of cramps surged through me, enough to make me pause.

Fuck. More Braxton Hicks contractions.

I'd gotten them a week and a half ago and Maverick had demanded we go to the hospital, thinking I'd started labor. But after wasting an entire day in the hospital to be monitored, the doctor sent me home, saying it wasn't time yet. I had an appointment on Wednesday, anyway. My doctor said she would likely induce me if I hadn't gone into labor yet. Little girl had seemed happy enough in my stomach when I'd gone in for my ultrasound on Friday. I'd last through the next two days. I was sure of it.

I breathed through the pain, letting it flow through me as it peaked and then receded, like a wave on the shore.

Thank God Mav wasn't here. He'd have already had the truck running and been ushering me into the passenger seat. Hopefully they were gone soon, then he'd never have to know.

...except they weren't.

In fact, they actually got stronger and more frequent over the next couple hours. Still manageable, but sharp enough to take the breath from my lungs for a moment. Fuck. Maybe I should just call Maverick. Try and see when he'd be home... He had said to call if I felt anything. But when I checked my phone, there was no service.

Ugh. Great. Guess they weren't kiddin' when they said this would be a nasty storm.

I looked outside. The sky was black and angry, a fierce wind whistling, but it wasn't *pouring*. At least not yet.

What was I supposed to do? Were Braxton Hicks contractions supposed to be this strong? I let out a sigh. I should've read at least *one* of the books Charlie recommended me. But I don't know... I'd tried reading them. There was so much medical jargon in it that I just...I didn't care. I imagined my water would break and boom we'd go to the hospital and I deal with all this shit with a medical professional.

I could ask Charlie, but that meant driving through the storm to get to her house. Another wave of pain cramped its way through me, stealing the air from my lungs and forcing me to lean against the countertop. Brandy leaned into my leg as I rode the wave.

As the pain finally ebbed, I glanced down at her. "What'dya say, girl? Wanna go for a drive?"

———

A DRIVE DOWN THE ROAD MAY HAVE NOT BEEN—OKAY, wasn't at all—my wisest decision. I may have underestimated how hard it was raining...and these fucking cramps. I wouldn't call them contractions, because if they were contractions...well then, this meant something else entirely and there was no way I was having this baby without Maverick here.

The thought alone terrified me. He was my rock, my support. He'd read all the books. Watched all the videos. He probably could deliver a baby at this point with how much he'd researched it.

Another wave of pain coursed through me, and I slammed on the brakes hard enough to make the tires lock up and slide through the mud before lurching to a halt. Fuck, fuck, fuck.

They were getting stronger. A lot stronger. And closer together. What had Charlie said... something about 4-2-1... No, that wasn't it. 4-1...

5-1-1. Five minutes apart. One minute contractions for one hour. Well, they were definitely happening frequently. And the last three felt like they'd go on for fucking ever.

Panic knotted in my chest. I couldn't be in labor. How? Had my water even broke? Wasn't it supposed to be like a huge gush? I pulled out my phone to check if I had service, but nothing. Not even a damn bar.

It's just cramps, Cheyenne. Nothin' you can't handle.

Easing off the breaks, I started for the main road again. Thank fuck I hadn't gotten it stuck. I needed to get to Charlie's so I wasn't alone. Maybe she had service. But the wind and rain were so strong it took everything in me not to go off the road. Tree branches littered the ground almost everywhere I looked.

The barn came into view and a familiar maroon truck along with it. The headlights pierced through the fog and rain and a sigh of relief escaped me. Thank God Cash and his dad were back. I parked and hopped out, forcing Brandy to stay in the truck.

"What the hell are you doin' out here?" Bad shouted, poking his head out of the window of his truck.

My clothes were soaked through by the time I made it close enough for him to hear me. "We have a fuckin—" Another contraction barreled into me, and I slammed my eyes closed. Forcing air into my lungs, I breathed through the pain until it finally ebbed once more. Wiping water uselessly from my face, I focused on Bad.

"What the fuck was that?" Cash asked in the passenger seat.

"Well, fuck," Bad grumbled. "She's in labor, dipshit."

Hearing someone else say it out loud sent a wave of terror through me. I didn't want this to happen like this. I needed Maverick here.

"My service is shit. I need to get ahold of Mav."

"Where the hell is he?" Bad asked. "Wait, get in the damn truck. You're fuckin' soaked."

I hopped into the backseat, closing the door behind me. "Him and Ryder are fixin' some fence out in the back pasture."

Cash scoffed. "In this fuckin' weather?"

"They lost a couple cows. They didn't really have a choice."

Bad growled out a curse. "I can't believe Mav ain't here."

"I was fine before he left. This started like half an hour after. But I couldn't get a hold of him because of the storm."

Cash pulled out his phone, the home screen lighting up. "I gotta couple bars." Unlocking his home screen, he called Maverick, handing me the phone.

"What the hell do you want, Ca—"

"It's not, Cash," I interrupted, some of my nerves easing at the sound of his familiar, deep voice.

"Chey?" Fear rang in his words. "What's wrong?"

"I... I think it's time."

"Fuck. Where...you...comin..." Static and wind chased away his words, before the phone call dropped entirely. Because of course it fucking did. I let out a growl as I clicked on his name again. But it just went straight to voicemail.

"Shit! What the hell do I do?" My hands trembled as I tried to call him again but no answer. The phone wouldn't even connect. When I glanced at the screen the two measly little bars were gone. "What do I do? What do I do? I can't do this—" The words died on my lips as I gripped the door handle hard enough I thought it might break. "Fuck," I growled, drawing the word out in a long breath as I rode through the wave of another contraction.

"Cash, start a fuckin' timer on your phone. Every time she has a contraction, note it. See how far they are apart." Bad looked back at me. "We needa get you to the hospital."

"What about Mav?" I hardly even recognized my voice. It sounded shrill, high-pitched, pained. "I can't do this without him."

"Chey, what matters right now is gettin' you somewhere safe to deliver that baby. Mav will be there." Bad's words were calm, sure, but it did little to stop the fear flooding through my veins and trickling down my spine. I couldn't be in labor.

"Maybe it's just Braxton Hicks?" I offered, but even Cash had the common sense to shake his head. I sighed in defeat. "I need to tell Charlie. See if she can keep an eye on Brandy for me."

"I didn't see her Tacoma in the driveway when we pulled into the ranch," Cash replied.

"Alright. Well, can we drop Brandy off at the house and I'll change? Then we can go."

Bad frowned, almost like he was going to argue, but finally sighed.

It took us another five minutes just to get back down the road. Thunder and lightning had joined the fray, along with hail that pelted down so hard I was surprised the windshield hadn't broken. I'd had another contraction in that time—the longest so far.

How the fuck was I going to do this? What if Maverick couldn't get to the hospital in time? What if I had to deliver the baby alone?

I can't do this.

We got back to the house and I changed as quickly as I could through another two damn contractions before getting Brandy situated and myself back in the truck. We didn't even make it off the ranch. A huge branch from one of the trees lining the drive had fallen across the road.

"Well, shit," Bad grumbled.

"We could just off-road it," Cash replied with a shrug, spitting into his spitter cup.

Bad glared at him. "You can explain to your mother what happened to her truck when we break an axle."

"What're we gonna do? I can't—" Another burst of pain.

Cash's worried hazel gaze met mine as he noted another contraction. "They're comin' quicker," he said, glancing at his dad.

"Let's see what we can do," Bad replied, grabbing a pair of work gloves out of the driver's side door. "You stay here," he called to me as he opened up the truck and got out. I didn't even hear the door shut, that's how loud the rain and hail were. Cash growled out something under his breath and followed suit, leaving me alone and in silence.

I stared ahead, trying and failing to see anything through the windshield. Just blurry shapes that were darker in some places than others. I don't know how much time passed, but the contraction that pulsed through me this time brought tears to my eyes, knocking the air from my lungs so thoroughly I couldn't even cry out.

I pulled my phone out again, but there wasn't a single bar.

Bad and Cash climbed back into the truck a few moments later, both soaking wet and cursing up a storm.

"It's too fuckin' big," Bad growled out.

"What?" I sniffled. "What does that mean?"

Cash offered me what I think was meant to be a reassuring grin. "It means we ain't gettin' off this ranch."

My chest squeezed, my heartbeat drowning out the sound of hail and rolling thunder—no small feat. "But...the baby."

Another hopeful grin from Cash. "We've birthed baby calves before...how much harder can it be? Right, Dad?"

Tears rolled down my cheeks, fear and dread coiling around my heart. I couldn't breathe. I wanted to throw up. I—another. Fucking. Contraction.

CHAPTER 57
Ain't Even Met You Yet

MAVERICK

I tried calling Cheyenne back. Again. And again. And again.

But it was no use. I couldn't keep a signal long enough to get the phone to ring. I paced back and forth, uncaring of the rain pelting down on me, soaking me to the bone.

Ryder frowned from his spot by the broken fence as I stalked for him. "You get ahold of her?" He had to shout over the wind and rolling thunder.

I shook my head. "I can't get a fuckin' signal."

"Shit..." His frown deepened as he glanced between me and the fence. What should have been a relatively easy fix had quickly turned to shit with the rain and mud. Not to mention, it was cold, wet, and so slippery that Ryder and I spent more time trying not to fall or get stuck in the mud than actually repairing the fence.

"What do you wanna do?" Ryder asked.

I blew out a breath and wiped a hand down my face, but it did little to rid it of water. My hat might as well be useless at this point. "I don't fuckin' know," I growled.

Had her water broke? Was she okay? God, I hated that I wasn't there for her.

I knew it. I just fuckin' knew something bad was going to happen. I'd felt it. Felt it like I'd felt this storm brewing for days now. But I'd never thought this would've taken us as long as it had.

"We gotta finish this fence or else we run the risk of losin' the herd... but I need to get back to her... Fuck." I fisted my hands at my sides—well, tried—and instantly regretted it. Pain speared through my right hand. I glared down at the stupid soft cast. I'd shattered most of my hand from my fight against the four by four, and had been scheduled for surgery a week later. It'd only been about three weeks since then.

Ryder chewed his bottom lip, like he was mulling something over in his mind. "You go back," he finally said.

"This ain't a one-man job though." I hated the idea of leaving him, but the thought of Cheyenne home alone, in this weather, and in labor... My heart raced in my chest, fear gripping it like a vice.

"You gotta get back to her. Take my truck, get ahold of Cash, and send him back to pick me up. I can fix this up enough so that no cows go through it 'til we can do somethin' more permanent. You be there for your girl."

"You sure?" I asked.

He nodded. "Yes. Now go, before this weather gets any shittier." He tossed me the keys and I made my way for the truck. Excitement mingled with the fear and unease in my heart.

This was it. She was coming and after today, nothing would be the same. I'd be a father. The thought still rocked me to my very core.

I'm comin', Chey.

...except I couldn't. Not as I put the truck in gear and the tires started spinning. Fuck. I tried to put it in reverse, but same thing. I slammed the car in park and opened my door to find Ryder tripping over himself trying to come over and help.

"It's this mud. Everythin's so slick. Here, let's see if we can drag somethin' over for the tires to catch on," he offered.

It's like everything we did was doomed to fail—each idea going more poorly than the last. My nerves were frayed, my patience shot to shit. I'd ripped off my cast in my frustration. It was soaked and caked in mud anyway, and I had no doubt after all the work I'd been doing, the way I couldn't stop flexing and fisting my fingers, I'd done serious damage. Doctor was gonna be pissed… But the pain was but a whisper compared to the panic pumping through my veins. The only thought driving me forward was getting to Cheyenne. Of making it back there.

Was the storm as bad where she was as it was out here? Was she okay? How was the pain? Had she gotten to the hospital? Fear spiked in me. *How* had she gotten to the hospital?

"Fuck it," I said, damn near throwing my phone when I glanced at the time. We'd spent close to another two hours trying to get out of this mess and still weren't any closer to getting out of there. "I'm walkin'."

Ryder nodded. "I'm coming with you."

"What about the fence?"

Ryder waved it off dismissively as he came to my side. "Fuck it. I ain't lettin' you walk back in this alone. We'll find whatever cows get out later. This is more important. Your daughter is more important."

Hope and worry warred in my heart. But with a determined nod of my head, I aimed in the direction of home.

CHAPTER 58
Growin' Up Raisin' You

CHEYENNE

I'd been wrong. So damn wrong. I'd been foolish enough to think this would be a breeze... After all, the rest of my pregnancy was. I'd dealt with pain. I'd broken bones. Torn ligaments. But this... Holy shit, this was on a whole new level.

The contractions were so frequent sometimes I didn't know when one started and the other ended. I'd taken a bath, I'd paced the house, Cash had even convinced me to line dance at one point.

But now... Well, now it was all I could do to catch my fucking breath.

Bad and Cash made a surprisingly good support team, though. Bad seemed to have hands meant for gripping tight. They were firm and calloused and rough as leather, but they didn't budge or falter as I held them through some of the nastier waves.

I sat in the arm chair in mine and Mav's room, perched on the edge, while gripping Bad's hand like my life depended on it.

Maverick still wasn't here. Not that it seemed likely for him to be with this storm. It was just as bad out, if not worse. The wind whipped around the house, rain and hail pelting against the roof and windows.

But the idea of him not being here... No. I couldn't think of that. I had to hold out hope. He'd be here.

He'll be here.

A groan of pain fell from my lips, tears welling in my eyes as I rode through another contraction. But this one was different. I can't even properly explain it, aside from just...pressure. So much pressure that I thought I might drown in it if it didn't go away.

"Um...somethin's happenin'. It feels different..." My voice was little more than a squeak as I tried to speak through the pain. "What's happenin'?"

Cash hurried to the left side of the armchair, a wet rag to wipe the sweat from my brow hanging over his arm, while Bad remained holding my hand on my right. "Shit. You think it's time, Dad?"

Bad's hazel gaze held a laser-sharp focus. "Only one way to find out."

Cash frowned, tilting his head to the side for a moment until realization finally dawned on him. His mouth dropped open before snapping shut. His Adam's apple bobbed once as his pleading stare flicked from me to his dad. "I...I can't," he stammered out.

"Someone's gotta check how dilated she is. You ain't got your hand in a vice-grip right now. You do it."

Cash looked at me, and I almost—*almost*—laughed. I'd never seen Cash Mooney embarrassed or bashful since meeting him. Didn't even know it was possible.

Another contraction swept through me. Another relentless wave of blinding, white-hot pain and pressure. *Shit.*

"Cash, you've made a fuckin' art of lookin' at pussy. Don't tell me you can't do it now," I growled out.

Bad snorted at my side, and despite the pain, the barest hint of a smirk tugged on my lips. Cash's shocked, mortified expression was just too good to behold.

He gulped, chewing his lip for a minute. "It ain't the same," he pleaded.

"If you ain't gonna help, then get out," I snapped, another swell of pressure pummeling into me. "Fu—" My head fell back as I slammed my eyes closed and tried to just breathe through it all. Tears slipped down my cheeks.

"I'll do it." Cash's words were genuine, soft, and earnest. Not a shred of the cocky cowboy I'd come to know.

My eyes shot open, gaze snapping to his.

He nodded, saying the words again. "I'll do it." Then, nodding and repeating himself over and over, as if it had become a mantra, he knelt before the armchair. "Okay, just um...just lean back. You sure you're okay with this?"

If another pulse of blinding pain didn't ripple through me just then, I'd have offered him some sort of form of encouragement, but the pained groan that came out of my mouth was the best I could do as I fisted the hem of the silky nightdress Aunt Violet had gotten me, bunching it up towards my stomach. Cash's gaze left mine for but a moment, but the way it snapped up to me only a blink later, complete astonishment and a trickle of fear shining in his green-gold gaze told me everything I needed to know.

"Holy. Fuckin'. Shit." His voice boomed over the storm. "Well, I ain't no doctor, but I'd say start fuckin' pushin'."

I thought the contractions were bad, but the fear and panic that bubbled to life in my chest and pumped through my veins with each labored breath I took was worse. Far worse. I couldn't do this. I just... I couldn't.

Not without Maverick here.

My breathing—or whatever you could call the shallow gasps I managed to suck down my throat—hitched, making my lungs burn at the realization I was going to be doing this without him.

My body trembled, and I couldn't stop shaking my head back and forth.

No. No. No. No.

"No. I can't! I can't do it!" I was up and out of the seat quicker than should have been possible, all but shoving Cash out of the way as I moved to brush past him—a bad idea as the pressure weighing down on me, urging me to push, brought me down to my hands and knees.

"Holy shit! Chey!" Cash's shout sounded far away as the worst contraction yet tore its way through me, forcing my entire body to shake.

The pressure was too much. Too unbearable. I sucked in sharp, shallow breaths, my gaze trained on the floor as I bit the inside of my cheek hard enough to draw blood. Anything to take away from the overwhelming pain and pressure building, building, building.

I couldn't do this. I couldn't do this. I couldn't—

Cash's face materialized before me, his hands cupping my cheeks. "Breathe, Chey. You got this."

"I can't, Cash. I—"

"Damn it, Chey. You can."

I shook my head, tears leaking down my cheeks and blurring my vision. "I can't. Not without Mav."

"You can and you will. I ain't Mav, but I'm here. Now I need you to buck up and push."

An ember of anger sparked in me at his words. Buck up? I'd like to see him do this. Push a fucking baby out with no medication. No doctor. Just a couple cowboys whose only birthing experience was with fucking livestock.

"Fuck you," I growled through another grueling contraction.

And damn him, but he flashed one of those bright, shit-eating grins of his. Like he knew, and was depending on my anger to push me through. "Come on, Trouble. You got this."

He glanced beyond me, and I followed his gaze to find Bad settling a thick layer of towels and anything soft for the delivery. He offered me a single, determined nod.

Well, damn. This was happening.

My heart thumped so hard and wildly I wasn't sure how it hadn't come out of my chest, but a rush of determination surged to life in me, mingling with the fear and panic.

"Okay," I whispered, blowing out a breath as I turned forward to meet Cash's gaze once more. "Let's do th—" My words fell away, a groan tearing from my lips as the overwhelming urge to push rippled through me. I didn't fight through the wave this time, I embraced it, let it flow and just...pushed, letting the air whoosh from my lungs as I bore down and let it out.

"Good. Chey. Good," Bad urged, calmly.

I sucked in a string of deep breaths, letting Cash wipe the sweat off my face with the towel. "You got this," he murmured.

With a deep breath in, another contraction pulsated through me and I pushed and pushed and pushed, expelling the air from my lungs in a slow whoosh once more.

Bad and Cash walked me through each contraction, each push, each breath, in tandem. Cash knelt before me, holding me as I clamped my arms around his shoulders and used his support to push down through the waves of unrelenting, agonizing contractions. He whispered soft words of encouragement, rubbing my back, trying anything to ease my fears and worries.

My entire body shook with exhaustion, my breath sawing in and out of my chest. The adrenaline and determination I'd felt moments ago dwindled and fizzled out like a firework. God, it hurt. And burned. I felt like I was on fire. It was fucking painful. Brutal.

"I...c-can't..." I sobbed after another round of pushing.

Cash pulled back enough to cup my face once more. "You can't stop now. You're almost there."

"One more push, Chey." Bad's deep, gravelly voice soothed some of the fear. "Come on. You got this. One more."

One more. I met Cash's determined stare.

He pressed his forehead to mine. "One more, Chey."

I swear, the shout that tore from lungs as I pushed through that final contraction damn near shook the house. Or maybe it was just me shaking so hard.

"Yes. Good. Good girl, Chey," Bad's words were like a balm as the pressure began to lessen and ease until...

A cry pierced through the room, rising above a clap of thunder. Lightning flickered, casting the room in a white glow for a moment. I sagged against Cash, my entire body trembling as tears fell from my eyes. And then Bad placed a little piece of heaven in my arms.

She cried and cried and cried, more like a banshee than an angel, but she was beautiful no less. Even covered in blood and amniotic fluid and God knew what else. But I wiped at it gently, so gently, with the swaddling blanket Bad had waiting for her arrival.

467

I'd done it... I'd actually done it. She was here. And every fear and doubt and worry I'd had since finding out I was having her vanished in that moment. The road leading here had been hard, and the road going forward would be full of dips and turns, and highs and lows, but none of that mattered. All that mattered, right here and right now, was this precious little being I cupped to my chest.

"She's gorgeous, Chey," Cash said, still kneeling beside me.

"He's right. I ain't seen many gorgeous babies, and that's includin' my own." Bad chuckled as he sat himself in the arm chair and pulled the rubber gloves off his hands.

"Hey! Mama said I was the best damn lookin' baby she'd ever seen."

"She was lyin', boy." He nodded toward my baby, who still fussed and whined, but had begun to settle as I held her against me. "That right there is."

A smile curved my lips as I met each of their gazes before looking back down at the being I'd created. "Welcome to the world, my little storm cloud. This here's your Uncle Cash and your Grandpa Bad."

As I glanced up at them once more, I found both men's eyes lined with silver.

CHAPTER 59

I Don't Wanna Go To Heaven

MAVERICK

My clothes were drenched, leaving my skin chapped and chafed, I'd lost my boots to the fucking mud a couple miles back, and my hand throbbed and pulsed so badly that the wind licking at my fingers felt like sharp claws raking over flesh.

But the sight of the house sent my heart thumping wildly in my chest. A surge of adrenaline drove me forward, my feet eating up the distance between me and that beacon of light. Between me and Cheyenne. I pulled away from Ryder, picking up speed as I raced onward. The hail had stopped for the moment, but thunder still rolled, followed by the occasional lightning strike, and non-stop rain. I ignored it all as I reached the gravel driveway leading up to the front porch.

A familiar maroon truck sat in the driveway, but Cheyenne's was nowhere to be seen.

Did that mean they were here? Or had they taken Cheyenne's truck to the hospital? I couldn't imagine they'd do that. But maybe I'd have some damn service in the house and could get ahold of someone.

Fifteen feet.

Ten.

Five.

The front door opened inward, and Bad loomed in the entryway.

"Where is she?" I breathed, but as I made it to the porch, he pressed a hand to my shoulder, the wait of his stare paralyzing me in place. "Is she okay?" I croaked.

A slew of emotions I'd never expected to see in Bad shone in that usually hard, hazel stare. "They're doin' great."

They.

The breath left me in a whoosh. "She-she had her? Fuck!"

Guilt and frustration warred with the excitement churning within me, wilder than the storm overhead.

Bad gripped both of my shoulders. "Hey. Hey, it's okay. She's okay... they're okay."

How could I have missed it? A flicker of rage rippled through me, but I pushed it down, down, down. All that mattered now was that Cheyenne was okay. That they *both* were okay.

"C-can I see 'em?" I whispered, the words all but dying in my throat.

Bad's lips curved upward into a soft grin as he stepped aside.

My breathing was ragged and shallow as I crossed the threshold into the house. The living room and kitchen were neat and tidy as usual, but the light leading down the hall to our bedroom glowed. On shaky legs, I padded toward the room, the squelch of my wet clothes deafening compared to the quiet singing dancing on the air.

My feet stopped working altogether as I entered our room, finding the most beautiful sight awaiting me. Cheyenne's soft singing broke away into nothingness as her gaze snapped up to clash with mine.

She looked...well, she looked absolutely gorgeous sitting perched up against the pillows of our bed. Her wild curls were pulled up into a messy bun high on her head, little wisps falling to frame her face. There was this glow about her, almost like it came from within. And her eyes shone with warmth. So much warmth and love and light.

"Well, you ready to meet your daughter, Maverick?" My legs almost gave out at her words.

Your daughter.

Tears welled in my eyes as I moved toward the bed, coming to a stop a few feet away. I didn't want to get too close—I was covered in mud and shit and grime.

"Y-you guys both are okay?" I asked, swallowing past the lump in my throat.

Cheyenne's smile chased away the cold lingering in my bones and the fear lurking in my heart. It was radiant. She angled herself toward me, and I got the first peak at the most precious thing I'd ever laid my eyes upon.

"Wanna hold her?" she asked.

My hands trembled, and as I glanced down at them the sight stopped me in my tracks. "I'm filthy. I—can I change first?"

I didn't want to. I didn't want to spend another moment with them out of my sight, but the thought of holding her for the first time in the state I was in just didn't sit right with me.

Cheyenne's laughter reminded me of a babbling brook. "Of course, cowboy. Just hurry."

I bit back a wave of tears as I nodded. A warm hand slapped my shoulder, and I glanced over to find Cash. "I got you some clothes already. They're in the bathroom for ya."

I hadn't even registered that he was here, didn't even have the words to speak now. So, I just nodded. He squeezed my shoulder reassuringly and tilted his chin toward the bathroom. "Go."

I washed my hands for a full two minutes, trying to rid anywhere that would touch her of so much as a speck of dirt. After changing into new clothes, I stared in the mirror.

This was it.

Blowing out a deep breath, I made my way back into the room. Cheyenne smiled at me once more as I moved to the edge of the bed.

"Come on, don't be shy. She's been dying to meet her daddy for the last hour."

An hour. She'd had her an hour ago. Guilt niggled at me, but as she handed me the most beautiful treasure I'd ever beheld, all that doubt washed away.

My hands shook as I held her before me, studying her, committing every tiny detail of her to memory. Forever ingraining this moment in my soul.

Dear Lord, she was beautiful. A soft dusting of light brown hair. The smallest, most perfect little button nose. Tiny fingers and perfect little toes. And eyes blue as her mother's. I hoped they never changed. Never dulled or darkened, but shone like turquoise pools for the rest of forever.

"Hello, there Oakleigh M—"

"Oh, I wanted to talk to you about that." Cheyenne's voice held a timid note to it. I frowned, meeting her worried gaze. "I was thinkin... Oakleigh doesn't fit her."

"You don't think?" I asked, curiosity drawing my attention back and forth between her and the baby.

She chewed her lip and shook her head, her brows knitting together. "No. I just... I love the name, but it isn't *her*."

"What're you thinkin'?"

"What about Stormie Mae? I thought you know, with her spectacular entrance and all..." Her words trailed off.

A smile tugged on my lips as I eased myself onto the bed beside Cheyenne, careful not to disrupt the most precious little gift I'd ever gotten to hold. "Stormie Mae..." I nodded, bringing her up before me so that I could press the softest whisper of a kiss to her forehead. "It's nice to meet you."

Cheyenne leaned into me. "Little storm cloud, this here's your daddy. He's the most amazin' man you'll ever meet. He's gonna love you and cherish and take care of you for the rest of your life. You're the luckiest girl in the world."

Daddy.

The warmth and love in her voice broke me. Tears welled in my eyes, my throat closing as my heart clenched so tightly, I thought it might stop entirely. And when I glanced up at Cheyenne, tears streaming down her cheeks, I knew as long as I had her and this baby... Well, it didn't matter how dark life ever got, because I had the brightest lights to guide me through it.

———

BAD HAD MADE SURE NOT TO CUT THE UMBILICAL CORD, SO I had something to do with the birth. Getting to have him, Cash, Ryder, and Chey all there in the same room to see...well, it felt almost surreal.

The next few hours, the next few days really passed in a blur. Feedings, changings, doctor's appointments—for both me and Stormie Mae. She was healthy as can be, my hand though... Well, let's just say I'd gotten an earful from the doctor. She'd been equally as furious as impressed that I'd managed to even attempt to mend a fence with my hand in the state it was in. I'd done a bit of damage though, so another surgery was in the works for the following week. The splint they had me in now was bulky, and prevented me from doing much, but it gave me an excellent excuse to be stuck on baby duty.

Stormie's cries carried through the room from the bedside bassinet Cash and Ryder had set up in the room for us. Cheyenne stirred beside me, but with a kiss to her forehead, I murmured quietly, "It's okay. I got this."

I'd gotten pretty good at managing to change diapers one-handed so that I could help in any way I could. And heating up bottles. Chey struggled to produce much breast milk, but it didn't stop her from trying relentlessly. She had an appointment with one of the nurses at the hospital later on in the morning to see what they could help her with. But in the meantime, we were supplementing with formula.

I eased out of bed and moved to Stormie's bassinet, drawing her up into my arms as I went through the motions that had become so instinctual, so natural, in just a few short days. Deep down—subconsciously— I think a part of me feared that I wouldn't have a connection with her, but I'd never been so wrong. She might not share my blood, but this little girl was mine, through and through.

After changing her and heating up a bottle, I settled into the rocking chair I'd made in her room, rocking gently back and forth as I fed her. "And how are you this mornin' little storm cloud?"

I watched her in quiet awe as she fed, in pure disbelief that this was my life now. She was mine. I'd always assumed I never deserved love. Like I'd done something to deserve Ashleigh... and I was so starved for just a shred of her affection that had Cheyenne not come into my life, I'd have continued down that dark, endless road of unhappiness.

But now, I had Chey. I had Stormie. I had a family. Everything I could ever want. And I'd never been so grateful. My life was whole. It was good. It was full of love. And I would fight like hell to keep it like this for the rest of forever.

As the sky began to lighten slowly outside an idea came to my mind. Fuck, I needed to hurry. Clutching Stormie in my arms, I made my way to our room, lightly rousing Cheyenne.

"Hey...hey wake up, Chey."

She blinked away sleep and squinted at me. "Hm?"

"Come on, I wanna do somethin', but I need y'all there with me."

"What is it?" Her brow furrowed for a moment before smoothing, almost like she realized the need in my eyes, the desperation in my voice. With a nod, she sat up. "What time is it?"

"Six. We gotta get out there by sunrise."

She rose from bed and we both got ready quickly. I'd already gotten Stormie Mae ready for the occasion, putting her in the warmest outfit I could find in her drawers.

Cheyenne shimmied into a pair of jeans and top before noticing me watching her. The smile she gave me sparked desire and love in my chest. She came over to the armchair where I sat holding Stormie, leaning down to press a kiss to Stormie's forehead before tilting my chin up to look at her.

Cheyenne had settled into motherhood easily despite what she thought. She approached each new situation with determination and ease, going with the flow when things got overwhelming instead of being rigid. I was completely in awe of her.

"I love you, cowboy," she murmured against my lips. Her kiss held the same warmth and desire that shone in her eyes.

"I love you too." Holding Stormie with my good hand, I drew Cheyenne in close with my splinted one to the back of her head, deepening the kiss for a moment.

Her lips curved upward as she pulled away enough to look at me, I couldn't help the words that fell from my mouth. "I'm so proud of you."

Her gaze narrowed slightly, lips tugging downward. "Why?" The question was earnest, genuine. Like she didn't understand just how truly amazing she was.

"You amaze me every day with how damn strong you are. How kind and warm and open you are." I pressed a soft kiss to her lips before resting my head against her forehead. "Motherhood looks damn good on you, Chey."

Tears welled in her eyes, but she flashed another dazzling smile my way as she kissed me once more. "Thank you."

"I mean it," I urged.

She nodded, a single tear leaking down her cheek. "I know. And it means more than you know."

Within ten minutes, I'd gotten us all loaded up into my truck and drove us down to the barn. The sky was lightening at an alarming rate now—not that it really mattered in the grand scheme of things, but... I don't know, I just liked the idea of this moment being captured at dawn. Sunrise had always been my favorite time of day, when the world was just waking up, the sun chasing away the darkness of the night.

"Here, this way. I put her in one of the big turn outs last night," I said, ushering Cheyenne to follow after me as I got Stormie out of her car seat and cradled her to my chest.

"Who?" Cheyenne asked, following behind me.

The red filly whinnied from the other side of the pasture as I came up to the fence. Opening the gate, I walked in, urging Chey to follow. Brow furrowed in question, she followed, settling at my side as the filly loped toward us.

"What's goin' on?" she asked, her voice more curious than anything.

The horse slowed about twenty or so paces from us, coming to a walk as she came closer. I glanced between her and Stormie, who watched in silence in my arms. She was always so alert, examining the world through those ridiculously blue eyes of hers. It's like she was takin it all in...even though I knew she really couldn't see any of that, at least not yet with her field of vision being so limited. But if this is how she looked at the world now, I couldn't imagine how curious and observant she'd be as she grew.

"I don't know if you believe this, but I think that our horses choose us. Not the other way around. Call it fate or luck or just God's hand at work, but I think each horse comes to us when we need 'em. You needed her through the pregnancy, and now..." my words broke off as the filly took a final step forward, eyeing Stormie Mae with her deep brown, soulful gaze.

"I thought you were gonna sell her."

Knickering softly, the horse nuzzled Stormie's head, letting out a soft exhale through her nose.

A grin warmed up my face as I watched them. "Every cowgirl needs a good horse. And if this cowgirl is as wild as you, she's gonna need the best."

I glanced over to find Cheyenne crying, her blue eyes swimming with tears, but the smile on her face held the power of the sun. She pushed up on her tiptoes to kiss me. I savored her warmth, her kiss, and when she pulled away, my chest felt so full of love it might burst entirely.

"Thank you, Maverick," she whispered, sliding an arm around my bicep and leaning into me. "Thank you for lovin' me. For lovin' her. For givin' us this. Showin' me everythin' I've been missin', needin' my entire life."

I kissed the top of her head and she glanced up at me as I murmured, "Thank you for healin' cracks in me I didn't even realize hadn't healed. You saved me, Chey."

She smiled once more, and even though the sun peeked over the horizon, bathing the dark earth in its wondrous, warm light, it paled in comparison to her. "We saved each other."

I pressed another kiss to her wild curls, inhaling the familiar scent of her. "We needa name for that filly."

"Hmm..." Cheyenne looked at the horse. "What about...Calamity?"

I snorted. "Sounds pretty damn fittin', actually."

A soft laugh. "I thought so too."

My phone buzzed in my pocket, but I ignored it, not willing to let the perfectness of this moment go just yet. But when Cheyenne's phone buzzed next, a trickle of unease stirred in my chest.

Cheyenne's excited gaze met mine as she showed me the caller I.D. before answering it. "Is it time?" she asked. A pause, then a squeal from Cheyenne that upset both the filly—Calamity—and Stormie. I shushed them both, Stormie calming easily enough, even as Cheyenne all but vibrated as she spoke. "Keep us updated. Let us know if y'all need anythin'."

She hung up a moment later. "Charlie's water broke. Midwife's on the way. Ryder's gettin' the tub all ready."

I smiled, excitement of my own bubbling within me. Having a child had always been a forbidden dream of mine. I wanted nothing more than to be a father, but was always terrified of becoming like my own. But having the opportunity to raise my daughter up alongside my best friend, well, I don't think things could get much better at this point. Maybe if Cash somehow settled down and had a kid, but that wasn't gonna happen anytime soon.

I wrapped my free arm tighter around Cheyenne, kissing her gently, slowly, putting all the love I felt for her into that caress.

I'd always been taught that heaven was this place of perfection, where you could have anything and everything you wanted. No worries or fears. Only love and light. But holding Stormie Mae, kissing Cheyenne on land I worked for a living with a horse I bought and helped train, well...

I didn't need to go to heaven, not when heaven was right here in my arms.

The End

Cowboy Casanova

CASH

The sound of my phone ringing woke me from my slumber. A feminine groan—*groans*—forced my eyes open.

"*It's too early.*"

"*Turn it off.*"

I blinked away sleep as I leaned over the side of the bed, rifling for my phone. Maverick's name disappeared from the home screen before I could answer it. It didn't take long for the buzzing to start again, and the two girls in bed beside me to tiredly protest.

"Mornin', sunshine," I said with a chuckle, turning over to take in my bedmates. Tinleigh and Tinsleigh—twins. Double trouble of blonde hair, long legs, and curves meant for holding tight.

Man, were they fun.

"Where the hell are you?" Maverick's voice held that familiar layer of annoyance to it that made me grin.

"Havin' breakfast," I said, as Tinleigh—no, Tinsleigh turned over and ran a petite, manicured hand over my chest, down my torso and toward the sheet bunched up at my hips.

My cock sang in response, desire sparking to life like fireworks in my veins.

I could practically hear Mav's eyeroll. "You remember what today is?"

That was a dumb question. I rarely knew what day it was. They all sort of just blurred together after a while. But who needed a calendar or planner when you had Mav? He wouldn't let me miss anything. My cousin was nothing if not punctual. In fact, he might be more than punctual...not that there was a word for it. At least not one I could remember.

"Remind me again?" I asked, turning to meet the blonde's gaze, her brown eyes swirling with mischief as her hand continued its dangerous path.

The first brush of her soft hand on my cock sent a jolt of adrenaline through me. My eyes rolled back, my head hitting the pillow as I laid against the headboard.

"Charlie and Ryder are doing the reveal for the baby."

Oh, that's right. Mav, Chey, and I had waited around most of the day and night while Charlie was in labor, but in the end, Charlie and Ryder wanted to spend the night just the three of them. Mav and Chey had stayed in with little Stormie Mae, and I'd gone out solo.

Not so solo anymore.

Tinl—no, Tinsleigh started up a slow, steady rhythm and I bit back a curse as my nerves turned to live wires. "When's that again?" I got out, trying to stop the groan poised on my lips.

"An hour and a half. Don't be late." Mav's voice rang with finality as he hung up.

Well, Shit. Didn't leave me much time, but Big Daddy knew how to work under pressure.

Tossing my phone to the floor, I settled back more comfortably, my gaze taking her in.

"Who was that?" she asked, stroking my cock. Up and down, up and down.

I inhaled sharply through my teeth, before biting down on my bottom lip. "No one you gotta worry your pretty little mind about."

Tinleigh rose up beside us, a pout forming on her lips. "Hey, I want to play too."

I flashed her a grin. "Don't worry darlin', there's enough Big Daddy to go around... Now, who's ready to rodeo?"

Their laughter melded together, harmonizing into the most seductive melody. Goddamn, I loved twins.

———

MY BOOTS SCRAPED AGAINST THE BRICK AND CONCRETE lined steps leading up to Charlie and Ryder's porch. I glanced at my phone for the time. 11:45 AM. Only fifteen minutes late, which meant, by my own standard, I was early.

Muffled voices met me as I pocketed my phone and grabbed the front door knob, easing it open quietly.

Ryder's voice rose over the chatter. "We gotta wait til everyone's he—"

And there's my cue.

"Did someone call the doctor?" I crowed, loud enough to drag everyone's attention to me. Maverick's signature scowl was painted on his face. Ryder's grin was tight, but warmth and laughter danced in his eyes. Charlie and Cheyenne both smiled though—the latter's brighter than sunshine. Dad and Mama were there, along with Charlie's mom and Cason, who stood off to the right of the couch while Ryder's parents stood to the left. "Doctor Big Daddy is in the house."

"Oh, dear heavens." My gaze landed on Charlie's mom, and I fought to keep the smirk off my lips.

She'd always been a cold woman, but, I don't know...there was cold, then there was *her*. She was like a frost dragon who fed on Charlie's insecurities. I didn't like her. Never had.

I ignored her quiet grumblings as a much more welcoming voice joined the fray.

"Funcle Cash!" Cason darted from his spot, launching into my arms.

Warmth filled me. He was a good kid, and I loved hanging out with him. "How are ya, big guy?"

His face scrunched up, accentuating his freckles. "Hey, you never call me that. I'm little man."

I ruffled his hair. It'd grown since Charlie chopped off the mullet. A shame, to be honest—kid rocked it. "Well, now you gotta little... brother? Cousin?" I paused, trying to figure out exactly what they were. It was like Mav and I, if you thought about it. "Well, whatever little dude is, makes you not so little anymore. So you're now my big guy."

Cason's smile shone brighter than stadium lights.

"You wanna meet R—"

"No!" Both Ryder and Charlie shouted, startling the baby in her arms a moment. She rocked and shushed him easily enough. Motherhood looked good on her. But that wasn't a shock after how easily she took over raising Cason.

"Alright," Ryder finally said, loud enough for all of us to hear. "We better tell ya before one of us—" he snuck a grin at Cason "—slips." Ryder and Charlie exchanged a glance. "Wanna do the honors, darlin?"

Charlie's grin was full of mischief. "Welcome to the world, Railon Ryan Wright."

My brow scrunched up for a moment as I went through the name. On the surface it didn't sound at all inappro—a laugh bubbled up through me and out of my chest, loud as all hell. "Railon R. Wright. Railin' her right. Fuckin' love it."

Stroker's clap of approval sent a tidal wave of commotion through the room. Even Maverick grinned as he and Chey laughed amongst themselves. He held Stormie, looking more confident and sure of himself than I'd ever seen him. And something tightened in my chest at that. At seeing my cousin—my big brother, really—so happy. No one deserved it more than him.

Everything erupted into quiet chaos then, everyone fawning over both babies, talking, chatting, offering help wherever they could.

"So...Doctor Big Daddy?" Cheyenne chuckled.

"It's gotta nice ring to it, dontcha think?" I said.

She rolled her eyes but one of her bright, easy smiles tugged on her lips. Mav sure as hell lucked out with her.

Mama brought a cake from the kitchen a few moments later—Mav made it for the occasion. Because, of course, he did. In all his extra free time, being a new father, a roper, rancher, horse trainer, and a cake baker extraordinaire apparently. The pieces were divvied up, and the chatter continued.

My gaze fell to Ryder and Maverick, holding their babies in their arms. It was pretty cool seeing them enter this new chapter of life together.

Only way it would be cooler was if I had my own little rugrat. But that shit wasn't gonna happen anytime soon. No, I might be foolish, but I wasn't stupid. I was careful with the women I slept with. Responsible—despite what anyone else thought of me.

Nope, there'd be no little Cash Juniors anytime soon.

A pang shot through my chest, forcing a frown to my lips. I don't know exactly why, but the thought made me sad. I didn't want a kid though. Did I? I took a bite of cake. *Nah.*

No, I had Cason if I felt that bad about not being part of the dad club. Kid thought I farted rainbows or something and was a riot to have around.

But as I continued eating my cake in silence, the echo of that pang wouldn't go away. Man, could you catch hormones? Because I swear, I never was this sappy.

"I'll be right back," I grunted out to no one in particular, holding up my phone. But if anyone acknowledged me, they'd find no calls or texts on the screen.

I settled outside on the front porch, reaching for the snuff in my back pocket. The satisfying whack of smacking the can against my palm filled the air before I opened it up and scooped a finger in. With a sigh, I shoved it behind my bottom lip.

Growing up sucked. I mean, parts of it were cool, but well, I don't know, things were so much easier when I was younger. My worries so much smaller.

"So, what part of the Cash system are you at with this latest conquest?" Cheyenne's smoky voice to my right drew my attention.

My lips curved up into a grin. "*Conquests*," I emphasized.

Her blue eyes widened. "More than one?"

I nodded, a soft chuckle escaping me at the sound of disbelief in her tone. "Twins."

"Jesus Christ," she scoffed. "You are somethin' fuckin' else, Mooney. I mean...twins? How can you keep up?"

I barked out a laugh. It was funny, talking to Chey was like talking to the guys sometimes. She wasn't in the least bit fazed by my actions. "I don't know. I just got Big Daddy energy."

She snorted and nudged me with her shoulder. "You're horrible."

"I think you meant to say a legend."

Another eye roll as she turned to lean against the railing, her gaze flicking into the open front door for a moment before landing on me. Something shifted in her gaze in that short amount of time, a thoughtfulness and sincerity that wasn't there before.

"What's goin' on with you?" she asked.

I frowned. "Nothing."

She tilted her head to the side, every inch of her face exuding unimpressed disbelief. "You're actin' funny."

"I ain't actin' like anythin'."

"Exactly." She nodded. "You're always actin' a fool...but today, well it's subdued."

I shrugged, hunkering down a bit more into my stance as I leaned opposite her on the railing. "Today ain't about me."

"Again, how very un-Cash like. Everyday's about you."

Damn, she didn't miss a thing. My lips pulled up into a grin, but even I could tell how unconvincing it was.

I blew out a breath and turned to stand like her so we both faced in. Ryder and Maverick held their babies still and that resounding pang went through my damn chest again. I rubbed at it, but the movement did nothing to absolve the pain.

"I don't know... I guess I just thought it was gonna be us against the world for the rest of our lives. But Ryder's got Charlie. Mav has you. Now y'all are parents... things are changin'...except me."

"If you think we're gonna leave you in a cloud of dust, you got another thing comin' Mooney." She nudged me in the shoulder. "Those are your two best friends. Your fuckin' brothers basically. No one says you gotta have a baby or girlfriend to be part of the cool kids club."

I huffed a laugh. "Good, cuz it ain't happenin'."

Though a part of me, a small, traitorous, stupid part of me, wondered if that would be so bad.

Cheyenne eyed me for a long moment. "I get it. If you were to ask me year ago if I'd be settled down with a kid I'd have told them to fuck off and poured myself another shot of whiskey. I had no desire for any of that. The brick and mortar house, the guy, the baby. Why would I want that when I could be wild and free and young?"

I chuckled. "What changed?"

Her gaze went back to my cousin and the love and desire in her eyes charged the air with its intensity. "I finally had a reason to stop runnin'. To want more than just a string of hook ups or a casual fling. I wanted a life with Maverick."

I nodded, a traitorous image swirling to life in my mind—long hair the color of raven's feathers, eyes the color of amber, and miles of smooth copper skin.

Shut it down.

Funny how ten years had gone by but some things just never changed. I'd never rid my mind of her. Of ten summers ago.

"So are you still lookin' for the right girl?" she asked, her gaze settling on me. "Or have you already found her and lost her, and now no one lives up to her?"

Well, damn.

Was I an open fucking book or something or was she just really damn astute? I never felt like I was that easy to read. It was a part of the persona, the facade. You couldn't get hurt if you didn't let anyone in right?

I tilted my head to the side and spit into the planter. "There was a girl once."

She nodded. "And there's no way of gettin' her back?"

Nope, that ship had sunk, along with my heart, that summer day all those years ago. After that, I swore I'd never let myself get hurt like that ever again. Never bare my soul to someone only for them to stomp on it and leave it out like it was last week's laundry.

You couldn't break your heart if you didn't have one right?

Chewing my bottom lip, I couldn't help the scoff that escaped me. "Not a chance in hell."

Acknowledgments

This book was such a labor of love. It was my first ever "sequel" and while it's still considered a standalone, it still has sequel vibes. I laughed, I cried, I fought myself and my judgment through this story, but I am so so incredibly happy with the end result. Maverick and Cheyenne's story means so much to me, and I hope you enjoyed it.

I could not have done this without so many different people.

My number one, always and forever: Cody. If it weren't for you, this book wouldn't be done. Thank you for the constant love and support and belief. Thank you for wrangling our feral children so I could hunker down and write any chance I got. Thank you for holding me through tears of frustration, cheering me on when things were working, and believing in me when I didn't believe in myself. I love you. Always.

My Aussie Bestie: Clare. Not everyone gets to have a best friend as selfless and kind and wonderful as you. And not everyone has a best friend who will fly from Australia to Texas just to meet you. I am so glad for your friendship, your undying support, and the countless memories we have made through writing together. I hope I did Maverick justice. He wouldn't be who he is without your fierce love of him! Thank you for being there to write with, drink with, and cry with over zoom. Our weekly writing sprints will forever be a highlight of my week!

To the friend I didn't know I needed so desperately: Amy. I am so glad that you stumbled upon Forever After All. I'm so glad you loved it, but I'm even more glad for the friendship that blossomed because of that book. Your chats, your advice, your friendship have been something that I will cherish forever. Thank you for being amazing!

To my Hype queen, beta, and friend: Amanda. You are the kindest soul, and I am forever grateful for your constant, undying support. Your love for the MRC boys gives me so much life, and I love the friendship that blossomed out of you reading this book! I hope I did it justice. Your advice and thoughts were so appreciated!

To the lovely, beautiful soul: Megan. You are amazing! Your advice, love of this world and general support were so absolutely appreciated! I remember being so incredibly discouraged about Mav and Chey's story before you came into the picture, and I am so thankful for out chats and your help beta-ing this book!

About the Author

Shelby Storme is just a girl who loves tattoos, animals, crystals, and writing steamy romance. For as long as she can remember, storytelling has consumed her soul. She's a California transplant living in small town Texas with her amazing writer husband, a sweet-as-pie son, and a sassy little daughter. When she isn't writing she is working as a competitive gymnastics coach and a freelance editor. She loves rodeos, Country music, and Texas sunrises—all of which inspired her series